Welcome to the adventure

Where loyalty matters, magic runs deep,
and nobody stands alone.

2

LISA CASSIDY

THE DREADWATER GATE

THE INKWEAVER ARCHIVE

BOOK 2

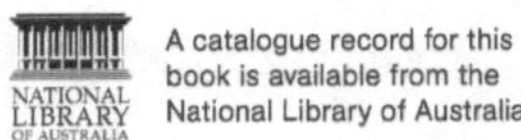

A catalogue record for this
book is available from the
National Library of Australia

National Library of Australia Cataloguing-in-Publication entry

Creator: Cassidy, Lisa, 2024 - author.

Title: *The Dreadwater Gate*

ISBN (paperback): 978-1-922533-13-5

Subjects: Epic fantasy fiction

Series: *The Inkweaver Archive*

First published in 2024 by Tate House

Cover artwork and design by J Caleb Designs

Map artwork by Chaim Holtjer

Also by me

The Mage Chronicles

DarkSkull Hall

Taliath

Darkmage

Heartfire

~

Heir to the Darkmage

Heir to the Darkmage

Mark of the Huntress

Whisper of the Darksong

Rise of the Shadowcouncil

~

A Tale of Stars and Shadow

A Tale of Stars and Shadow

A Prince of Song and Shade

A King of Masks and Magic

A Duet of Sword and Song

~

The Inkweaver Archive

The Nameless Throne

The Dreadwater Gate

The Wyvern's Cry

The Unleashed Storm

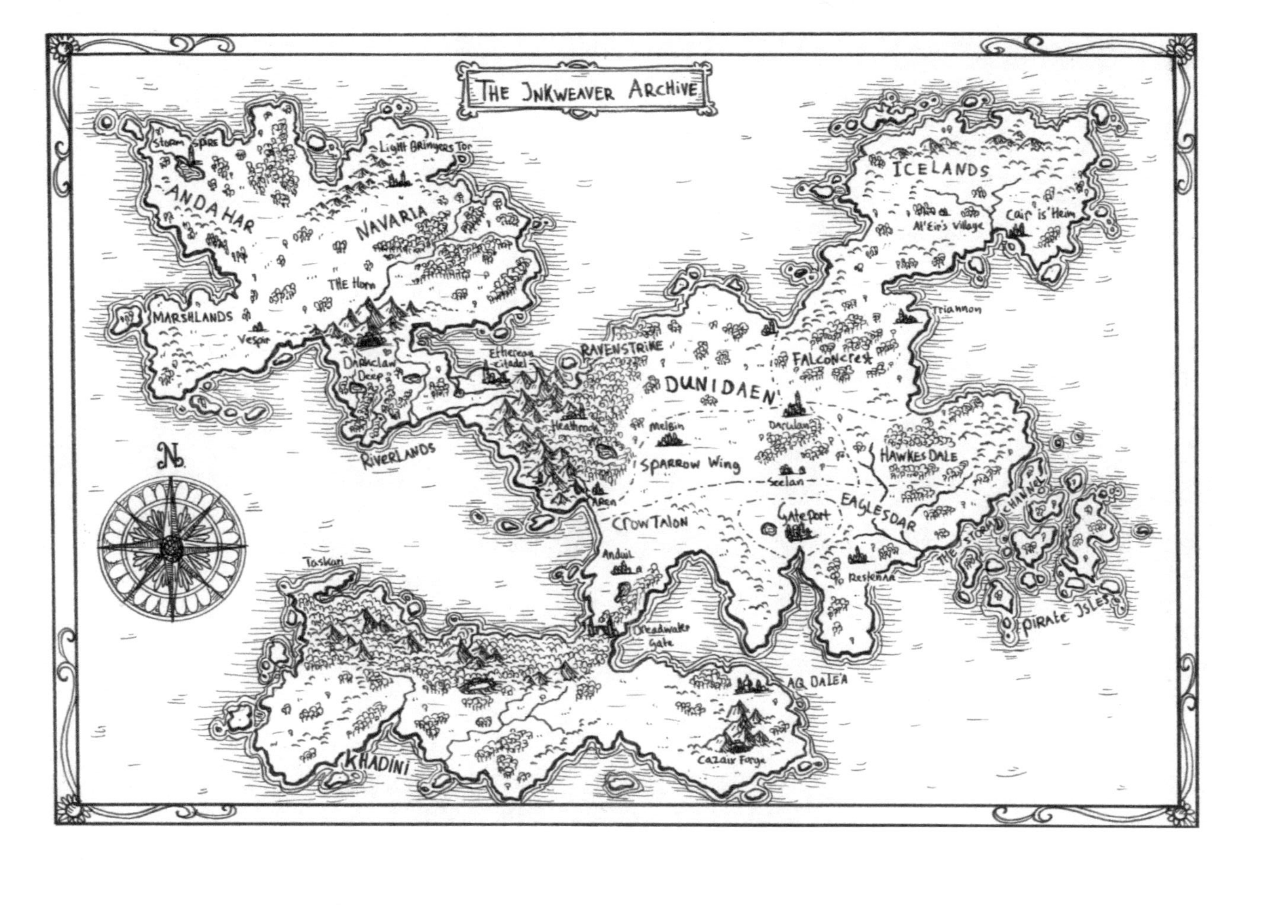

THE INKWEAVER ARCHIVE
N.
ANDAHAR
NAVARIA
ICELANDS
Storm Spire
Light Bringers Tor
Al'Eir's Village
Cair is'Heim
THE Horn
Triannon
MARSHLANDS
Vespir
Draaclan Deep
RIVERLANDS
Ethierean Citadel
RAVENSTRIKE
Heathrock
DUNIDAEN
Melgin
Daraclan
FALCONCREST
HAWKES DALE
SPARROW WING
Seelan
EAGLESDAR
Area
CROW TALON
GatePort
Anduil
Restennaa
THE STORM CHANNEL
Dreadwake Gate
PIRATE ISLES
Taskari
AG DALE'A
Cazair Forge
KHADINI

Chapter 1

The street outside The Ruined Arms was lively with music and chatter, an oasis of warmth and light in the midst of Heathrock's cold and gloomy air. Arya tied Zeke to a post outside and pushed through the front doors, weaving her way through the crowded interior straight to the bar, where she waved for the bartender's attention.

"I'm looking for Tiya," she said, pitching her voice above the noise.

The barkeeper gave her a strange look. "She's not here."

Damn. "She's not working tonight?"

"No."

"Is she back on tomorrow?"

"She's gone. Left about three weeks ago. No notice, no nothing. Just vanished." He shrugged. "Her stepfather sold the place. He's not here either."

"Who can I talk to who *does* know where I can find Tiya?" she snapped with impatience.

He gave her another shrug. "You want a drink? Otherwise, I can't help you."

Arya swore, turned to survey the crowded inn, and debated what to do next. She'd only come to see Tiya—it was the first chance she'd had since returning from SparrowWing with Rorin a few days earlier, and probably the only chance she'd have before leaving again, this time for the Dreadwater Gate.

It made no sense. Tiya had turned the Arms into a thriving business that was making serious money. Why would her stepfather sell it? And why had Tiya left without saying where she was going, or why? A shudder rippled through Arya at the thought that she might have been caught as a magic-wielder. Tiya had always been so careful, though. No, The Ruined Arms was a popular inn. If its owner had been discovered and brand-ed—standard policy in Dunidaen, where magic was feared and hated in equal measure—Arya would have heard the Raiders talking of it.

Pushing off the bar, she headed back out the doors.

Outside, she was engulfed by the icy night air. Winter was only a couple of weeks away. What if Tiya *was* in trouble? There was a city guard office a couple of blocks over. They'd be able to confirm whether Tiya or her father had been arrested or gotten into any trouble.

Arya wavered, unsure. She was supposed to be leaving in a few days to begin training with Ranier, leader of the Shadeweavers, to run the Dread-water Gate with Rorin, Darmanin, and Essa. The danger of training under a Shadeweaver, let alone the incredibly risky Dreadwater journey itself, was already weight enough on her mind. What could Arya do for Tiya?

Arya let out a sigh. Squared her shoulders. Tiya wasn't only her friend and occasional lover, she'd saved General Desomer's life a few months earlier, even if she hadn't been able to save his ability to walk. She deserved whatever help Arya could provide.

She crossed the busy street, giving Zeke's ears a rub as she passed, and ducked into a narrow alley between high stone buildings, her boots rapping on cobblestone. The quieter residential street at its opposite end was empty of foot traffic. Arya turned right, making for the city guard two blocks far-ther down.

It was dark, the lamps either blown out or not present in this area. Moonlight trickled through the gaps between buildings rearing high on either side. Worries continued to cloud her mind as she walked. She and Rorin would soon be facing the Dreadwater—to win him a cazaix blade and strengthen his claim as heir to Ravenstrike. A rite of passage no heir had survived for a generation. All while over the border to the west, the powerful ruler of Andahar threatened everything she loved.

And it was Arya the Nightstalker wanted. The true heir to the throne that he'd stolen decades earlier. Not that Arya had noticed the slightest shred of magic within herself. Or wanted anything to do with the Andahari throne.

Her home and family were here in Ravenstrike. Her future as general of its army.

Something whispered over her senses, pulling her abruptly from her thoughts.

She frowned, looking around her. While she'd been lost in worrying, the night seemed to have grown darker somehow. Thicker. Shadow was coalescing at the top of the street behind her.

She stilled.

The street was empty, lights on in some of the homes but nobody outside. The guard office was out of sight ahead. An odd hush had fallen. She could no longer hear the distant murmur of voices drifting over from the main street where the Arms sat. A little spot of warmth pulsed in her chest, and she was abruptly reminded of the dream she'd had two nights earlier. The golden wyvern. *Mine.*

Blinking, Arya chased away the distracting memory. Her fingers were curling around the hilt of her sword when she heard it.

A snuffling sound.

Fear closed over her chest so tightly she almost choked on it. It froze her in place. The darkness intensified, coming inexorably closer. The snuffling came again, followed by the click of claws on stone.

Arya wavered—run for the guard office, or circle around the dark streets to make her way back to Zeke? She shifted, ready to run towards the guard office—

A gloved hand closed over her mouth without warning. An arm wrapped around her middle. And Arya was dragged backwards into the alley.

It happened so fast and so quietly that she'd only just begun to fight back when her captor pressed her against the alley wall, hand still covering her mouth, and hissed in her ear: "Be quiet and still!"

Sweat broke out over her skin and her heartrate skyrocketed as she recognised that voice.

Ranier. Leader of the Shadeweavers.

Arya froze. Ranier's grip was vicelike. Beyond the alley, the darkness and shadow seeped farther along the street towards them. The closer it came, the tenser Ranier's body became, until it felt like being pressed against a slab of granite. His heartbeat thudded; he was as afraid as she was—and if anything, that made her even more terrified.

Then he moved, slowly, and she heard the faint rasp of a blade loosening from its sheath. Panic surged. Cold metal pressed against the bare skin of her throat. But Ranier didn't intend to harm her, he simply held the blade of his cazaix knife against her skin. He wanted her to feel it. This was a threat.

It burned, though, not the burn of cold metal on skin, but with heat and edge, like acid. But Arya didn't struggle. Instinct held her rigidly still.

The houses across the other side of the street faded from view, and Ranier pressed them both harder against the wall, trying to hide them completely in the darkness. Something moved deep in the shadow, claws skittered on stone. And that infernal *snuffling* sound that put Arya so on edge she felt like screaming. Ranier's hand on her mouth tightened and an odd sensation prickled on her skin.

The thing in the street hesitated, but after a long moment, it kept going. The dark shadow passed by and the houses across the street came into view again. Even then, Arya remained still, breathing quick, shallow breaths.

Eventually, after the rippling shadow had gone completely, and the sound of chatter and footsteps from the main street at the other end of the alley became audible again, Ranier let her go.

As soon as he withdrew the knife, Arya spun on him. "What the—"

He cut her off, speaking quiet and fast. "We leave tonight, in secret. I'll meet you by the lake gate in your walls an hour after midnight."

"What *was* that, Ranier?" she demanded, lifting a hand to touch the patch of skin on her neck that still smarted.

He lifted a finger to his lips. "Not to be spoken of, not so near it. Go back to your horse and head straight home, no diversions. I'll see you an hour after midnight. Don't be late."

"Ranier, you can't just—"

But he was already walking away, sinking into the shadows, and in a blink, he vanished from sight.

Chapter 2

The jittery remnants of fear and worry weighed on Arya as she rode back through the gates of Heathrock castle. A sharp sadness joined the discomfort when her fellow Raiders on the gates called out cheerful greetings.

She didn't want to leave home again so soon.

"Give Zeke water and grain, but don't unsaddle him," she told the groom before heading inside. Thankfully, the warlord's chamberlain was crossing the foyer as Arya came in, carrying a lantern.

"Arya." Peemla's smile was bright and warm. "Are you heading up to bed too? I can walk with—what happened to your neck? It looks burned."

"Long story." She grimaced. "I'm so sorry, but we're going to need your help tonight. I'm on my way to the warlord now."

The young woman waved her off. "Don't be silly. What do you need?"

"We have to leave to start Rorin's training tonight, an hour after midnight. I can't tell you why. Can you help get us organised, so nobody sees us go?"

Worry flickered over Peemla's face, gone as quickly as it had appeared. "Of course I can, although I don't understand why it has to be a secret that he's running the Dreadwater?"

"Our warlord needs Rorin to be confirmed as heir by the State Council of warlords. But nobody has survived, let alone successfully completed, the Dreadwater run in decades. If Rorin tries and fails and everyone knows he failed, in addition to the fact he's a mute..."

Arya trailed off grimly. But Peemla had a quick mind. She understood immediately that Rorin would never win the confirmation if he failed. "I'll get you prepared and out of here without any of my staff knowing a thing, don't worry," the chamberlain promised.

A few hours later, midnight having just come and gone, Arya hovered in the darkness outside the door leading out of the castle kitchens to the garden beyond. The fragrant scent of herbs filled her senses.

Peemla had made sure all her staff were abed so that nobody would see them departing, and she'd done all the work of preparing their packs of supplies alone. Now, the chamberlain stood in the kitchen, speaking with Rorin. Her shifting stance betrayed worry. He reached out to press a hand against her shoulder, a lightly reassuring touch. Peemla visibly relaxed and her shy smile crept over her face.

Arya's gaze turned in the direction of the main entry yard, where light and noise filled the night. To serve as a distraction for Rorin's secret departure, Thiara Ravenstrike had ordered an impromptu practice drill for her imminent travel to the informal Council of warlords to be held in SparrowWing State.

Which was just another worry on Arya's mind.

King Lucius Nightstalker of Andahar had recently expressed his deep displeasure at Dunidaen's inaction on finding the Andahari traitors the Nightstalker believed were inside their borders. Not insensible to the threat posed by the powerful Sky Lord king, the High Warlord had called the impromptu council of all Dunidae's warlords to discuss how best to allay the foreign kings concerns.

That was bad enough.

Worse, the meeting would also be an opportunity for Mathas Crowtalon to push his case to be High Warlord when Darien Eaglesoar stepped down at the next full State Council—only a year away. His only rival was Rorin's mother, and after recent events, when Arya had helped Darmanin escape his father and kill Crowtalon Lances in the process, he had ammunition to use against her if he chose.

Arya hoped Darmanin was all right. Ranier had said that he would make sure the young man joined them for the Dreadwater training, but she worried that Mathas might have caught him already. Their recent encounter had made clear that Mathas considered the death of his second son the only way to keep hidden the secret that Darmanin was a magic-wielder. A fact that, if widely known, would scupper any chance Warlord Crowtalon had of becoming High Warlord.

But it would also ruin Thiara Ravenstrike's chances. She'd practically raised Darmanin in her household after Mathas had thrown him out. Even though she remained unaware of Darmanin's magical ability, Arya doubted anyone would care.

The lively cacophony of whinnying, raised voices, hooves clopping, and the usual whistle of wind made Arya homesick already. Her place was with her army, and Arya wished she was riding with her warlord to the Council. Not only because she longed to be part of the discussions, but because *she* was the one the Nightstalker was looking for.

Not that any of the warlords knew that.

The icy wind from earlier had only grown stronger, and she tugged her cowl over her head and adjusted her cloak. A light snow drifted from the sky and dusted the garden. Out of habit, she scanned the skies, but they were clear enough for now. Just scudding grey clouds.

She let out a long breath. After the incident in the city earlier—she'd *never* felt fear like that—maybe it was for the best they were getting away from Heathrock for a while. Her gaze returned inside the kitchens as her fingers unconsciously traced the burn on her neck from Ranier's cazaix blade. Taze and Essa had arrived. Taze hovered close to Rorin, always protective of his charge, and was dressed identically to Arya in the multiple layers of his Raider uniform. Essa looked out of place, dressed in woollen breeches, jerkin, and cloak rather than the colourful dresses she preferred. She was the least enthusiastic of them all, a withdrawn expression closing over a face that was usually lively with character.

Now they were just waiting on the warlord to arrive to farewell her son.

A cleared throat drew her attention as a familiar Raider approached. She couldn't help a grin at seeing the scowl on Laskin's face. He was the only Raider apart from Taze who knew their true purpose.

Arya piped up. "This time it wasn't my idea, Laskin."

He grunted. "Then the warlord's even crazier than I thought. That's problematic."

Normally Arya brushed off Laskin's grumbling, but on this occasion, she agreed with him. Her gaze shifted to where Rorin, future heir to Ravenstrike State, signed enthusiastically, making Peemla and Taze break into chuckles. His cheeks were flushed in the cold, blue eyes bright, blonde curls hidden by his cowl. "I'll bring him back safe."

"And the other three?" Laskin enquired.

"We'll be fine," Arya said with a confidence she didn't quite feel. "You know Taze and Darmanin can look after themselves, and Essa isn't someone to be trifled with."

"How's the warlord going to explain Lord Rorin's absence from Heathrock, and yours and Essa's?"

"She's still figuring that out. We'd planned to discuss it with Magen tomorrow," Arya said. "I trust they'll come up with something good."

"Not sure which is most dangerous." Laskin scratched his beard. "Running the Dreadwater Gate into Khadini, or the months you'll spend alone with Shadeweavers training for it."

"Definitely the latter," she assured him with a grin.

"Good luck, kid," Laskin said quietly. "It won't be the same here without you."

"I'm going to miss you, old man," she said, equally serious. "Take care of things here while I'm gone, will you?"

He managed a smile. "You know I've always got your back."

Movement heralded Warlord Thiara Ravenstrike's arrival, her husband Matte at her side. Arya nodded at Laskin. "You're up."

He saluted and headed out of the garden. His job was to keep the Raiders on guard atop the lake wall from noticing any of them leaving through the side gate. As soon as he was gone, Arya approached Thiara. Proper goodbyes between them all had been said earlier, so Arya simply saluted and said, "Warlord. We'd best move. Laskin won't be able to distract the guards for long."

"Understood. Good luck to you all." The warlord met each of their gazes in turn, her incisive look imparting both confidence and expectation of success.

"I'll get home safe, Mother, Papa, but I'll miss you both." Rorin signed.

Matte drew his son into a fierce hug, murmuring something in his ear that Arya couldn't hear. Thiara merely squeezed his hand, but her hard features softened in a way they only ever did around Rorin. Rorin grinned and swept them both into his arms.

Once they parted, Arya and her warlord shared a look—she would keep her warlord's son safe—and then they filed out of the kitchen. Stepping out last, Arya glanced over her shoulder to see Peemla, Thiara and Matte watching them leave, all of them emanating worry.

A sharp pang went through Arya. It was going to be a long time before she saw her home again. Her family. She paused, lifted her hand to all three.

All three waved back.

Then Arya turned, her soldier's focus falling into place. From here on out there was no time for worries or missing home. It was her responsibility to get them all back home safely. She hurried the group through the wall gate, casting anxious glances upward as she closed it behind them. Her Raiders were trained to leave no gap in their patrol of the walls, and Laskin wasn't going to be able to distract them for long.

Taze moved suddenly, leaping in front of Rorin, hand at his sword. Arya reacted on instinct, reaching for her own blade, but it was only Ranier, emerging from the shadows along the base of the high wall. He didn't make any special greeting to his daughter, who stood huddled miserably in her furs.

"We have to move," Arya told him, with another glance upward. "Or we're going to get seen."

The Shadeweaver leader gave a sharp nod. "We'll be walking for a while. Follow close behind me and make sure you keep up. There'll be time for talking when we get where we're going."

Without another word he turned and strode south along the narrow path between the wall and the frozen lake, heading away from the castle's main entrance and the road that lead to civilisation. Arya let out an internal sigh. Wonderful. They were hiking up into the mountains. In the middle of the night. How pleasant.

Rorin caught the look on her face and signed, *"Cheer up. This will be fun."*

Arya snorted. "Nobody has ever described hiking in the Diamondfang mountains in winter fun, Rorin. Especially for no good reason."

"You and I both know there is good reason. Dunidae warlords value strength and grit above all else—and they see my disability as a weakness. If I successfully run the Dreadwater rapids, none of that will matter. I do intend to be warlord of Ravenstrike one day, Arya."

She respected the resolve she saw in his eyes, but wished he had any idea what he was in for. She wondered if he'd be as determined then. "You know I'll do everything I can to help you."

His mouth quirked in a bright smile. *"You have to. We're officially family now."*

The spark of joy that swept through her at the reminder she was now an adopted member of the Ravenstrike family still took her by surprise with its intensity. The fact that Rorin also took such obvious joy in it only made the feeling that much sweeter. She matched his smile and they grinned at each other for a long moment.

"You're not going to convince me so easily." Essa spoke from where she walked ahead. A dispirited air had hung around her like a shroud since learning she'd be joining them. "This is a foolish gambit, and I want no part of it."

Rorin and Arya glanced at each other in surprise. While Essa had been unenthused, she'd never said she didn't want to run the Dreadwater with them. Arya had just assumed she was anxious about how difficult and dangerous it was going to be.

"You don't have to come with us," Rorin signed, exaggerating the movements so they were more visible in the dark. *"We won't think less of you. You know that, Essa."*

"I *do* have to, actually." Bitterness filled her voice.

"What does that mean?" Arya demanded.

"It means that Warlord Ravenstrike told me that if I want to retain my position in her household, I had to come." Her mouth tightened. "Apparently my father made my attendance contingent on his help."

"I'm sorry." Arya hesitated, then offered, "I'll do my best to keep you safe."

"I'm not scared." Essa gave her a scathing look. "I just don't want to sneak into another country, put their lives *and* ours at risk in the process, and steal something for no good reason. Who cares figs if *I* have a cazaix blade? It's bad enough that holding one rates as some kind of measure of good leadership in this country."

Rorin looked at Arya in silent appeal, and Taze, walking just behind them to cover Rorin, stayed quiet too. Clearly neither knew what to say to this. For a moment there was nothing but the sound of their boots crunching through snow. Ranier hadn't looked back once.

"Look at it this way," Arya said after some thought. "If you do this, you'll be able to keep your position on the warlord's staff and one day become Rorin's chief adviser. *Then* you'll have enough influence to try and abolish the rite and develop better ways of measuring leadership."

Rorin looked at Arya in amusement. "*We've been family members for a whole two days and already you're choosing my future staff for me?*"

Arya arched an eyebrow. "You think you could do better than Essa?"

"You're not going to convince me this is a good idea," Essa said before he could reply, unamused. "So let's stop talking about it."

"*All right.*" Rorin accepted that. "*Arya's right though. When the time comes, if it's what you want, I make the same promise to you that I did to her. She will be my general and you my chief adviser.*"

"Assuming we survive the Dreadwater run, of course," she said sharply.

Taze winced.

"*Does the fact we'll get to see Darmanin soon cheer you up at all?*" Rorin asked hopefully.

Essa merely gave him a withering look.

Arya cleared her throat and shared a look with Taze, who shrugged. She was officially out of things to say. Best to leave it. They fell silent, focus becoming necessary as they started up a steep incline. The layer of snow on the ground deepened, making the hike more laborious.

Arya scanned the skies intermittently and wondered. She wondered if the Etherean warrior scouts had spotted her departure from Heathrock. She wondered what Elder Salyarin would make of it if they had. He hadn't visited her dreams again since two nights earlier when he'd begged her to come to the Etherean citadel and begin learning her heritage as a Sky Lord. To grow strong enough to become what the Nightstalker feared most—a genuine threat to his power.

She'd strongly considered doing what he'd asked of her.

But in that moment in Thiara Ravenstrike's study, when Thiara had given Arya her House's name, she'd chosen to remain with her family, to protect Rorin on his journey into Khadini. To protect *her* future as general of Ravenstrike's army. *This* was what she wanted. This was what she was meant for.

The path to being a Sky Lord and heir to Andahar's throne might offer the power and influence she'd always craved, but it was an uncertain path, one unlikely to ever eventuate. And the other potential Sky Lords ... always five, Salyarin had told her. Well, Darmanin wanted no part of Andahar either, as determined as Arya was to claim what he *did* want, Crowtalon State. Chiarn had fled from her and the protection she'd offered. Essa seemed content with staying in Heathrock too. And who knew who the fifth potential Sky Lord was. Arya might never meet them.

The terrain grew increasingly difficult, and multiple times they had to slow down to traverse dangerous terrain in the darkness. Ranier's route didn't have them heading into the heights of the mighty peaks though. Instead, they weaved through the foothills.

Dawn was cresting on the horizon, casting the peaks in a glorious pink glow, when Ranier finally slowed. They emerged from the trees into a snowy clearing, walled at one end by sheer granite rock, to find the Shadeweaver leader halted in the middle of the clearing, apparently relaxed.

But Arya's gaze went straight to the tall figure waiting for them, dressed in the motley layers of the Shadeweavers. His alert posture showed that he'd heard them coming.

Darmanin Crowtalon.

A pang of joy went through her, though she stayed where she was, watchful, when Rorin immediately ran to embrace his foster-brother. Once she'd scanned their surrounds carefully, and satisfied herself they were momentarily safe, she switched her attention to Darmanin. A long breath of relief loosed as she looked at him properly.

He looked good—maybe a little taller, a little wilder with the stubble coating his jaw and roughness to his hair. But his light grey eyes were bright as Rorin hugged him, and he offered a small but genuine smile to Arya, Taze, and Essa. Arya relaxed further when she saw that smile.

"Did something happen?" Darmanin asked Ranier. "You moved the meeting time up."

"Circumstances required the change." Ranier finally pushed back the hood of his cloak. "Besides, the sooner we get started the better." He looked unchanged from the first time Arya had seen him; shaved head despite the cold, jagged scar running from eyebrow to mouth, and a shimmering violence in his dark eyes that made you want to stay at least a few steps away from him at all times. He wasn't keeping an eye on any of them the way Arya and Taze were watching him—he felt himself in no danger from any of them, even all together.

Unlike the first time she'd met the Shadeweaver, Arya now knew that confidence was warranted. A glint appeared in his dark eyes, as if he'd read her thoughts and remembered the time she'd attacked him. How quickly and easily he'd dispatched her. But he said nothing of it. Instead, he lifted his voice. "Leanir, you can come out now."

A man emerged from the trees at the other side of the clearing, lowering a nocked bow. The assassin casually slid the arrow back into his quiver, then tugged back his hood and smirked. Leanir's dark hair was severely shorn, stubble coating his jaw, but she would never forget that smirk, those cold brown eyes, the killing look in them.

How had she missed him in the trees?

The last time Arya had seen the Shadeweaver assassin, it had been on the roof of a building in Heathrock city, where she'd chased him down after he'd tried to assassinate Rorin and badly injured General Desomer; a man she loved and admired.

A snarl ripped from her throat, and she drew her sword with a sharp ring. But she'd taken only a half-step towards Leanir when Ranier materialised between them. Leanir's eyes gleamed at her over Ranier's shoulder, full of challenge.

"Touch him and our deal is over," Ranier said, quiet menace reverberating through his words.

"What is he doing here?" Arya demanded.

"He will make the Dreadwater run with you."

She laughed, the sharp notes of it pealing through the silent clearing, but it stilled abruptly when she realised he was serious. "He tried to kill most of the people here only a few months ago. How stupid do you think I am?" she asked incredulously.

"You are under my protection," Ranier said. "He will not touch you."

"That's nice, but your word means nothing to me," she said flatly. Her gaze remained steady on Leanir even as she spoke to Ranier. The assassin stayed silent, lips curled in a smirk. He was enjoying this.

Ranier continued, simply. "You either accept his presence or you leave. Those are my terms."

Her temper flared. They were *always* doing things on Ranier's terms, and she was sick of it. She stepped back and sheathed her sword. "We can train for Khadini just fine without you."

"Arya. A moment?" Darmanin asked quietly.

She held Leanir's gaze for another heated few seconds before tearing hers away and following Darmanin a few steps away from the group. "What?" she snapped at him.

When he spoke, it was for her ears only. "You understand as well as I do why Rorin needs to do this. Why *I* need to."

She gave him a withering look. "Being killed by a Shadeweaver assassin isn't going to help either of you be confirmed as heirs to your respective States."

"Ranier has given his word Leanir won't touch us. I will vouch for that."

"Why do you put so much stock in that man's word?"

"I've never seen him break it, not once. He wears it like a badge of honour."

She searched his gaze. "Do you really trust Rorin's life to that?"

He didn't look away. "Not just Rorin's, but yours too. And Essa's."

"Even if that's true." Arya huffed a breath. "Dar, come on. You really want to go on such a dangerous journey with that man?"

"I'd rather not." He gave her his little smile. "But consider this. Ranier has made the Dreadwater run before. He knows what it takes to survive and return successfully, and not only has he agreed to train us, but he's also insisting that his daughter goes along. If he's sending Leanir with us, there's a reason for it."

Darmanin was right. She would have seen the same thing, but her temper had taken over at the sight of Leanir smirking at her. Even so. "I don't understand why he's sending Essa, Dar. Look at them—not exactly overflowing with familial love. Maybe he doesn't care about her as much as we assume he does."

"You're the only one of us with experience in combat and surviving outdoors. In rough terrain. In bad weather. Maybe you're good enough to keep Rorin safe, but Essa too? Leanir could be an asset."

"We'll have to watch our backs around him the entire time. That's not an asset, Dar, that's a liability."

"I told you, Ranier has given his word. He won't touch us."

Raven's balls. Arya turned abruptly and walked back to the main group, Darmanin following. "If Warlord Ravenstrike knew that I allowed Rorin to remain in close company with the assassin who tried to kill him, she'd murder me herself."

Ranier smiled. "Nobody here is going to tell her."

Arya threw up her hands in defeat. "If he makes so much as one threatening move, I'll kill him."

Leanir smirked. "You mean you'll try."

"Enough," Ranier said. He didn't raise his voice. His tone didn't change. But the violence contained within those words leaped across the space between them. Leanir flinched. It was miniscule, but it was there. "Arya, if he tries to hurt you while under my protection, you won't have a chance to kill him. The Shadeweavers will beat you to it."

"And I'm supposed to trust that?" At her side, Darmanin coughed a smothered laugh.

Ranier stared her down. "You're in or you're out. Decide now. I will not waste my time debating with you."

"We're in," Arya said, mutinous. "But I'm done with the secrecy. We're here, as you asked. Tell us what happens now."

"You'll stay with me for the next six months while I train you to run the rapids. The first thing to know is that six months is nowhere *near* enough time to prepare you properly. Mathas Crowtalon spent years training, and we were full grown men when we did it." Ranier crossed his arms over his chest, revealing a hint of the inky black tattoos that wound over his wrists. "Your warlord has a troublingly high level of confidence in the five of you."

"It's less about confidence and more about timing," Darmanin observed.

The next official State Council was just over a year away. By then, both Rorin and Darmanin would be old enough to be put forward to be confirmed as heirs to their States. They didn't have years to train. They had to be back from Khadini inside a year.

Still, Ranier's words had Rorin paling, and Essa huddling deeper into her layers. Arya and Taze shared a look of tacit agreement. Running the Dreadwater was an incredibly dangerous gamble to begin with. She wasn't sure a reduced training period made much of a difference to that.

"There's a storm coming." Ranier glanced at the sky. "We're going to move to a safe location. Once there, we'll talk more. Leave your packs. One of my people will retrieve them."

Arya baulked. "What about our supplies?"

"You won't need them."

Nobody moved.

"I'm leaving," Ranier said. "Keep up or lose me. Your choice."

He turned and moved with a quick, graceful, stride into the trees. Leanir fell into step behind him without a word. Rorin and Essa went next, Taze close behind. Arya waited for Darmanin to fall in and joined the group at the rear.

She let out a sigh as her legs began to burn again, her breath coming faster.

She had a bad feeling about this.

Chapter 3

For a long time, the silence of the forest was broken only by their rasping breaths and boots crunching through ankle-deep snow. They'd been walking for hours, when Rorin and Essa started flagging. Arya and Taze, in their heavy layers, didn't last much longer—the Raiders were a mounted force, and an hour's drill training every day didn't quite build stamina for long periods of hiking. Only Darmanin seemed to move as easily as Leanir.

Ranier, while he had to have noticed them struggling, made no effort to slow or give them respite. The distance between him and Leanir and the rest of the group lengthened, until Darmanin dropped into the space between them, making sure the trailers didn't get disconnected.

As had been trained into her very bones since day one of Raider training, Arya scanned their surroundings constantly. Weather, predators, Shadeweavers ... all could kill quickly and without warning in the Diamondfang. She glanced at Ranier. His presence probably meant they only had to worry about the first two.

After all, he had apparently saved her the previous night. A shudder went through her at the memory of that darkness, the snuffling sound, the click of claws, and the overwhelming sense of fear and vulnerability she'd felt. Her gaze lingered on the Shadeweaver leader. He knew what it had been. She had to know too.

The weather closed in, and even Ranier's pace slowed as they struggled up a long incline against a squealing wind. At the top, they reached a dead end; a sheer rocky section of mountainside. Arya came to a halt, her pride resisting the urge to hunker down and desperately suck in air like Rorin and

Essa were. While they watched, Leanir pushed aside some thick brush that had been placed artfully to conceal a cave entrance, and waved them in.

Inside, chopped wood sat in a neat pile to one side of the cave, and crates of supplies stacked at the back. Wind whistled as a strong gust kicked up and snow began coming down.

"This will be long cleared out by the time you can report its location to your Raiders," Leanir said coldly as he noticed Arya studying the interior.

She merely gave him a smirk.

"Get a fire started," Ranier instructed. "Then we talk."

Essa and Rorin sank to the ground, still catching their breath, heads hanging between their knees. Arya gave Taze a quiet order to keep watch on them, while she and Darmanin got a fire going.

By the time they were seated around crackling flames, a kettle filled with snow heating over it, the storm was gusting outside. It was almost dark, despite being early afternoon, and the temperature had plummeted. The sweat Arya had worked up now chilled her skin and she, like the others, huddled as close to the fire as she could.

"That's the first thing that's going to have to change," Ranier said, pointing between Arya and Taze and Rorin and Essa. "You run the Dreadwater as equals, not as bodyguards and warlord's son." His gaze set on Rorin. "They don't make your fires for you because you don't know how or because you're too soft and tired. What happens if you get separated?"

"*I agree,*" Rorin signed, Taze translating for him.

"I don't expect anyone to carry my weight for me either," Essa said. "So quit being condescending and start training us."

Arya smothered a smile. Ranier might be incredibly dangerous and skilled, but he didn't know them. The Shadeweaver looked between them, his expression calculating. Eventually, he said. "You all know how to sign with Rorin?"

"We do," Arya confirmed.

Ranier turned to Leanir. "Then you'll need to learn it as well. It will be a unique advantage."

"*I'm not teaching it to him,*" Rorin signed.

"It *is* an advantage," Arya added after translating. "And not one I'm surrendering to a Shadeweaver assassin."

"I don't need any advantages," Leanir said. *Nor do I need any of you* were his unspoken words, clear from the expression on his face.

Ranier's silence filled the space, clearly disapproving. Yet when he spoke again, he seemed to have put the subject aside for the moment. "You'll be entering Khadini via the Dreadwater Gate—the place where the Dreadwater river tumbles over cliffs and flows along the narrow spit of land that joins the landmasses of Dunidaen and Khadini. That entire section of river is dangerous rapids."

Taze lifted a hand. "I understand going through the Dreadwater Gate is traditional, but if cazaix blades are the goal, why couldn't we smuggle ourselves into Khadini on board a trading ship instead? Wouldn't that be safer?"

"Two reasons. First, being considered successful at running the Dreadwater is conditional on going in via the most dangerous way possible. No warlord will consider you a success unless you go in and out through the Gate."

Arya didn't miss the rolling of Essa's eyes, and couldn't help saying, "Raven's balls, I'm starting to agree with Essa. Dunidae tradition is ridiculous."

"You don't say." Ranier gave her a look, then continued. "The second reason is that Khadini ports are locked up tighter than Icecliff Fort in a winter storm. Emperor Atan uq-Danresan is even more paranoid than his predecessors. He knows every foreigner wants the Khadini cazaix *and* the secret to making it. Arriving ships are searched top to bottom by the Rangers, the elite soldiers of the Khadini army. Everyone stepping off a ship is searched, and then they're searched again before they get back on. They do not get lax about this. *Ever.*"

"Okay, but if the Dreadwater Gate is the only other way in, the Rangers must know that too," Arya said.

"There is a single gap in their ability to surveil the entire Dreadwater, and you'll have to exploit it successfully to get in. It's a supremely difficult thing to do, and getting caught and killed or captured ends most journeys before they've even begun. The Rangers have been known to use poisoned arrows, so even if they don't land a kill hit, you still die. That's why the practice stopped."

Arya reached up to rub her suddenly aching temples. She'd known this would be hard, but hearing the details was reducing whatever small amount of confidence she'd started with.

"If you manage to pilot the rapids successfully and make landfall in Khadini, you'll have to remain unseen at all costs. The four of you and your fair skin are going to stand out like snow leopards in the desert. If you're spotted, your travelling papers will be demanded. Since you won't have those—they're only granted at Khadini ports *after* you and your ship have been searched—well ... best-case scenario, you'll be arrested and thrown into one of their labour camps." Ranier looked around, making sure they heard him. "Trust me when I say that's not really any better than being executed outright."

Arya sneaked a look at Taze, then Leanir, at their brown skin that wasn't any different from the Khadini. Maybe the assassin's presence in the group *would* be helpful. Could that be why, in addition to his fighting skills, Ranier was sending him with them?

"Khadini is nothing like you've experienced before. It's tropical. Humid. The landscape is entirely different. Your best chance of getting cazaix weapons is at the cazaix forge in the far southeast of Khadini, the only place in the world where it's made and stored. To get there, you'll need to travel the breadth of the country without being discovered." He paused abruptly. "How good is your Khadini?"

After sharing a glance with the others, Rorin signed. "*I wasn't taught any more than the basics of Khadini and the Icefolk tongue. It didn't seem practical.*"

Arya looked away when Taze translated and Ranier swung his gaze to her. She'd barely paid any attention in the lessons she'd shared with Rorin.

"I remember a little from our lessons," Darmanin ventured.

Ranier gave them all a contemptuous look. "Then assuming you're able to make it across the country without being able to communicate at all with anyone there, you'll have to breach the security of the forge, steal your cazaix weapons, then make it all the way back. If you survive *that* far, you then need to get back along the Dreadwater without rafting the waters—the currents are too strong to raft against."

Another thick silence held once Ranier finished.

"*I'm going to die*," Rorin signed with false cheer, then looked at Arya. "*Will you attend my funeral?*"

"As long as you promise to come to mine," she muttered.

"This is not a joke." Essa straightened, green eyes flashing orange in the flamelight.

"No, daughter mine, it's not," Ranier said. "So you'd all better be sure about this. I can help you, but only if you're fully committed. Preparing for the run will be the hardest thing you've ever done, but only by giving it everything you have will you have any chance of succeeding."

"I'm in." Darmanin spoke without hesitation.

"*Me too*," Rorin signed.

Arya sighed. "So am I."

"And me," Taze followed.

Essa said, "You say we have a choice, but because Rorin is here, Arya and Taze don't have a choice, and neither do I. This is madness."

"Ah, but you *do* have a choice. And your choice is to remain a member of Thiara Ravenstrike's household." Ranier held his daughter's gaze. "Isn't that right, daughter mine?"

Essa let out a breath, but after a moment she merely shook her head and looked away. Rorin had turned white, and he looked between Taze and Arya as if he'd only just realised what his determination to do this meant for them.

"I am a soldier, Rorin," Taze said quietly. "My life will always be inherently risky. I don't see this as any different to my posting at Icecliff Fort. More, you are not just my lord but my friend. I *do* choose this willingly."

"*And you?*" Rorin demanded of Arya.

She let out a long breath. He deserved an honest answer. "Yes, you being here means I must be here too, for a whole host of reasons, not least of which is that you are my family and I will always protect you. And if I'm honest … I doubt the wisdom of doing this. But it is my warlord's command. And that I will always follow."

"Will you?" Ranier cocked his head, quick as a striking snake.

"You doubt that?" she challenged.

A smile ghosted his face. "You do not strike me as the type to be happy following anyone unquestioningly, Raider."

She held his gaze and said nothing.

Ranier stood in one single movement. "Make yourselves a substantial meal tonight, and ensure you get as much sleep as you can. It will be the last time you have the opportunity for either of those things for a long while."

Arya watched him leave, disappearing into the storm.

After a moment, she rose to her feet and followed, finding him a few paces beyond the entrance, snowflakes already dusting his shoulders. He'd been expecting her to follow.

"What *was* that, back in the city last night?" she asked without preamble, keeping her voice low.

"A threat I saved you from."

"Why would you save me from anything?"

Even in the dark, she could see his eyes glimmer. "I made a deal with your warlord."

That wasn't the full truth. Not even close to it. "What is going on between you and her?"

"Go back inside, Arya. You need as much rest as you can get." He turned and strode away, disappearing into the swirling snow. Arya shivered, watching him go. In three strides he'd vanished from sight, walking out into a snowstorm like it was nothing.

Her gaze narrowed. Secrets and lies eddied around the Shadeweaver leader like bees around fresh flowers.

Who was Ranier, truly?

Chapter 4

From the very first day, Ranier made them run.

"If Khadini Rangers are on your tail, you can't stop no matter how exhausted you are," he said on the first morning as they staggered along behind his apparently endless stamina. An hour into the run, Leanir and Darmanin still moved easily, but everyone else laboured. Arya had begun to worry about how little air she was managing to suck into her lungs. Was she imagining her light-headedness? "Success in running the Dreadwater hinges on mental strength. Your mind can will your body to keep going much longer than your muscles can. We're going to keep running until you learn that."

And on it went. Day after day.

They stumbled through thick snow, snapping tree branches and crashing through into frozen streams. When their breath burned like fire in their chests, and their legs turned rubbery with exhaustion, backs and knees and ankles aching, Ranier made them keep going until one of them finally stopped, vomiting everything they'd eaten that day into the snow.

When that happened, Ranier would stop with a huff of disgust, "Rangers and their dogs are going to hear you emptying your stomachs from miles away," and let them rest for a half hour. Then he made them start running again. On and on until each of them collapsed on the ground, unable to move another inch.

That usually happened by midday.

"Khadini Rangers use tracking dogs to help them cover the border region either side of the Dreadwater rapids," he lectured during one midday break as they sprawled, exhausted, on the ground. "If they get your scent, you're in trouble. The way you get out of it? You outrun them. Dogs are quick, but they're not long distance runners at speed. You can use terrain to lose them too—like climbing a rock face or fording a river too rough for them to cross. Move downwind of them, if you can."

None of them responded to this—they were too busy trying to suck in enough air to stay conscious.

"On your feet," he snapped.

Arya pulled herself upwards with a groan, leaning down to help Rorin up. He tottered on rubbery legs, but to his credit, made no complaint. Ranier set off, leading them through a section of thick brush that emerged after half a mile at a rocky mountainside.

Essa halted beside Arya, her weight leaning against Arya's side. Arya wasn't sure the young woman knew she was doing it, but she adjusted her stance to help take Essa's weight. She and Rorin were so far coping with their physical misery with what Arya considered impressive fortitude. She wondered how long that would last.

Ranier waited until he had their attention, then pointed at the rockface. "Climb it."

Arya let out a breath of dismay. It wasn't particularly high—perhaps four times her height. And there were handholds enough to make it climbable without any expertise. But slipping and falling near the top could cause serious injury, and their legs were shaky and exhausted from running.

Without comment, Leanir began climbing, moving swift and agile. Everyone else merely stared at him. Arya wondered whether she had the energy to even walk over to the rockface, let alone climb it. Even Darmanin seemed reluctant.

"Why aren't you following?" Ranier asked, ice in his voice. He was wearing a low collar today, and the edges of his tattoos were visible twining around the base of his neck. In her less exhausted moments, Arya itched to get a better look at them. She swore they looked different than the last time she'd caught a glimpse of his neck.

"I'm honestly not sure I could climb a set of steps right now, let alone a rock wall," Essa said.

"*What she said,*" Rorin echoed.

Ranier surveyed them, then asked abruptly. "Which of you knows exactly what crossing the Dreadwater Gate entails?"

Arya glanced around, met a lot of shrugs. Nobody answered. She'd assumed the gate was some kind of formal marker that indicated the line of the border, like a column or statue or similar on the banks of the river.

"The Dreadwater flows south from Lake Darkin in Crowtalon, but where it hits the Khadini border it tips over a large rocky shelf—a waterfall about half a mile long." Ranier smiled without warmth. "That's the single gap in the Khadini surveillance of the Dreadwater. You'll be climbing down the cliff face *behind* the waterfall, hidden from sight until you reach the banks of the river at the bottom."

"So running *and* climbing will feature prominently in your lesson plans, I take it?" Arya said.

He snarled, "Get up that rockface now. Don't make me ask again."

It was *that* tone, so nobody considered arguing further.

"Taze, lead the way to show us the easiest path," Arya ordered after a quick scan to judge everyone's level of exhaustion. "Dar, you and I will go last. I'll shadow Essa, and you watch Rorin."

That way if either fell, she and Darmanin would at least be able to attempt to arrest their fall. Not that she was sure she'd be up to catching anyone. Her arms, strong from swordplay, gripped and lifted her easily from handhold to handhold, but each time she needed to brace or push off her legs, they wobbled alarmingly.

Rock and dirt rained down from Essa's boots into Arya's eyes and mouth, which she did her best to ignore. Taze went slowly and deliberately, showing the two inexperienced climbers the best path upward, and together, even though painfully slowly, they got to the top.

Arya groaned as she hauled herself over the edge and slumped to the ground. Everything hurt. She wanted to sleep for a year before moving another inch.

"Thanks, Arya," Essa said quietly beside her. "I'm sorry I'm such a liability."

"You are no liability, Essa Varsoth," Arya said fiercely, leaning close to make sure her words were clearly understood. "You'll be as strong as us in no time. And that incredibly smart brain of yours is something the rest of us don't have and can't train for."

Essa looked away, as she often did when someone complimented her, but Arya hoped her words had hit home.

"On your feet!" Ranier snapped the moment he reached the top behind them.

"Oh, good. More running," Arya said. "Just what I was hoping for."

Rorin chuckled silently, and even Darmanin gave his little smile. Taze helped Essa up, and Arya touched her shoulder lightly. "Run in my steps, it will make it easier on you."

"You're not here to make things easier for her," Ranier said, overhearing. "Daughter mine, you run up front. Arya, you take the rear. Let's go again."

Essa's spine straightened, and she did as ordered.

And they started running.

***

By the time Ranier let them stop that day—as the sun began sliding down behind the mountains—nobody was running anymore. It was more like staggering, than running. But they were still on their feet.

He'd brought them back to the cave, but the crates of supplies were almost all gone. "There's enough for tonight only," Ranier said. "From tomorrow, you'll start foraging for your own food and making your own shelter. I'll show you how. I also expect you to set a watch tonight. You can't sleep unguarded in Khadini."

Leanir was the least exhausted of them all, but Arya wasn't trusting him on watch, so she took the first watch herself, assigning Darmanin next.

The stone was cold at her back as she settled at the cave entrance, staring out at the darkness and away from the light of the fire inside that would ruin her night vision. A light snowfall drifted from the dark sky. Every muscle in her body ached and she was so weary she could have fallen asleep in a blink. Once she realised that, she forced herself to her feet. Sitting was too dangerous.

The tired chatter of the others drifted from inside, along with the crackling of flames. Rorin appeared to bring her food and water, which she accepted gratefully, then told him to go back and sleep. "You're going to need it."

They were also going to wake up horribly sore the following morning. Arya winced at the memory of each morning so far. Stiffened and aching muscles and bitterly cold air, which made it all worse.

"You're the leader."

Ranier's appearance out of the darkness made her start, and she swore inwardly. He could have slit her throat before she'd had any idea what was going on. He was as good as Leanir at moving around without a trace, and it made her intensely uncomfortable. Still, she didn't want him to know that, so she merely shrugged and said casually, "That surprises you?"

"The way you got them up that cliff, how you rallied their spirits at the top. You're the leader," he said this not as a question, but observation of fact. "You're careless though. You put yourself at risk to protect the others. If Essa had fallen, she'd have taken you both to the ground. You would've tried to stop Rorin if he'd fallen too. It is a strategic error for a leader to risk themselves so. Fix that."

"Why do you care?"

"Because there are bigger things at stake than your friends' lives." His gaze set on the sky above, looking westward. Something like sadness was etched on his face. It was the first time she'd ever seen him look truly human.

"How was it that you ran the Dreadwater with Mathas Crowtalon?" she asked. She'd never heard how Ranier had become leader of the Shadeweavers, or who he'd been before that. He couldn't have always been a Shadeweaver, not if he'd been close enough with a warlord's heir to run the Dreadwater with him.

"You're aware that his first wife, Andrian's mother, died in childbirth when she and Mathas were both very young?" He kept his gaze on the sky as he replied, voice distant, as if he wasn't entirely with her. "Mathas re-married not long before making the Dreadwater run. There were … ties … between my family and that of his new wife. I went with Mathas on her behalf, to ensure he returned safely to her."

Arya looked at him in surprise. Mathas Crowtalon wouldn't have taken a wife from any but a warlord or vicelord's family. Which meant… "You're from a noble house, then?"

"Of sorts," he said evasively, before he turned pensive. "Mathas was charming back then, thoughtful, kind. It seemed to me that he loved his wife very much, that she was a balm to him from the grief of losing his first wife."

Arya wondered how Mathas had changed from that man to the one whose cold negligence had contributed to that wife's death, the one who was willing to kill his own son. "Is *that* why you took Darmanin in when Mathas threw him out? Because of these mysterious family ties."

"I took Darmanin in the same way I take in all magic-wielders and those with nowhere else to go."

She took a step closer to him. "Are you related to Darmanin, Ranier?"

He flicked her a glance, amused. "Not by blood."

"And how did you go from a 'close family friend' of a warlord's wife to leader of the Shadeweavers?"

"That's none of your concern, Raider. I give you only what you need to know."

She frowned. "Need to know for—"

But he was gone then, back inside the cave, silent as always.

Arya thought on his words after he'd gone, curiosity helping her stay awake despite her weariness.

Ranier had revealed more than he'd realised.

Because if Darmanin was Andahari like the Etherean elder claimed, then that Andahari blood had to have come from his mother. Mathas Crowtalon was Dunidae, descended directly from a Dunidae warlord's house. And Ranier had just admitted to being a close family friend of Darmanin's *mother's* family. Close enough that he went on a dangerous journey to help protect the man she loved.

When you added that together with Essa, Ranier's daughter, also having Andahari blood from somewhere... and not only Andahari blood. Both Darmanin and Essa were potential Sky Lords.

She'd always assumed that Essa had gotten her Andahari blood from her mother, but now ... Arya let out a surprised breath, gaze cutting inside before returning watchfully to the forest around them.

Ranier was probably from an Andahari Sky Lord House.

Chapter 5

Winterfest passed without remark. Every day Ranier pushed them a little bit farther, a little bit faster, always past the edge of their strength and beyond. He led them over increasingly difficult terrain and sent them up longer and more difficult climbs. They moved higher into the Diamondfang, where the air was thinner and colder and made their lungs burn.

And the Shadeweaver leader kept pace with them step for step.

When they flagged, he told them mental toughness could push them through it. When they baulked at a dangerous section of cliff face, he told them they could either figure out how to manage it now, or do it while Khadini Rangers were shooting at them. He never once softened or showed any mercy for their physical distress.

In the short periods between runs, he showed them how to forage for food—including how to tell what was poisonous—and how to build shelters from what was around them. He taught them to hunt and trap the hares and foxes that were hardy enough to survive winter in the mountains. He also showed them which plants would encourage healing if they were injured or sick.

"There's a compound that counteracts the effects of the poison the Rangers use on their arrows, and you'll take the herbs for that with you," Ranier explained one morning in the pre-dawn as they roused themselves. "But you'll have to travel light, and there's always a chance you lose your packs, so learning to treat wounds and injuries with what you can find around you is crucial."

"You said Khadini was tropical, that the landscape is different to anything we've experienced," Essa pointed out. "Yet you're teaching us to forage in the freezing depths of a Diamondfang winter."

"True." He met her gaze. "But if you can survive in the depths of a Diamondfang winter, then how much easier will it be when the days and nights are warm, and you don't have to dig through snow to find what you need?"

Realisation spread over her face. "You're deliberately making our training even harder than we'll find the Dreadwater run."

He gave her a satisfied smile. "A clever mind, daughter mine."

"Plant life will be different in a tropical climate, though," she said. "Animals, too."

"Yes. Both will be more plentiful." He gave them a smile full of teeth. "I'd steer clear of the snakes, though, if I were you."

"Tell us more about these labour camps," Arya asked a short time later. "You said that ending up in one wasn't any better than execution if we're caught."

"If you get put in one, you're never getting out," he said flatly. "And if you *do* get put into one, your life expectancy drops to a handful of years. It's hot, back-breaking work in their pit mines or oil digs, and there are no rest days or breaks. They work you until you drop."

"*The Khadini emperor does this to his own people?*" Rorin signed.

Ranier nodded after Taze translated. "It's the cheapest way for him to mine the iron Khadini needs to make cazaix, and extract their precious oil, the country's two biggest exports."

"I suppose paying his citizens to do the work in reasonable hours with proper food and breaks would be far too much of an administrative and financial burden," Essa said.

"Yes, and you treat your criminals—including magic-wielders who've never broken a law in their lives—so much better here in Dunidaen," Ranier replied smoothly.

Rorin and Essa shared a look. "*We're going to change that. One day.*"

That night, on first watch, Arya sat thinking. As had become routine, once Ranier let them stop for the day, they'd wearily built themselves a shelter, foraged for food and started a fire.

By then, Essa had been too exhausted do to more than drink some water and eat a handful of rabbit meat before curling up in her blankets and falling asleep. Rorin seemed to have more energy—Arya suspected that was due more to his determination to succeed than anything else—but they'd both grown gaunt in the past weeks, all fat stripped from their frames, dark shadows under their eyes. And yet they kept going, grimly applying themselves to each task Ranier set them.

Taze, too, had returned to his too-thin frame, but he was adjusting well to the increased physical hardship. Arya had counted each one of her ribs easily while having a quick wash that morning. Darmanin and Leanir alone seemed unchanged, only perhaps even sharper, harder than they'd been before. Arya wondered whether one of them could die or be badly hurt in this training Ranier was putting them through.

If he would *let* that happen.

Her stomach growled. She ached everywhere, and never seemed able to get *quite* enough rest or food. She couldn't imagine doing another long run the following day, let alone scaling a dangerous cliff face.

She'd do it though. If only because she'd never allow herself to falter in front of Ranier or Leanir. Or Darmanin, she admitted to herself, gaze falling on his sleeping form. He was no longer the boy they'd known, not since that night with his father in the forest. The memory of being ambushed by the Crowtalon warlord after helping Darmanin escape him, of watching Darmanin's shadowhound leap for his father's throat ... He would have killed Mathas Crowtalon if Arya hadn't stopped him. She still didn't understand how she'd done it. Hadn't wanted to think about it. Pushed the memory away now.

There had never been much childishness in Darmanin, but now it was all gone, burned away to leave a hardened and fierce young man. He and Rorin were of an age, yet when they stood side by side now they seemed worlds apart.

An adult Darmanin was not someone Arya could control like she had when they were young. His magic made him dangerous, especially when added to his corrosive anger towards his father and implacable determination to be named heir to Crowtalon. If he succeeded in running the Dreadwater, he'd grow even more dangerous.

Had her warlord thought about that? Darmanin would always be an ally to Ravenstrike after what Thiara Ravenstrike had done for him, and because of his firm friendship with Rorin. But he had a mind of his own.

"I am beholden to nobody."

Her memory of Darmanin's words—days after first meeting him—came back to Arya with a starkness that made her shiver. Would she be able to hold him back if tested again, like she had that night with his father? She wasn't sure.

"You doing okay, Captain?" Taze hunkered down beside her, interrupting her thoughts. He'd been scouting their perimeter for danger before seeking his blankets. A close call with a snow leopard the previous night had made them more watchful.

"I worry about Essa and Rorin," she admitted.

He looked at them both. "They are too thin and exhaustion dogs them constantly. But they rise each day, and they make no complaint and they keep going."

Arya glanced at him, considering. Memory filled her then, of the days she and Taze had spent as Nameless on the streets in Aren, snuggling together with other hungry orphans in any empty building they could find for shelter, subsisting on scraps. Determined, each day, to survive. And she thought of what they'd become because of it.

"Ranier is forging them into steel," Taze said. "And I don't think they will shatter in the process." He flashed her a smile. "I could do with a little less running though."

She hesitated. "How are you doing, Taze?"

"I am a soldier in service to my warlord." He shrugged. "It's what I signed up for, and it was my free choice."

"Is it what you want, though?" She shifted uncomfortably. "I've never thought of either of us as *having* choices before." She and Taze were Nameless. They'd joined the Raiders because it was their only escape from a life on the streets. Their best path to shelter and clothes and three meals a day.

Taze was slow to answer, as if carefully considering his words. "It is clear to me that Thiara Ravenstrike is your warlord, that you have sworn yourself to her body and mind. And that is good." He held her gaze. "But Rorin Ravenstrike is mine."

"Good," she eventually said, giving him a nudge with her elbow. "Rorin is a fortunate man."

"I'll take next watch, Captain. Let Essa sleep a little longer."

"No," she said. "You were right. Ranier too. We might not be there to take watch for her in Khadini. She'll be fine."

Taze smiled, then went to his blankets.

***

Two months in, when a day of running and climbing left them merely weary, rather than shaking with exhaustion and collapsing into dead sleep each night, Ranier began teaching them to move silently and without leaving sign of their passage.

"Rangers can follow days' old sign," Ranier explained as they ran one day, winding up a narrow goat track towards the summit of a mountain, the air growing thinner as they climbed. "I'll show you how to move while leaving as little sign as possible, or to fake a trail and send those tracking you in the wrong direction."

"Don't we need to learn how to raft rapids too?" Essa asked one morning as they set off.

"I'll teach you to make a stable raft, but..." He swept his arms around them. "There's nothing in the Diamondfang that can approximate the Dreadwater. It is the one thing you will not be able to prepare for."

"How did you do it?" Arya asked. "When you trained with Mathas?"

"There are some rougher sections of the Dreadwater just south of Lake Darkin in Anduil. But those are in populated areas of Crowtalon State, so we cannot go there."

The final months of winter saw them running quick and light through the snow and scrambling into the heights of the mountain peaks. Ranier taught them the antidote to the poison the Khadini Rangers used on their arrows, but warned them that it needed to be made up freshly, administered fast, and would take time to be absorbed into the body and work.

They began having more success foraging and improving shelter construction, meaning they slept more easily at night and rose feeling better in the morning. They survived two blizzards without help, and Arya started thinking about how useful all these skills would be if she taught them to her Raiders too.

It would improve them from an elite mounted cavalry to a force that could more confidently and successfully fight a battle in the mountains if an invader came from the west. Or the Shadeweavers grew out of control.

It was a thought she filed away.

"I've been keeping us away from predators," Ranier announced briskly one night. Winter had officially ended by then, although it will still be some time before the high mountains felt the first touch of spring. "I will no longer be doing that. Tomorrow you start learning to read their sign. If we encounter a wolf, snow leopard, or bear, it will be up to you to manage it."

***

Their first encounter with a bear was sudden and violent. They emerged from a thick copse of trees onto the banks of a frozen lake where the ice bear crouched, waiting for fish to come near its icy surface. It rounded on them with a mighty roar, teeth bared and claws swiping at Rorin, who was in the lead that morning. Arya reacted faster than anyone else, diving forward to knock Rorin aside and taking the blow on her shoulder. The padded layers of her Raider uniform kept those razor-sharp claws from drawing blood, but the blow was hard enough to send her flying.

She landed hard, wincing as pain shot through her shoulder. By then, Ranier had vanished, and the others had drawn weapons and scattered, forcing the bear's attention to split.

Arya snapped orders as she rolled to her feet. "Essa, back into the trees, but slow. Rorin, you too. Taze, Dar, cover them. Leanir, shoot the damn thing—aim for the eyes!"

Roaring in fury, the bear went at Darmanin, who was closest. Quick-footed, Darmanin backed away, drawing the bear's full attention on him and away from where Rorin and Essa were retreating into cover.

Arya glanced at Leanir, saw where he was positioned, then shared a look with Taze. The two began shouting, waving their swords. Arya ran in behind the bear, poked it in the back. It spun away from Darmanin, roaring in frustrated anger, and as it turned, it moved right through Leanir's field of fire.

He felled it with a single arrow.

Ranier re-appeared as they gathered around the bear, looking down on it in satisfaction, but his face was stony as he addressed Arya. "What did I tell you about throwing yourself heedlessly into danger? That swipe could have killed you."

"And I would do it again. Rorin was in its path."

"He needs to be able to stand up for himself. And you will get yourself killed before your twenty-first birthday if you don't stop to think about your actions."

"Rorin *can* stand up for himself," she snapped. "But the bear came out of nowhere. He had no time to react. *I* did."

Rorin, who looked shaken, signed. *"Thank you, Arya. Ranier, we will pay better attention to our surroundings from now on."*

"You need to listen to me on this, Arya Ravenstrike."

But despite Ranier's anger with her, it was Leanir who took Arya's attention as they settled back into a run. He'd listened to her snap order in the moment, and because of it, they'd felled the bear quickly and without anyone getting hurt.

Could she trust him to do the same once they were away from Ranier?

***

From that morning on, they were more careful of where they trod, deliberately keeping out of the path of the mountain's predators rather than engaging them.

Arya wasn't sure what Ranier thought of that approach, but they weren't going to encounter any of these animals in Khadini and she had decided the risk of injury wasn't worth it. None of the group, Leanir included, disagreed with that direction when she gave it.

One night they sat around a fire, weary but alert enough to spend some time relaxing by the flames rather than curling instantly into their blankets to sleep. It was an unusually clear night, spring having finally arrived. The night air remained cold, however, and Arya sat as close to the fire as she could, her right leg extended out before her, a hand absently rubbing her knee. The constant running and climbing was bothering the old injury she'd sustained the night Leanir tried to kill Darmanin and Rorin.

The assassin sat across from her, his attention focused on waxing the string from his bow. Some weeks earlier, Ranier had begun having them run with a full load of weapons and pack. Arya's sword rested just by her right leg, never far from reach.

Ranier had disappeared when they'd begun making their shelter for the night, as he always did. He was always back in the camp by morning, sometimes returning before midnight, sometimes in the early hours. She assumed he was managing Shadeweaver business during his absences, though how he was doing that from the middle of the Diamondfang, she had no idea.

One by one, the others sought their blankets. Leanir was on watch, so Arya stayed awake, unwilling to trust him. Despite her best efforts though, soothed by the fire's warmth and that of the blanket around her, Arya fell into a doze.

And dreamed of the wyvern again.

The dream had the same unreal quality as before—like she was both inside and outside of it at the same time. Air ran over her skin, soothing and delightful. His wings were spread wide, and ... he was *flying*. He was hungry, too. Arya's stomach rumbled with echoing hunger pangs. The rich scent of sheep drifted on the wind, and he banked sharply—

The dream segued.

She was back in that place where the darkness was heavy with a hatred that was *alive*. Something hissed, and she spun, seeing nothing, but feeling exposed. The horrific white face of the nazal flashed, teeth bared, turning towards her. "*I know you're near,*" it hissed, the words raking through her. "*So close. But where? Where? Where?*" She felt it touch her mind in triumph, and she screamed, surging awake.

The scream had been silent, fortunately, because around her, everyone slept on. Across the fire, Leanir's gaze glimmered as he watched her, but he said nothing. She took a deep breath to steady herself, then promptly froze.

That *hatred* she'd felt in the dream. The same one from the nightmare she and Essa had shared not long before leaving Heathrock. She recognised it.

It was the same thing she'd felt that night in Heathrock.

Ranier appeared from the shadows to her left.

She didn't try to hide her annoyance at how she'd failed to notice him approach. Again. "What do you *want?*"

"We need to talk."

He was gone again before Arya could protest. With an irritated sigh, she pushed herself to her feet and followed him into the night. Ranier waited in the shadows of a drooping tree. There was something different about him. He was tense, his watchfulness even more tightly focused than normal. "Do you plan to go to them after the Dreadwater run?"

"Go to who?" she asked.

"The Etherean."

Arya shifted in surprise, then cursed herself for betraying her reaction.

"Essa is my daughter," Ranier said. "Do you truly think I don't know what she is, what she will become?"

Wariness crept through Arya. She already suspected Ranier was Anda-hari—how much of what Salyarin had told her did he *know?* All Arya could think to do was play dumb and try to draw him out. "Essa's parents are Shadeweavers. I think it's fairly obvious what she would have become. Isn't that why you sent her to join our household, to give her a different life?"

"Essa's mother was no Shadeweaver. I met her in Khadini, in fact."

Curiosity leaped in Arya, and she couldn't help asking, "When you made the Dreadwater run?"

He didn't answer. "Essa needs to do this if she's going to survive what lies ahead, as do you, but she should go with you after, to Salyarin and his people. They can teach you both some of what you need to know."

If Ranier *was* from a Sky Lord House, then he knew exactly what his daughter was. But surely he couldn't know about Arya? Nobody knew her identity other than Salyarin. Fear trembled through her at the idea Salyarin might have betrayed her to the Shadeweaver leader. "What lies ahead for Essa is to be Rorin's chief adviser. I don't think being able to run all day and climb cliffs is going to help her with the political wrangling of the warlords. The clever mind she has now is all she needs for that."

"Enough." He made a cutting motion with his hand. "You have many gifts, Arya Ravenstrike. You are quick and strong and a confident strategist, not to mention the power that rests inside you. But you will not regain Andahar on those things alone."

Arya stilled, the panic creeping back. "Regain Andahar? What are you talking about?"

An impatient huff. "You are twenty years old. There is no way Salyarin hasn't reached out to you by now. You are too dangerous to be left lying about untaught. You and Darmanin both."

"I have no idea what you're talking about."

His mouth curled in a snarl, then. "I know everything about you, Arya Ravenstrike. *Everything.* I have knowledge that would bring you to your knees. That could destroy both Mathas Crowtalon *and* your precious war-lord."

Arya froze. She felt that threat with every fibre of her being, but still... "If that was true, you'd have wielded that knowledge by now. The warlords are your enemies."

"There is a worse enemy across the Diamondfang. One that is coming for Dunidaen, sooner or later. All he needs do is find and destroy you and Darmanin and Essa and Leanir, and whoever the fifth is, and—"

"Leanir?" Arya stiffened, gaze darting back towards the camp, horror sweeping through her. The emotion was strong enough to have her forgetting all her denials. "No. He is *not*—"

Ranier's mouth twisted in genuine amusement. "You already know he is your fourth Sky Lord."

That day in the Heathrock city square. The twang of the arrow that had taken down General Desomer. How Arya had known, in the next breath, that the second arrow was coming for her. That tug in her chest, like a thread linking her to something, or some*one* else. Like the thread that had pulled, warning her Darmanin was in danger the night Leanir had come, or the one Chiarn tugged when he'd used his magic on the fires outside Seelan.

Realisation crashed down over her. The same thread she'd pulled hard that night in the forest with Mathas Crowtalon, *forcing* Darmanin to stop attacking his father. Forcing him to obey her.

Arya shook her head. No way. Chiarn was bad enough. It couldn't be Leanir.

"I see it on your face, Raider. You can't hide from me," he said, dark eyes glittering.

She crossed her arms over her chest, taking a steadying breath, seeking a way to get back on the front foot. "You're drawn tight tonight, Ranier, more so than usual, *and* you're back at camp early. What's happened?"

He didn't even blink. "It took longer than I would have liked, but I've received a full accounting of events at the High Warlord's impromptu Council months ago. The Nightstalker's demands have grown. If the Dunidae don't hand over those he's looking for by the State Council next year, he will pay a personal visit to whoever is voted the next High Warlord." Ranier paused. "Not even your doddering High Warlord Eaglesoar is under any misapprehensions about what that means."

"A declaration of war," Arya murmured. She did a quick calculation in her head—after how long they'd been with Ranier, the State Council was now ten months away. "How much do the warlords know of those the Nightstalker is searching for?"

"The Nightstalker informed the High Warlord that he knows potential Sky Lords live, and that they're not in Andahar. But it seems he knows little more about you as yet. I suspect if he did, he'd have included them in his missive."

Arya let out a long breath. "Good news." At least if the Nightstalker knew nothing about them, they could keep hiding.

"There's worse news," he said. His hand slid towards his cazaix knife, almost unconsciously, Arya thought. "Murders in Heathrock city. Particularly gruesome ones where the victims were left completely unrecognisable. One was found inside a locked room with the doors and windows fastened from the inside."

"Isn't murder a regular activity for your people?"

"The victims were magic-wielders."

Arya fought to hold back the shudder that went through her, but suspected Ranier didn't miss it. "What was in the street that night?"

"A nazal."

She flinched, and he caught it.

"Salyarin *has* communicated with you, then. I thought as much. Then you know what a nazal is, how dangerous they are to you."

She rubbed a hand over her face, hated how it trembled slightly. "You think the nazal was behind the recent murders?"

"I don't think it, I know it." He stepped forward, stabbing an index finger into her chest. "*You* are the Stormrider heir. *You* are the one the Nightstalker hunts. If his nazal don't find you, if they don't hand you over to him, then he will come for Dunidaen. The warlords can only hold him off so long. I am training you to run the Dreadwater, both to gain the strength and mental toughness you need to face the Nightstalker, but also to get you and my daughter as far away from Heathrock as possible while a nazal is a breath away from finding you. But after you're done, you need to learn your magic. All of you. Or you will die."

Arya blinked. *Stormrider.* That name echoed through her so profoundly she barely heard the rest of Ranier's words. A long silence held after he finished. Eventually she cleared her throat. "*I* get to decide who I am, Ranier, and I've already made that choice. I am Arya Ravenstrike, future general to Warlord Ravenstrike. Salyarin hasn't been able to convince me otherwise and you won't either."

"And what makes you think you *get* a choice?"

"I am beholden to nobody," she repeated Darmanin's words to Ranier, feeling their rightness as they settled in their chest.

"We'll see about that." Ranier shrugged. "Tomorrow you leave for the Dreadwater Gate."

Her head came up, quick as a snake. "It hasn't quite been six months yet. Those reports you received scared you. You're not sending us because we're ready. You're sending us because you fear the nazal finding us here."

"There is very little in this world that scares me, Raider," he murmured. "But ... yes."

Before she could ask anything further, he'd disappeared into the dark.

Arya swore, kicked out at the trunk of the tree, and felt the satisfying thud as it landed. The Shadeweaver leader knew her identity. How?

And what did that mean for her? It made her position even more tenuous. Warlord Ravenstrike now unknowingly sheltered three magic-wielders under her roof, magic-wielders wanted by a dangerously powerful foreign king who wouldn't be put off.

He *would* come for Dunidaen. As little as Arya trusted Ranier or his motives, she knew he was right about that.

And ... the wyvern. He was real.

Her wyvern. The wyvern of an Andahari Sky Lord.

Salyarin told her a wyvern would be born for her, that she had magic, and she'd always used the lack of those things to push back on his insistence she take up her place as heir to Andahar. But now, suddenly, she had both.

She opened her gloved hand, stared at her palm. What was her magic? Where was it? Was it nothing more than the threads of *something* she felt connecting her to Darmanin and Essa and Chiarn and Leanir? Or was something else simmering away inside her readying to break out?

Arya suspected she'd just learned the name of the Sky Lord House she was descended from. The true ruling family of Andahar.

Stormrider.

Chapter 6

Arya didn't sleep at all, the cold digging deep into muscle and bone as she lay there and stared out into the darkness.

If Ranier was right, a nazal was in Heathrock. Hunting them. Her wyvern was a real thing. And his existence only marked her more deeply as the one the Nightstalker wanted more than anything—

The Stormrider heir to the Andahari throne.

Familiar frustration beat at her. She had no desire to mess with Andahar or the Nightstalker. Neither did Darmanin or Essa or Chiarn. They didn't *want* any of it.

She'd thought by doing nothing, keeping a close eye on the border, she could hold him off until he lost interest or realised there was no threat coming for him. But the Nightstalker wasn't going away, no matter what she did. It was time that she accepted that.

Arya rolled over, staring up at the clear, star-filled sky.

What if accepting it meant Dunidaen going to war because of her?

Dawn saved her from her spiralling thoughts, though the mood was grim when everyone roused from their blankets. It seemed nobody had slept well. Ranier was snappier than usual, and everyone but Leanir recognised Arya in one of her moods.

"*What is it?*" Rorin asked.

Arya gave a little shake of her head. Leanir was watching them with far too much interest in his dark gaze. How much did *he* know of what Ranier had told her?

"He knows nothing," Ranier murmured at her side, as if reading her thoughts. "It was safer that way. For you *and* him. I've kept him alive all these years, but it will be your job to win him to your side—I highly recommend doing that before trusting him with any of this knowledge."

"And how much exactly do *you* know, Ranier?" She turned to hold his gaze. "Who are you?"

Instead of answering her question, Ranier lifted his voice to address all of them. "There's no more for me to teach you. Not in the limited time you have. Today we hike down to the foothills, then south through the Wraith Forest. From there you'll make for the Dreadwater Gate."

"*We're not going via Heathrock?*" Rorin asked.

"We can't." Arya answered. "By now your mother will have given everyone a story about where we are. We can't risk anyone seeing us and undermining whatever that story is."

Ranier added, "It's likely Crowtalon has spies watching your home."

She gave him a quick glance. It wasn't Crowtalon that Ranier was worried about. It was the nazal stalking Heathrock city. And if a man like Ranier was afraid of them ... then they were truly something to fear.

Rorin conceded, turned to Ranier. "*You will send my mother a message that we have departed for the Dreadwater Gate?*"

"I will do better," Ranier promised. "I will see you safely to the Gate itself."

***

Just over two weeks later, dressed as simple travellers on cheap horses, they'd travelled through Ravenstrike and SparrowWing and into Crowtalon State without incident. The warm early summer weather made the travel pleasant, although the passage of time also reminded Arya that it was now barely eight months until the next State Council and Rorin's confirmation hearing—not to mention the High Warlord vote.

Ranier's escort also meant they could lean on the Shadeweaver network for supplies and discreet places to sleep—though Ranier was careful that they never saw anyone he interacted with, and Arya doubted the gang would ever use any of those safehouses ever again.

Thiara Ravenstrike had paid a high price for the Shadeweaver leader's help, but Arya was forced to admit carrying out this mission would have been infinitely more difficult without it.

She'd begun to wonder, though, about Thiara's history with Ranier. Arya had never forgotten that interaction with her warlord at Windfall Fort years earlier, where her warlord had essentially ordered Arya not to hand herself over to the Nightstalker. As if she'd known Arya was the one he was looking for. And she'd never raised it again. Never intimated she thought Arya any more than a Nameless Raider from the streets of Aren.

Yet now it turned out Thiara had been planning all these years with Ranier—linked to Andahar himself—for her son to run the Dreadwater Gate with what turned out to be four Andahari Sky Lords.

Coincidences didn't exist when it came to Warlord Thiara Ravenstrike.

"What do you know about your father?" Arya asked Essa as they rode side by side one morning.

"Very little," she said. "He's never spoken about himself, even when I asked."

"Did you know that he knows about us?"

"No!" Essa's eyes went wide with shock, before frustration and fury flashed over her face. "He told you that?"

"Recently, yes, and don't ask me how, he wouldn't say." Her jaw tightened. "It's not a good feeling, the sense that the strings of your life are being pulled by somebody else."

Essa paused. Then continued. "I assumed my mother must have been my Andahari parent. But..." she trailed off.

"But what?"

"I've seen his tattoos before. When I was little. His chest and back. Arms too. I walked in on him undressing to bathe. He didn't see me see him." Essa turned to Arya. "The artwork is exquisite."

Arya let out a breath. "Like your art. Does he have the same magical ability as you?"

"He can't, or *he'd* be the Sky Lord the Nightstalker is looking for, right? And it makes more sense someone *gave* him the tattoos. Perhaps a family member with the same magic I have?"

"Essa, I'm pretty sure your father is from a Sky Lord House." She explained how she'd come to that conclusion. "And I think there's more to the connection between him and Rorin's mother than either of them has told us."

"I've always wondered why he sent me to the Ravenstrike household. It seems now it was because he wanted me to run the Dreadwater. But there were other ways he could have prepared me to do that."

"If I didn't know better, I'd suspect he wanted us to grow up together. Forge a bond." But then why not send Leanir to the Ravenstrike household? That would have been harder to explain to Thiara, though.

"That would suggest he's far more invested in the Nightstalker and Andahar than he's letting on." Essa paused. "And I've always truly believed he cares very little for either Dunidaen or Andahar."

They fell silent, both lost in their thoughts.

***

Once inside Crowtalon, they circled Lake Darkin, travelling out to the east to avoid the main roads, before joining the banks of the Dreadwater south of Anduil, Crowtalon's capital.

Arya wondered how Darmanin felt, passing so close to the home where he'd been born and spent the early years of his life, but he said nothing, and his gaze rarely shifted in that direction. Maybe it had ceased being home for him the moment his mother died.

The countryside grew more isolated the farther south they travelled, small villages dotting the landscape. One morning, Rorin was the first to spot the smudge against the distant horizon.

Throughout the day, the smudge separated into two distant hazy outlines that slowly resolved into stone towers. They reared impressively high into the sky—far taller than those at Icecliff Fort—beyond anything Arya had seen before.

"The Dreadwater Gate," Ranier announced, breaking the silence that had fallen for hours. "The towers stand on opposite banks of the Dreadwater where it flows over the cliffs into Khadini. Hundreds of years ago, the Dunidae built the gate to guard the entrance to their kingdom. Pretty, but ultimately useless, since what sensible Khadini army is going to attempt invasion by scaling the cliffs underneath a waterfall?"

Arya and Essa shared a glance. Arya had always put Ranier's references to 'their kingdom' and 'their warlord' to the fact he was a criminal who didn't consider himself a part of Dunidae society. But now she figured it wasn't that at all.

It was because he *wasn't* Dunidae. He was Andahari.

Knowing that, part of her yearned to ask him questions, to understand more about Andahar and Sky Lords and what had happened when her ancestors fell to the Nightstalker's blade. But she buried that part of her down deep. She didn't need to know any of it to be general to Warlord Ravenstrike. Besides, it wasn't like Ranier had ever demonstrated a willingness to answer her questions. Nor did she trust anything he told her. He was still the leader of a violent criminal network.

The towers grew steadily closer, rearing above the tree canopy. To their left, the waters of the Dreadwater river seemed to flow restlessly, the current speeding south towards the border. Soon Arya could make out a high bridge connecting the two towers about two thirds of the way up. Her heart leaped with fierce glee at the thought of standing on that bridge, so high above the world, the wind no doubt rushing past.

They camped overnight a short distance from the Gate, concealed in thick brush and without a fire, and roused in the pre-dawn hours. Leaving everything but their packs behind, Arya and the others trailed after Ranier through the dark woods. The area was so isolated it was unlikely anyone was around to see them, but they moved silently through the brush as Ranier had taught them anyway. Neither Ranier nor Arya put it past Warlord Crowtalon to have watchers at the Dreadwater Gate.

They reached the Gate as the first glow of sunlight touched the horizon. Arya caught glimpses of roiling blue ocean through the trees out to the southwest, beyond the clifftops. Ahead—through the Gate—the Dreadwater river cascaded off a sharp precipice. A morning mist hugged the surface of the water, giving the space between the towers the mysterious air of a portal to another world.

Arya glanced around. Rorin stared at the Gate, transfixed, while Essa and Darmanin wore expressions of resignation and grim focus respectively. Leanir was watching the trees behind them. Taze gave Arya a nod and smile. She grinned back.

Ranier left them waiting while he went to scout the tower on the western bank, but it wasn't long before he returned. "That low cloud bank is thick enough that any Khadini Rangers below won't be able to see us up here. Let's go."

On reaching the tower, Arya pushed through a rotted wooden door that hung from one remaining rusted hinge. The large circular space inside was empty, its original stone flooring layered with moss and debris. She crossed with quick strides to an open balcony that looked down over the water-fall—no doubt purpose-built for a line of archers to fire on anyone trying to scale the cliff behind it.

Time and weather had crumbled the balcony railing to almost nothing, so she stepped right up to the edge, a slight breeze blowing her hair back from her face. To her left, the Dreadwater tumbled out of the fog before plunging down in a massive curtain of flowing water that crashed to rocks a mile below and flung spray high into the air.

Once clear of the waterfall, the Dreadwater continued through a long ravine that joined the landmasses of Dunidaen and Khadini. Blue ocean twinkled to the east and west. The ravine sides were thick, tree-covered terrain, rocky and steep. As hard as she stared, the distance was too far to make out anything beyond the tree canopy. If Ranier was right, those trees would be heavily patrolled by Khadini Rangers.

Essa appeared at her side. "I suppose it's too much to hope that you've changed your mind?" she asked.

Arya let out a breath. "No, I haven't." As dubious as she had been about the sense of this mission, after learning about the nazal, she thought taking Rorin and those she loved so far away from Heathrock might be the best thing for them all. "How about you?"

Essa's mouth quirked in a smile. "I'm really glad I'm not afraid of heights."

Arya laughed, shoulders relaxing. "You and me both."

"Have you had any more nightmares since..."

"One." Arya hesitated. She hadn't told the others yet about the nazal in Heathrock—there hadn't been an opportunity to speak to them without Leanir listening in. "What about you?"

"None. I wonder what it means."

"It's a good thing," Arya said, her frustration leaking out. "*This* life is our real one, Essa, no matter what your father or Salyarin says."

Essa held her gaze. "Of all the times I've heard you say those words, that sounded the least convincing."

Arya's shoulders sagged. "He's going to come for us no matter what we do. I realise that now, Essa. But that doesn't change anything. It doesn't change what I want."

"I don't want *any* of it." Essa's words were low, impassioned, raw with despair. "I don't want to fight, Arya. I don't want to hurt people, no matter the cause. I don't want to have the people I care for constantly at risk."

Struck, Arya reached out to touch her shoulder. "Essa..."

"I want a cottage by a stream in a sunlit forest where I can listen to birdsong in the morning and the trickle of water when I go to sleep at night. I want my parchment and inks and brushes, and a morning stroll into the village for a fresh pastry. I want to spend a month every year travelling to places I've never been and visiting friends before coming back to my cottage and my solitude. That's what I want."

Essa hadn't shifted her gaze from Arya's during that speech, and there was so much meaning in there. So much honesty. Arya didn't shy away from it, accepted the rare and precious insight she was being given into her friend, as painful as it might be.

Because there was no family in that life. No man or woman at Essa's side, or children, or even close friends. But it sounded beautiful nonetheless … even if that life would drive Arya mad within a day, she could see how it would fit Essa like a glove.

"Essa, I—"

"There you are." Darmanin's words interrupted, his brisk strides echoing across stone as he exited the tower. "We need to get moving."

Arya cleared her throat, let her hand drop from Essa's shoulder. Darmanin frowned slightly as he glanced between them. "Everything okay?"

"Just admiring the view." Essa smiled, as if her moment of vulnerability had never happened, and she turned and walked past Darmanin into the tower.

"The Nightstalker isn't going away, Dar," Arya said, feeling unusually helpless. "And I know you want to ignore that, pretend it doesn't exist. But every time I say aloud that my life is here, I feel the lie in my words. It's stronger every time. Essa has already figured that out and I think you know it too."

"This is what I know, Arya." Darmanin let out a breath. "I know that each day from now until we die, we will wake up and make choices. Big ones and little ones. Ones of consequence and ones that seem tiny on the surface of it. And it's those choices that will determine the course of our lives."

She considered that for a moment. "And if the choice we one day face is between what we want for ourselves, and accepting what Salyarin tells us we need to do in order to protect those we love?"

"Then we make that choice when it comes." He smiled a little. "But right now, we are about to make the Dreadwater run, so I suggest all our focus be on surviving that."

She took a deep breath, dispelling all her maudlin thoughts, and followed him back through the tower. "I can do that."

Chapter 7

Early morning sunlight streamed through the trees as they gathered near the banks of the Dreadwater. Its deep green waters ran swiftly, the roar of the waterfall so close they had to raise their voices to be heard. Ranier waited while they checked their packs for the final time, then secured them—and their weapons—to their backs and settled into the weight.

"Are we ready?" Rorin signed, looking admirably calm. He'd grown another inch or two in the past months, and while he was still thin, it was all wiry muscle. The young heir was as ready as he was ever going to be for this.

"I want to say something." Arya looked at them all in turn. Her adopted brother, a man she loved more than anything in the world. Her wary and fierce foster-brother. Her truest friend and the smartest of them all. And her fellow Raider, a man who'd already been through incredible danger at her side and come out victorious. Even though they had Leanir to contend with, confidence filled her.

She could do anything with this group.

"We are doing this together, as a team. Remember that. No matter what happens, we keep faith with each other." She looked at Leanir. "Until we come back through that Gate, we're a team. Leanir too. Our best chance of survival is to stick together."

Leanir smirked. "Rousing speech. Very nice. Go team."

"Leanir," Ranier warned.

A simple word, but Leanir immediately cleared his expression and simply nodded. "If you mean that, Raider, then I'll hold to it too." He hesitated, then, "My word on it."

"*Not just a team,*" Rorin added, flicking a look of surprise in Leanir's direction. "*A team of equals.*"

Darmanin nodded and held out his hand. Arya took it, then Rorin took them both, then Taze, Leanir, and Essa until they were all gripping hands.

"Let's do this," Arya said before letting go.

Without a word, Ranier moved. He led them along the riverbank all the way to where it reached the foundations of the western tower. He waded into the shallows and made his way around, one hand pressed against the stone. And then, where the tower wall began to curve away from the water, he stepped onto a narrow dirt path leading to the clifftop.

"This will take you under the waterfall, where you can begin the climb down," Ranier said. "You should be back here within a month if you move fast. I will send a message to Warlord Ravenstrike to inform her that you've passed through the Gate. My part of this deal is done."

The Shadeweaver leader stepped aside, giving them room to pass him onto the trail.

As agreed, and as they'd practiced over and over in the Diamondfang, Leanir took the lead, Taze following, Essa and Rorin in the middle, and Darmanin and Arya bringing up the rear.

Light dimmed as the muddy trail—a narrow track at the top of the precipice—wound under the gushing flow of water. They paced its length, determining the best place to start the climb. Soon Leanir pointed at a section just east of the centre, and Arya nodded.

He sat down on the edge, turned carefully, and began to lower himself down.

One by one, they followed.

The climb was just over a half mile, but they had the entire day to do it. The height had seemed dizzying looking down from the tower above, but because of the thick cloud still hovering over the top of cliff face, they couldn't see the bottom once they'd started climbing.

For the most part, there were plenty of solid hand and footholds in the craggy rock—they'd made much more precarious climbs in the Diamond-fang—and the greatest danger came from its damp and slippery surface.

The packs and weapons weighed them down, made balancing harder, but again, Ranier had made them do far riskier climbs with even more bulky weight strapped to them.

Nobody talked. It was impossible to tell how far sound would carry—with the breeze blowing in the right direction the sounds of conversation could conceivably be heard by Rangers a couple of miles away.

Hardened and well-practiced as they were from Ranier's training, they reached the bottom by early afternoon without incident, sweating and tired, but with energy left. At the base of the cliff, water had hollowed out the rock into a cavern of sorts, so they remained well hidden by the curtain of falling water.

"Stage one achieved," Taze murmured, face lighting up in a smile as they gathered in the dim light of the cavern. "We're in Khadini."

Arya returned his grin. "Now stage two."

They lowered their packs to the ground before unstrapping the large square wooden planks—already nailed together—four of them had carried. Leanir, the fifth, unstrapped the long wooden poles that had been attached to the outside of his pack. Working together, they used the straps to lash the planks together, and within a half hour they had a sturdy raft.

By then it was mid-afternoon.

"Eat, drink, and rest. We go as soon as the sun gets low," Arya ordered. They'd need some light to be able to navigate the rapids, but couldn't afford to be too visible out on the open water to Ranger scouts. Dusk would have to do.

Arya took watch while the others rested. None looked adversely affected by nerves or the climb down, although the usual ebullience in Rorin's manner was muted.

As the orange glow of dusk filled the cavern, they shouldered their packs, then carried the raft around the curtain of falling water, hunkering down on the banks and studying the river as far along as they could. The fading light made anything beyond a hundred metres or so impossible to see, but there were no shouts or cries of alarm, and no sign of human movement, so Arya gave the go ahead to move.

Pushing their craft into the water, they waded in and carefully climbed to sit crossed legged on it. They almost overturned the craft twice, but eventually they were all aboard. Arya, Taze, Rorin, and Darmanin sat at the four corners of the raft, each holding a pole. Essa and Leanir were in the centre. Leanir kneeled, his bow held ready, quiver of arrows beside him. He would be their sole defence if they were spotted and attacked while on the water.

The first little fission of doubt rippled through Arya. This was the one part of the mission Ranier hadn't been able to train them for. For this, then, they'd have to trust the balance and teamwork they'd forged over the past three months.

"Hiking along the ravine walls is not an option," Ranier had insisted when Arya suggested doing that instead. "The space is so narrow the Rangers will pick up your passage, and you will not be able to fight your way through. Rafting is your best and only chance."

Arya closed a hand over the doubt, strangling it before it could take root. Then, she took a breath, straightened her shoulders, and looked around. "Ready?" she asked them.

"*Ready, Arya.*"

"I'm ready." Darmanin's grave tone.

Essa sighed. "Let's get this over with."

"Ready, Raider," Leanir murmured, archer's gaze already scanning the ravine tops above them.

"Me too, Captain," Taze said.

Arya lifted her pole and reached out, pushing them off the riverbank. Almost immediately, the current picked up the raft and sent them floating into the middle of the Dreadwater. They picked up speed quickly and within seconds they were free of the constant mist hovering over the waterfall and into the rapids.

Water rushed around them, roaring as it crashed into the sharp rocks poking above the surface. Arya leaned back when the raft dropped suddenly and careened towards a clump of rocks.

"Poles on the right!" Darmanin called.

Arya and Rorin pushed their poles out to propel them away from the rocks. The raft jerked wildly, and Arya swayed. She managed to get her balance, just before Taze poled them away from another rock. A second later, the bottom of the raft scraped along an underwater obstruction and jerked upwards. Taze and Darmanin crashed into each other, almost sliding off the raft. Water flowed over Arya's boots and Rorin's pole flew from his hands.

Arya swore, glancing around, trying to identify the safest route through.

Another glancing blow sent the raft into a spin and for a long moment they had no control over its movement. They slammed into another obstacle, and Rorin teetered alarmingly. Darmanin grabbed his arm just in time and he managed to re-balance himself.

Arya squinted. It was hard to make out much in the fading light, but she couldn't see the end of the ravine yet. A faint hiss caught her attention, and she looked around with a frown, swaying to keep her balance as Darmanin pushed them away from another rock and they plunged a short distance before hitting the water again. Her eyes caught on a dark shape embedded in the wood at her feet.

An iron-tipped dart.

"We've been spotted!" she called urgently, but her words were drowned out by the raft scraping over rocks just under the surface. Wood splintered and the corner of the raft where Taze sat cracked apart. With a shout, he toppled over and fell into the churning waters.

"Taze!" Essa screamed, lunging to catch his hand, but he was already gone.

Arya looked frantically between the water where Taze had disappeared and the top of the ravine wall, where distant figures ran along the top of the cliffs, following their passage.

"Leanir, give us cover!" she snapped.

A bow twanged as Leanir began firing.

"Can anyone see Taze?"

Essa and Arya desperately searched the water, but it was nearly dark, and she could barely see the rocks, let alone Taze.

And they were moving so fast.

A dart clipped her jacket, tearing a hole but not penetrating her skin. "We're open targets, we have to get off this raft," she shouted, ducking as another dart whispered past her ear.

"The end of the ravine is just ahead," Darmanin called back. "We can make it."

"There are too many of them," Leanir said as he loosed two more arrows into the darkening sky.

Another dart sank into the wood at Essa's feet.

"Hunker down," Arya shouted, shifting her body to try and cover Essa. "Make yourself a smaller target."

A pile of jagged rocks appeared ahead. Distracted, they didn't react in time to steer away from it. The raft crashed into it, the front breaking off entirely. Darmanin and Rorin tumbled into the water.

"RORIN!" she screamed, looking desperately around her. "DAR!"

Leanir had stopped firing. He held his wrist, just above where a dart protruded from the back of his hand. Arya stared at it. If that was a poisoned dart...

"I can help." Essa bravely crawled towards him, reaching for the small pack at her waist where they carried their healing supplies.

With only Arya left to guide the remains of their raft, they spun out of control and swept around a bend. She gave a gasp of relief at seeing the end of the gorge ahead, the landscape opening up into Khadini proper. She hunched her shoulders, trying to make herself as small a target as possible, and do enough steering to get them there.

It was almost full dark now, which would inhibit the archers. Leanir was trembling, though, and a sheen of sweat covered his skin. Essa yanked out the dart and then thrust his hand into the water, seeking to clean it out.

The raft dropped abruptly, riding another unseen rapid, and crashed among more rocks, before smashing completely apart. Arya plunged into the water with no time to catch her bearings before being tossed violently about. Water filled her mouth, and she fought her way to the surface, coughing and gasping for air. The water was warm compared to the icy lakes and streams of Diamondfang.

She'd barely broken the surface when the current gripped her. The weight of her pack and weapons held her down. Her fingers fumbled at her sword belt, unbuckling it, and letting it loose from her waist. Then, kicking out, she made it back to the surface to gulp in another lungful of air. Her pack dragged at her, but she refused to leave all her supplies—she wouldn't last in Khadini without them.

Her leg slammed into a rock underwater, and the force of it sent her body flying into another rock. Her shoulder clipped it, and the current dragged at her again. Arya managed another gulp of air. Another kick out. Another grasp for something steady. But in a flash, her head hit a rock.

And everything went black.

Chapter 8

Arya washed ashore onto the pebbled banks of the Dreadwater. She came to with a gasp, pain tearing through her shoulder, her head pounding. Dizziness spiralled through her, and for several moments she could do nothing but suck in air and fight to keep her stomach from emptying. Once the dizziness faded, she moved her head more cautiously.

It was dark, and the rush of the river drowned out the sound of anything else that might be nearby. Water soaked her clothes and hair. The air around her was thick and warm. Her vision remained blurry. Her lower legs were still in the shallows.

And she was alone.

Grimacing with pain, she staggered to her feet, cradling her left shoulder, and doing her best to ignore the spinning in her head. The open riverbank was the most dangerous place for her to be—it was the first area the Khadini Rangers would search. Overhead, a full moon provided some light, but she couldn't see very far into the thick forest that pressed close to the riverbank. A quick scan of the shore showed none of the others had washed up nearby.

To the north, the ravine loomed. She'd made it through and into Khadini proper.

Agony pulsed in her shoulder, and after palpating it gently, Arya worked out that it was dislocated. Next, she felt the wound on the back of her head. Already a lump swelled there, and her fingers came away sticky with blood, though the bleeding had slowed to a trickle.

Her dagger and the small knife inside her right boot had made it through the rapids. Everything else, including her pack of supplies, was gone. Her shoulder had likely been dislocated by the pack being wrenched off in the water.

A faint sound came over the rushing of the river, and she stilled, doing her best to parse it. It was quiet. And then it came again.

The barking of dogs.

Shit. Shit. Shit.

Don't react, Arya. Plan! General Desomer's familiar voice was clear as day in her head, helping dispel some of the grogginess of what was probably at least a mild concussion. This was why she'd trained.

She had to find the others and get them away from the riverbank, clear of the Rangers.

She slowly slid her lame arm out of her jacket, then turned it into a sling that she tied tightly across her chest, keeping it immobilised. Arya took a few deep breaths, waiting for the agony of moving her arm to subside. The sound of barking was still distant. She hoped it would stay that way.

She jogged south along the river, looking for signs of anyone else, stepping from rock to rock as Ranier had taught her so that she didn't leave any trail. Her soaked clothes were a problem—each droplet falling to the ground filled with her scent would make it easier for a dog to track her. There wasn't much she could do about that. If she found the others before the dogs got the scent, then they could run their way out.

But she had to find them first.

The distant sound of barking was growing louder, and anxiety crawled between her shoulder blades.

Arya came across disturbed mud on the riverbank and sobbed with relief. These marks were clear—more than one person had come ashore. She crouched low to study the ground in the dim light and followed the tracks into the forest. Fortunately, they hadn't gone far, and Arya emerged into a small clearing to find Leanir prone on the ground, curled in a fetal position, shaking so hard his teeth were chattering. Essa crouched over him, rummaging around in her pack, which had a large tear in its side. Taze paced, sword drawn, eyes darting around, wary for danger.

No Rorin or Darmanin. Arya's stomach sank.

"Everybody okay?" Arya asked, stepping into the clearing. Essa gave her a relieved nod before turning back to her pack.

"Captain!" Taze's shoulders crumpled in relief. "Essa and I are fine. Are you—"

"Rorin, Darmanin?" she interrupted.

"We haven't seen them," he said. Despite his soldier's brisk reporting, his jaw was set, betraying deep worry.

Arya crossed to Leanir, crouching beside him and Essa. The Shadeweaver's skin was slicked with sweat, and even in the dim light she could see the veins sticking out on his neck and the backs of his hands. She glanced up at Essa. "How is he?"

"I've cleaned the wound, but the poison from the dart is in his blood," she said briskly, finally pushing her pack aside as it became obvious what she needed wasn't in there. "We need to make the antidote Ranier taught us, and fast, but my pack was damaged in the river and the mortar I carried is gone. I've only got the pestle. Taze and Leanir lost their packs entirely."

Despair settled in Arya's chest. The herbs that made up the antidote had to be ground together freshly—it became useless if not used quickly. "I lost my pack in the river too."

Leanir groaned, teeth chattering. "Of course, you did."

Silence fell over the clearing. Arya's thoughts raced, trying to push aside her growing panic so she could figure out what to do. The barking in the distance was a constant reminder that they had little time to do anything.

"We need a bowl of some kind," Taze said. "What if we whittled some wood?"

"No time for that," Arya said. "The dogs will be on us as soon as they pick up a scent."

Abruptly Essa turned, digging through her pack, then yanking parchment and a narrow stick of charcoal—she'd wrapped it in some kind of plastic material to keep them dry.

"Essa, no!" Quick as a blink, Arya grabbed her wrist. Revealing her magic to Leanir could be a death sentence.

"You said it yourself. There's no time for anything else."

"What about the nazal?" Arya demanded.

"What's ... a..." Leanir's teeth chattered. "Nazal?"

Essa yanked her wrist free of Arya's grip. "We're hundreds of miles from Heathrock *and* Andahar, Arya. I'll take the risk."

Before Arya could argue further, she settled on the ground, cross-legged, and began to draw. Leanir tried to look at what she was doing, but his eyes soon glazed, and he let out a groan. Blood pearled on his mouth where he'd bitten through his lip in his shaking. Arya listened to the dogs in the distance, looked again at Leanir's trembling form ... and she sat back to let Essa work.

"Watch our backs, Taze," she murmured.

"Yes, Captain."

With quick, sure, movements, Ranier's daughter began sketching Leanir's curled body, the clearing around them, and then ... right near his head, a mortar.

Arya stared, struck by the intricate detail of the drawing, the pure focus on Essa's face as she made stroke after stroke. Once she was finished, Essa pocketed the charcoal, then held the parchment in both hands and closed her eyes.

Even as Arya watched, unbelieving, the ground near Leanir's head shimmered and the mortar she'd drawn blurred into life. "There!" Essa said in satisfaction.

Arya stared from the mortar, back to the parchment. "You're amazing," she said.

At her words, Leanir craned his head, eyes widening in something approaching shock and surprise when he saw the mortar. In the next breath he let out a groan and curled up, eyes closing over.

"Those dogs are getting closer," Taze warned.

"I'm mixing the tonic now," Essa said, admirably calm as she tipped the small packet of herbs she'd already gotten from her pack into the mortar and began grinding them. "Won't be long."

Taze looked Arya over. "You're hurt."

"A dislocated shoulder. Bump on the back of my head. Nothing life threatening."

"I'm done." Essa drew a wad of something sticky and pungent out of the mortar and pressed it against Leanir's mouth. "You need to chew and swallow."

He did as she bade, clearly struggling to chew around his violent trembling. Arya hoped it tasted as bad as it smelled. His throat worked as he swallowed, then he sagged back against the ground, eyes sliding closed.

"Ranier warned us it would take time to work, and the poison was in his system for a while," Essa murmured. "He won't be able to outrun tracker dogs tonight."

Arya rubbed at her aching temples. Rorin and Darmanin were still out there somewhere, and she couldn't leave until she found them. But if Leanir couldn't run, then he was a liability she had to figure out what to do with.

The assassin coughed, and his eyes slid open. His limbs and muscles seemed to be relaxing, and an echo of his smirk crossed his face. "Looks like you'll get your wish, Raider. You can walk away and leave me here to die."

"I should," she snapped. "You tried to kill my brother and you ruined my general's life. I told you on that roof in Heathrock I was going to kill you one day, just like this."

"Then take your opportunity, Raider. You won't get another one."

Everything in her wanted to do exactly that. His death was only justice after the things he'd done. She wavered, hesitating.

She'd given her word.

She shook her head. "We are a team until we go back through the Gate. But it's no longer viable for all of us to pursue the cazaix. We should cut our losses. I'll go after Rorin and Darmanin. If possible, we'll continue on for the cazaix. But, Taze, you're going to get Essa and Leanir back over the border."

"We just got here," he protested.

An idea unfolded in her mind, step by step, one she thought Desomer would approve of. "Yes, but we need to adjust to the circumstances. I will lead the Rangers and dogs away from you to give time for Leanir to get back on his feet. Then, you three will head back over the border, and leave plenty of sign of your going that the Rangers think we *all* gave up and went home. That way Rorin, Dar, and I will be clear to carry on without pursuit."

Essa gave her a look. "Arya, you're in no shape to stay ahead of a pack of hunting dogs."

"We should leave Leanir here as a distraction while we get clear," Taze said.

"We're not leaving him," Arya said, her own frustration at the situation making her snap the words. "I'll kill him myself someday, but not when I've given my word not to touch him. That's an order, Taze."

His jaw tensed, but he didn't protest any further.

"Why do *I* need to go back?" Essa asked. "Taze could stay with Leanir and I could come with you."

"You never wanted to be here in the first place."

"Dammit, Arya." Essa kicked the ground in equal frustration. "That doesn't mean I want to abandon you."

"You need to convince the Rangers we've all gone back over the border, so the more tracks they see, the better," Arya said. "Rorin and Darmanin need the cazaix—the rest of us don't."

"What about provisions?" Essa asked.

"Ranier taught us to forage. I'll be fine."

"What if you're forced to fight?" Essa continued. "That shoulder won't hold up to—"

"I'm right handed, I'll be fine."

"Arya—"

Arya recognised the stubborn light in Essa's eyes and didn't have the energy for a lengthy argument. "Essa, please stop fighting me on this."

Essa glanced between Leanir—who'd now stopped trembling but whose eyes were closed and limbs slack—and Arya. "As soon as you've drawn them away and Leanir is on his feet, we'll catch their attention and make a run back to the Dreadwater Gate."

"Thank you." Arya gave her a relieved smile, then turned to Taze. "I need you to push my shoulder back into place."

Taze put his pack down and sheathed his sword, then came over to grip Arya's shoulder. He didn't hesitate; he simply manipulated the joint back into its socket in one quick movement. Arya swore as agony flared hotly, and he worked quickly to re-bind her left arm tightly against her chest with her jacket. Tears ran down her cheeks, and she gasped for air, gritting her teeth until the pain eased.

"Take this at least." Essa passed her the small pack of herbs she'd been wearing at her waist. "It won't weigh you down, and Taze still has his. There's willow bark in there for the pain."

"Thanks." Arya took the pack, squeezing her hand softly in the process. Essa squeezed back before letting go. "Good luck."

"Take care of yourself, Captain," Taze said. "Make sure you come back home safely."

"I will if you will," Arya promised, managing a smile for them.

Essa lifted her hand in a silent wave of farewell.

Arya forced herself into a loping run she'd mastered over the brutal months of training with Ranier. She doubled back to where she'd come ashore, then turned west into the trees, moving directly towards the barking. She got close enough that she could make out the distinct sounds of individual dogs, then she turned south for a short distance.

There, she hunkered down against a tree, resting and waiting for them to hit her trail. If it worked, they'd turn south after her and never get close enough to the riverbank to catch the scents of the others. If they went east for the riverbank instead ... well, she'd have to make a noise, enough to draw their attention her way.

As she rested, she went over her plan again, Desomer's voice in the back of her head urging her to think, to make sure she covered all contingencies. A sharp wave of fear and worry for all her companions swept through her, and she ruthlessly squashed it. Worry wasn't going to help.

The tenor of the barking changed, becoming at once high pitched and frantic.

They'd caught her scent.

Arya waited until she could tell which way they headed. Within minutes, she spotted pinpricks of torchlight coming in her direction, bobbing up and down as the Rangers followed their dogs. A man shouted, and someone replied.

They'd turned south after her.

Not waiting an instant longer, Arya rose to her feet and ran, striking southwest, away from the river and the border, plunging headlong through the trees, pushing aside branches and making enough noise for several people—just to make sure they followed her.

Arya sprinted, knowing she needed to stay ahead of the dogs until they began to tire, at which time she could slow her pace and return to the ground-eating jog Ranier had taught them to keep up for hours.

Branches thwacked her as she pushed through foliage, incurring tiny cuts and scrapes on her hands, face, and neck, and she narrowly avoided a turned ankle as a narrow path she was running along suddenly turned into a steep incline. Hot fear flashed at how close she'd come to disaster. But she couldn't afford to slow down and be more cautious—from the tenor and closeness of the barking, she was barely staying ahead of the dogs. She pushed herself, ignoring the burning in her lungs and the stabbing pain in her left shoulder, and praising Ranier with every single breath for how he'd prepared them for this.

After several miles, the dogs began falling back, and she could have sobbed in relief. The increasing pain in her shoulder, mixed with exhaustion, was beginning to make it hard for her to think clearly. Khadini was appreciably warmer than her home and sweat slicked her skin and soaked through her clothes in a way she'd never experienced before. She slowed to a more manageable jog, still heading away from the river.

Now she just had to run until they gave up.

Eventually, the barking faded entirely from hearing. When she looked over her shoulder, there were no pinpricks of light, just the darkness of the forest. Arya emerged onto the banks of a stream, and took her opportunity. She waded through water—blessedly cool on her sweat slicked skin—as high as her waist before running up the opposite bank, making sure to leave tracks in the mud. Then, she backed up, carefully placing her feet in the marks she'd already made. Once back in the water, she began wading down the middle of the stream.

She kept going for a mile or so. The stream continued in an easterly heading, and she guessed it might be a feeder to the Dreadwater. On that hope, when she waded out of the water, she continued along its banks, moving back into a jog.

Arya forced herself to keep going until her legs trembled underneath her and waves of dizziness began sweeping through her body. Crouching down, she scooped up mouthfuls of fresh water and drank.

Then, with the last shreds of her energy, she reached upwards and grabbed hold of a low overhanging tree branch. After bracing herself against the inevitable pain, Arya used her good arm to scramble up into the tree, grunting with the effort. It was a clumsy attempt, but eventually she managed to drag herself onto a sturdy branch. There she sagged, catching her breath, and waited for the pain in her shoulder to subside. Once it did, she settled with her back to the trunk, and closed her eyes. A couple of hours to give her body the rest it needed, then she'd go looking for Rorin and Darmanin.

At first, sleep seemed impossible. The moment she stopped moving, worry and fear for her companions flooded her. The anxiety of not even knowing whether Rorin and Darmanin had made it out of the water was a live beast clawing at her chest. Darmanin was a survivor, and Rorin had become physically hardened in a way he'd never been before over the last few months. They were both strong in their own ways.

But … if they had made it out of the water, they were alone, and she wasn't there to help them. They'd be okay.

She'd repeated it to herself over and over until, eventually, pain and exhaustion dragged her under, and she slipped into sleep.

Chapter 9

Arya woke to the music of birds warbling and water gurgling. A shaft of morning sunlight pierced the canopy above and warmed the back of her neck. She opened her eyes, shifting out of her cramped position without thinking. Her left shoulder launched a severe protest, and she hissed in pain. Her head pounded too, and she could feel the stickiness of dried blood down the back of her neck.

Her entire body felt like she'd been run over by stampeding horses.

And it was *hot*. Stickily, palpably, so.

Stifling a groan, Arya slowly uncurled, stretching out her arms and legs one at a time. Fresh pain throbbed in her body, but she'd become loose enough to begin a slow descent out of the tree. Her boots landed in the stream with a splash. Slowly, wincing with every movement, she soaked herself in the water. Its coolness was a pleasant relief.

After a long drink, followed by tightening the sling on her left arm, Arya felt marginally better. And the only cure for her stiff muscles was movement.

She had to find Rorin and Darmanin.

She started off at a limping walk along the banks, heading in the direction of the Dreadwater, then moved into a jog as soon as her muscles and joints loosened enough. The forest was quiet, the sunlight warm, and her speed increased as her body warmed. Frequently she paused to listen for the sounds of search dogs or Rangers, but it seemed the search had shifted focus.

By early afternoon, Arya was once again soaked through with sweat, and her stomach growled with hunger. The humidity made it feel like breathing through soup. She heard the rush of fast-flowing water that signalled she was approaching the Dreadwater, and slowed her pace, ensuring nobody was around before emerging from the trees. The water gleamed dark green.

Turning north along the banks would potentially take her closer to the Rangers and their dogs but given both Rorin and Darmanin had fallen into the water before Arya, it seemed more likely they'd washed ashore further north than she had.

So, she turned north, extra vigilant now. She heard snatches of the roaring rapids on the afternoon breeze, and the forest grew thicker as it wound towards the rocky ravine. Then, just as she assumed, came the faint barking of dogs.

She held still for a long moment, trying to ascertain which direction the barking was coming from, but the breeze was faint. It was too difficult to tell. If she kept going, she risked running right into the search parties. But if she turned back now, she might miss Rorin and Darmanin entirely.

Arya kept going until, thankfully, she found what she was looking for. Tracks leading from the edge of the water into the forest. She hunkered down, studying them. Water had sloughed away most of the imprints in the muddy bank, but even so, she thought the marks had been made by only one person. Rorin's boots had a distinct imprint, one she recognised from hours upon hours of following his steps in long runs through the Diamondfang.

Hope flared. He'd been on his feet, so he couldn't have been badly hurt.

She followed the tracks into the trees until they ended in a small clearing, where all her burgeoning hope vanished in a blink, replaced by despair. The rich soil here was scuffed and gouged with multiple sets of prints. There were clear signs of a struggle, and marks where something heavy had been dragged away—a body, by the looks of it.

Even though she circled again and again to be sure, there was no sign of Rorin's distinctive boot print leaving the clearing. He'd been captured. He must have washed ashore right into a patrol of Rangers.

Arya hesitated, trying to beat back her rising panic to decide what her next move should be. Her first urge was to follow the tracks, catch up to the

Rangers and try to get Rorin back. But she couldn't forget about Darmanin. If she kept moving upriver, she might find him. Getting Rorin back would be easier with Darmanin's help, but if she took too long trying to find Darmanin, any chance of tracking Rorin would be gone.

The answer came immediately. She couldn't abandon Rorin, not under any circumstances. Once Rorin was safe, they could both go after Darmanin. And part of her knew Darmanin would be fine.

Arya rose to her feet, spotting the drops of dried blood in the dirt at the same time her ears caught rustling in the trees behind her. She spun as three Khadini warriors emerged from their places of concealment, and quickly realised her mistake. Rangers, she assumed.

They'd set a trap.

Raven's balls. Desomer would have a fit when he learned she hadn't checked for something as simple as an ambush.

The closest Ranger said something unrecognisable, a challenging note in his voice. She eyed him flatly, daring him to come at her. All three held their swords ready, and carried knives strapped to their chests and legs. No armour though. They wore loose pants tucked into sandals and sleeveless jerkins. Their arms were roped with wiry muscle, and they moved with the grace of well-trained swordsmen.

The Ranger spoke again, contempt in his dark eyes as he addressed her. She couldn't understand the Khadini words but understood the gesture to get on her knees well enough. Arya ignored him, her gaze returning to the blood she'd spotted right before the soldiers appeared. The splatters followed the tracks of a body being dragged through the mud. Not enough to signify a mortal wound, but still...

Rorin's blood.

A tide of anger rose in her chest. These warriors had harmed her brother. Arya's mouth curled in a silent snarl, and she held the Ranger's gaze as she yanked off the sling binding her shoulder and drew her dagger.

"Come on then," she said.

The warriors came at her as a group. Their aggression only tipped her rising anger into white hot fury. A red haze descended over her vision as she thought about Rorin struggling against these warriors, about how they'd drawn blood and carried him off.

A burning sensation heated her skin, like a physical manifestation of her fury. The Rangers faltered, staring at her face, confusion and wariness in their expressions. She didn't know what they'd seen to make them halt, but she took advantage of it, leaping at them with a blood-curdling cry. Her anger seemed to bleed out into her dagger, the strength of her arm, and her strike carried enough force to bury her blade to the hilt in the closest Ranger's chest, shearing through bone and muscle like a hot knife through butter.

Arya yanked it out with a spray of blood that spattered across her hands and face, then flew at the next two warriors without pause. She countered their attacks with almost insulting ease. Both lay dead at her feet in moments, and then her anger had nowhere to go. It roiled inside her, seeking an outlet, like electricity burning through her, almost painful but not quite.

Her fingers uncurled, her dagger dropping to the ground, and she stood with her feet spread apart, head hanging, breathing hard, fighting to contain whatever it was demanding to be loosed inside her. She didn't understand what was happening.

This wasn't just anger.

Realisation crashed down over her with the final bit of clarity she had left.

This was magic storming inside her, trying to get out.

No! Arya fought it with everything she had, pushing it down, stifling it, unwilling to acknowledge it or what it would mean. It was a desperate inner war, but gradually she began winning it. And then, as soon as she had control, whatever was surging inside her winked out of existence.

As it did, blackness descended over her vision, and she realised she was falling, a distant part of her noticing the pain spiking in her shoulder as she hit the ground.

And then the nazal had her mind, and it was wrenched away from the clearing in Khadini and trapped in their darkness.

Malice filled the darkness, threat tinged with triumph. The shadowy face of the monster faced her, mouth twisted with glee. But though she only saw the one monster, there were more with it, somehow … their voices…

"*We see you. We hunt you. We see you.*"

The hissing whispers came over and over, echoing between them. At least three, she thought, maybe four of them. But only one she could see, flashing in and out of the darkness, taunting her with its horrifying visage; white, papery skin and gleaming red eyes. Sharp, pointed teeth bared in triumph. Their whispers ripped through Arya's already tender mind, and she cried out in agony. Tendrils of something *dark* reached for her, and she recoiled in horror.

"*Ours now. Filthy Valheran. Useless. Weak. We see you. We hunt you. But where?*"

Arya fought to escape and wake herself, but she couldn't, she didn't know how. She struggled anyway, terrified into a panic by the creatures surrounding her.

All at once a haunting cry echoed through the darkness. The beauty of that cry hit Arya hard, cutting through her terror and restoring her sense. Gold flashed. Widespread wings and a lashing tail.

He was here. The wyvern. Somehow, he was here.

Her heart leaped at the same time as she instinctively reached for him, to warn him of the danger, to tell him to get away, to flee.

The nazal turned their attention away from Arya and focused it on the wyvern. He appeared before her, flooding the darkness with golden light, rearing high, covering her from their searching gaze, a long, serpentine head and teeth bared with the same fury that had roped through her at the sight of Rorin's blood.

And the hunger on the nazal's face as they regarded him terrified her to her core.

They wanted the wyvern as much as they wanted her.

"Go, get back!" She tried to get herself in front of the wyvern to protect him. As soon as her hand touched his silken scales, a jolt of energy catapulted through them both before exploding outwards in a circle of golden light. The nazal were thrown from the darkness, as were Arya and the wyvern.

She saw Essa in her mind then, as if watching from a distance, the woman's features set in determination as she stared ahead of her. *Essa.* Arya didn't realise she'd called out, but Essa turned, eyes roving behind her. "Arya?" But then she was gone. There was a flash of Darmanin then, pressed against a tree trunk, and Chiarn, playing music at in inn she didn't recognise. And finally Leanir, standing still as a statue, bow hanging loosely from his left hand.

She reached for all of them, not knowing why or even how, but they were there, the threads of them, and they slid into place like a perfectly made key into an oiled lock. Her wyvern cried again, low and haunting, and she thought there might be echoing cries, other wyverns.

But then everything broke away and she sank into an exhausted slumber.

***

By the time Arya woke, it was unclear how much time had passed. The sun was high in the sky, and she was still lying in the middle of the clearing. It took a few moments to remember what had happened, and she sat up, groaning at a stab of agony from her stiffened shoulder. She'd half expected to find herself surrounded by nazal or Rangers, but the clearing was quiet aside from the chirping of birds in the nearby trees and the soft rustling of the breeze through the branches.

The monsters had found her, though. After all these years they knew her. She was sure of it. Maybe not her name, but ... whatever had happened to her when the Rangers had attacked ... they'd sensed it. Sensed *her*. And they'd recognise her magic if they crossed paths. Or if she used it again.

Tentatively, she reached inside herself, trying to see if that roiling storm of magic was still there.

Nothing.

Relief filled her, and she tried again, harder this time. Nothing, not even a glimmer of what had been there. Good. She hoped it stayed that way.

She searched inside herself, trying to see if she could sense the wyvern or reach him while she was awake. She had no more success with that than she had reaching her magic. It was probably for the best, now the nazal had found her.

She couldn't keep sitting here.

Arya forced herself to her feet, favouring her shoulder and grimacing as she caught the scent of rotting flesh. The fallen bodies of the Rangers nearby were beginning to bloat in the warm air, and the sweet smell of decay drifted towards her. Her stomach roiled, and she took deep breaths until it calmed.

She'd been lying there at least a day, then.

Her head pounded. Her limbs trembled with fatigue. After tugging her water flask free, she drank her fill, then returned to the river to re-fill it before going back to the clearing.

The dead soldiers had carried minimal supplies with them, but she took all of what they had, ravenously shoving a handful of some kind of sticky rice and herb ball into her mouth. She attached another waterskin and rope to her belt and slung one of their swords over her uninjured shoulder.

The tracks milling about the clearing were further confused by the ambush party, but after some careful study, she worked out which direction they'd taken Rorin. The trail was faint. The tracks led in a south-westerly direction, well away from the border.

Arya started running, knowing she might already be too late.

It was hard not to give into despair, to feel like she was already too late, even as she ran. Rorin was captured, she had no idea where Darmanin was, and the other three members of their party were risking their lives trying to get back to the Dreadwater Gate. At least if her visions had been real, both Essa and Darmanin were alive and well enough to be on their feet.

The terrain was so different to anything she'd known. The foliage was thick and green, the air warm and alive with the scents of flowers and the rotting mulch on the forest floor. And it was hilly, so much so it was hard to get a sense of her surroundings, of where the trail might lead. At least the rich, loamy ground meant tracks were easier to follow.

The trail left by the Rangers brought her down a steep incline to where a dirt road had been cut into the side of the hill. On its opposite side, more forested slope continued steeply downward. The sound of water rushing below drifted up to her, even though it was hidden from sight by the thick foliage. Birds continued to sing, bright and happy.

She stopped at the road, easing aching legs and using her sleeve to wipe away the sweat dripping down her face. Her heart fell when she saw tracks of multiple horses passing by in both directions, their hoof prints sinking deep into the soil. There were signs of carts, too. When she spotted the cluster of hoof tracks and manure just off the side of the road where the track ended, she cursed under her breath. The Rangers had had horses waiting for them. Which meant they could be anywhere by now.

The road was empty, but she could hardly walk openly along it, even if she knew which direction to head in. Taking a deep breath, she hunkered down over the tracks, trying to see if she could pick out the freshest. By looking closely enough at the verge where the horses had been waiting, the markings *looked* like they'd turned west.

Arya started running.

Chapter 10

Dawn the following morning found Arya running parallel to the road. She'd allowed herself a couple hours rest overnight before forcing herself onwards. Opening her eyes to find a brightly coloured snake staring at her—only a few inches from her head—had prompted a hasty and undignified disembarking from the tree she'd slept in. Ranier had taken great pains to explain how venomous Khadini snakes could be, and she hadn't regretted the momentary panic, despite feeling sure the creature was laughing at her.

Her shoulder had felt slightly better when she awoke, and though the running jarred it, it was a duller pain than before. The thick forest and rising hills seemed endless. She'd seen it laid out on a map before, of course, but the markings of the jungle-like terrain marked out across almost the entire northern third of the country on Desomer's maps hadn't prepared her for the reality.

The road had so far curled for miles without much traffic coming in either direction, and without passing through a village or town. Despite that, the surface appeared well-tended, which indicated it served an important purpose, or at least had once. In Arya's experience, rarely used rural tracks were left entirely to the mercy of weather and time. Perhaps the road was used to ferry supplies and weapons to the Rangers patrolling the territory around the Dreadwater Gate

Mid-morning, she finally reached a fork in the road. She slowed to a halt. There was no marker, no sign, just the dirt surface splitting off in two different directions: west and south. Ruts in the surface of the road leading south indicated heavy carts travelled frequently along it, and it was almost double the width of the other one.

The jungle birds sang merrily around Arya as she tried to decide which way to go. If she chose incorrectly, her chances of finding Rorin would vanish. Instinct had her carefully examining the edges of the road for a short distance in either direction. Picking out the tracks of those she was following as distinct from any other was impossible, but...

A wide grin swept over Arya's face when her peripheral vision caught a flash in the sunlight shining through the canopy. A piece of flint. Rorin's—whittled into the shape of an arrowhead one night as they'd sprawled exhausted by the fire after one of Ranier's training sessions. He'd dropped it because he knew if she was alive and well, she'd be following him. It was lying on the verge of the road leading west.

Arya tucked the flint into her pocket and continued west.

***

Within an hour, she approached the first town. She'd already had to conceal herself in the foliage lining the road twice as horse-driven carts passed by heading east. Legs burning as she crested a rise, Arya found herself looking down into a small valley. The road wound into it and through a huddle of buildings before continuing up the western valley wall. A swift-flowing stream bisected the valley from north to south.

Arya studied the village as best she could from a distance. The valley floor had been cleared for farmland, and there was enough movement—farmers at work in the fields, lowing cattle, carts, and horses moving in and out—to suggest a bustling village. The road went right through it, so Arya couldn't keep following it—she'd stick out instantly with her fair skin and golden hair. There wasn't enough cover to circle around in broad daylight either, only open fields.

She'd have to hike around the steep valley wall.

By the time night fell, she was sweaty, exhausted, and being feasted upon by the bugs that seemed to come alive at nighttime in this blasted place.

Arya longed for the cold snows and open expanse of the Diamondfang with a fierceness that took her breath away. Once she'd circled back to the road, she decided to push through and keep going through the night, figuring daylight would likely force her to take cover again if she was heading into a more heavily populated area.

But as dawn's pink glow lit up the horizon the next morning, Arya struggled along the road as it weaved backward and forward up another steep incline. When she reached the top, the forest ended abruptly and cleared back to a distinct edge. Her ground-eating jog slowed to a halt as she regarded what was below her. The entire area ahead had been cleared, the rich brown loam like a scar on the landscape where it formed an open pit mine that spread out for miles.

Arya had learned about mining during those endlessly mind-numbing lessons Desomer had forced her to attend with Rorin's tutor, because Ravenstrike relied on its eastern gem mines for a good portion of its revenue. But those were underground mines. Dark and narrow and dangerous.

She'd never seen anything on this scale.

The pit was astoundingly deep and dug down like an oddly shaped amphitheatre into the earth. Rows cut into the sides as it wound down to its bottom, which had to be at least a mile deep, if not more. Raw, bare, earth was open to the rising sun.

But this was no ordinary mine. A tall metal fence, topped with barbed wire, ran the entire circumference of the open earth. From the looks of it, Arya thought there had to be miles of fencing. And as far as she could tell, there was only one entrance, a set of closed gates about a half mile further along the road.

Then, as she stood there and studied the place, there was movement at the western edge of the mine. She stared into the distance, trying to make out what was moving, and eventually realised.

A long line of people snaked their way down to the pit floor.

Horses and carts came into view, trundling down from massive log warehouses set along the southern edge of the pit, inside the fence. To the north, the water of a massive lake glittered green in the sun. The wire fence stopped at the water's edge, the only break in its circumference, and it looked like one of the roads up from the mine led directly to the water.

This was a Khadini labour camp.

Arya wasn't sure whether to be relieved or horrified. Rorin must have been brought here. It was exactly what Ranier had told them would happen if they were captured and not killed outright. It meant she'd found Rorin, finally. But it also meant he was a prisoner, which was a death sentence.

Arya ducked into the trees, maintaining the cover of the canopy, and chose the tallest tree she could find to climb. Once settled, with a good view of the mine, she studied its operations.

And planned, as Desomer had taught her, carefully and without emotion.

The fence was the height of two tall men, and climbable, even with the barbed wire, but there was absolutely no cover amidst the cleared ground surrounding the pit, and anyone scaling it would quickly be spotted by the continuous patrols of mounted guards riding the perimeter—a pair passed by the main gates every couple of minutes.

Even if she managed to get over the fence without being seen—perhaps at night—the open sides of the pit were just as exposed. Carts moved along the pathways transporting whatever was being dug up, and a lone figure walking would be spotted immediately.

It was hard to get an exact count, but she estimated a couple thousand workers crawling over the bottom levels of the pit. Finding Rorin would be impossible unless she happened to stumble across him almost immediately. She kept watching as night fell, but hope slowly faded. The workers returned in a long snaking line up the western side of the pit when the light grew too dim to work, but it was too far to see where they went once they reached the top.

There were so many of them. Did Khadini truly have so many criminals? Surely not. But how else did so many thousands end up in the mine?

By the time it was fully dark, the patrolling guards had lit torches along the fence line, placed close enough together there were no gaps in the light shining over the area along the fence.

So much for climbing over under the cover of darkness.

A sleepless night followed, in which Arya tried to come up with a plan to get Rorin out. Every plan she came up with she was forced to discard as unworkable. It was useless.

To get Rorin out, she would need his help, as well as a better understanding of the inner workings of the mine. She considered returning to the border, searching for Darmanin before coming back for Rorin. But she couldn't see how two outsiders was any better than one. And she had no trail to follow to find Darmanin. By the time she did, *if* she even did, Rorin could be hurt or worse.

Ranier had said that anyone put in the mines could have their life expectancy measured in years, months even. Her chest tightened painfully at the mere thought of Rorin there.

She only had one viable option.

As soon as dawn's light lit up the sky, she dug a hole just off the road, inside the tree line, and buried her stolen sword and dagger and knife. Rising to her feet, she glanced ahead at the mine, and behind her, where the border of Dunidaen lay.

"I don't want to hear it," she muttered to Desomer's voice in her head, telling her she was stark raving mad. She wished the crusty old general were with her right now.

Taking a deep breath, Arya left the cover of the trees and walked down the road. The early sun was already hot on her back. The pit loomed even larger ahead of her, enormous in scale, dwarfing anything she'd ever seen before.

The guards saw her quickly, dispelling any doubts she might have had about their general alertness. Shouts echoed through the morning and then the gates opened, and four mounted guards cantered out. She stopped and waited, hands in the air and palms out to demonstrate she was no threat. They circled her, kicking up clods of dirt from the road. Grit flew in her eyes and mouth. One of them shouted at her in Khadini.

She caught the word 'Dunidae' in there more than once.

"This has got to be the stupidest idea I've ever had," Arya muttered to herself, not really regretting her choice. She owed so much to Thiara Ravenstrike that there was no question of doing everything she possibly could to get Rorin free, and that was apart from the simple fact that he was her brother.

When Arya didn't respond, but didn't move to attack either, they slowed their horses to a walk, and the soldier shouted at her again, a demanding note to his voice.

Arya shook her head. "I'm sorry, I don't speak Khadini."

Unexpectedly, the guard behind her kicked out with his boot. She grunted and fell forward, hitting the ground hard. Before she could get up, he'd dismounted and pressed his booted foot into the back of her neck. Dirt filled her mouth as he ground her face into the road. Another guard dismounted, yanking her arms behind her back and tying her wrists tightly together. Her shoulder screamed in agony but she didn't fight them, just breathed through the pain.

One of them yanked her unceremoniously to her feet, barked something unrecognisable, then re-mounted his horse. She swayed, blinking blurriness from her vision, tears trickling through the dirt on her cheeks from the pain in her shoulder, and mixing with the blood seeping from her nose.

The guard ahead gestured in the direction of the gates, then turned his horse that way. The four guards stayed in a close circle around her until the gates swung closed behind them. Then they peeled off and two new guards—on foot—took an arm each and unceremoniously dragged Arya to a nearby cart before tossing her into the back of it.

Arya grunted in pain and lay there, reminding herself that antagonising the guards would only make things worse. She had to stay alive and as healthy as possible if she was going to help Rorin. The cart lurched into movement and trundled over bumpy surface for a good long while before creaking to a halt.

They were still at the top of the pit but had arrived at a cluster of wooden buildings on its northern side, not far from the dam. The guards dragged her out of the cart and hustled her over to the nearest building where they promptly shoved her through the open doorway.

Unable to keep balance with her wrists bound, Arya stumbled and fell to the floor hard, groaning at the impact. Her old knee injury made itself known, pain stabbing down her left calf. An instant later they hauled her back to her feet. Not far away was a fire pit, flames roaring merrily inside it, and beside it a bellows. The air was oppressively hot.

A shirtless smith worked nearby, hammer clanging down and shaping a piece of metal. She couldn't quite make out what it was. He was so focused on his work he hadn't realised they'd entered so one of the guards shouted at him.

The smithy plunged whatever he'd been hammering into a bucket of water. It hissed and steam rose into the air, making the room even hotter. The guards dragged Arya closer to the fire pit. Sweat slicked her skin, turning the dirt on her skin to rivulets of mud. The smith left his work and came to the firepit, reaching out for a rod that hung nearby.

Shit. Arya's heart sank as she abruptly realised why she'd been brought here.

Immediately she began struggling, fighting to get free of the guards' hold on her. But they were too strong and held her firmly in place as she yelled and cursed. Inexorably, they turned her around, so her back was to the fire. One loosened the rope binding her wrists enough to be able to twist her right arm, turning the inside of her forearm towards the firepit and then tearing off the sleeve of her shirt.

"Get off me, you bastards!" she screamed, struggling for all she was worth. "Get away from me!"

They laughed and only held her more tightly. She heard the hiss as the brand was lifted from the firepit, and craned her neck over her shoulder, trying to see what was happening. The end of the brand glowed red-hot.

"If you touch me with that thing, I'll kill you all!" she roared.

It was no use. She couldn't get free. While the soldier held her right arm locked in place, the smith pressed the red-hot brand into the pale flesh of her inner forearm. Arya screamed with the agony of it, tears running down her face, and anger burning through her. Her entire arm felt on fire, skin blistering, heat overwhelming.

The anger fuelled her enough to break their hold, if only for a brief second. The burning brand slid against her flesh, sending more agony flaring though her. Her stomach heaved and sweat poured off her.

She screamed from the very depths of her being.

It burned so badly that she thought she might pass out, and then the brand was lifted away. The sweltering room smelled like burned flesh, and she gagged, doubling up. One of the guards re-tightened the binding on her wrists.

Arya, breath sobbing, tears of agony flooding her cheeks, sagged in their grip as she was dragged back outside and tossed into the cart again. One guard yelled something at her, but she ignored him. Her right forearm burned unbearably, and she mustered the courage to look at it. Her struggles meant the brand hadn't left a clean mark—instead a lightning-shaped welt, angry red and blistered, ran from her wrist halfway along her forearm.

The cart lurched into movement, beginning a long, winding journey down into the pit. Shivering with shock and pain, she allowed herself to slump boneless in the cart, conserving energy while she could. For a moment she was overwhelmed by the certainty that she'd made a fatal mistake, that she'd never get out of this place. She might even die here.

But then she realised that they must have done this to Rorin too. Her brother. How afraid and despairing he must be, and in pain.

She would get Rorin.

And then hunt down every guard who'd done this to them.

And make them pay.

Chapter 11

A bell rang across the mine. Like clockwork, everyone in the dormitory rolled out of bed, pulled their threadbare clothes on, slid feet into worn sandals, and headed for the door. Arya followed as the line from their dormitory snaked into the communal eating building. There she put spoon to mouth—watery oats, and not near enough—just like everybody else.

A second bell sounded, cutting through the clutter of murmured conversation and spoons scraping against clay bowls. Before the first echo had died away, everyone around Arya rose to their feet, whether they'd finished eating or not. She *had* finished eating—in almost two weeks, Arya had already learned that it paid to eat as much food as was put in front of you as you could—and obediently joined the line filing out of the eating hall and towards the pit entrance.

They worked every day without respite, spending daylight hours down in the pit, either taking a pickaxe to the rock in search of iron ore or helping to shift the waste rock into carts to be hauled away. The amount of waste rock was staggering. The ore they did uncover was taken to the top of the pit where it was transported to the cazaix smelter in the south. The soldiers guarding them didn't hesitate to use the whips they carried if they thought a worker was slacking off. To them, being too tired or sick to work fell under this category. If you were ill or injured, you worked until you got better or you died. Arya now understood why Ranier thought a sentence to the mines as bad as execution. It essentially was an execution order—just one that took time to be carried out.

This morning, as always, when each worker passed the guards, they were handed a flagon of water. Without it, they'd keel over from dehydration before midday in the oppressive heat and humidity. But they received nothing else, including food, until they returned at dusk.

As Arya walked, the sloshing flagon bumping against her hip where a sword once had, sweat already slicking her skin, she contemplated the fact that, by her count, she'd been away from Heathrock for almost seven months, making it mid-summer in Ravenstrike.

The State Council was six months away.

It was a daily ritual, using the long walk down into the pit to assess her position, scan every face she could see for Rorin, and try to figure out how to escape the moment she found him. The focus on planning kept her from losing hope with each day that passed without finding her brother among the thousands of her fellow prisoners. There were just so many of them. And they were given no freedom of movement.

It had been a lonely time.

Nobody in the mine understood Dunidae, and though she'd been able to pick up some basics of Khadini by careful listening, she couldn't speak it. And even if she *was* able to ask her fellow prisoners whether they'd seen Rorin, their wariness of her was obvious. She might be a prisoner like them, but it was also clear she was a foreigner, and they probably guessed she'd come to steal their cazaix.

Arya's gaze caught on the lighting-shaped scar on her right inner forearm, mostly healed over now, a red line against her skin. She *had* learned that the brands were a way of preventing escape. It was a clever tactic. A branded person found anywhere outside the labour camp would be quickly recognised as an escapee, and re-captured and returned.

A shout from a nearby guard jolted Arya from her thoughts. The man two spots ahead of her in the line was moving too slowly—the result of a badly bruised and swollen foot, sustained two days earlier from a pile of falling rock. He quickened his limping pace, pain tightening his features, and they filed past the guard, gazes carefully averted. They were halfway down the pit now, crossing between shelves—as Arya had come to consider them—via wooden ramps sturdy enough to hold the horses and carts that frequently traversed them.

The man directly ahead of her in the line leaned forward to mutter something to the prisoner who'd been reprimanded; his shoulders and back were stiff and his hands were clenched into white-knuckled fists at his sides. Whatever the man in front of Arya said to him made him chuckle, though, and Arya watched the tension drain from his body.

The exchange wasn't unusual. Arya had marked the man ahead of her from almost her first day in the mine, for a couple of reasons. His name was Kulan. Physically he wasn't any different from the other Khadini men here—tall and too-thin, brown hair and beard grown long and scruffy—but it was his behaviour that set him apart.

He never did anything to incur the guards' wrath, was always submissive and obedient, but Arya hadn't failed to notice how often he diffused tension between prisoners, or prisoners and guards, and how he quietly worked to keep the prisoners' morale up.

And he did it in such a way that she was pretty sure nobody else noticed.

When she'd noticed *that,* she started to pay more attention to other things. Like the fact that a handful of other prisoners—so far she'd counted twelve, a mix of men and women, in a range of ages—deferred to him. In small ways only, never enough to make it obvious to the guards or other prisoners. And yet Kulan was young, probably no more than a year or two older than Arya.

He was deliberately discreet, and those who deferred to him were discreet about it too. It made her curious. Was there some kind of danger in the guards or other prisoners knowing who Kulan was?

So she kept paying attention, wondering if she might be able to use her knowledge somehow. To find Rorin. To escape.

Planning for that was never far from her thoughts.

A flicker of movement at her side drew her sharply back to the present. The guard had noticed Kulan's exchange of words with the injured man in front of him, heard their shared chuckle, and strode after them to cuff the back of Kulan's head. "Quiet!"

Arya responded without thinking. "Hey!" she protested, uselessly, in Dunidae. "He didn't do anything." In fact, he'd been helping to calm his fellow prisoner.

The guard turned his glare on her, then struck Kulan again, this time drawing blood. Kulan winced, lifting a hand to the trickle of blood down the back of his neck. At the sight of it, the injured prisoner gave an inarticulate cry and jumped at the guard, swinging his fist into the man's face. The guard staggered back, and the prisoner leaped on him, tackling him to the ground.

The prisoners around them backed away as quickly as they could, shouting. Though Arya had no idea what they were saying, it seemed they were telling the prisoner to stop attacking the guard. Kulan crouched over the two fighting figures, trying to draw off his fellow prisoner before he could do too much damage.

But it was too late. A second guard came running at the fracas, raising his whip.

"He's just trying to stop the fight!" Arya shouted. "He's trying to help."

But the guard ignored her. He cracked his whip across Kulan's back. The man cried out in agony, but before he could scramble clear, the guard snapped the whip again, and again. The soldier's face was twisted with anger and contempt. The first guard had gotten the best of the prisoner he was wrestling, and his fists and boots pummelled the weaker man's body.

As Arya watched, that *thing* inside her rose with her anger. It happened every time her temper flared now, rising like bile in the back of her throat, and each time she had to fight it back down.

And each time it was harder.

Whatever had happened against those Rangers in the forest three months earlier, it had unlocked something inside her and whatever it was didn't want to be kept restrained.

Her magic.

Now, desperately, Arya fought it down—losing control here could have disastrous consequences, not to mention it might allow the nazal to entrap her mind again. She lived in constant terror of that happening. But the magic surged inside her, battering at her defences, refusing to be contained.

In the end, needing to do *something* before she exploded, Arya launched herself at the second guard as he lifted the whip to bring it down on Kulan again. She hit him cleanly, and her shoulder rammed into his chest. They crashed to the ground. Arya landed on top and drove her fist squarely into his jaw before he could recover.

He cursed and tried to draw the dagger sheathed at his waist. She grabbed his wrist with both hands and managed to twist his arm as he drew it out. The blade fell to the ground with a thud. The guard twisted violently, throwing her off him. He rolled above her and tried to pin her hands above her head. She kicked up with a knee, missing his groin by inches as he moved aside. But she pushed with his movement, shoving him away, muscles bunching, preparing to leap on him again.

But another pair of arms grabbed at her, and hauled her back. More soldiers had come running, and now two of them had her by each arm, holding her firmly as she struggled. The guard she'd fought came to his feet, spitting blood and dust. He shouted furiously, then lashed out. He backhanded her, snapping her head back. Hot blood trickled from a split lip. A second fist followed up with a heavy blow to her stomach. She sagged, gasping, winded badly. Another punch, to her kidneys, then a final backhand to her face.

All the surging magic inside her drained away as if it had never been.

Arya hung lifeless in the guard's hold, barely conscious, breath wheezing. More loud chatter among the guards before she found herself being dragged away. Then, somewhere along the journey, she passed out.

***

Arya stirred, letting out a soft groan as her battered body made itself known. She was sprawled on a hard floor in a hot, oppressive space. The scent of blood, excrement, and old sweat filled the air. She dragged herself into a sitting position. Every inch of her body hurt. She looked around. The cell was dim. The walls were built from the same logs as all the other buildings in the compound, and a single door with a small window set into it was the only way out—and the only source of light. And she wasn't alone.

Kulan sat in the opposite corner, leaning forward gingerly so his back wasn't touching the wall. He gave her a wary nod when she met his gaze. An attempt to stand made her ribs protest stridently, so she gave up and remained seated. She settled as comfortably as she could against the wall and pointed at her fellow prisoner. "Kulan?" she ventured.

He nodded, then pointed at her, eyebrows raised.

"Arya," she replied. "Arya Ravenstrike."

He said something else but spoke too quickly for her to pick out any of the words. She shrugged, to which he seemed to guess her difficulty. He shifted closer, moving into the dim light cast from a window. Beneath the beard and grime coating his olive skin, he had fine features, with deep green eyes. He spoke more slowly this time, and with a heavy accent that made it hard to parse the words, spoke in Dunidae. "How ... you come here, Arya Ravenstrike?"

"Dreadwater." She aimed for words that should be common to both Khadini and Dunidae. "Cazaix."

His disgusted eye roll was obvious even in the dim light. She didn't understand the next word that came from his mouth but would have bet all the gold she didn't have that it was a curse word.

Arya merely shrugged, too excited by his use of Dunidae to worry about what he thought of her. "You speak Dunidae?"

Before he could respond, footsteps sounded outside, the door opened, and a flagon of water and a clean cloth were tossed inside—presumably to clean the wounds on Kulan's back. The door slammed closed. Arya pointed to the supplies.

Kulan scowled, but eventually said, "Yes ... please."

He sat still as she moved closer to him. She began to clean his wounds. "So you *do* speak Dunidae?"

"A little. If you ... speak slow. Simple." Kulan let out a noisy huff. "Why ... help us?"

"Angry. You hadn't done anything wrong." She carefully cleaned out the long cuts on his back from the soldier's whip. "Your friend?" she asked. She wondered why he hadn't been put in the cell with them.

Kulan's face tightened in worry. "Tefel?" Then he shrugged, gaze dropping to the floor.

She didn't ask anymore, giving him a moment before asking her next, most urgent question. "Kulan, I'm looking for someone. Like me. From Dunidae. A ... young man. Light hair. Blue eyes."

"In this mine?" He seemed puzzled.

"Yes." She tried her best to speak slowly despite how eager she was. "Do you know which ... sleeping room he is in? Where?"

His puzzlement deepened. "You ... the only Dunidae in here."

Her heart plummeted even as she searched his gaze. "But ... so many people here. You can't be sure?"

"No Dunidae here, Arya." He shook his head decisively, then pointed, as if at her fair skin and golden hair. "Stands out. Prisoners talk. No other Dunidae or I would hear."

It felt like all the air had been sucked out of the already airless cell. Arya stared wordlessly at him.

All for nothing. If Rorin wasn't here, then...

She'd given herself up for nothing.

Chapter 12

For hours after Kulan's revelation, Arya sat staring at the opposite wall of the cell, despair clawing at her like a live creature. Where *was* Rorin? Was he okay? What if he needed her help, and she'd trapped herself in this blasted place?

Kulan tried to get her to eat her share of the slop they'd been delivered, but she refused everything but the water.

"Upset?" Kulan asked quietly.

She shook her head, unable to speak of it.

Eventually, as the sun set on the jungle surrounding the mine, Kulan broke the silence, his face bright, as if he'd thought up something clever. "You and me … long time here. I teach you Khadini?"

She let out a long breath. She didn't want to learn Khadini, or break another piece of rock, or do anything but scream her frustration and despair into the air. But her brain saw the sense in Kulan's offer. Being able to speak Khadini, or at least make herself understood, would be crucial if she was ever going to get herself out of this place.

So she could find Rorin, and the others.

So she turned to her head toward him. "Okay."

"Good." He shifted closer to her so they could see each other better in the fading light, then gave her a sympathetic look, like being Dunidae meant she was probably simple. "We start … easy."

She forced herself to focus on his face and what he was saying, determined to learn quickly. And as they began, her thoughts creaked to life, the despair dropping away and allowing her soldier's focus to return. There was more than one way learning Khadini from Kulan could help her.

There were secrets hovering around her fellow prisoner, and learning from him would give her an opportunity to probe at those secrets.

And just maybe ... part of her suspected that whatever he was hiding might help her escape and find her family.

***

In the days that followed, Kulan taught Arya the building blocks of pronunciation in Khadini. It was starkly different from Dunidae, more guttural and with different rules around sentence structure. However, unlike her insufferable, tedious lessons with Rorin's tutor, leaning a language seemed to come easily to Arya.

Once she'd picked up enough to understand more of what Kulan was saying and ask better questions, Arya learned they were likely to be held in the cell for some time.

"They will lose two workers for a time," he said, referencing the guards. "But stop wider problems from breaking out. By the time they send us back, tempers will have died down and an example will have been set."

Their lessons were a welcome distraction from endless worry about Rorin and the others, as well as hunger and listlessness; food came once a day and was minimal. Kulan pointed out that being put in the cells had to be enough of a punishment that anyone placed in them would never want to come back. He was a good teacher, with a sharp sense of humour that enjoyed teasing her mercilessly whenever she mangled a pronunciation.

She'd briefly considered offering to help him improve his Dunidae, but ultimately discarded the idea. Best to spend as much time as possible on learning the language of the country she was in, and had to escape from. Kulan had little need to be fluent in Dunidae, as much as she would have relished the opportunity to ridicule him over *his* terrible pronunciation.

"I thought you Dunidae had finally given up on attempting to steal cazaix from us," Kulan said one afternoon, two weeks into their isolation. His voice was full of contempt, gaunt face tight with displeasure. "Running the Dreadwater Gate is a very stupid thing to do."

"It is," she agreed. There was *something* in Kulan's manner—a cockiness, a self-assuredness with a hint of condescension—that niggled at her. It reminded her of something, but she couldn't quite figure out what.

She caught a flash of white teeth as he grinned. "You did attack a guard on a stranger's behalf, though, so perhaps you are a stupid person."

Arya scowled. Sometimes she wasn't sure whether she liked or was intensely irritated by Kulan. "Next time I'll leave you to be whipped."

"You should have," he said. "We are both in here, when only I should be."

Arya took a moment to figure out what she thought were the right words. "Sometimes ... not okay to watch bad things and do nothing. No matter what."

There was a long, heavy, silence, and then Kulan said simply. "You are right."

She gave him a curious glance. "Who are you?"

"I am Kulan," he said guilelessly.

She left it alone.

For now.

On another afternoon, as they both lay sagging in the sweltering heat of the afternoon, Arya's stomach hollow with hunger, Kulan asked, "Why did you run the Dreadwater Gate when nobody has for so long?"

Arya let out a breath, trying to figure out the best way to explain so he would understand—she didn't yet have the Khadini words for a lot of what she wanted to say but Kulan refused to let her use Dunidae unless she was truly stuck. "I came with my brother. He is the son of a ... leader, but he cannot speak."

"So he must prove himself by running the Dreadwater and stealing our cazaix?" Kulan nodded understanding, then rolled his eyes. Hard. "Still stupid."

She huffed a conceding laugh. "It *is* stupid."

"But you thought he was here? Why?"

"That's a long story," she hedged, having no wish to drag it all up. She worried that Kulan was still a relative stranger, even if they were bonded by sharing an isolation cell. So she changed the subject. "How did you end up in here?"

"I do not like the emperor's rule." He took a moment. "He bleeds us. He looks after his commanders and nobles while others go hungry. He treats women as slaves. Taxes are very high."

Arya waited. None of that explained why Kulan was in the mine camp.

"I am among those who believe it will be necessary to remove him." Kulan finished. "It is the only way."

Arya was surprised. Kulan was a rebel. To be so disloyal to one's ruler, it was hard for her to understand. The rightful ruler of Andahar had been deposed in just such a rebellion by the Nightstalker, and look how that had turned out for everyone. Yet what would she do if Mathas Crowtalon one day became High Warlord of Dunidaen? The thought chilled her. And made her think. "So that's how you ended up here. The emperor's soldiers know you ... think this way?"

Kulan's eyes flashed with momentary anger. It was the first time she'd seen such strong emotion in him, yet the depth of it made her wonder how much of his light-hearted self-assurance was a façade. "Yes. I was a fool and made a mistake."

She let that sit for a moment, holding his gaze. "I see how you are treated in here by some of the other prisoners. They are like you ... dislike the emperor's rule?" Silence fell, and she watched him steadily for a long time, considering. "I think you do not plan to stay in this mine for a long time?"

A brief hesitation, and then, he said, "I do not."

"Neither do I, Kulan."

Footsteps sounded outside. A guard barked at them to move away from the door, and they shifted obediently to sit along the back wall of the cell. The door swung open, a guard slid two trays of food inside, and the door was closed and locked.

Arya and Kulan waited until the guard's bootsteps retreated before going to retrieve their food. Two large mugs of lukewarm water each, a crust of bread, and a bowl of soup with unrecognisable vegetables swimming in it.

Kulan settled against the wall, drained the entirety of one cup, then looked at her. He was tense, like her words had made him uneasy. "How long have you noticed the others?"

"Many weeks. They don't tell anyone. They protect you." She paused, then. "I have protected you too."

Kulan nodded, picked up his spoon. "Perhaps we help each other?"

Hope leaped in her chest. This was exactly the leverage she'd been hoping for. She smiled. "Perhaps we could."

***

"We have been waiting for storm season," he explained the following morning. Neither of them had slept well. They tried to move about in the cell during the day to keep muscles loose, but the constant hunger kept them lethargic, and moving was an effort. At least Kulan's back was healing cleanly. "Khadini storms are very ... wild." He made a big gesture with his arms. "So big nobody will see us escaping. Nobody will notice us gone before morning."

"How many people will escape with you?"

"I will not risk them by telling you."

That was okay. She already knew who they were. "Have you a safe place to go after you escape?"

Kulan nodded. "It isn't close, but once there, we will be safe."

"How long to get there?"

"A week, maybe more. The storm might make things slow until it passes."

Arya considered that, finding some irony in being in Desomer's position for the first time ever. "You won't make it."

Amusement glinted in Kulan's eyes. "I have planned this very carefully."

"You will get caught," she said firmly.

He stared at her, green eyes opaque, and she wondered if she'd made him angry. "Why?" he asked eventually.

"The guards here have horses and tracking dogs. If we escape on foot, they'll catch us quickly, even if they don't notice straight away." Arya paused, searching for the right words. "The forest is thick, but muddy ground is good for tracks. Easy to follow us."

She saw the desire to protest spread across his face, but after a moment, he gave a sharp nod. "You are right. But there is no other way. We must hope the storm destroys our trail."

"Too dangerous to rely on hope. But," Arya said. "not if we take the horses with us."

Kulan was already shaking his head. "My people cannot ride. Only soldiers and nobles learn to ride horses here. It is a mark of status."

Arya swore. Putting untrained riders onto horseback was a recipe for disaster, even in clear weather. But in the middle of a bad storm? "Then we need a different plan. Or you will fail."

He let out a long breath, clearly making an effort to swallow that cockiness of his, then asked grudgingly.

"Will you help us?"

The grin was already spreading across Arya's face as she settled back against the wall, mind racing. "You'll take me with you?"

"You help, you come with us," he promised.

"Then I will fix your problem. I will make our escape plan so good that they will never catch us."

It would be just like playing a game of stones with Desomer.

Chapter 13

Despite her determination, and having a new ally, Arya's plans for escape didn't get very far. She and Kulan were released after three weeks in the cell, and as soon as she was out, Arya focused on finding out where the guards' horses were stabled.

It wasn't good news. The barn was on the opposite side of the pit from where the workers slept and ate, which meant if they attempted to escape at night, they'd have to cross the entire pit edge—over a mile long—to get to the horses. With the well-lit perimeter and sheer number of patrolling guards, doing that without being seen would be impossible.

Arya considered just one person sneaking over—perhaps to set the horses loose or bar entry to the stables somehow to delay the guards chasing them—but even one person making that distance without being seen was unlikely, not to mention the stables were *inside* the fence. If the horses were set loose, it wouldn't take long for the guards to round them up again. It wouldn't be enough of a delay.

"Then we have to escape on foot like I originally planned and move as fast as we can," Kulan said stubbornly one night. By now her Khadini had improved enough that they could speak with minimal pauses.

"Then you're doing it on your own," she said. Kulan was confident, charming, and clearly good with people, but he'd clearly never been taught tactics or strategy. Not like she had. She wondered if that was how he'd come to be caught. "You won't get clear of this place on foot, not unless you have a safe place within an hour's run that can't be found or scented by the Ranger guards and any tracking dogs they bring."

He deflated.

"Also, you're never going to get fourteen people through that fence without being seen by the patrols, even at night, and even in a storm."

His head came up sharply. "What?"

"I told you," she said patiently. "I pay attention. You may not be willing to tell me how many of your people are here, but I figured it out on my own. There are twelve."

Alarm flashed in his gaze.

"I want out of here as badly as you do, Kulan."

"You're very smart, but, Arya, trust me on this if nothing else," he said earnestly. "In a proper storm, visibility will be bad. It is impossible to watch the entire fence line in such conditions, and we can take down a single pair of patrolling guards if they catch us."

Arya studied him for a moment. He wasn't exaggerating or dismissing the risks. He believed what he was saying. She just hoped he was right. If they were caught at the fence, another opportunity for escape would be nigh on impossible. "We still have to figure out a way to deal with those horses."

"What if we poison their food, kill them before we escape?"

"We still have to get to them to do that. And where are you obtaining enough poison to kill so many animals?" She held his gaze. "We have one chance at this, Kulan. If we're caught, we won't be rebranded. We'll be killed."

"Okay, Arya," he said. "You devise a plan and we do it your way."

***

Arya twisted and turned on her cot, a restless sleep gradually sinking into a deeper slumber that opened suddenly onto a moonlit night sky. Stars glittered like diamonds and the breeze was crisp against his scales.

Her wyvern.

He felt her presence immediately and let out a delighted cry. An answering delight swept through her, but before either of them could do anything more, they were *taken*.

Ayra couldn't have described it any other way.

The glorious night sky faded, replaced by an inky blackness so deep it made her feel as if she was sinking. She couldn't feel the wyvern anymore. She couldn't feel anything.

The distant scrabble of claws. A sibilant hiss infused with triumph.

"We know you. We recognise your magic now."

This time Arya couldn't tell if it was one monster's voice in her thoughts or multiple. Could barely even process the words her terror had struck so deep. The snuffling sound they made pounded dread deep into her soul, the hiss of their voices ripping at her mind.

"Who are you? Where are you? You can't escape us, Sky Lord heir."

Arya fought then. She had to hide as much as she could from them, had to get free before they saw any more information about her. Or they'd find her. But it was a weak struggle, her fear so overwhelming it was all she could do not to simply give in. The nazal who'd caught her mind held her easily, like a cat toying with its prey, the others gathered around it, joining its glee. She felt something clawing through her mind, tearing at it, digging for ... and then it saw. The pit mine. The workers.

"Ahhhh." The triumph shifted to avaricious delight. *"There."*

"Khadini." The word hissed through all of the monsters.

Arya surged awake, head throbbing, heart pounding, sweat slicking her skin. Unable to lie still a second longer, she sat up and swung her legs over the edge of the cot, head falling into her hands as she fought to calm her breathing. It was still dark, the long dormitory around her quiet apart from the soft sounds of sleeping.

They'd *let* her go this time.

Because they knew where she was.

And they were coming for her.

Lingering dread and fear jangled Arya's nerves the following morning as she filed into the eating hall as she'd done every day for what was now almost two months. But the mind-numbing routine was a balm today. Walk in, collect a bowl of gruel and some bread, sit down, eat it, wait for the bell to ring, then line up and march down into the mine to pound at rockface all day.

She had to get out of the mine.

It was no longer just about getting free to find Rorin and Darmanin and Taze. Now, it was about saving her own life.

The nazal knew where she was. With every strike of her pickaxe the words beat through her in a constant refrain. If they found her here … she was unarmed, her body thin and weakened from endless labour and not enough food and rest. She'd never be able to defend herself properly.

Would they know her from being close enough to sense her magic? Would they kill everyone in the mine to make sure they got her if they couldn't pick her out? She didn't know the answers and that only compounded her fear. What if she got everyone in this mine killed because she'd let the nazal see her location?

She had to get out before they got here. That was the only option.

If the nazal was still in Heathrock, then she had weeks. But if it was closer … or the others were closer … she couldn't tell from the nightmares where *any* of them were. Ranier had implied only one nazal was in Dunidaen but she couldn't know that for certain.

When Arya trudged back up the mine wall that night, almost delirious with exhaustion, it was to find there'd been a shakeup of sleeping and working groups. This was done regularly, to prevent prisoners forming close attachments that could lead to planning escape or attacks against the guards.

When she learned that she and Kulan would be placed in the same working group and dormitory for the first time, she almost sobbed with relief. Until now, they'd had opportunities to talk briefly during meals, but had been careful not to let it happen too often that the guards would take notice. Now they'd have their nights, and even days of working—as long as they were discreet—to plan.

Maybe there was hope that she could get herself out of this place before the nazal got here.

Arya took her bowl and moved to sit in the nearest empty space along the long bench seats facing the tables. It was only once she'd settled, spoon digging into the slop, that she idly looked up to scan the room—a soldier's habits never died—and met a stunned gaze staring back at her, several long tables away.

Arya froze, spoon halfway to her mouth. Her heart literally leaped in her chest. And then it plummeted to her toes.

Essa.

It took everything she had not to jump over the tables and run to her friend, and from the tensing of Essa's shoulders, she was having a similar struggle. Arya knew she was staring too long, that someone would notice, but she couldn't find it in her to look away. Her fingers curled around her spoon so tightly it cut into her palms.

She eventually forced herself to look away, to concentrate on her food, to eat every bite of the unappealing slop and never look in Essa's direction again. Why was Essa here? How had she been captured? Why hadn't she crossed back through the Dreadwater Gate? But none of that mattered. Because the nazal were coming for her.

And now Essa was stuck here too.

Cold fear closed around her heart, dispelling the brief uplift in mood she'd felt upon seeing her friend alive and well. It lay across her shoulders like a heavy weight, tightening the muscle into twists and sending an aching throb up the back of her neck.

She didn't taste a bite of her food.

When the bell sounded, Arya rose with everyone else, determinedly not looking Essa's way. She forced herself to look at the ground, follow the line, climb the steps into her newly assigned dormitory building. The whole way, the fingers of her left hand tapped against her thigh in agitation.

As soon as the guards closed the door behind them and the clang of the bars lowering echoed through the long room filled with narrow cots, Arya spun, looking for Kulan. Maybe one of his rebel prisoners could—

"Arya!"

Unbelievably, Essa was there, pushing through the prisoners choosing their sleeping places, eyes alight.

The guards had put them in the same dormitory group.

Almost swaying with the relief of it, Arya took two running steps forward and threw her arms around Essa. The shorter woman crashed into her, sending them both rocking, and Arya clutched her tightly, the breath loosing from her lungs, the joy of it pricking tears in her eyes. They were betraying their relationship to everyone else in the dormitory, but Arya didn't care, *couldn't* care. Essa was alive, and here. For a glorious moment it didn't matter that the nazal were coming, just that she had a part of her family back with her.

"What are you doing here?"

They both spoke at exactly the same time, then laughed, letting go of each other.

"Arya?" Kulan's voice broke in. "Who is this?"

Arya swallowed back the tears that still wanted to fall. "Kulan, this is Essa, one of my companions from the Dreadwater run. Essa, Kulan. Oh, Essa, we have so much to talk about."

***

"We couldn't get anywhere close to the Gate," Essa explained later, as they huddled together in the dark on Arya's cot. As usual, the exhausted prisoners had rolled straight into their new cots and fallen asleep, and as far as Arya could tell, all of them slept. Still, they kept their voices to barely audible murmurs. "Even with you drawing the dogs away, there were so many Rangers combing the area that it was impossible to slip through. We had no choice but to turn east and swim across the Dreadwater to the opposite bank." She paused. Then smiled. "Turned out to be a good thing. That's where Dar washed ashore."

Hope surged in Arya's chest. Her hand covered a cry that tried to escape.

Essa touched her shoulder in sympathy. "Rangers followed him on that side of the river too. So we split up, Taze with Leanir to try and get to Darmanin, and me to draw the Rangers away."

"And they got you." Arya took her hand, turned it over. It was impossible to see the new brand clearly in the dim light, but it didn't appear to be weeping or infected. "How is your arm?"

"Sore, but it's a clean burn." Essa gave a little shrug. "I'm pretty sure I succeeded in drawing them away from Dar and the others, though, so it was worth it, especially since it brought me to you."

"Oh Essa."

"Don't sound like that. I made my choices, and this is where I choose to be."

"I wish you hadn't." Arya swallowed, the fear rushing back, making her hand tremble where it held Essa's. She let go before her friend could notice. "The nazal are coming."

Essa stilled. "Tell me everything."

So Arya did. It didn't take long, and when she was finished, Essa had that look in her eye that meant she found something intellectually interesting. "Does it seem to you that only one of the nazal has the ability to capture our minds, or reach our minds, or whatever it is they're doing during our nightmares?"

Arya's gaze narrowed in thought. "Now that you say it … I always *feel* more than one, but, yes, I only get the sense that one of them has hold of me. The others are there, but a step removed. Ugh, it's impossible to explain. I hate magic."

"Can you put a number to how many you sense?"

Arya shrugged. "Four, maybe five, but honestly, Essa, I can't tell them apart in any way. They could be different monsters each time."

"But you don't think so?"

Arya hesitated, then, "No."

Essa's gaze narrowed. "That's interesting."

"Is it?" Arya snorted.

Essa touched her hand where it still trembled. "I understand your fear, I feel it too. When they had me in that nightmare, I've never felt so vulnerable, so full of horror. But take heart, Arya. You were planning escape anyway. We just need to make it happen faster."

Arya nodded, finding it easier to be honest in the darkness and the still-there cascading relief of having Essa here with her. "At least with you here, I think we have a real chance of getting out."

Essa snorted. "If you haven't managed it yet, I can't see how I'm going to help."

Arya chuckled and squeezed her hand before letting go. "Oh, dearest Essa, those of us here have determination and strength in spades, but none of us have your brain."

She slipped off the cot and padded over to where Kulan slept. Or didn't, because his eyes slid open the moment she approached him. She gestured for him to follow, then went back to Essa. Soon Kulan was seated on the narrow bed with them.

"Kulan." Arya held his gaze in the dim light, finding it an effort to switch back to Khadini after being able to speak so easily in Dunidae with Essa. "I trust Essa with my life. She would never betray you. I understand she is a stranger to you. But either she comes with us when we escape or I'm out."

His jaw tightened. "I don't like ultimatums. And you forget that who I place *my* trust in risks the lives of my people."

"Essa is an asset; I swear it to you. We can help."

He still wavered, gaze shooting between them, eyes narrowed with uncertainty.

"You won't succeed alone," Arya said. "And I won't either. But together we can do this."

"Fine." Kulan shifted his gaze to Essa, a challenging note in his voice. "What do you think of our situation?"

Essa considered for a moment after Arya translated. If she understood from Kulan's voice that this was a test, it didn't seem to bother her. "If the horse problem can't be solved, then we need to make it irrelevant," she said finally.

Both Kulan and Arya stared at Essa in astonishment. Arya had already opened her mouth to translate her words into Khadini for Kulan's benefit, but Essa had spoken in Khadini. Albeit heavily accented, but easily as fluent as Arya had become.

"What?" Essa asked. "Did I say something wrong?"

"You speak Khadini?" Arya hissed.

"Sure. A little bit of Icelands dialect too." She shrugged. "I taught myself years ago. I had nobody to practice with, so my pronunciation is a bit off."

"A *lot* off," Kulan snorted, then at a glare from Arya said, "but close enough to understand."

Arya shook her head in admiration. Of course, Essa had taught herself another language for fun. "All right, how do we make the horse situation irrelevant?"

"We make it so there's no trail for them to follow. It doesn't matter how many horses or dogs they have if they don't know which direction we went in or where we're heading." Essa flicked a sideways glance at Arya. The same applied to any nazal coming looking for them after they'd escaped.

"That's impossible," Kulan declared. "We can't go anywhere without leaving some kind of trail, particularly in a storm where the ground will be muddy. And even if we didn't, there are only three directions we can go in. East, west, or south. The north is blocked by the lake."

Arya looked up sharply at those words, the hint of an idea coming to her.

"What about smuggling ourselves into the carts that transport the iron ore out of here?" Essa suggested.

Kulan shook his head. "The carts are too small, and only shielded by a piece of canvas. One person might be able to escape that way, if they got lucky, but not so many of us."

"Essa is right," Arya said. "In fact, she's a genius."

"I am?" she asked dryly.

"You are. When we escape, we'll do exactly as you said. We'll leave no trail behind. We'll go where they think it's impossible for us to go."

Essa caught on quickly. "The lake?"

"We'd need a boat for that." Kulan glanced between them both like they were mad. "And not only do none of us know how to sail, a storm would make navigating the lake far too treacherous."

"We don't need a boat," Arya murmured, thinking of the mortar and pestle, of a girl pinned underneath a fallen crate. "We have Essa."

"What does that mean?"

Arya ignored Kulan, looked at her friend. "Could you do something on that scale?"

Essa cocked her head, thinking about it. "I've never tried before. But I think … I'm confident enough to try."

"That's good enough for me." Arya turned to Kulan. Normally she'd want to test *all* elements of a plan before settling on it, but they didn't have time for that. Not anymore. And if the nazal were coming, it wouldn't matter if they sensed Essa using her magic, as long as they couldn't follow her away from the mine. "If you and your people can get us from here to the lake without being seen by the guards, Essa and I will get us all clear of the mine in a way the Rangers won't be able to follow."

"How?" His gaze narrowed.

Arya shook her head. "Best not to be too specific. Too many people are involved in this as it is. We'll need parchment and charcoal though, or quill and ink, and a way of keeping it dry if the storm brings heavy rain. Can your people get those things?"

"Probably. Maybe." He looked unhappy. "I don't like not knowing the details."

"You'll have to trust us. Trust me." Arya held his gaze. She wasn't going to betray Essa's magic to Kulan, even though they'd become friends as well as allies. Not with the nazal hunting them. Time enough for him to learn *if* they escaped the fence. "Or at least trust that we want out of here as badly as you do."

He let out a long breath, glancing uncertainly between them. "I'll think on it," he said eventually.

"Fair enough." Arya glanced around the room. "But we have to go soon, Kulan. Too much longer and we risk our plans leaking to the guards."

"The storms will be here soon enough," he said. Too casually. She considered telling him about the nazal, but that risked him losing trust in her. Without the help of Kulan and his people they'd never get out. So she simply smiled and let him go.

"How long do you think we have?" Essa asked in a murmur once he'd gone to his cot.

Arya shrugged. "It's been two days already. We might have three or four weeks, *if* the nazal was still in Heathrock when he found me. Or it could be here in days if it was closer."

"Sleep, Arya. We'll figure this out." Essa smiled and left.

Arya stretched out on her cot, muscles weary. But her thoughts kept her from sleep.

What if the nazal came before the storms arrived?

Chapter 14

Two weeks passed. Kulan refused to attempt escape before the storms arrived, and as desperate as she was to get out, as much as she felt time ticking down like a death sentence, Arya knew he was right. They needed the cover of the weather. A failed escape wouldn't help her and Essa avoid the nazal. Even so, with each day that passed her anxiety wound tighter and tighter until her stomach was full of knots she couldn't relax, not even in sleep.

"We go at the first storm," Arya said firmly, as they discussed the specifics of their plan one night.

Kulan narrowed his gaze at her. "Until Essa arrived, you were the one preaching patience. Now you seem eager to rush things. What's changed?"

"The longer we wait, the greater the chance the guards learn of our plans. Too many people know the details. Even if you trust all of them, it's inevitable." She let out an anxious breath, as genuinely worried about this element as the nazal. "It's already been too long for comfort."

He seemed to accept that, and they moved on. One of Kulan's people had managed to lift some parchment and charcoal from one of the guards' rooms when he was assigned cleaning duties. Another rebel swiped waterproof oilskin to wrap it in from one of the cart workshops.

Kulan looked intensely curious when he handed the items over to Arya, but she refused to tell him what they were for. Already she was trying to figure out whether Essa could use her magic without Kulan or the rebels seeing what she was doing ... but she doubted there was any way to conceal what her friend would be doing.

And what if Essa failed?

Arya shook her head, refused to think about it. They had to go, and this was their best chance. If they stayed, they died. And she had faith in Essa.

"How will you know the storm is coming?" she asked Kulan.

"We learn the signs from a young age, especially those whose livelihood depends on farming, or on fishing," Kulan explained.

"How much notice will we get?" Essa asked.

"Six hours, give or take."

Arya nodded, stared out the window to the north, wondering if that was going to be enough time. Wondering what they'd do if it wasn't.

***

They planned each night, as soon as everyone was asleep. When necessary, Kulan would pass information or instructions to his twelve rebels across the other working groups. Arya hated this part—it was their biggest vulnerability. If even one of them spoke carelessly of escape, or was punished due to an unrelated infringement and told the guards everything, they'd be lost.

"But if we don't tell them our plan, have them memorise it, then all will be chaos on the night of escape. That introduces greater risks," Kulan pointed out.

It was true, and so she allowed it. "Along with sharing our plan, impress upon them the need for good behaviour," she told him. "If they're placed in isolation for an infraction, they'll miss the escape."

One night as they went over the final details together, Essa asked Kulan, "Do you really plan to leave everyone else behind when you go? Are your rebels special enough to warrant freedom over everybody else?"

Arya stifled a sigh. This was Essa, kind to a fault sometimes.

Kulan shrugged. "If we tried to free everyone in this camp, most would be caught again within hours. The punishment would be severe; they'd be killed, if not severely beaten."

"You don't think that's their choice to make?"

"We can't save everyone, Essa," Kulan said quietly. "One day, we hope to remove the emperor, and then we can abolish these camps, but until then, we must make difficult decisions."

"And *we* have to focus on Rorin and Darmanin and Taze," Arya reminded her.

"I know." Essa nodded. "It is the rational choice."

But still. The word unspoken between them all. They were leaving thousands of people behind to continue eking out a miserable existence.

Once Kulan slipped off to his cot, Arya stopped Essa before she could leave too. "Have you thought about the risks, of using your magic in the escape?"

"You mean because of the nazal hunting us, and that if they're close by when I use it, they'll learn to recognise *my* magic as well as yours?"

Arya winced. "Exactly that."

"We need to get out, Arya, and this is the best way. If I don't do it, then I'm fair game anyway when they arrive."

She knew. It was why she'd suggested it even knowing the risks. "I just want to make sure that you're okay with the danger. My magic, at least, I think that's what it was, tried to break out soon after we washed ashore. I passed out and the nazal caught my mind almost instantly. I worry about that happening to you."

Essa froze. "How did you get free?"

"I'm not sure, to be honest. But my wyvern was there. I think he helped me break away from them somehow."

"Your wyvern." Essa lifted a hand to her mouth. "It's all true, isn't it, what Salyarin told you. I keep hoping that it will all turn out to be wrong somehow, but it's not."

"No, it's not," she said.

After a moment Essa's shoulders straightened. "I'll take the risk, Arya. We have to get free."

***

The first storm of the season approached as they were down in the mine working. Arya was digging out a section of the pit wall when she noticed two members of her work detail scanning the skies. An hour later, she glanced over at Kulan working a short distance off, and when he caught her looking at him, he looked away and gave a discreet head nod. Followed by two more in quick succession.

It was their pre-arranged signal.

A storm was coming. Her pickaxe thundered into the rock with more energy than usual as her anxiety and anticipation found an outlet. As afternoon arrived, Arya watched the sky slowly darken above the jungled hills framing the eastern side of the pit mine. The first thing she felt was joy. Then hope. Both leaping through her like a cresting wave.

They were going to get out. Before the nazal got to her.

But as the jubilation settled, she became more aware of the storm itself. She was well accustomed to the snowstorms and blizzards of the Diamondfang, but this seemed another beast entirely.

The oncoming behemoth had a crackling energy she'd never felt before. It was in the heaviness of the air, so thick it felt like wading through water, and the zips of electricity that had the little hairs on her forearm standing on end.

The guards rang the end of workday bell just after midday. Astonished, Arya nonetheless didn't hesitate to fall in line with the workers filing back up to the top of the pit. This was the first time the pit guards had *ever* ended a workday early.

These Khadini storms must be something.

The dark clouds rolled inexorably down the hills towards them as Arya reached the top of the pit. The air had turned soupy and the humidity made it hard to breathe.

Once inside the dormitory, most of their fellow prisoners took the opportunity for extra rest and sprawled on their cots to sleep, but Essa and Arya stood at the window, staring out in wonder. The black stormfront swallowed up the hills surrounding the mine and left an odd twilight settling over the area.

"I've never seen anything like it," Essa breathed.

"Give me a good old blizzard any day." Arya was more dubious. Although she couldn't deny the energy fizzing in her veins.

The skies opened up abruptly. One moment there was nothing, and in the next, heavy sheets of water fell to the ground, drumming like thunder on their roof. The wind kicked up, first a brisk wind, then a gale, screaming its intensity, bending the trees halfway to the ground.

"You think we'll survive outside in that?" Essa asked in a low voice.

Arya smiled, looking to put her at ease. "It will be a great opportunity for a shower." She was less worried about the storm than the lake. From the narrow glimpse she had of it from their window, she could see frothing waves crashing against the shore. "You think you can manage that?"

Essa let out a long breath, but determination firmed her jaw. "I hope so."

"Kulan was right about cover." Even as they watched, the light grew so dim, the rain so heavy, that they couldn't see even the closest dormitory hut. The lake faded entirely from view. No mounted guard would see anything other than what was right in front of them. *If* they were even out patrolling in this.

As if speaking his name had summoned him, movement came from her left; Kulan rising to his feet and moving to the window beside his bed. The window frames were painted over to prevent easy opening, but they'd been scraping it away for weeks and now it slid up—any sound it made muffled by the drumming of rain on the roof.

They'd planned this out. There was no hesitation or talking. Kulan swung himself out of the window. Essa followed. Arya was third, pausing only to run her gaze over the darkened room. It was doubtful their fellow prisoners were all asleep given the ruckus of the storm, but she could only hope anyone watching them leave wouldn't sound the alarm.

Arya's sandaled feet landed in what was already mud outside, and she reached up to slide the window closed behind them. The warm drops of driving rain soaked through her thin clothing instantly. Thunder roared, sounding like it was directly overhead. As if on cue, the rain increased in strength. The wind tugged at her hair and clothing as it gusted around them.

The three made straight for the nearest dormitory building, unable to see the log frame until they were upon it. Kulan reached up, banged a pre-arranged signal on the glass, then moved aside and waited. The window slid open, and two women and a man quickly slipped out.

They nodded and clapped Kulan on the back before filing off into the rain, heading to the meeting point by the northern fence. Kulan, Arya, and Essa ran along the side of the dormitory, mud splashing from their sandals. Arya's hair was plastered to her skull, and her clothes stuck to her like glue. The wind and rain were so heavy, moving felt like swimming. Water filled her mouth whenever she opened it to breathe.

At the end of the building, she stopped and looked in both directions. There was a wide open space between them and another building that ran along the fence. It was otherwise quiet. No alarms sounded through the night, and she couldn't hear any voices over the storm. Looking back around the corner, she could see nothing but the driving rain.

Kulan made a 'go ahead' gesture and they split up, dividing the remaining dormitory buildings between them. Another roll of thunder ripped through the sky as Arya splashed through mud to her assigned dormitory, giving the same knock on the window. By the time she made her way to the rendezvous point, one of the rebels was already at work cutting through the fencing with stolen cutters.

Kulan ran up behind her with the last of the rebels. They waited silently for the fence to be cut. Arya stared through it, but despite how close it was she could barely make out the lake, though she could hear its water roaring. She glanced at Essa, soaked and dripping at her side, and wondered how this was going to go.

Then, more thunder rolled overheard, lightning dividing the sky. The storm was right on top of them.

Arya doubled over as the *thing* inside her roared to life.

"Arya?" Essa's voice came distantly, almost inaudible over the storm.

The rebel cutting the fence made a gesture of triumph and stood back, pulling a large section away that they could all file through. Arya stumbled after them, dizzy, fighting an internal battle.

No, no, no. She couldn't explode here. Not without knowing how to control it. It would mean disaster.

Thunder pealed again, this time accompanied by a flash of blue lightning that sizzled into the mud only metres away. Her blood raced. The wind gusted, swinging the fence back towards her as she went through. A jagged piece of wire ripped along the top of her forearm, drawing blood. She swore. Blood trickled from the wound, but it didn't seem particularly deep, so she ignored it and kept going.

Another lightning flash caused a redoubled surge of Arya's magic that she had to fight back. Kulan shouted something that she couldn't hear over the storm.

"Arya!" he yelled again, almost directly in her ear this time. "What now?"

She managed to focus enough to look at Essa. The woman gave her a firm nod. "The tarp!" Arya said.

He'd had it wrapped around his middle and now quickly unwound it.

"Kiraya, Rifal!" he snapped an order to two of his rebels, and they helped him hold it over Essa's head, giving her some cover from the rain. Even so, water flowed from its edges in a falling curtain of water. If Arya hadn't been so occupied fighting back what was surging through her blood, she'd have been worried about Essa staying dry enough.

"Arya, what is happening? We can't linger here." Kulan called over another roar of thunder.

"Just be patient," she managed. She breathed hard, trying to focus, realising it was a losing battle. What would happen when she exploded? Nothing good, surely. Her hands were clenched into fists so tight she was sure her nails were drawing blood.

"Essa," she groaned.

Essa had the parchment and charcoal out and was sketching quickly. From the looks on the faces of the nearest rebels, they thought she was mad.

Every time the storm surged, Arya's magic surged with it.

Then one of the rebels cried out, then another, then they all turned, staring in shock and astonishment at the lake.

The waters parted.

Arya glanced at Essa's parchment, saw the woman had sketched a path through the lakebed, with the waters rising high above on each side. But her friend was trembling, jaw taut with focus, skin deathly pale even in the dim light.

"Go!" Arya bellowed at Kulan, taking the tarpaulin and pulling it over her and Essa like a cloak. "Quickly." She swore at another surge of her magic. "Don't know how long she can hold it."

He hesitated. His gaze shifted between them with something like surprise, some kind of dawning realisation. If she hadn't been fighting so desperately to hold herself together, she'd have wondered at that look.

"Go, Kulan! Please."

After only a moment's more hesitation, he snapped an order and set off at a run into the lakebed. His rebels streamed after him.

"Can you walk and hold the parchment at the same time?" Arya shouted to Essa.

"I need to focus to hold it in place." Essa managed, her voice a rasp. "But the water is so strong, it's fighting my hold. I don't know if I can."

Even as Arya looked at the parchment, the edges were beginning to dampen. Something told her that once it got soaked, the lake would go crashing back into place. Lightning flashed and she groaned, the magic surging again. Her tether on it was loosening, rapidly.

"Arya!"

Something in Essa's voice gave Arya the focus she needed to look at her, to pay attention. Essa was holding out her hand, the other one maintaining a death grip on the parchment. "Take my hand."

So Arya did.

And her magic exploded.

Into Essa. The woman sucked in a deep, energising, breath. Her shoulders straightened and light flashed into her eyes. The walls of lake water steadied—the rebels were well into it by now—and held.

And Arya and Essa crashed into their magic, bright and strong and binding.

"Let's go!" Arya shouted.

Still holding hands, Arya holding the tarp over them, she and Essa plunged forward into the lakebed, running free and easy, bolstered by their shared magic.

Part of Arya was aware of the mud and slimy growth of the lakebed, the burn of running muscles, the weight of her soaked clothes and sandals, but the rest of her was lost in magic. In what Essa had created. In the electrifying bond between them.

"*Arya? Essa?*" It was Darmanin's voice, and she saw him in her mind's eye as clear as day, weary and scruffy, but alive. "*Where?*"

"*Dar!*" Essa said joyfully.

Leanir's face flashed into their minds, dark and dangerous, and as he saw them his brown eyes narrowed. "*What is this?*" She thought she heard the voice of the Etherean elder, but it was too quick to grab onto. And then there was Chiarn, walking along a quiet road, fiery copper hair in a neat queue. He stopped, frowning, and looked around him. "*Arya?*"

A wyvern cried, and another. More strength surged through the bond.

But then she heard the sibilant hiss, felt the familiar dark magic of the nazal. It, or they, were close. And it had sensed their joined magic.

Its shriek of thwarted anger tore through her, bringing a surge of panic. But in the same moment that panic started threading through Arya, it all blinked out, the initial surge of their combined magic fading.

Arya came back to herself, still holding Essa's hand fiercely in hers, almost stumbling on a loose rock in the lakebed.

"You okay?" Essa gasped out.

Arya nodded. "Can you hold?"

"Linked to you, yes."

From then on, they saved their energy for running and holding the powerful lake at bay. Eventually, gasping and stumbling, they reached Kulan and his rebels, who'd arrived at the far northern shore and were staring back at them in wonder.

Arya scrambled up the banks, dragging Essa's exhausted form after her, and then they finally came to a halt. Her magic was gone as if it had never been. Drained entirely or faded enough to repress, she didn't know.

"Let go now, Essa," Arya mumbled. "Let go or the nazal will follow."

Essa let out a breath, something like a sigh, and she ripped the parchment she'd been clutching into pieces and let them drift into the driving rain.

They all stood and watched as the two halves of the lake came crashing back together. Water sprayed as it surged up the shoreline before receding to its usual level.

"Well," Essa said in satisfaction. "They certainly won't be following us that way."

At her words, the rebel prisoners started smiling and laughing and slapping hands in triumph. Arya had only just begun to wonder why they weren't showing more shock or wariness about what Essa had done when Essa swayed and fell into a dead faint.

"Essa!" Arya caught her just in time, dropping to her knees in the mud, then Kulan and his rebels were surrounding them, assisting her get back to her feet.

"Is she okay?" Kulan asked in concern.

Arya nodded. There was a new thread she could feel now, and it was pulsing gently. Essa was just exhausted. "She'll be fine in a bit. We should keep moving," Arya told Kulan.

His eyebrows shot skywards. "You're not planning on explaining what just happened?"

"Not now. Not while we're still so close to the mine," she snapped.

He still looked concerned, glancing at Essa. "Are you all right to run? It's a long way to where we need to go."

"I'll be fine."

One of Kulan's biggest rebels gently took Essa onto his back, her small frame seeming to rest easy there, and they set off in a line with Kulan in the lead.

Soon the lake was swallowed up by dripping jungle, but Arya's gaze was focused ahead. Elation and worry both burned bright inside her.

What had they just done?

Chapter 15

Essa woke as the storm finally moved past them, immediately insisting she was fine to run. Kulan pushed them onwards, heading steadily northwest, only stopping for brief snatches to drink whenever they passed a stream.

He finally let them stop for a proper rest at dawn, choosing the banks of a swift-flowing river. By then Arya's legs were trembling with weariness. Months of poor food and rest had taken a toll on the elite physical shape she'd been in from Ranier's training. Still, the Shadeweaver leader had been right. Her mental strength had allowed her to push through, keep going.

"They may not even know we've gone yet, not until they do a headcount," Kulan crowed in delight as they all waded into the delightfully cool shallows, soaking themselves and drinking. Birdsong filled the morning, a hot sun already shining through the trees.

"We're not clear yet," Arya warned. "The others in our dormitory may have reported us. Besides, anyone seeing us right now will know we're escaped prisoners. We have no supplies and no way to carry water."

"Worry not, my Dunidae friend." Kulan smiled widely. "We are heading into the most isolated area of Khadini. There are none out here to notice us. And as you have already seen, water sources are plentiful, and there will be enough berries and nuts for us to scavenge as we go. We are maybe four days or so from our destination. The only thing we need worry about is stepping on a snake or coming to the attention of a hungry panther."

"Then maybe it's time for us to part." Arya was increasingly uncomfortable with how far they were travelling away from the Dunidae border, not to mention the cazaix smelter. And Kulan had helped them—she didn't want to risk drawing the nazal to his people, even though the creatures shouldn't be able to track them from the mine if they kept their magic contained. "Essa and I need to find our companions."

He frowned as he glanced over at where Essa rested, back against a tree, eyes closed, then gestured for Arya to follow him. He waded out of the water and along the banks, far enough the trees hid them from the sight of his companions. Once clear, he lowered his voice. "You didn't tell me she was an Inkweaver. I thought you were both Dunidae?"

Arya kept any reaction from her face, and said carefully, "I don't know what you mean."

Kulan cocked his head, confused, as if he were made uncertain by her answer. "Inkweaver is one of the Andahari Sky Lord Houses," he said. "Their Valheran can turn what they draw or paint into reality."

"How do you know anything about Andahari Sky Lord Houses?" It was Arya's turn to be confused.

"How do you *not* know about them?" He made a dismissive gesture.

"Essa *is* Dunidae, Kulan. We both are. That's why I don't know anything about what you're saying. We were born in Ravenstrike State and have spent our whole lives there," Arya said. She needed to kill any notion of his that they might be something else before he spoke of it to anyone else in Khadini.

The confusion on his face only deepened.

Arya needed to be clearer. "Kulan, if you or your rebels breathe a word that suggests Essa might be anything other than Dunidae, her life will be at risk."

He chuckled. "I know that. It's why I was surprised she used her magic so openly. The Nightstalker will be actively searching for her if he learns of her existence. We owe her a great debt for risking herself so."

"You know about..." Arya trailed off. She had no idea how, but Kulan clearly already had too much knowledge ... knowledge that could hurt them. She rapidly rethought her approach. It might be safer to be honest with him, so he understood how important protecting Essa's identity was. "He already is, Kulan."

Kulan sucked in a breath, eyes widening. "Then you are in far greater danger than being caught by the Rangers again. Has her wyvern—"

"No more information." She cut him off. "You have to make sure your people say nothing," she said. "Please, Kulan. Promise me you can keep them quiet."

"Where we are going, my people will—"

"Essa gets to choose who knows this about her." She held his gaze.

"Understood. I will ensure my people say nothing." He bowed his head. "You have my word."

She let out a breath of relief, hoping that was enough. "Thank you."

He nodded. "Now, about what comes next. You are free to choose your path, of course, but you will have a better chance of staying free if you remain with us."

Arya was already shaking her head. "I'm not interested in being kept safe. We need to find our companions and get home to Ravenstrike." She didn't even care about the cazaix anymore. Not now the nazal were in Khadini too, or on their way. She just wanted them all safely home.

"Yet you don't know where to even begin looking for them," he pointed out. "Once we are safely at our destination, I will spread the word among my network, asking them for reports of your friends. This is your best chance of finding them."

"He's right."

Arya started at the sound of Essa's voice, and looked over as she approached, still pale, one hand rubbing her forehead as if she had a headache. "Arya, if we go on alone, where would we even start?"

"You don't think hiding with a rebel network the emperor is hunting isn't just as dangerous?"

"The emperor will not go where I am taking you," Kulan promised. "Arya, Essa, you have won us our freedom. We owe you a large debt. I will do all I can to find word of your friends."

Arya mirrored Essa, rubbing at her temples. She hated every step she took that increased the distance between her and Rorin and Darmanin and Taze.

But Kulan's logic was solid. And if Essa agreed that was the best way too... "All right," she said. "Thank you, Kulan."

He smiled at them both. "Get some rest. We'll move on soon."

He left them, padding back through the trees to his rebels. Essa turned to Arya. "What were you talking about before I joined you? You were so tense."

Arya relayed what Kulan had said. "It's dangerous, him and his rebels guessing at what you are."

"We don't even know what I am," Essa said drily. "But ... Inkweaver. I like it."

Arya's mouth quirked. "So do I."

"What House is yours?" Essa asked curiously. "Do you know?"

Arya hesitated. "Your father mentioned the name Stormrider once. I don't think he meant to, but..." she trailed off. Even now, it made her uncomfortable. Naming herself as something other than Arya Ravenstrike.

Curiosity lit up Essa's face, and she mused, "Hmmm, Arya S—"

"Don't," Arya snapped. "That's not me."

Essa read it all on her face. "Knowing more details makes ignoring the Sky Lord thing even harder, doesn't it?"

Arya sighed. "This is why I love you, Essa. You never let me get away with anything."

Essa smiled, bright and full. "And I love you because you never hate me for it."

***

They ran all day and into the night. Once again Arya was grateful for Ranier's training. Kulan set a punishing pace, and that was completely apart from the regular inclines and tricky terrain. Every foot had to be placed carefully to avoid injury.

And the humidity.

Arya wondered if she would ever be dry and sweat-free again. Still, the respect dawning in the rebels' expressions as they watched Arya and Essa keep up with them step for step didn't fail to give her a smug glow of pride.

"It's difficult to rely on horses in much of the country because of the heat and terrain." Kulan mentioned. "So running is often the quickest way for messages to pass between villages and towns and communities. Official messengers spend their whole lives running, but most Khadini run from childhood too." He smirked. "It is surprising to see a Dunidae keeping up with one of us."

Kulan led them steadily northwest, through unending jungled hills, the birdsong their only company. Occasionally they passed signs of human passage, and often used the dirt roads or trails winding through the thick foliage.

One morning, they struggled up a particularly steep incline.

"How many people live in this region?" Essa asked.

"Most of the villages are much closer to the southern edges of the jungle, but you'll find the occasional one here in the isolated reaches. Many of these people spend their whole lives out here and never leave."

Arya waited until they reached the top and she could catch her breath again before asking, "Why do you rebel against Emperor uq-Danresan?" He'd given her a limited answer the last time she'd asked that question, but now her grasp of Khadini was better, and she wanted to understand more of what drove him.

"Because he cares about himself more than his country. Or his people," he said bitterly. Kulan looked away, clearly unwilling to discuss it any further.

Arya tried a different subject. "Do you have family?"

Teeth flashed as he smiled. "A brother. Younger than me, only fourteen. He keeps nagging to join my warriors, but he is too young. I wager that hasn't stopped him from training with them the moment I left home."

"Is that where we are going? Your home?"

Kulan nodded. "It is not where I was born, but it is the home I choose. I will be sad to leave it." He cut himself off. "It's a beautiful place, and it will be safe for us. It is one of the few places in Khadini that the emperor's warriors will not venture into because of how isolated it is."

"How serious is the opposition to the emperor's rule?" She looked at him curiously, asking a question her warlord would want to know—especially if she achieved her ambition to become High Warlord. "Does it genuinely threaten to topple him?"

"I am one leader of many, and none of us alone have anywhere near the strength to challenge the emperor's army, not unless we unify our forces. And even then, I do not think we are strong enough yet."

"What prevents you from unifying?"

"The rebel groups are disparate, scattered across Khadini, and formed in isolation, their goals shaped by their local circumstances. That means we all want different things or have differing views on how best to unseat the emperor." He let out a breath. "I was making initial attempts at unification when I was captured. I was foolish—too open about what I was doing. The emperor's spies picked up word of it and his Rangers laid a trap for me."

"Why didn't they just kill you?"

Kulan shrugged. "I'm of more use digging up their iron ore for them until I keel over. Nobody escapes from the mines and so in their minds the threat is still dealt with."

One of the rebels running close behind them snorted. Arya glanced over her shoulder in surprise. It was Kiraya, the youngest of their group. When they looked at him, he said pointedly to Kulan, "They would have killed you if they had known—"

"Enough, Kiraya," Kulan's tone was sharper than she'd ever heard from him before.

Essa, running ahead, glanced briefly over her shoulder. The look on Kulan's face forbade any further pushing on what Kiraya had said, so Arya reverted to her original question. "It sounds like these rebels place their own individual interests over the good of the country. That doesn't seem much different from how you describe Emperor uq-Danresan."

Kulan shrugged. "I should scout the trail ahead, make sure it is clear."

Arya let him go as he increased his pace, moving to the front of the pack. She looked back at Kiraya, hoping he might expand on what he'd said, but the young man's expression was closed, and he deliberately avoided her eyes.

***

Kulan roused them early on the fifth day, as the sun rose on the horizon. They crested a steep rise and came to a halt, catching their breath. They'd reached the northern coast. The hill they stood atop sloped down to the pristine sandy shores of an azure bay. Jungled hills framed the bay to the south and east, but the western headland snaked out a little further into the ocean, curling around, almost in a protective gesture.

And while jungle covered some of it, the longer headland's eastern face looked like bare, sandy cliff face. Arya stared harder, her gaze picking up snatches of colour gleaming in the morning sunlight … she blinked, thinking her vision was spotting, but the colour was still there.

Beyond the bay stretched open ocean. Something inside Arya ached at the sight. Directly northeast across that body of water was Dunidaen. Only a handful of days sail would carry her to the eastern shores of Crowtalon or SparrowWing.

She wanted to go home.

Essa shifted beside her, staring in the same direction, and they shared a quiet glance of shared longing.

"We'll get a boat from there." Kulan's voice broke the reverie, and when Arya looked where he pointed, she could see the cluster of huts along the southern shore of the bay, hidden amidst the canopy.

Her eyes widened. "A boat to where?"

He grinned. "You'll see."

And then he set off running.

***

Kulan brought them to a halt while they were still in the jungle outside the village. He sent Rafal ahead to make sure all was well. As they waited, Arya caught the scent of woodsmoke on the air, mixed with something unfamiliar but sweet. Whatever it was made her stomach grumble in hunger.

It wasn't long before Rafal and another man appeared, moving with quick strides through the trees. The second man broke into a wide grin of relief the moment he caught sight of Kulan. "Praise everything you have returned to us, Dostari. We heard you had been captured and thought you were lost."

At Arya's side, Essa stiffened and shot a questioning glance at Kulan, but his attention was on Rafal and the villager. "What is it?" Arya asked her in a murmur.

Essa shook her head slightly. "Later."

Kulan returned the man's warm hug. "I was imprisoned in a labour camp but managed to break free. It is good to see you, Tashwan."

Tashwan was still beaming from ear to ear as the hug ended. "I assume you are heading for Taskari?"

"Yes. Is it safe to head out there?" Kulan asked.

"It is, Dostari. We haven't had a navy boat sail past in months. I'll row you out there myself; I have already sent my two sons to prepare the boat." Tashwan's gaze finally shifted away from Kulan and fell on Arya and Essa. Immediately a frown filled his face. "Who are they?"

"These are my friends, Arya and Essa," Kulan explained. "They saved my life in the camp, and we could not have escaped without their help."

Tashwan's mouth curled in disapproval. "They're Dunidae."

"They are," Kulan said firmly, and Arya's shoulders relaxed in relief as he held to his word. "And they are trusted friends. I owe them my life, Tashwan."

"It is true," Rafal's soft voice rumbled, echoed by the other rebels. "We owe these Dunidae a large debt, Tashwan."

Tashwan considered these words as he settled a long look on Arya and Essa. Eventually he let out a long breath. "Then that debt is mine also, Rafal uq-Kalan, Dostari. I will see you all safe to Taskari. Come, the breeze is fine this morning and I can have you out there by midday."

"Where exactly are we going?" Arya asked again.

Kulan grinned as he set off after Tashwan. "You'll see soon enough, Arya Ravenstrike, and then you'll understand why any attempt to describe it is useless."

His energy was infectious, and Arya tossed a smile Essa's way as they ran after the others and into the village. The day was bright, the sun warm, and they were going to see something new.

For the briefest of moments Arya's worries fell away and she simply breathed in the warm air and *lived*.

Chapter 16

Villagers waved and called out greetings to Kulan and his companions as they walked out onto the sands where several fishing boats were pulled up above the tide.

Crystal blue water lapped around Arya's calves as they pushed Tashwan's boat out and climbed aboard, Arya and Essa settling comfortably together in the prow, thrilled for the chance to rest their weary legs.

Arya's gaze turned to Kulan, who was in deep conversation with Tashwan as he supervised two younger men—his sons—rowing them out into the bay.

"He's not what he pretends to be," Essa said.

"What do you mean?"

"That word Tashwan used, *Dostari*, it's the Khadini signifier for prince. It's only used to address those of the royal family."

"How do you know that?" Arya asked, rather stupidly.

"If you'd paid attention in our lessons, when Rorin was being taught how to address foreign leaders when meeting them, you would know it too. If you were addressing the Icefolk prince, you would use *er'fin*."

Arya snorted. "You know very well that I rarely paid attention when Rawson started droning on."

Essa didn't laugh. "We should be careful of what we're getting ourselves into."

"I hear you," Arya said.

Kulan appeared, balancing easily as he stood behind them. "That looks sore," he said, pointing at the cut on Arya's arm.

She grimaced. It throbbed, and the wound looked red and angry. "It's not closing like it should. I think it might be infected."

"We have healers at Taskari."

"That's what your home is called?" Arya asked. "Taskari?"

"It is not so much a name as a description. I think in Dunidae you would call it a peninsula."

Arya turned as Essa straightened suddenly beside her. Her friend's gaze had taken on that look of intense fascination it got when she came across something new. They were well out into the middle of the picturesque bay now, and the western headland was much closer.

Soon Arya could make out high cliffs tapering down to a sandy beach at the point. Her eyes widened when she discovered that the bright colours she'd glimpsed from the top of the hill miles away were actually a multitude of shade cloths that looked to be functioning as roofs of some kind. On the northern end of the peninsula, jetties reached out into the ocean like spokes in a wheel. Fishing boats in different sizes bobbed peacefully alongside them.

As Tashwan directed his sons to row straight for one of the jetties, Arya's gaze remained fixed on the cliffs, staring in wonder. The eastern face of the peninsula sloped down to the bay, featuring many narrow pathways worn into the rock. Rope bridges swung idly in the afternoon breeze joined sections of path. Areas where rock jutted out had been turned into dwellings—roofed by the riot of multicoloured shade cloths that had been visible so far away.

Kulan shifted beside her. "What do you think?" He was grinning as he watched Arya and Essa take it in.

"Why would people choose to live on the side of a cliff, when they could live along the shores of the bay?" Arya asked.

"Originally, because they had no place else to go. Taskari began as a haven for those who weren't accepted in the villages. They were enterprising and hardworking and built this city with nothing more than what they had with them," he said. "Now it serves as a safe haven of sorts for others too, but you will learn about that soon enough."

"It's wonderful," Essa said, eyes alight. "How does the community sustain itself?"

"The surrounding ocean is rich in fish stocks, and those who live on Taskari have become adept fishermen. And the jungle is rich in fruit and vegetables." Kulan cocked his head. "My rebels bring other supplies in when we can, and I have contacts that will trade on our behalf."

Arya glanced at her friend, a smile coming unbidden. Essa being enamoured of something was always a delight to behold. As reserved as she was, as much as she held back the core pieces of herself, she also wore her heart on her sleeve. "Perhaps you could make your cottage here, one day."

Essa looked at her, a flicker of hope in her green eyes. "You think?"

"I do think." Arya glanced at Kulan, who was frowning at this exchange.

Tashwan's sons soon had their small boat bumping up against a jetty, skilfully piloting it into a narrow gap between two fishing boats roughly the same size. Rafal jumped out to affix a rope to the mooring post.

"Thank you, my friend." Kulan shook Tashwan's hand, offered a nod to his sons. "I am in your debt."

Tashwan bowed his head. "There is no debt. I would do anything for you, Dostari. Be safe."

In Dunidaen, the phrase 'my word on it' was a way of formally making a promise or vow, a serious binding. Arya was beginning to realise that owing a debt was a similar formality in Khadini. She filed that away to be conscious of when speaking their language.

Arya and Essa followed Kulan and his rebels along the ramshackle jetty, glancing back to see Tashwan and his sons already rowing back into the bay. The cliff face towered over them, and she had to crane her head uncomfortably to be able to see the distant cliff tops.

At the end of the jetty they stepped off wood onto sand covered rock, a wide cavern entrance looming before them. Kulan said a few words to his rebels, dismissing them to find their families, before turning to Arya and Essa. "Over time those here dug into the cliff, expanding existing spaces and creating tunnels to link them together, all to increase the available living space," he explained.

"It's amazing," Arya said, meaning it. As desperately as she missed the snow-tipped mountains and icy air of her home, she was fascinated by Kulan's home, at how *different* it was to everything she knew.

He smiled. "Come on. I want to see my family, and Arya, you need to get that arm seen to."

The light dimmed once they were inside the cavern, and Kulan led them across a sandy floor and into one of three tunnels leading upwards. Essa stumbled along last, head craning to take in everything. The path took a steep upward incline for a short distance before exiting onto a narrow bridge leading across the open cliff face. A salty breeze whipped Arya's hair in her face and she pushed it back in irritation. The bay was already far below, twinkling turquoise.

On the other side of the bridge, they entered another tunnel. Three young men coming the opposite way stepped back politely to let them pass. As soon as they saw Kulan, their eyes widened in stunned surprise, and they muttered welcomes, almost falling over themselves in doing so. Kulan thanked them, but didn't stop, and their eyes rested curiously on Arya and Essa.

The two exchanged glances. The deference and respect Kulan commanded was becoming increasingly obvious.

Halfway up the cliff the tunnels in the rock became much wider, and there were proper pathways across the outside. They exited a tunnel into a wide atrium that was open to the sky above and filled with stalls and people.

"One of three markets on Taskari," Kulan explained as they wended through the crowd. Although Arya and Essa received as many stares of curiosity as they did of suspicion, Kulan seemed unconcerned. "This is where we barter or buy our food and other essentials, but it's as much of a social gathering place as a market."

Back outside, they walked up a path that split at the top into three smaller trails. Kulan turned onto one that followed the rock face horizontally a short distance before turning into a short flight of steps leading down to a dwelling roofed in a bright blue and green shade cloth.

"Anyone home?" he called out as he moved down the steps, excitement in his bouncy stride. "Your favourite son and brother has returned!"

A skinny youth was the first to appear at the sound of Kulan's voice, his young face lighting with stunned delight when he saw who it was. "Kulan!"

"Kader!" Kulan caught the boy up into a fierce hug before letting him go. "You've grown again!"

"I'm going to be taller than you!" Kader beamed, before his gaze fell on Arya and Essa. "Who are they?"

"My friends, Arya and Essa." Kulan turned to them. "And this is my brother, Kader."

Arya held out her hand as Essa ventured a polite smile. Kader was a mirror image of his brother, with the same olive skin, curls of brown hair and bright green eyes, only younger and healthier and without a beard. "It's nice to meet you, Kader."

"Welcome to our home."

"Kulan, is that really you?" An older woman appeared, wiping her hands on a cloth before tucking it into her belt. Joy lit up her weathered but striking features at the sight of Kulan. "*Kati!*" Kulan spoke the Khadini word that meant 'mother.' He swept her into a hug as tight as the one he'd given his brother.

She clung fiercely to him, tears streaking her cheeks. "You've been gone so long. We heard you'd been captured, but we've had no other word and assumed the worst. Nobody lives long in the mines."

"I was taken to the pit mine near the Dreadwater. But all is well now, Kati. I escaped, and I am safe."

"Kati, Kulan brought visitors," Kader broke in, curiosity alive in his expression.

The woman's eyes widened as she turned to Arya and Essa, and said simply, "You brought Andahari?"

For a second Arya reeled and Essa stiffened in shock, then both of them just as quickly tried to hide that reaction.

"We're from Dunidaen," Arya said. "I'm Arya Ravenstrike and this is my friend, Essa Varsoth."

Disapproval filled the woman's features, which seemed sculpted perfectly to display that exact emotion. "Oh. So you came for cazaix."

"Yes," Arya admitted, trying not to quail under that stare. It was even more intimidating than Desomer's.

"Arya saved my life in the pit mine." Kulan seemed unbothered by his mother's look. "We could not have escaped without her and Essa. I owe them a large debt."

Some of the disapproval faded from her face. "In that case, much can be forgiven. I am Yarmana." Her voice filled with formality as she spoke those words, and at her side Kulan twitched. "I am honoured to meet you both. You must be exhausted and hungry. Please come in."

Kulan shook his head. "Arya needs to see a healer first. She has a wound on her arm that I fear is infected."

Yarmana frowned in concern. "Then you'd best take her straight to Tomin."

"If you give me directions, I'll go myself," Arya offered. "You should spend some time with your family, Kulan."

"I'll take her," Kader offered, glancing between his mother and brother. "She'll be safe with me, and I can bring her back here when Tomin is done."

"Thanks, little one." Kulan ruffled his brother's hair. "You take good care of her."

"Your debt is mine. I won't let you down, Kulan," he said.

"You will be welcome back here once your wound has been treated, Arya," Yarmana said, barely able to tear her shining eyes from Kulan's face. "And Essa, you must be hungry and tired. I can offer you a meal and a comfortable sleeping place."

"I'd like that." Essa beamed at Yarmana. "Thank you so much for your hospitality."

Arya touched Essa's shoulder. "I'll see you when I return."

Kader was a bundle of irrepressible energy as he led Arya through a rabbit warren of caverns, tunnels, and pathways to a quieter corridor not far beyond the market they'd passed through earlier. Here, he stopped at a smaller cavern with a brightly coloured curtain hanging across the entry.

He swept the curtain aside and motioned Arya through. A small chime sounded at their entrance. She found herself in an open cavern, where a woman sat at a table. Behind her was a cabinet filled with drawers. Two curtained entryways sat either side of the cabinet, and the muffled sounds of low conversation came from one of them. The woman's eyes widened at the sight of Arya with Kader. "Kader, what brings you here?"

"My brother has returned." Gleeful excitement filled his voice and lit up his face. "This is Arya—she is his guest. Arya, this is Raysa, Tomin's apprentice *and* his niece."

Raysa, who looked not much older than Arya, and had the same golden hair and fair skin, looked stunned. "You must be so happy. Taskari will be thrilled to know Dostari Kulan is safe and sound."

Kader nodded. "Arya helped him escape and return to us and so we owe her a life debt. That's why we're here—she has an infected cut. We hoped Tomin could look at it."

"Welcome, Arya." Raysa turned her attention to Arya, who was still processing the fact that the woman was clearly not Khadini. "Come with me. Tomin is with another patient right now, but he can see you next. I'd offer to take a look at your cut, but my uncle prefers to see all new patients himself."

Kader cheerfully wished her luck and told her he would wait outside for her to be finished. Arya followed Raysa behind one of the curtains and found herself in a small cavern furnished with a low cushioned table, two chairs, and a row of shelves filled with supplies.

"You're Dunidae?" Arya asked.

She laughed, a musical sound. "No, actually. I'm Andahari. You'll see plenty of us here on Taskari. Tomin won't be long."

Raysa bustled out before Arya could ask anymore. And a short time later, the curtain drew back, and *another* blonde-haired, fair-skinned man entered, carrying a steaming bowl of water. He was much older than Arya, probably in his late fifties, and wore a neatly trimmed beard that framed a weathered but friendly face.

"Hello, Arya. I'm Healer Tomin." He paused after placing the bowl on the low table, raising an eyebrow. "You look far more surprised than you should be to see a healer in a healing centre."

"I didn't expect to see two Andahari here!" she blurted out.

He laughed at that, a warm sound that instantly relaxed her. Tomin pulled the second chair closer to her and sat down. "Show me the cut, please."

Wincing a little, Arya rolled back the tattered sleeve of her shirt, revealing the inflamed wound along the top of her right forearm. Yellow fluid leaked from it.

He took gentle hold of her wrist so that he could get a closer look. "How did you get the cut?"

"From a jagged piece of wire fence." She explained how they'd cut through it to escape the mine.

Tomin nodded, his eyes twinkling at her. "It's infected, but I have great confidence you'll live if we clean it out and treat it properly."

"Good news." She chuckled. "Thank you."

He gave her a quick smile. "Don't thank me yet, I've got to clean it first. It's going to hurt."

Tomin rose and went to the shelves on the wall, fishing out a couple of small pots and some bandaging. After seating himself again, he drew a soft cloth from the bowl of warm water and began thoroughly cleaning the cut. He didn't shy away from ensuring he got all the way inside the wound to clear out the pus, and it stung. Arya gritted her teeth through it all. Once that was done, he gripped her wrist and took another good look at the now-clean wound.

"It's small enough I don't think it needs stitches." He rotated her forearm slightly, then stiffened when he caught sight of the healed burn scar on the inside of her forearm. His grip tightened.

"That's just the labour camp brand. It healed up fine," she explained.

There was a moment of odd silence, and when he spoke again, his voice had a distant quality to it. "The shape is different than the brands I've seen."

"I fought when they gave it to me. The brand slipped right as they pressed it to my skin," she explained, confused by his reaction.

He looked up and smiled, his hold loosening so quickly she wondered if she'd imagined his reaction. "The burn looks well healed, as you say. I'll put some of this unguent on your cut and bandage it up for you."

He was quiet as he skilfully mixed the ingredients from two of the small pots, then rubbed the resulting paste into the wound, making sure to pack it deep inside. Arya swore inwardly as pain burned through her arm, but after a little while the sting was soothed by a delightful cooling sensation.

"You'll need to keep this covered at all times," he said as he bandaged it, covering almost her entire forearm.

Arya frowned. "I thought wounds did better if they were left open to air?"

"Generally, yes, but this unguent works best when pressed close to the broken skin, and I want to be sure infection clears completely." He finished the bandaging and sat back. "Please come back to me every morning and I'll clean and re-bandage it for you."

"Thank you," she hesitated. "I don't have any coin with me at the moment."

"I'm told you helped Dostari Kulan escape the pit mines, so consider this the thanks of a grateful Taskari resident." He smiled. "I'm a curious fellow, so I do have a question, if you'll permit me?"

"That depends what the question is," she said.

He chuckled. "Fair enough. I ask only your name and your origins, Arya."

"That's easy." She relaxed. "I am Arya Ravenstrike, from Ravenstrike State in Dunidaen. I'm a captain in their army, the Raiders."

"Ah," he said lightly. "I'd assumed you were Andahari from your colouring."

"My colouring?"

"Yes. Golden hair and blue eyes are common among us Andahari river-folk, as you can tell from looking at Raysa and me," he said. "It was nice to meet you, Arya. Don't forget to come back tomorrow morning to get that seen to."

"Thank you, Healer Tomin." She hopped off the bed and offered him her hand.

He shook it. "Just call me Tomin."

It was only when she was walking back to Kulan's home with Kader that she noticed the reddened marks still on her wrist from where Tomin had gripped it so tightly.

What had bothered him so?

Chapter 17

The following morning, Arya sat at a small table in Yarmana's home eating a strangely spiced, but delicious, flatbread. Essa—never an early riser—slept on in the room they'd shared. The call of seabirds drifted through the curtained doorway, and the air was already warm. At least here on Taskari the sea breeze cut through the humidity.

"Is there any magic in Khadini?" Arya asked. It was something she'd never wondered before.

A shadow crossed Yarmana's face. "We are a magic-less people. That's part of the reason we so jealously guard our cazaix. It isn't just the powerful Andahar Sky Lords that it protects us against—all our neighbours have some magic in their peoples."

"We are terrified of our magic-wielders. So terrified that no general would be able to tell you how many or how powerful they are, let alone how useful they'd be in battle against another kingdom."

"That was not always the case," Yarmana said. "The Nightstalker created far more change in the world than just replacing the ruler of Andahar and closing down its borders."

"The Icelands have magic, then? I'm aware of the Etherean and their healing powers."

"They do, but it is kept closely hidden." Yarmana said. "Even though it's limited, the Icefolk need their trade with Dunidaen to survive, so they've all but buried the fact they have magic. The Etherean had to cut off contact entirely—they don't have the strength of arms to protect themselves if your Dunidae attacked."

Arya nodded, gaze contemplative on her plate. The Icefolk were renowned for their elite warriors, so she understood why they felt comfortable still engaging with Dunidaen. But how much important trade was *Dunidaen* missing out on because its hatred of magic-wielders made other kingdoms wary of dealing with it?

A moment later, Kulan bounded through the entrance with a burst of energy. She empathised. While they were all still gaunt and weak from months of mine labour and the long run northwest, being free and somewhere safe was a bubbling, warm, energising feeling. "Have I come in time for your morning voseni, Kati?"

Yarmana gave a long-suffering sigh from where she stood over a steaming pot. "I fear my voseni is the only reason you visit me. Sit down and I will bring you both a mug."

"You are in for a treat, Arya. One cup of Kati's voseni, and the wear of months in the mine will drop away like it was never there." Kulan dropped into the seat beside hers. "Where's Kader?"

"Already gone to join the fisherman," Yarmana replied. The older woman gave the contents of her pot a final stir before carefully pouring a dark, steaming liquid into three tin mugs. She handed one to an eager Kulan before placing the other in front of Arya and then taking a seat with her own.

"I have missed this." Kulan breathed in deeply of the steam coming off his drink and closed his eyes in pleasure.

"Go on, Arya, try it," Yarmana encouraged. "You will find it strong and perhaps bitter at first, but let it sit a while and I think you will find it as good as all Khadini do."

Arya lifted the cup to her mouth and sipped. The taste was bitter on her tongue, the liquid almost viscous in its consistency. She swallowed, making a slight face as more acrid bitterness filled her mouth.

"Try a spoon of honey." Yarmana pushed a small honeypot across the table.

Arya obligingly added a spoon and stirred the drink before taking another sip. The sweetness cut through the bitter edge, and her second mouthful went down a lot easier. By the time she'd drunk half the cup, she was beginning to adjust to the taste. A steady warmth burned in her stomach and then spread throughout bone and muscle, leaving her feeling an odd combination of content and energetic.

"Good, isn't it?" Kulan asked.

"It's not bad," she admitted. "What is it?"

"In your language, you would call it something like hot bean juice." He fumbled with the Dunidae words, then reverted to Khadini. "The voseni beans grow here in our jungles—they need the heat and humidity to survive. We've tried exporting them before, but the Dunidae and Andahari both turn their nose up at the bitter taste. The Icefolk love it though and always buy from us during the trading months when the eastern seas are calm enough for passage through the storm channel."

Arya nodded understanding. While ship passage along the eastern coast of Dunidaen between the Icelands and Khadini was limited to when the seas were calm enough—the storm channel was named for its dangerous winds and currents—nobody was willing to sail the longer distance around Andahar since the borders closed down, *or* circle further east around the Pirate Isles and come under attack.

For a few peaceful moments the three of them sat and sipped their voseni. Arya got the sense the drink was as much a ritual as anything else, something perhaps Khadini families did together.

Eventually, Yarmana turned to Arya. "Kulan tells me you need our help?"

"Arya crossed the Dreadwater Gate with four other companions, but they became separated. She needs to find them," Kulan said.

Yarmana scowled. "That stupid Dunidae rite of passage. I didn't take you for a fool, girl."

Arya bit her lip, once again intimidated by the woman's glare. Essa was right about this whole journey. Arya had been determined to help Rorin do what he needed to become heir, but none of them had thought—or cared—how the Khadini felt about Dunidae robbing them. "I have no excuse, Yarmana, only an explanation. My brother, Rorin, is the heir to our

State, but he is a mute. To be accepted as a warlord in Dunidaen, he had to do something to prove himself to the other warlords."

"Impossible to be a future warlord if you are dead," Yarmana observed. "The only thing Emperor uq-Danresan and his Rangers treat more harshly than rebels are those that try to steal our cazaix."

"I understand," Arya acknowledged. "Cazaix gives Khadini an important strategic advantage."

"The metal is certainly stronger and more durable than the iron in your Dunidae sword," Kulan said. "But its true importance comes from its ability to deaden Sky Lord magic. A cazaix arrowhead lodged in a Sky Lord's body, for example, would cut their access to magic until it was drawn out. A prison cell made of cazaix bars would prevent a Sky Lord accessing their magic while they are inside it. There was a time when having such a weapon was critical to our survival."

Arya blinked, startled by a sudden realisation. She'd been so busy refusing to acknowledge her heritage that she hadn't thought about what would happen if she, Darmanin, and Essa succeeded in stealing a cazaix weapon—what effect it would have on them? Surely Ranier had thought of that ... she frowned. What was his game?

"Arya? Did I speak too quickly?" Kulan asked, catching her hesitation.

"No, it's all right. It just takes me a moment to catch up sometimes." She shifted, then ventured. "Are you aware of the Nightstalker stirring?"

Kulan and his mother shared a look. "We know of the agreement your High Warlord made with him three years ago, and why." Kulan let out a breath. "To be honest, we are hoping it remains a Dunidae problem. Khadini is not the stable and prosperous country it was decades ago when we united with you against the Nightstalker."

Neither is Dunidaen, Arya thought. Not with Crowtalon and Ravenstrike duking it out to be High Warlord. How much of that did the Nightstalker know?

Yarmana reached across to take her son's hand and squeeze gently. A moment later, she turned to Arya. "We will do what we can to help. Kulan has probably told you we have networks stretching across most of Khadini. I will put the word out, but first, I will need information on your companions and the last place you saw them."

"I was separated from Rorin, and our companions Darmanin, Leanir, and Taze, soon after washing ashore on the banks of the Dreadwater. I followed Rorin's trail until it became clear he had been captured by Rangers. It's how I ended up in the pit mine with Kulan—the trail his captors took led almost right to it, so I mistakenly thought Rorin had been taken there." She then explained where Essa had last seen the other two.

"Describe them for me," Yarmana ordered.

Arya described their colouring and rough height, "Taze and Leanir won't stand out as much here. But Leanir is ..." She hesitated, not wanting to scare them off. "He's a hardened warrior and it will be hard for him to hide that."

Yarmana nodded and rose from her chair, laying a hand on Arya's shoulder. "I'll do what I can."

Arya watched her leave, then turned to Kulan. "How is your mother involved in your work?"

He smiled. "Emperor uq-Danresan may dismiss women as those who belong by a hearth rearing children, but my mother dispelled me of that ill-informed view a long time ago. She runs a network of informants that is un-paralleled. If your companions have been spotted anywhere, my mother will hear of it."

She frowned, already beginning to feel antsy now that she'd reached a place of safety and had a good night's rest. They'd been gone from home so long, and the State Council was only four months off. Taking into account the weeks it would take to get back to Heathrock even if they safely got back across the Dreadwater Gate, not to mention the nazal. As long as Arya and Essa didn't use their magic, the monsters wouldn't be able to track them to Taskari, but she was still reluctant to remain in one place too long, or put any of the people here at risk. "I would feel better if I could go out looking for them myself."

"Where would you start?" Kulan scoffed. "No, it is better to wait until you have information before going after them."

She sighed. "I'm not very good at sitting around and doing nothing."

Cloth rustled as Essa appeared, yawning, pushing aside the curtain hanging across the entrance to the room they'd slept in. "Morning."

"Here." Arya rose and poured a cup from the pot still simmering. "Have some hot bean juice."

Essa made a face. "You want me to drink *what*?"

"It's called voseni." Kulan said. "Drink it, and eat some flatbread. Then, if you like, I will take you both on a tour of Taskari."

Essa nodded in delight. "I'd like that!"

***

Unlike Arya, Essa was not won over by the voseni, so Arya drank hers while Essa wolfed down the flatbread and Kulan filled her in on how his mother was going to help find Rorin and the others. Outside, the sun was hot against the cliff face and a pleasant salty breeze whipped around them. The ocean gleamed azure and many boats were scattered across its surface into the distance. Even as Arya watched, one of the boats unfurled their sails and started skipping across the ocean's surface towards the jetties.

"I have a question," Arya said as Kulan began their tour.

"Go on," he said.

"Yesterday your mother assumed Essa and I were Andahari. And Tomin's niece implied there were many Andahari living here. Is that true?"

Essa flicked a glance her way, but otherwise didn't betray any particular interest.

"It is. At least a third of the Taskari population is from Andahar. Kati assumed you were Andahari because you look so much like one, Arya." Kulan smiled at her. "Come, it might be better to show you."

He led them on a steady incline through the maze of dwellings, bridges and tunnels that made up Taskari. Close to the top of the cliff, they came to a rope ladder. Sunlight from above filled the space.

Kulan gestured toward it. "After you."

Arya gripped the rough rope of the ladder in her hands and clambered up. It wasn't long before she reached the top and scrambled onto a grassy clifftop. Down to her right was the bay, but out to her left and straight ahead was endless open ocean. The clifftop was mostly flat, running about half the length of the peninsula before it turned into the thick jungle that carpeted this area of Khadini.

After stepping aside to give Essa room, she ran her gaze over the groups of men and women gathered on the grass. All were undertaking some form of combat training. There were archers shooting at targets, swordsmen drilling in pairs, and even a few groups learning the basics of unarmed combat.

The sight instantly made her yearn for home. Icy mornings in the drill yard with her Raiders, or riding patrol with them through the Diamond-fang. Her right palm twitched, wanting to be wrapped around a sword hilt and swinging it through the air.

If only they were home right now. She wished for it so badly that her stomach hurt.

"You okay?" Essa seemed to sense her sadness.

"Just a little homesick."

Essa shook her head. "I'll never understand your love of wielding a sword or snapping orders."

"Just as I'll never understand how you hate the idea so much."

Kulan pointed. "Roughly half of those you see are warriors under my command. The rest are Andahari."

She'd already noticed as much. Many of those training had the olive skin and dark hair of the Khadini, but just as many were tall, with lighter hair and skin like Tomin and Raysa.

Like her.

"They're refugees, aren't they?" Essa asked.

He gave her an approving smile and pointed north across the ocean. "Roughly four days sail north is the southern Andahari coast. The Anda-hari here are riverfolk who fled during the Nightstalker's coup. They came looking for safety, only to find the previous emperor unwilling to accept so many refugees settling in his country. He didn't trust them and refused to allow them to assimilate into Khadini towns and villages. So, they found themselves stuck here at Taskari, essentially in limbo."

Here Kulan paused to make sure they were both following his words. Even Arya was fascinated and echoed Essa's eager nod.

"Those Khadini who lived here then took the Andahari in and gave them safe haven. In return, the riverfolk taught us to build fishing boats and sail, which allowed the whole community to rise out of subsistence living. We will never be wealthy, but nobody here goes hungry anymore. Fishing became our livelihood, and in return our warriors teach the Andahari to fight."

"What do you mean by the term riverfolk?" Essa said.

He shrugged. "My understanding is that Andahar is divided into regions, and the riverfolk are those that come from the Riverlands—the region along their south coast and the closest point of Andahar to here. There was a lot of violence and instability in the years before the Nightstalker stole the throne, and the riverfolk were the strongest allies of the true Andahari royal house. They bore the most severe consequences after the coup."

Arya ignored the curiosity that niggled at mention of her ancestral family, and instead asked, "It has been decades. Why are they learning to fight now?"

"I think it helps them to feel stronger, more in control, to know how to defend themselves if they ever needed to again."

"They surely can't feel fully safe here," Essa pointed out.

Arya shivered, despite the warmth of the sun on her back. "It must be awful, to be trapped in limbo, unable to make a proper life here or return home."

"I agree." Something in Kulan's voice reached her, telling her he knew exactly how that felt.

Essa caught it too. "Are you ever planning on telling us who you are?" she asked him.

As Kulan opened his mouth, pretend puzzlement on his face, Arya fixed him with a glare. "Essa knows what dostari means," Arya said.

Kulan turned away, arms crossing over his chest, but after a moment he turned back, and he gave them a brief, formal bow. "I am Kulan uq-Danresan."

Essa gasped and Arya's eyes widened. "uq-Danresan?"

"I am the emperor's younger brother," he confirmed, a hint of bitterness in his voice. "I was fourteen when he took the throne on our father's death and gave the execution order to remove all other potential heirs. My mother took Kader and me and fled—because we were still children we lived in a different part of the palace, and the executioners went for my older siblings first."

Arya stared, not knowing how to even respond to that. Essa had no idea either—she looked incredibly uncomfortable. Eventually, Arya asked. "How many siblings did you lose?"

His jaw tightened. "Three brothers, two sisters."

"I am sorry, Kulan. I cannot pretend to imagine such a loss." Her chest clenched just thinking of it. It had been hard enough losing Raider comrades—but they had died doing their duty and proud to serve their State.

"You can imagine," he said. "It's in your eyes every time you speak of finding your Rorin."

The sheer impossibility of a world without Rorin killed Arya. She nodded, looking away so they wouldn't see the tears trying to well in her eyes.

"Is it a normal custom to execute all potential heirs when ascending the throne?" Essa asked.

"It is not, but has been done in the past. I would *never*." Kulan's voice hitched, then trailed off.

"*That's* why you kept your identity hidden at the mines, why Rafal and the others hid it too. If the soldiers found out who you were, they would have executed you outright," Arya said.

"Yes. My own people know who I am, but most of the wider rebel network does not. It would be incredibly dangerous for Kati and Kader if my identity were more widely known." He looked troubled. "Though eventually I will have to reveal it if a rebellion is to succeed."

Arya cleared her throat, pointed to the training fighters. "Could we join them?" She wanted to start rebuilding the strength in her body as soon as possible. Not to mention regain the quick footwork and reflexes needed for swordplay.

"You would be welcome to join us." Kulan smiled. "Essa?"

"No thanks." Essa shook her head vehemently. "But if that market we passed on the way here sells parchment and ink, I'd love to draw while you train. The view up here is stunning."

Kulan dug in his pocket and offered her some coins. "They will definitely have what you need, Inkweaver."

Essa blinked at the name and seemed to hesitate. "What do you know of House Inkweaver?"

Again, Kulan looked puzzled, as if surprised to be faced with neither Arya nor Essa knowing anything about Essa's heritage. "Not enough to answer all your questions, I suspect. If you would allow me to tell one of the Andahari here, in confidence, of course, they could—"

"No," Arya said firmly. A little shiver ran down her spine at the thought of the nazal out there. Had they reached the mine yet and found her missing? "We tell nobody. It's too dangerous."

Kulan glanced between them, as if guessing that Arya hadn't told him everything. "I understand. House Inkweaver were the scholars of Andahar, as I understand it. Responsible for holding its store of knowledge. That is all I know. Andahari are quite tight-lipped about the secrets of their Sky Lord Houses."

"Thanks, Kulan." Essa waved and headed back down the rope ladder.

Arya followed Kulan as he headed towards the drilling fighters. Already her shoulders were loosening, and her breath was quickening.

A sword back in her hand again, even a wooden one.

It was going to feel good.

Chapter 18

One morning several days later, when Arya made her daily pilgrimage to Tomin to have her cut cleaned and re-bandaged, the healer invited her to dinner with his family.

"It's very kind of you to offer," she said. She instinctively wanted to keep a distance from any of the Andahari on Taskari. Not only did she not want her, or Essa's, identities discovered, their presence made her uncomfortable, like an itch in a place you couldn't reach. "But I wouldn't want to intrude."

"Nonsense. It will just be myself and my nephews, and Raysa. We'd love new company at the table to liven the conversation. Bring Kulan and his family, and your Dunidae friend ... is it Essa?"

"I'll ask, and if they're free, we'll come."

Did she detect a little *too* much casualness in the way he threw out Essa's name?

It turned out that Kulan *was* pleased by the invitation. "Tomin is a respected leader among the Andahari community, and keeping relations between our two peoples on good terms is a priority for me," he said. "The ability to use Taskari as a safehouse relies on it. One traitor leaking word to the emperor, or his Rangers, would destroy everything."

They strolled together to Tomin's home as a fiery sunset lit up the bay. Arya had found herself slowly being seduced by the beauty of Taskari. Even the unrelenting heat was becoming more bearable—and it was honestly nice not to wake with stiffened and sore muscles every morning that took ages to loosen in the bitter cold. And walking around with no more than a shirt and loose breeches was unexpectedly freeing.

Kulan and Kader led the way with Yarmana, and Arya and Essa brought up the rear. "Be careful, tonight," Arya said to Essa, slowing their pace so they fell a bit farther behind.

Essa's gaze narrowed. "Why?"

"Because I think Tomin is curious about us, and I'm not sure why."

"I imagine the arrival of a couple of Dunidae here is enough to excite curiosity. I'm sure they rarely, if ever, get foreign visitors," Essa pointed out.

"That's true."

Essa flashed her a smile, clearly catching the unease still in Arya's voice. "I'll be careful."

When they arrived, Tomin waved them in and introduced Arya and Essa to his family. "You've met Raysa, and these are my nephews, Daarin and Atarin. Raysa is Daarin's wife."

"It's nice to meet you," Arya said. Both young men were tall, with Daarin obviously being the oldest and Atarin looking closer to her own age.

"My uncle tells us you're both from Dunidaen," Daarin said, just as polite.

Arya tried to stifle a sigh of impatience. She *hated* small talk. Thankfully Essa stepped in easily. "That's right. We're from the north, Ravenstrike. You have a lovely home, Healer Tomin. Thank you for inviting us tonight."

"We're so pleased you said yes. Now come on in and sit down. No need to linger awkwardly in the doorway."

He showed them to seats around a circular table, and Atarin and Daarin served the food, which it appeared Tomin had cooked. There was seasoned fish baked over coals with grilled green vegetables that Arya didn't recognise. Tomin's food was different again from the meals Yarmana had made for them, but Arya found the fish delicious. From her delighted smile, Essa clearly felt the same.

Talk flowed easily. Tomin seemed a natural conversationalist, and both Kulan and Essa jumped in seamlessly if things lulled. Arya didn't have to do more than smile and answer the occasional question. They spoke of the differences between Dunidae and Khadini and the things they liked to read—though Arya did notice none of the Andahari spoke of their original home.

Later, with everyone full and relaxed, she asked the question that had been simmering since the first morning she'd visited the clifftop. "Why are your people so eager to learn and maintain your fighting skills?"

The four Andahari glanced at each other, but by unspoken consensus they left Tomin to answer the question.

"We cannot go home," he said. "The Nightstalker maintains a close watch on the coastline of the Riverlands region. His soldiers kill any who attempt to leave or arrive." His mouth twisted a little. "He has a long memory."

"We don't want to raise bad memories, but we are curious," Essa said. "We obviously know of the Nightstalker in Dunidaen, but beyond the fact that he rules Andahar after a coup that led to the closing down of our borders, we know little. Could you tell us more about him?"

Arya only barely managed to avoid shooting a look at Essa, who had just vastly underplayed their knowledge of the Nightstalker. But it was an excellent way of trying to get the Andahari to open up while simultaneously downplaying their own connection to Andahar.

"I also wish to be respectful of your past," Kulan said into the brief silence that followed. "But given what happened three years ago, it would perhaps behove all of us to learn more about this king."

The mood at the table darkened, the looks shared between the Andahari heavy with sadness. Eventually Tomin spoke. "We do not like to speak of it, but you are right, Dostari. It concerns us deeply that the world seems to have forgotten the threat he poses."

"You think he does still pose a threat, then?" Kulan frowned. "Wouldn't he be getting pretty old by now?"

"The Nightstalker is Valheran, and one with unnatural powers." Daarin spoke, jaw set. "We believe that has something to do with how he managed to succeed in his coup. He is stronger than any single Sky Lord has been in the past, stronger than should be possible."

"Whatever happened all those decades ago, it twisted his mind," Tomin said, gaze distant, as if he were looking straight back into the past. "He is a man no more. At least, there is very little left of the man inside the monster."

"How do you know all this?" Arya asked.

"Daarin and Atarin were born here at Taskari, but I fled here with the first of the refugees from the Riverlands." Tomin's voice shook with remembered pain. "I watched the Nightstalker and Xaphistryl raze my entire town and everyone still in it when he arrived. It took him mere minutes."

There was a beat of silence. Kulan and his mother shared a look, and he reached out to take and squeeze her hand. Essa didn't seem to know what to do or say, and Kader glanced around the table with wide eyes before dropping his gaze to his empty plate.

But Arya had to know.

"If you can't go home, then what is the purpose in learning to become warriors?" Arya asked.

"We are preparing ourselves," Raysa said, tears of determination glistening her eyes. "For when the time comes for us to go home and fight for what is ours."

Daarin placed a reassuring hand on his wife's arm. "Raysa feels very strongly about that, as do most of us here. We believe that an heir to House Stormrider will one day come to lead us home, and they will bring their Valheran *cairdre* to fight with us and destroy the Nightstalker."

The words rebounded through Arya so strongly she was momentarily speechless. Salyarin had told her more than once about who she was, and she'd come to accept it as fact, but even then it had only been a nebulous thing. Nothing that meant anything to anyone else because nobody knew of her. It was something she'd been able to ignore because it was unachievable.

But that wasn't true.

These people *hoped* for her.

Tomin continued, "I am not as hopeful as the younger ones. The Nightstalker was thorough in tracking down and killing all of the Stormrider family, *and* every existing Sky Lord. He has monsters at his disposal that continue to hunt any born with Valheran potential."

Something clenched tight and fierce inside Arya, from the same place her magic leaked out of. Her family had been *exterminated*. No, she reminded herself, Rorin was her family. House Ravenstrike and the Raiders were her family.

"Even so, the magic of Andahar ensures that Sky Lord potentials will continue to be born within the Valheran family bloodlines." Atarin insisted. "There were twelve Valheran Houses, all with the potential to bear Sky Lords. The Nightstalker cannot kill every potential born, not forever. The world is too large."

Raysa nodded fiercely. "It is why he sent his creatures into the Diamondfang three years ago and attacked Ravenstrike, I am sure of it. There are potentials out there, and he knows it. He's looking for them."

"Given the hunters at his disposal, it's more than likely he's found and killed them by now." Tomin gave her a sad smile. "But what is life without hope?"

It was on the top of Arya's tongue, to tell them that he hadn't found them, that the Nightstalker was getting increasingly impatient with Dunidaen. But she couldn't risk it. The words stuck in her throat.

And then the moment was past.

"Indeed," Kulan said softly. To his credit, his quick glance in Essa's direction had no remonstration in it. Arya felt it anyway, and swallowed, suddenly wishing she'd never come to this dinner. She wished she'd never walked into the pit mine after Rorin that day, never met Kulan, never come here and found people that claimed her. "These hunters sound terrifying. Do you know much about them?"

Tomin's mouth tightened. "They are magical—created by the Nightstalker, I'd say. Unnatural. Powerful. I saw one tear apart... No. I am sorry, I cannot talk of them any further."

"We have brought the mood down," Essa said, smiling lightly. "What awful guests we've been. I'm sorry, Tomin."

"As am I." Kulan said easily. "It is in my nature as dostari to ask questions, but tonight should be a relaxing dinner among friends."

Tomin shot Kulan a sympathetic look. "It is hard to separate a cause from life when you are its leader. It won't be easy to unite the rebels under you, Dostari."

His shoulders straightened and a fierce light shone in his eyes. "We will never defeat my brother unless we do. And Khadini cannot go on as it is. Something has to change."

A heavy silence fell over the table before Atarin smiled and clapped his hands. "Let's talk of something more light-hearted. I wanted to know more about this silly Dunidae ritual of sailing along dangerous rapids in order to prove your manhood or whatever you call it?"

They all laughed.

***

After dinner, they strolled back to Yarmana's home. Arya lagged, deeply troubled. Essa was equally quiet, lost in her own thoughts, while Kader left them to go and see some friends of his.

Before they reached Yarmana's house, Arya let them all go on ahead and stopped at a flat section of path that looked out over the dark bay. It was a balmy evening, and a soft breeze blew across her skin. But even the peace of the ocean spread out below her couldn't calm her discomfort.

Kulan settled at her side a few moments later. "I'm sorry if dinner disconcerted you."

"It's not your fault, or theirs." Arya let out a breath. "Kulan, after what the emperor did ... was becoming a rebel what you wanted to do? Or what you felt you had to?"

"Both," he said simply.

She searched his gaze. "So you never wished for another life? Becoming a farmer perhaps, or blacksmith, or anything else."

He frowned. "I'm not sure I ever *had* another choice. My family will be in danger as long as my brother sits the throne. Yet if it were only that, perhaps

I could be content with them hidden safely here. But my brother's rule is hurting my people, and that I cannot stand, not when I am in a position to do something about it."

"I'm Dunidae," she said forcefully. "I'm going to be general of Ravenstrike's army, and I'm going to stand at Rorin's side when he becomes warlord. *That's* my life. *That's* what I want."

Kulan was silent for a long moment, and when he spoke, it was barely audible. "I'm going to assume from your reaction at dinner and your words just now that Essa isn't the only Andahari of the two of you," he said quietly. "And knowing you as I have come to .... *you* are the Stormrider heir, aren't you? The one Raysa and Daarin were talking about."

She turned to him, fear rippling through her. "You can't tell them. Please. You can't tell anyone."

"Your secret is your own," he said. "And you should choose the life you want, not the one people force on you."

"You don't think I have a duty to save the people of Andahar?" she asked.

He considered that. "I think Andahar has been under the control of a despot for decades, and unseating him will be well-nigh impossible. Tomin is right that we all need hope, but there *is* no realistic hope of unseating such a powerful ruler. He will die eventually, and perhaps then Andahar can determine its own course without any Sky Lord ruling them. They might even be better off for it in the long run."

Arya wondered what Salyarin or Ranier would make of that argument. She wondered what *she* thought of it. Eventually she gave herself a shake. "Ugh. I'm so sick of *thinking* about all of this, and worrying about Rorin, and just sitting here and not being able to do anything about any of it."

His smile flashed out. "You've been here barely ten days."

"I know," she grumbled. "I told you, I'm not very good at sitting still."

Kulan shifted closer, his voice dropping. "I can suggest a remedy for that."

Arya lifted her eyebrows and leaned in. "Is that right?"

"I can promise an excellent distraction from both our troubles." He reached out to trace his fingers down her arm, raising a little shiver of reaction. "Stay with me tonight."

He was certainly confident, and she could use what he was offering. She'd be lying if she claimed she wasn't attracted to the rebel prince. Still she searched his gaze. "As long as it's only a distraction. I'll be gone soon, and we probably won't see each other again."

"Distraction and pleasure, Arya." He slid his hand into hers, and tugged her gently against him. "That's all. I promise."

A night of distraction from all her worries, where she only needed to focus on the moment, the physical pleasure.

Arya welcomed it with open arms.

Chapter 19

Arya woke the next morning tangled in Kulan's sheets, warm and snug. A languid contentment replaced the restlessness and discomfort she'd felt after dinner the night before. She stretched and yawned.

"You talk in your sleep," he said beside her, still half-asleep.

"I do not!" She sat up indignantly, only for one of his arms to reach out and draw her back down.

"Yes, you do," he said, then kissed her.

The curtain being yanked back from across the entrance broke them apart, and Kader stepped in. He was breathing hard, eyes bright, and he took in the two of them with a quick glance before facing his brother. "A messenger came for you this morning, Kulan. He waits with Kati."

"We'll be right there," Kulan said.

Kader smirked, then whirled, and left as quickly as he had come.

"It's barely been ten days, not long enough for most of Kati's network to have even received a message asking about your companions, let alone sent back a reply," Kulan said, correctly reading Arya's hopeful look. "Don't get your hopes up."

Kulan tossed the sheet off and strode naked across the room towards a wide basket where he appeared to keep all his clothes piled in together. Arya hunted her clothes around the floor, discarded from the night before, and yanked them on.

"Will this upset your mother?" She waved to the rumpled bed. Such matters didn't cause any comment among Raiders and working folk in Dunidaen, but Rorin doing the same ... problematic might be the best way to describe it. Nobles—women in particular, which never failed to set Arya's teeth on edge—had to be careful about affecting their chances of a good marriage.

"Not at all. Kati would have already known you didn't sleep there last night and probably guessed the rest. She is smarter than all of us put together except maybe your Essa." He crossed the room to kiss her soundly. "Come on, let's go and drink some voseni and hear this news."

***

Two steaming mugs awaited Kulan and Arya as they entered Yarmana's home. Essa gave Arya a smile, then winked when Kulan wasn't looking. "I'm glad you found a way to distract yourself," she said as Arya sat beside her.

"Are *you* okay?" Arya searched her gaze.

"I'm honestly not sure how I feel." She gave a little shake of her head, like she often did when she didn't want to talk about something.

Arya looked up as Yarmana joined them at the table with her own cup of voseni. She carried a piece of crumpled parchment and looked worried. "Kulan, Safal uq-Rasaya is on his way here." Kulan's eyebrows shot up and he reached out for the parchment, eyes scanning its contents while his mother kept talking, "He has heard about your escape and travels here to meet with you and plan rebel affairs."

"He is less than a week away." Kulan rubbed his jaw. "Still, that is enough time to prepare. This is good news, Kati!" As an aside to Arya and Essa he explained, "Safal is the strongest rebel leader apart from me. He is critical to our unification efforts."

"Safal knows the location of Taskari?" Arya asked sharply, all her soldier's instincts rousing.

"He is one of the handful of rebel leaders who do, yes," Kulan admitted.

Yarmana said quietly, "Safal is fiercely loyal to the rebel cause, no matter which region they come from. He wouldn't betray Taskari's location to the emperor."

Arya shared a glance with Essa. She wasn't sure she trusted that as much as Yarmana and Kulan seemed to, yet they knew the man better than she did.

"Does he know your identity?" Essa asked.

Kulan shook his head. Arya relaxed slightly.

"Arya, Essa, there is news for you also." Yarmana turned to them. "My contact thought I would be interested to know that Safal recently added three warriors to his group—she made a point of mentioning it because one of them is raven-haired and fair-skinned."

Hope flared in Arya's chest, banishing all her concerns about Safal as if they'd never been. She and Essa shared an excited glance. It had to be Darmanin. And could the other two warriors be Leanir and Taze, assumed to be Khadini by Yarmana's contact and therefore not worth describing? If so, how had they ended up falling in with a rebel leader?

"Are these warriors travelling here with Safal?" Arya asked.

"Yes."

"But no news of Rorin?" Essa asked.

"No, I am sorry. Still, I wouldn't worry yet. The Dreadwater is a long distance from here. If my contacts in that region have seen your Rorin, I may not hear of it for some time."

"I understand," Arya said. "Thank you."

"Take heart, Arya." Kulan reached out to squeeze her hand. "Yesterday all of your companions were lost to you, bar one. Now you have news of another, and even better, they are coming here."

"I appreciate everything you have done for us." Arya managed a smile and took another sip of her voseni. It tasted different than usual today, the honey not cutting through the bitterness as much as usual. She looked over at Yarmana, planning to ask if she hadn't added as much, but the older women just gave her a little knowing smile.

"I added some herbs to yours this morning, Arya. It will affect the taste a little, I'm sorry."

"Oh." Arya tried not to flush. Yarmana had saved her from having to ask Tomin for herbs she could use if she planned to continue sharing Kulan's bed. She shuddered at the thought of bringing another Stormrider heir into the world, a tiny baby for the Nightstalker to hunt. And with Kulan ... another uq-Danresan heir the emperor would want dead. "That was thoughtful. Thank you."

The usual silence fell then, all of them sitting in comfortable quiet to share their morning voseni. As usual, though, Arya was the first to break it, unable to sit still for too long. As soon as she took her final sip, she rose to her feet. "I'd best go and see Tomin to get this arm re-bandaged before training. I think it must be the most looked after wound in all of Taskari."

"He does take an interest in you," Kulan said. "Say hello to him for me, and I'll see you later."

Essa joined Arya, leaving Kulan and his mother huddled together, discussing Safal uq-Rasaya's message in hushed tones.

"When Dar arrives, especially if it is Taze and Leanir with him, it's time for us to leave," Essa spoke. "We can't afford to get mixed up in Khadini politics. And I don't want to lead the nazal here, Arya. They've surely reached the mine by now and found you gone."

"I agree." Arya frowned. She felt for Kulan and his cause, but it wasn't hers. Her responsibility was getting them all home safely—with or without the cazaix at this point. "Crossing Khadini will be easier if Taze and Leanir are with us, and I don't like waiting for news of Rorin either. It's been too long already."

They arrived at the cavern where Tomin worked, the man himself in the front room giving instructions to Raysa. He smiled at their entrance and waved them through. "Good morning to you both."

Essa smiled at Tomin, then touched Arya's arm. "I'll see you later."

"I hear Safal uq-Rasaya is on his way here." Tomin spoke conversationally as he unbound Arya's arm.

"News travels fast in Taskari. Do you ever worry about being caught up in a Khadini civil war?"

"Sometimes," he conceded. "The Khadini here have been wonderful in how they've taken us in, but I admit the fact that Taskari is the safehouse for

Kulan's rebels discomforts us. We have nowhere else to go, and their fight is not ours."

"Would you fight with them, if it came to it?" she asked.

He finished examining the now closed-over wound and leaned back to reach for fresh bandaging. "No. But if the emperor's soldiers came to Taskari, they would see us no differently from the rebels. If they didn't kill us outright, I've no doubt they'd ship us back to Andahar or imprison us in their pit mines. Both are a death sentence."

Arya thought about that as Tomin wound fresh bandaging around her arm, again covering most of the skin to her elbow. What *could* the Andahari do if Emperor uq-Danresan's soldiers came to Taskari? When the silence lengthened, he mistook it for her disquiet and looked up with a quick smile. "There is little use in worrying about things we cannot change."

"You should go to Dunidaen," she said. "Take your boats before the emperor's soldiers arrive and sail for SparrowWing State, not Crowtalon. Even better, make straight for Aren in the southwest of Ravenstrike if you can get that far. You're right, Tomin, the Khadini fight isn't yours. You have a way out. Use it."

He eyed her. "You think your Dunidae would treat us any differently?"

"Helden SparrowWing is a traditional warlord, but a good man. I cannot guarantee that he would let you stay, but it would be worth trying," she said. "And if you made it to Ravenstrike, you will find shelter with me."

He didn't look away. "Is that so?"

"I will be general of Ravenstrike when I return home, Tomin. My warlord is a hard, ruthlessly practical woman, but I will do all I can for you."

"Why?" he asked the question without accusation in his tone, but it still felt like a test of some kind.

"Because I can," she said simply. Maybe if she couldn't be their lost heir and lead them home again, she could at least offer them a new home if they needed it. And safety.

Tomin glanced down for a moment, tying off the ends of the bandage. When he looked up again, there was something she couldn't quite make out in his gaze. "If Taskari comes under threat, I will bring my people to you, Arya Ravenstrike."

Something shifted between them. A promise. Maybe even an inevitability.

She nodded. "And I will keep them safe, Tomin. My word on it."

Chapter 20

Arya and Essa were breakfasting with Yarmana when Safal uq-Rasaya arrived at Taskari. The previous days had dragged. Arya had done her best to work out her restless energy with drill training and long runs with Essa up and down the peninsula, rebuilding the physical sharpness Ranier had developed in them. Yarmana's cooking had put the flesh back on their bones and a healthy glow to their skin. But even so, Arya's leg jiggled constantly that morning as they sat together, unable to rid herself of the anxiety.

The thud of running feet interrupted Essa querying Yarmana about how bartering worked in the Taskari markets. All three looked up as Kader ran in, flushed and breathless. "Two boats are rowing up to the jetties. It has to be Safal uq-Rasaya and his retinue. Kulan has gone down to meet them and asked me to let you know."

Hope surged in Arya, and she leaped to her feet, Essa only a second behind.

"Go." Yarmana smiled at them. "We will speak later."

Kader spun and ran back out the door, Arya and Essa hot on his heels.

The three raced through the cliffside community, breathing easily despite the warmth of the day and the number of steps to negotiate. Kader slowed the pace as they reached ground level and emerged into the sandy cavern open to the shoreline where all the jetties terminated.

Kulan was there, speaking with a handful of his warriors. Arya recognised Kiraya and Rafal from the mine camp. They looked up when she and Essa joined them. "Which jetty will they tie up?" Arya asked.

Kulan stood stiff, sober and steady, his amiable demeanour absent this morning. "Just wait."

"Which one?" Essa cut in.

Kulan shook his head. "I need to be the first to greet them, not you. Please, be patient. If your companions are with Safal, it will not be long before you can see them."

Arya rolled her shoulders, shifted from foot to foot impatiently, as Kulan gave his rebels instructions. "Rafal, round up some warriors and organise food and voseni for the meeting chamber," he instructed. "We must receive Safal and his warriors as respected guests and provide proper hospitality. Kiraya, Tanifa, you will stay with me."

"Kulan, they approach!" Kader's voice rang out from where he hovered at the cavern opening. Rafal dashed off, calling to two women hovering nearby to join him.

Kulan turned to Essa and Arya. "I won't ask you to wait here, but please remain behind me until official greetings are conducted."

He led the way out into the sunlight, Kiraya and Tanifa at each shoulder, Arya and Essa trailing behind. The hot sun beat down on their skin despite the early hour. Arya's gaze jumped ahead, towards the boats tying up. A man, presumably Safal uq-Rasaya, had disembarked and walked towards them, tall and lean and moving with a warrior's grace. Like Kulan, two warriors flanked him.

But Arya looked beyond him, searching. Several figures moved around securing the newly arrived boats, but her gaze fastened instantly on the tall young man she would recognise anywhere in the world. That thread in her chest gave a little tug.

Darmanin Crowtalon.

She and Essa shared a single, delighted glance. Kulan halted ahead of them. Safal stopped too. As the two rebel leaders exchanged formal greetings, Arya and Essa slipped around them, Arya's longer legs quickly carrying her ahead of Essa as she broke into a run. "Dar!" she shouted.

With the shout she gave an instinctive tug on that thread between them. He spun instantly, gaze searching and then landing on Arya and Essa. His sharp features transformed then, eyes widening in combined surprise and joy.

In the next breath, he'd pushed aside a man in front of him and swung over the boat railing and onto the jetty. Arya reached him and they collided, arms wrapping around each other, holding on as tightly as Arya knew how. She breathed in the scent that was so familiar, so uniquely his, felt his stubble graze against her cheek. Almost as quickly, they realised how fiercely they were hugging and released each other to step back.

Then Essa arrived and Darmanin reached out to clasp her shoulder. "Dar!" Essa's eyes sheened with tears, one hand lifted to cover her mouth, the other to touch his hand where it rested on her shoulder. "You're well."

"You have no idea how good it is to see you both," he said in that quiet, deep voice of his.

Arya went to speak, but Darmanin lifted a finger to cut her off, then pointed over his shoulder where two other men had followed him off the boat. She'd been so caught up in seeing him, she and Essa both, that they hadn't even noticed.

"Taze." Her smile widened into a grin, which he returned with a matching grin and a snappy salute. At his side stood Leanir, wary and aloof, and she gave him a nod of acknowledgment, before turning back to Darmanin. "No Rorin?"

"We've seen no sign of him," he said. "You?"

"He was captured at the Dreadwater. I tried following the trail they left but lost it. I have no idea where he is now. You're all right, though?" she asked him, searching his face and body for any sign of injury before shifting her gaze to include Taze and Leanir too.

"We're good, Arya," Taze replied. "And you both?"

"Just this." She raised her bandaged arm.

"And I have a nice new scar." Essa pointed at her labour camp brand. "It's so good to see you. We've been so worried."

"Arya?" Kulan's voice caught her attention. Safal uq-Rasaya and his warriors were being escorted into Taskari by Tanifa and Kiraya, leaving Kulan alone on the jetty. "You have found your companions, I take it?"

She couldn't help the smile that spread over her face. "Yes. Kulan, allow me to introduce Darmanin Crowtalon, Taze Nameless, and Leanir."

"Welcome to Taskari," he said, every inch the polite host. "I am Kulan."

Darmanin's eyebrows went up slightly, and Arya wondered whether it was because of the almost challenging tone Kulan had introduced himself with. Darmanin bowed his head and replied in rough Khadini. "Thank you for your welcome."

Kulan didn't smile. "Please, come inside. Arya and Essa will show you around." He turned to Arya, and lowered his voice. "I ask you to keep my identity secret, as I have yours, at least while Safal is here."

"I won't say anything. Good luck, Kulan," she said.

His smile widened, and he was gone, whirling to stride along the jetty and catch up with Safal.

***

"What's the story with this place?" Taze asked. The five of them sat around a table in a communal drinking hall not far from Yarmana's home. They'd been there for hours, with Arya and Essa taking turns filling them in on how they'd come to be at Taskari. As far as Arya knew, Kulan and his warriors were still in discussions with Safal uq-Rasaya and his entourage.

"You tell us how you got here first," Essa said. "Arya and I have talked too long already. How did you end up with Safal uq-Rasaya's warriors?"

Taze glanced at Darmanin, ceding the story to him. Leanir had barely participated in the conversation so far, his attention more on studying the room and the people in it than his companions. Arya suspected it was a mixture of disinterest in them and the instinctive need of an assassin to map his environment. A little shiver of worry went through her. Leanir was a contract assassin, so nobody at Taskari should be in danger from him. But he seemed to like killing. She resolved to keep a close eye on him.

"Taze and Leanir caught up to me several days after I left the Dreadwater. I hadn't made it far because I spent most of my time evading Rangers while searching the eastern riverbank for signs of any of you," Darmanin explained. "Once they told me what had happened, we got clear of the Rangers, and then looped back around to search for a safe place to cross the Dreadwater and search for your trail. Or Rorin's or Essa's."

Darmanin lifted his drink to take a sip and Taze picked up the tale.

"But we ran into another Ranger patrol. It wasn't looking good for us—they had numbers on their side—until Safal and his warriors joined the fight. They'd been tracking the Rangers, apparently, with the intent to ambush them."

"Once the Rangers were taken out, Safal's people captured us," Darmanin said. "It took some time to get our stories across since none of us spoke Khadini."

"And when we did, they almost executed us outright for daring to try and steal their cazaix." Taze said.

Darmanin's expression darkened. "Until Leanir here made an offer—that we would join them and fight alongside them if they freed us."

Leanir spoke for the first time, delivering a flat glare in response to the censure in Darmanin's voice. "Joining them gave us the ability to move around Khadini, as well as access to food and weapons. It also allowed us to *live*."

Arya frowned. "Even so, I'm surprised a rebel leader was willing to take three foreigners into his retinue just like that."

Darmanin glanced around, then lowered his voice. "The man is making clear efforts to build his numbers. From what we can gather, he's been increasing the number of attacks on Ranger patrols, seeking to de-stabilise the region. We are not trusted, but they want our fighting skills." He cast a glance at Leanir. "Leanir noticed them watching us fight the Rangers. They were impressed. Maybe you can provide some context that explains why? We still understand very little Khadini."

"I think we can." Essa gave Arya a knowing look. "We seem to have stumbled into the middle of a brewing civil war."

Arya explained what Kulan had told her about the rebel efforts.

"So Safal and Kulan are trying to unify all the rebel groups?" Taze asked. "That's quite the undertaking. No wonder Safal is stepping up his efforts.

He must think it will impress the other rebel leaders, make them choose him as overall leader."

"It also explains why he needs warriors, and good ones," Darmanin said.

As if summoned by her speaking his name, Kulan entered the cavern. He lifted a hand in greeting but didn't come over. "I'll be back in a bit," she murmured to her companions.

Arya picked up her mug of ale and weaved through the tables to join him where he'd taken a seat on a bench against the wall. He smiled in greeting, but it didn't hide the lines of tension around his eyes.

"Do you want a drink?" she asked.

"No." He rubbed a hand over his face. "I need to keep a clear head while Safal is here. I could use one though, after today's discussions."

"They didn't go well?"

"Safal is cagey and won't say what he truly thinks. It's all flowery words and dissembling. I understand why he's wary—after all, look what happened to me when I wasn't careful—but it gives me a pounding headache," Kulan admitted.

"I know how that feels," she said, and a moment of comfortable silence fell between them, Arya sipping her ale. She watched a small group of musicians play in the corner.

"Your companions are interesting." Kulan broke the silence. "Not what I expected."

Arya followed his gaze to where it rested on Darmanin and the others sitting together, still chatting away. "How so?"

"One is a soldier much like you, a good man, I think. The one with the hooded gaze is a killer, a man I do not want near anyone I love. Your fair-skinned friend—he is very dangerous too."

"Why do you say Dar is dangerous?" she asked. He was intense, certainly, driven too. But she'd never thought of him as a danger to them.

He glanced at her in surprise. "It is not obvious to you?"

"Maybe I just know him better than you," she said, feeling defensive of Darmanin. "We practically grew up together."

"Yet you do not call him a brother like you do Rorin?"

Arya paused, unsure how to explain that.

Kulan shrugged, letting it go. "Unlike you and Essa, your companions show no interest in making friends here."

Arya sighed, acknowledging that. They'd behaved with nothing but chilly politeness to anyone they'd met at Taskari.

"Dar and Leanir don't like anyone much, and Taze is still feeling his way—he's very protective," she said. "And they don't know you like Essa and I do. Don't take it personally."

"I won't," Kulan said. "I don't need the regard of some Dunidae boys, Arya. I am a dostari."

She huffed at that; it was the thing she liked least about Kulan, his cockiness. "How are the discussions going, apart from being frustrating?"

Kulan sighed, and he reached up to rub his clean-shaven jaw, a habit of his when he was thinking something over. "Safal has a proposition for me," he said.

"Go on." Arya settled back on the seat, took a sip of her ale.

"We both want to unite the rebels into a single force, but he believes that there must be a meeting of all the rebel leaders in person to agree on such a unification, and I don't disagree. He's been working hard on our plans during my imprisonment. Arya, Safal has secured an in-principle agreement from the other rebel leaders to attend a meeting." Eagerness shone from Kulan's face. "That's why he travelled here as soon as he heard I was free—he wants to move quickly."

"Could it sound more like a trap?"

Kulan chuckled. "Safal is a trusted ally, Arya, and this is everything I've been hoping for. It is a risk, though, to have us all gathered in one place. That is what makes me hesitate, and it is why Safal has organised the meeting so quickly. Best it happens before my brother's spies get wind of it."

"All right," Arya said. That logic made sense, and if Kulan trusted Safal, it was probably for good reason. "It sounds like you've made your mind up already."

"I would like to agree, but I have a favour to ask first. I've come up with a possible solution to managing the risk of all the rebel leaders being gathered in one place."

She took another sip of ale and waited for his question.

"Will you take command of my warriors to keep the area secure while we hold the meeting? My people are committed and loyal, but they don't have your training in tactics or strategy. And neither do I—I was too young when Kati fled the palace." His jaw tensed, clearly reluctant to admit that. "We must be ready for all eventualities, but you can plan for them better than I can."

Arya shook her head. "I sympathise with your plight, but I need to find Rorin. Now that I've found my other companions, we can't afford any more delays."

He leaned closer. "If you agree to help me, I will give you a guide to take you directly to the cazaix smelter after the summit. Then, once you have your cazaix weapons, my warriors will escort you safely to the border and stage a diversion so that you can climb to the Dreadwater Gate without detection."

"I can't do any of that until I find Rorin," she said.

"We will look for sign of him as we travel to the summit. If we have no luck, we wait for word from Kati's spy network. Either way, once the rebel meeting is safely conducted—no matter the outcome—I will hold to my word about escorting you to the cazaix and then back to the Dreadwater; whenever you find Rorin."

Arya looked at him for a long moment, before rising to her feet and draining the remnants of her ale. "I need to discuss it with the others."

"Of course. I will wait."

They looked up as Arya approached, and Darmanin slid along the bench to make room for her. "Kulan has a proposal for us," she said, outlining what he'd offered. "What do you think?"

Darmanin's jaw tightened. "I think the politics of Khadini's rebels has nothing to do with us. We should leave on our own to find Rorin."

Essa raised an eyebrow at him. "You know the way back to the Dreadwater, do you? A way that avoids Khadini towns and Ranger patrols? And you have somewhere to start looking for Rorin?"

His eyes flashed, but a moment later he conceded. "Point taken."

Arya looked at Essa in surprise. "I thought you wanted to leave as soon as Dar and the others arrived too?"

"I did. But that was when we had no other option but to wait for news of Rorin and then make our own way. Kulan's deal offers us a much safer way of retrieving the cazaix and getting over the border. It increases our odds of success significantly, and with little risk. You can command Kulan's warriors and keep the rebel meeting secure with your eyes closed and both hands tied behind your back."

Arya had to smile. That brain of hers.

"I don't like to delay finding Rorin, but I suspect it would take us longer alone to find him," Taze said, looking troubled. "I think Essa is right."

"Dar, we will get back home, I promise you," she told him, reading the unhappiness still in his expression.

"I have no doubts on that score, Arya." He rose suddenly. "I'll see you all later."

"I'm off to bed too," Essa said, and Taze rose with her.

Finding he was left alone with Arya, Leanir gave a shrug. "The reasoning is sound." He didn't wait for a response for rising and stalking off.

She smirked, but the amusement faded from her face. Everything Essa said made sense. She was sure even Desomer would think taking Kulan's deal the best strategic option.

But her worry for Rorin grew with each moment that passed.

After a moment she shook off her concerns and rose. Jumping into something too quickly to save Rorin was how she'd ended up in the pit mine. And it was something Ranier had warned her about repeatedly.

Arya parted from them and walked over to re-join Kulan, giving him a little bow. "We accept your offer, Dostari uq-Danresan."

Chapter 21

The following morning, Kulan formally agreed to Safal's plan. The rebel leader and his entourage left Taskari that afternoon—deciding it would be safer for the two groups to travel separately to the meeting location.

"This is good news for you," Kulan said when Arya protested at the speed of developments. They were in his living space, sharing a late cup of mead.

"How so?" she asked.

"We leave tomorrow, Arya." A smile teased his mouth. "The meeting is in two weeks, and it will take us almost that long to get there. You can finally stop sitting still."

Instead of excitement, she scowled. "It's never a good idea to rush such an important meeting."

"My brother has an efficient spy network. It is not as good as Kati's, but it will pick up news of a rebel gathering if we plan too far in advance," he repeated this logic patiently. "If we are all to meet, it must be done quickly."

That was a fair point. And Essa had been right the previous day; Arya's experience meant she didn't really need much time to plan for something like this. "Where are we going?"

"Farther than I'd like." Some of his good humour faded. "We'll go east, circling to the north of the pit mine and keeping to the jungle most of the way. The meeting spot is a few days' journey west of our capital, Aq Dale'a."

She frowned. "So close to your brother?"

"I don't like that aspect of it either." He heaved a sigh. "But the location is in an isolated valley—far from any large towns or villages. The other rebels will be loathe to leave the cover of the jungle also, and it is the most central location for all to travel to. If we want them all to come, we can't expect them to have to travel too far."

That all made sense, but still it made her nervous.

Kulan chuckled, seeing the discomfort on her face. "What motive would Safal have for betraying me? He wants the emperor gone as fiercely as I do, and fighting among ourselves only takes us further away from our goal."

"I'm not suggesting that Safal will betray you, but are you as confident in these other rebel leaders as you are in him? Are you confident your brother's spy network won't learn of your meeting?"

"I am as confident as I can be," he said. "Arya, we must take risks if we are to succeed."

She let out a long breath. "I still don't like it, Kulan."

"So you keep saying." He stepped closer, settled his hands at her waist. "But the meeting location is no more than a week's swift run from the cazaix smelter, so this is actually more good news for you."

"I have to get you and your warriors safely through this meeting first," she pointed out. "And to do that I need a lot more information than what you've told me so far."

"We'll have many days for me to tell you all the little details," he said, and then he kissed her. "For now, I propose more distraction from our worries."

***

Yarmana made Arya a final cup of voseni at dawn, which they sat and drank together in peaceable silence. Kader gave her an awkward farewell hug before darting out to join the fisherman. Kulan swung by for a cup of voseni to take with him and told Arya he would meet her by the jetties once he'd gathered all his warriors.

When Essa woke, Arya rose and drained the remainder of her cup. "I'm going to miss this."

Yarmana stood too, reaching out to squeeze her hand. "I wish you both all the best. You are welcome in my home anytime. If I hear any news of your Rorin I will send a messenger straight to Kulan."

"I will never forget how you've helped us," Arya said. "I hope one day I will be able to repay the debt I owe you."

"There is no debt," Yarmana said. "Go with happiness."

Leaving without looking back, Arya found Darmanin, Taze, and Leanir waiting for her outside Yarmana's home.

"I have someone to see before leaving," she told them. "You're welcome to come along, or Essa can take you straight down to wait at the jetties."

"We'll come," Darmanin said.

***

Tomin greeted her at the entrance to his healing rooms, his eyes widening at the sight of the others filing in behind her. "I heard you were leaving with Kulan today."

"I thought I'd best come and get this arm looked at one last time, or you might hunt me down," she joked. "Tomin, these are my companions." She introduced them one by one.

Tomin offered his hand to each with a warm smile. "I'm pleased to meet you."

"And you," Darmanin said. Leanir merely scowled and went back outside into the hallway, where he stopped and waited with evident impatience. Essa, as wary as Arya was about being near the Andahari since that night's dinner, gave Tomin a warm smile but then left to join Leanir.

"Tomin is Andahari," Arya told Darmanin and Taze. "There is a very large Andahari community living among the Khadini here."

"Is that so?" Darmanin said, his expression giving no indication what he thought about that.

"Come along," Tomin said. "Let's have a final look at that cut."

Darmanin and Taze waited outside while Tomin unwrapped the bandaging and took a close look at the healed cut on Arya's right forearm. It had stopped itching days ago, and she probably wouldn't have even noticed it anymore if it weren't for the bandaging.

"The redness will fade with time," Tomin said. "I'll bandage it with the unguent once more, just to be thorough, but tomorrow when you wake, remove the bandage and throw it away."

She smiled at him. "Thank you for taking such good care of me."

"It was a pleasure to have known you, Arya," Tomin said. "I truly hope to see you again."

"I would like that," she said. "You remember our deal?"

"I remember." Tomin smiled, breaking the sudden heaviness. "You'd best be off. Keep that dostari safe, won't you? I think he's Khadini's best hope. And ours."

"I'll do my best," she said.

***

The first part of their journey was almost enjoyable. They ran as long as there was daylight, a swift, ground-eating, pace. The jungle around them was green and bright. Birdsong filled the humid air and Kulan's warriors were experienced enough to keep them from accidentally treading on a dangerous snake or moving into the territory of a jaguar or panther. But even the beauty of the jungle grew tedious after a while. And the sweat that permanently slicked their skin was a haven for the bugs that flew at dusk. Arya found herself constantly itching.

A week into the journey, a storm hit. They sheltered through the worst part of it, watching as wind bent back the trees, but then had to keep moving. Warm, driving rain made the ground muddy and treacherous, and it was impossible to keep dry.

The rain dogged them all the way to the meeting point. When Kulan suddenly called a halt, halfway along a muddy trail in thick forest, Arya was surprised. The trees and hills that surrounded them, water still dripping from their leaves, looked no different than the terrain they'd been running through for days.

"We are no more than an hour or so from the meeting point," Kulan explained, then chuckled and lifted a hand to forestall Arya's protest. "No,

I am not suggesting we go straight to it. There's a village to the south that we can use as a safe base while we're here."

"How do you know it's safe?" Arya asked, deeply unpleased. More people she didn't know. And they were too far from Taskari for them to be members of Kulan's rebel group.

"The villagers are not rebels, but they give us supplies and shelter when they can. They risk their lives to do so, Arya, and that is how I know I can trust them. Even more, like most villages in this region they are poor, and so helping us is an extra burden on them. I will first scout ahead to ensure it is safe."

"Then I am coming with you," she insisted.

"I will come too," Darmanin said in Dunidae, making Arya start. She hadn't realised he and Taze were paying close enough attention to figure out what was happening.

"And I'm not going to be separated from you all again." Essa added.

Kulan smiled. "Be my guest. I ask only that you stay out of sight until I confirm the area is safe for those of fair skin to walk around."

Leanir gave a sharp shake of his head as soon as Arya looked at him. No, he didn't want to go with them. "You'll keep watch for Kulan's warriors while we're gone?" she asked instead.

Kulan snorted. "They don't need—"

"Humour me," she said sharply, growing irritated with his dismissal of her companions, even though she shared his view of Leanir. "Leanir?"

"I will watch," he said.

***

They ran in a single line behind Kulan, Arya glad for the sun finally shining through what had been days of rainclouds. She'd been wet for almost two days straight, and it was lovely to finally dry off a little in the hot sunlight, even though the humidity in the air meant her clothes didn't dry past 'damp.'

Birds started chirping in the trees, as happy as the humans that the storm was over. The sun also brought out a bright yellow snake that slithered across the trail mere inches ahead of Kulan. He paused, waiting for it to disappear into the undergrowth, before continuing with a smile tossed over his shoulder, "Steer clear of those. There's no antidote to their venom."

Eventually, Kulan slowed as they reached a deep pool fed by a swift-flowing steam. A proper road, albeit narrow, led away from the opposite bank. Grooves made by a cart were ground into its muddy surface.

"That leads to the village eventually, but we're heading for a farm on its outskirts. It's not far along the road," Kulan called over his shoulder as they rounded the pool and then splashed through the stream. "If the people there tell us the area is clear of patrols, we'll hole up at the farmhouse until the summit tomorrow. That way we limit the exposure of the rest of the village to our presence."

Arya tapped his shoulder, stopping him before he started along the road. "Are these people loyal to the rebel movement in general, or you in particular?" she asked.

He hesitated, then, "Me. When my mother fled the palace in Aq Dale'a with Kader and me, we hid out here until it was safe to move on. The other rebel leaders don't even know about the farm."

"Good. Let's go." Her shoulders relaxed. In her experience so far, Kulan and his mother both inspired genuine loyalty. She felt better about these villagers now she knew the connection was to him, and not to other rebel leaders she didn't know.

Farther down the road, the trees began to thin until they reached the edge of cleared farmland. Waving grasses swept back and forth in a slight breeze. A farmhouse sat almost a half mile straight ahead, away from the road. Smoke curled lazily from its chimney. Fields, both tilled and fallow, lay in all directions, and farm workers dotted the landscape. Further on, Arya could just make out the roofs of a town beyond another patch of jungle.

Kulan paused. "Things would not be so calm if there was danger. Still, if you wish to come with me, Arya, I recommend your companions stay back while we make sure. They can cover us if there are any unexpected problems."

"Agreed," Darmanin said before Arya could. "We'll watch your back."

"If anything happens," she said, "keep yourselves safe first, and warn Kulan's warriors. Don't come after us. Remember that our priority is finding Rorin."

"She's right," Essa cut in before Darmanin could protest further. "Go on, both of you. I'm aching for a home-cooked meal and a wash."

Kulan grinned and set out along the road with a quick, eager, stride. Relishing the open space, Arya nonetheless reverted to patrol behaviour, scanning her surroundings with a constant, sweeping gaze.

The farm workers looked up with interest as she and Kulan appeared, many of them tipping their hats or offering a friendly wave—clearly recognising him. Arya they looked more puzzled about, but since it was clear she was with Kulan, they let her pass without comment.

They were halfway to the farmhouse when her peripheral vision caught sudden movement off to her left; one of the farm workers breaking into a run towards them. Arya spun, her hand closing around the hilt of her sword, body ready to fight.

Then she stilled.

The worker's strides were familiar. And as he came closer, he began waving wildly, almost jumping into the air in his enthusiasm. He had messy sun-bleached blonde hair and sparkling light blue eyes, and newly broadened shoulders filled out the sleeveless cotton shirt he wore.

Arya's eyes widened. It couldn't...

"RORIN!" she roared, unable to believe her eyes. "RORIN!"

In a heartbeat she broke into a sprint straight for him.

"Rorin." She gasped his name as they crashed together in the middle of the field.

Rorin picked her up off the ground and swung her in a circle with unfettered enthusiasm. She threw her arms around him, tears welling in her eyes as relief tumbled through her. She hadn't realised how much she'd worried for, and missed him, until now.

They spun in that field for what felt like forever, but eventually Rorin put her down, and they grinned foolishly at each other.

She had her brother back.

Chapter 22

"*A*rya!" In his excitement, Rorin's signing was barely readable. "*Are you well? I can't believe you just appeared like this! Where have you been? Are you okay?*"

"I'm fine," she told him. "And you? I can't believe how much you've changed."

It was true. The gangly seventeen-year-old she'd known five months ago was gone. In its place was a lean, strong young man who sparkled with strength and confidence. But before he could reply, Darmanin was there. His grey eyes glowed, but he came to a more restrained halt, giving time for Essa to fly past him and into Rorin's arms. Rorin hugged her fiercely, then reached out to sling an arm around Darmanin's shoulders and hold on tight. Then Taze was there too, and Rorin made a face when he tried to salute, instead hugging him as tightly as he had the others.

For a moment they all stood there in a close huddle, smiling unabashedly at each other, surprise and delight and relief filling the space between them.

"*I am well now,*" Rorin signed eventually. "*But there is much to tell you.*"

"We have so much to tell you too," Essa said. Tears glistened in her green eyes.

"Arya?" Kulan's voice interrupted them; he'd come after her, but stood a short distance away, giving them some space.

Arya turned, grinning. "Kulan, this is my brother, Rorin Ravenstrike. Rorin, this is Kulan."

Rorin's eyes widened. "*This is Dostari Kulan? They adore him here.*"

Kulan offered his hand as Arya translated. "I have heard much about you too, Lord Rorin."

"*I am honoured to meet you.*" Rorin shook firmly. "*You are safe here, Dostari. All is well. The last Ranger patrol came through a fortnight ago.*"

"Good news, Lord Rorin." Kulan turned to Arya. "I am glad you are re-united. Are you happy to remain here while I fetch my warriors?"

"Of course. Be safe."

"Always." He smiled at her and left, long strides carrying him back across the fields towards the forest.

Another wondering silence fell between them, and Taze chuckled. "What now?"

"*How did you all fall in with Dostari Kulan?*" Rorin asked, his eyes still wide. "*I still can't believe you're actually here. Wait, what about Leanir?*"

"What is this word you keep calling Kulan?" Darmanin asked sharply. "Dostari?"

Rorin's face fell as he realised what he'd inadvertently let slip. "*I'm a fool. I should never have—*"

"It's all right," Arya told him. "Dar, Taze, it isn't our secret to share. At least not while we're here. After we're home though, I'll explain every-thing."

Darmanin didn't look happy about it, but gave a sharp nod. Taze seemed puzzled but happy enough to wait. Arya turned back to Rorin. "It's a long, story, but in short, Kulan, Essa, and I helped each other escape from a labour camp," she replied. "We found Darmanin, Taze, and Leanir a while after. Leanir is back with Kulan's warriors while we made sure the farm was safe. How did you come to be here in this village?"

Rorin's face tightened and some of the light faded from his eyes. "*You look hungry and in need of a wash. I'll take you up to the house where you can get both those things. After that, we can talk properly.*"

***

The woman who owned the farm—Rorin introduced her as Armani aq-Yaraya—greeted them warmly. There were streaks of grey in her dark hair where it was pulled back in a neat bun, and her hands were chapped, her clothing patched. Still, she showed no hesitation about having unexpected guests arrive on her doorstep and didn't flinch at the news that Kulan was bringing twelve of his warriors. She also clearly doted on Rorin; her tart instructions to him about fetching soap and towels and showing them to a stream behind the house to wash were edged with clear affection.

Essa and Arya were rinsing suds from their hair when Tanifa and another of Kulan's female warriors arrived, joining them to wash days of grime from their skin. Chatter from the male warriors out of sight farther down the stream drifted to them in the steamy afternoon air.

Relieved to be clean and fresh again, Arya strolled with Essa back to the farmhouse, hair dripping down her neck. There they found Leanir, prowling the boundaries of the house with his watchful air. "Found any assassins?" Arya asked.

He scowled.

Her smirk faded. "Nobody here is to be touched, you understand me?"

Something flashed in his eyes. "You really think me a monster, don't you?"

"What have you ever done to make me think otherwise, Leanir?"

His gaze met hers unflinchingly. "I could ask you the same question."

Sighing, Arya followed Essa into the farmhouse, following the sounds of movement into a great kitchen. Armani handed them steaming bowls of rice and some kind of stew. The scent was delicious and had Arya's stomach rumbling. "Your brother is waiting to speak with you," Armani told her in Khadini.

"Thank you. For the food and the welcome," Arya said, bowing her head in thanks. "We are in your debt."

"There is no debt, not for Dostari's companions or Rorin's family," Armani said.

In the room beyond the kitchen, the window was open, allowing the breeze to enter. Rorin sat on a chair opposite Darmanin and Taze, fingers flicking while the other two devoured their food. His eyes lit up when Arya and Essa entered. Arya sat across from her brother, gaze raking over him again. He looked good, but she hadn't missed the shadows lurking in his eyes earlier. "How did you end up here?"

Rorin lifted up his shirt. A long, ragged scar puckered the skin from his navel to halfway up his ribs. Essa's gasp was audible, and beside Arya, Darmanin's hand where it wrapped around his spoon turned white-knuckled.

The scar looked healed now, but Arya's experience told her it had come from a life-threatening wound. Her eyes shot up to meet Rorin's, horrified. He'd been badly injured, and she hadn't been there to protect him. Suddenly her appetite was gone, and she put down her spoon.

"The Rangers captured me almost as soon as I washed ashore," Rorin explained. *"For days they had me trussed to the back of a horse travelling steadily east. I have no idea where they were planning to take me. One night, they tied me loosely enough I was able to use one of Ranier's techniques to get free. I grabbed a weapon and managed to cut loose the tethered horses before they discovered me. I fought my way to the last horse, but one of them cut me good as I was mounting. I rode free, but I had no idea where I was going, and I was losing a lot of blood. At some point I fell from the horse and passed out."* Rorin paused there, hand lifting to his ribs as if in remembered pain. *"Armani was on her way back from trading in Desira, the nearest large town, and found me sprawled unconscious on the road. She hid me in her cart and brought me back here. The wound took a long time to heal, and it's only recently that I've gotten my strength back. I was about to leave, to start searching for you all."*

Silence fell after he finished, Arya's stew still untouched before her. He'd come so close to dying and if anyone else had found him fallen on that road … well, she owed Armani an incredible debt.

"Eat, Arya," Rorin said gently. *"I'm well, now, and I'd like to hear all your stories."*

So she ate, and the four of them took turns relaying everything that had happened since that night on the Dreadwater. Rorin looked progressively more upset the more they told him. He pressed close to Essa, seated beside him, and at one point, he reached across the table and grabbed Arya's right arm. Before she could object, he pulled up her shirt to reveal the red, lightning-shaped scar on the inside of her forearm.

"*You gave yourself up for me*?" he demanded.

"I was convinced you were in there," she said. "But it worked out in the end. I met Kulan in there, and then Essa arrived, and we got out together."

He gave her a look, as if he knew full well she was glossing over the hard parts. "*Thank you, Arya. I will not forget it. Ever.*"

"I would do it again," she said. "You are my family."

He leaned over and hugged her tightly, and for a moment she felt such relief that he was alive and well and they were together that she thought she might cry.

"What do we do next?" Taze asked as Arya pulled away, ruthlessly tamping down on her emotions.

"*We get what we came for*," Rorin signed. "*The cazaix.*"

"We must hold to our agreement with Kulan," Arya said, explaining the details to Rorin. "I still think that's our best play anyway. His rebel meeting will only take a day, and his help after to reach the smelter and get back to the Dreadwater Gate will be invaluable."

Rorin shrugged. "*If you have given your word, then that is what we will do.*"

Arya relaxed further into the chair, stomach full. "You know that we have been gone almost four months? They must all think we are dead."

"Ranier said we should be in and out within three weeks. That turned out to be a tad optimistic," Essa said, smiling.

"It's not the Shadeweaver leader we need worry about, but your mother, Rorin. She's going to be furious we made her think you were dead," Taze said.

Arya laughed. "You're probably right."

"If my father hears word we died running the Dreadwater Gate, it will be an unmitigated triumph for him," Darmanin's gaze was distant.

Arya nudged his shoulder with her own. "Then even if he does hear of it, we must make certain he is quickly disabused of that notion."

A little smile curled at his mouth. "Indeed."

"I can't wait to see the look on his face," she murmured.

"Not that I want to bring the happy mood down," Essa said, glancing curiously between Arya and Darmanin. "But Mathas Crowtalon isn't even close to our real problem once we return. The nazal are—"

"I don't want to talk about that now." Arya rose, pushing her chair back with a screech. "There are more immediate challenges facing us. The nazal can be dealt with once we're home with the proper resources."

Rorin looked uncertain. *"Has something happened since we parted?"*

"Essa will fill you in," Arya said, heading for the door. "I'm going to find Kulan. Start planning the security for this summit."

It wasn't Essa she was annoyed with. But every time it felt like things were going to be okay—they'd found Rorin, they'd secured help to find the cazaix—the damned Nightstalker was always there to remind her nothing was all right.

***

"What's got you steamed?"

Arya tensed as she approached Leanir in the back garden. "I'm looking for Kulan. Have you seen him?"

"He's with his warriors in the barn. Planning for tomorrow."

"And you're not listening at the door?"

"I couldn't care less about Kulan or his rebels or his ridiculous ideas of taking down the emperor. I'm here to get cazaix, and because I gave my word, I'm now stuck traipsing around after you."

"It's not like I want to be stuck with you either, Leanir," Arya said. "Why did Ranier send you with us?"

A smirk lightened his expression. "An answer for an answer. What do you say, Raider?"

Arya considered. It was a risky agreement to make with someone she trusted so little, but learning something more about this man who was apparently one of her Sky Lords could be highly valuable. "Do your worst."

"Don't give me false denials." He took a step closer, and she instantly went on the defensive, but he didn't attack, only lowered his voice. "What is your magic? You reached out to me when you and Essa escaped the mine. I felt her too. And it definitely wasn't me doing the reaching. So what is it?"

"True answer, Leanir?" Arya shrugged. He wasn't going to get the value he was after in this little exchange and she didn't need to lie either. "I don't know what it is. And I don't want to know. My question—what is *your* magic?"

While frustrated anger rippled over his expression, he seemed to believe her. Even so, he hesitated to respond.

"We made a deal," she reminded him.

"I can influence your perception of reality," he said, words short, jaw tight. "Make you see what isn't there or conceal something that is."

Her eyes widened in realisation. "That explains so much." Why she couldn't land an arrow shot on him for one. Why he always seemed a step ahead when they fought. "So why did you agree to run the Dreadwater with us?"

"The deal was for one question only, Raider." Leanir stepped away. "No more deals."

"Fair enough."

But when Leanir turned away, presumably to return to his patrolling of the farm, Arya closed her eyes, took a breath, and fumbled for the thread that connected them. It wasn't there, not initially, but she found Darmanin's and Essa's easily, and from there, Leanir's. Although it was much weaker than the others.

Arya tugged it. Hard.

And an instant later she found her back slammed against the wall of the farmhouse, Leanir's knife at her throat. "Don't you dare." He snarled the words in her ear and the sheer ferocity in them shivered through her body. "Never again, Raider, or my blade opens your throat."

She met his gaze, unafraid. "*Could* you kill me? I'm not so sure."

"What *was* that?" He was furious, still vibrating with it. But there was also fear lurking in his eyes.

"He really told you nothing," she said. Ranier hadn't lied about what Leanir knew.

"About *what?*" He ground out.

Slowly, ever so slowly, Arya pushed off the wall and stepped away from Leanir's knife. "I need to go and speak with Kulan and his warriors. The sooner his summit happens securely, the sooner we can all get what we came for and go our separate ways."

"Raider—"

"A question for a question, remember, and you just said no more deals."

As she walked away, Arya was tempted to tug on the thread again, to see if she could stop him attacking her this time. In the end she decided against it. They still needed to work together to get home to Dunidaen safely, and Leanir's rage and fear had been a potent combination.

Still, it was good to know that he was tied to her in the same way Darmanin and Essa were. And Chiarn too.

She held power over Leanir. And now he knew it.

Chapter 23

They left Armani's farm and headed east, camping overnight a couple of miles from the meeting point, a small valley west of Aq Dale'a. Arya sent Tanifa to scout the area under the cover of darkness. She returned to inform them that the lip of the valley was ringed by watchers. "Not Rangers, though."

Not liking the sound of that, Arya rounded on Kulan. "One of your rebel leaders is clearly in place ahead of us," she said.

"If we had arrived first, you would have done exactly the same thing," Kulan pointed out. "Or am I wrong?"

She huffed out a breath. That was true. Still ... something about all this didn't feel quite right to her.

"*A valley is the perfect place for an ambush,*" Rorin signed, easily reading Arya's unease.

"It's also a location that can be controlled from all sides, and not somewhere a Ranger patrol or villager will accidentally stumble across," Kulan said.

Darmanin looked at Kulan, gaze glimmering in the dark. "You asked Arya to make sure you were safe. She knows what she's doing. If she is uneasy, there is good reason for it."

Kulan's mouth tensed. "You deploy my warriors as you wish, Arya, you have full control. But I'm not calling off this meeting, or simply not showing up, just because you're a little uneasy."

"Fair enough," she conceded.

And then she rethought her approach to guarding the summit.

Kulan's warriors went to sleep late, after she spent hours going over her strategy and ensuring they knew what they needed to do. Part of her wished for Laskin and Charlin and Kait and her original unit of Raiders. They'd have known how to do this with their eyes closed. But Kulan's warriors were eager and willing to do what she asked.

She hoped that would be enough.

***

The next morning, Arya ran along a narrow track, heading north into deep jungle. Rorin paced beside her, and behind them, Kulan and Darmanin, with Taze and Kulan's warriors bringing up the rear. The dostari had initially only wanted to bring a retinue of five warriors. Arya had overruled him, insisting he bring all twelve of those who had accompanied them from Taskari.

"You asked me to ensure the meeting is secure. I can't do that properly with only five soldiers. Twelve is already pushing it."

Kulan had still demurred. "I can't afford to look weak, like I need so many to keep safe, or worse, that I don't trust my fellow rebels."

"And your people can't afford you to be dead," she'd told him. "Unless you think Safal uq-Rasaya or one of the other rebel leaders is a better leader for Khadini than you would be?"

That had ended the argument.

She'd *lost* the argument with Rorin, Darmanin, and Taze when they'd insisted on coming. Darmanin had simply given her that steely look that told her literally nothing would change his mind, and Rorin had informed her that she was his sister, not his warlord, and therefore couldn't give him orders. Taze simply pointed out he was Rorin's bodyguard and therefore obligated to come and make sure he was safe.

Essa, thankfully, had no interest in joining them, and Leanir unsurprisingly had also chosen to remain at the farmhouse. He'd been even more silent than usual since their interaction. It made her uneasy, and she was glad not to have him at her back for this.

Now, Arya glanced over at Rorin, wishing he wasn't with them. Worrying about his safety was a distraction she didn't need, but even when she'd used that argument on him, he'd still insisted on coming. *"I won't be separated from you again,"* he'd said repeatedly.

"We're nearly there," Kulan spoke, breaking Arya from her thoughts. They'd been running up a steady incline for some time, but the forested slope made it hard to tell how far ahead the summit of the valley was.

Arya slowed to a halt. All Kulan's warriors gathered around her. They weren't her highly trained and incredibly efficient Raiders, but they knew this territory, they knew how to fight, and they had heart.

Keeping her voice low amidst the birdsong around them, Arya repeated the plan once more. "Kulan, Kiraya, myself, Rorin, and Darmanin will move into the valley openly—Kulan's official entourage," she said. "Tanifa and Rafal, you know your instructions?"

Rafal nodded. Tanifa grinned. Around them, their warriors shifted in anticipation. They were ready.

"Good. Remember, you do nothing unless we're threatened. If all is quiet, let the meeting take its course, then slip away and meet us back at the camp tonight. But if there is any danger at all, you come to our aid and you kill without hesitation." She set her gaze running over all the warriors as she said this and got a reassuring series of confident nods. "Good luck," she told them. "Now, go."

Rafal and Tanifa made a sharp gesture, and the warriors split into two groups before melting away into the surrounding jungle.

"Ready?" Arya asked Kulan.

"Absolutely." His green eyes were firm with purpose.

"Then we're right behind you."

Kulan strode forward, Kiraya at his side. Arya, Taze, Rorin, and Darmanin falling in behind him. They reached the top of the valley wall soon after, unsurprised to find two Khadini men waiting, armed, and dressed for fighting.

"These are Safal's warriors," Kulan said.

One of the guards stepped forward. "All is secure. Please proceed to the meeting site. If you follow the trail from here down into the valley, it will take you straight there. A tent has been set up with refreshments and chairs."

"Have the others arrived?" Kulan asked.

The guard nodded. "We await only Kenlaya aq-Taransi. The rest have come through."

"We'll do our best not to keep you out here too long." Kulan gave them a warm smile and a nod and walked past. Every inch of Arya was taut with tension as she, too, passed the guards, her back vulnerable. But there was no attack, and they passed unmolested.

Arya glanced at the ground, then over at Darmanin and Taze. They gave her little nods.

"*What?*" Rorin signed, catching the look.

"Nothing," she said. "Yet."

The valley wall on this side wasn't as steep, and the trail was relatively easy to traverse. In the distance, Arya could hear the rush of water. She instinctively took the lead and pushed the pace, not wanting to get trapped in such an obvious ambush point. Her gaze scanned their surrounds constantly.

But soon the trees thinned, and they emerged into flat ground. The path continued a short distance before ending in a wide, cleared space along the banks of a rushing river. Where they'd expected a gathering of rebels, however, there was only grass waving in the breeze. There was no tent. No chairs. No refreshments.

A trap. The thought whispered through Arya's mind.

"The trail must continue farther," Kulan said, puzzled.

"Wait here." Arya touched his arm, preventing him from leaving the cover of the trees. "Let me take a look."

"Be careful," he said.

"Always."

She stepped out of the trees onto the grass, stance wary, hand hovering near the hilt of the sword Kulan's warriors had loaned her. A bird called. Something slithered through the trees not far off. The river flowed. No sounds of people talking though. No footprints on the ground. There'd been no other tracks in the mud at the top of the valley wall either, where Safal's guards had told them almost all the leaders had already passed through.

Arya moved into a jog across the grass, gaze scanning the ground for signs of people or the trail they were supposed to be following to the meeting point. The trees at the other end were as empty as the cleared space, but here she saw traces of mounted riders.

Disquiet flashed into outright worry.

Kulan had told her only nobles and the emperor's soldiers rode horses. Yet those were Safal's warriors at the top of the trail.

He was working with the Rangers to betray Kulan.

And he'd *almost* had them out on open ground. Easy targets.

Arya spun, boots kicking up the muddy ground as she sprinted back across the clearing. "It's a trap! Go back!" She yelled not for Kulan's benefit, who was close enough to hear a much quieter call, but because she needed everyone in the valley to hear her words.

Darmanin and Taze were already shepherding Kulan back along the trail up the valley wall, Rorin in the lead, as Arya reached them, legs burning from the flat-out sprint.

Safal sprang the trap anyway.

The first sign of attack was the high pitched whistle of an arrow flying, barely missing Kulan's head and forcing him to duck. It had come from somewhere ahead.

There were archers ahead of them on the trail. And no doubt mounted warriors would be coming up behind them. It was how she would have designed the ambush.

Arya shouted, "Keep as low as you can and push the pace. We need to break through whatever cordon they've set up and get clear. Keep to single file so they have less of a target. Faster!"

She took the lead and pushed them into a faster run, covering Kulan's front, giving Darmanin a quick look as she passed him. He nodded imperceptibly and dropped behind Rorin as Taze moved ahead of the young heir. Kiraya took up position immediately behind Kulan, protecting his dostari as best he could with his body.

More arrows came at them, whispering through the trees, but the trail was narrow, surrounded by thick forest, and the runners made themselves difficult targets. Arya had forced Kulan's betrayers into a backup ambush plan that wasn't as good.

The whistling stopped, but into the ensuing silence came the thunder of hoofbeats. Arya read the sounds quickly—mounted riders coming at them from ahead *and* behind. And they were probably well-trained Rangers.

"Faster!" Arya shouted. "When we hit the riders, we strike east into the jungle, but we stay together. Don't let yourselves become separated."

As they rounded a bend in the trail and came upon a group of Rangers cantering down towards them, the rest of Kulan's warriors had responded to Arya's first alarm call. Rafal and Tanifa had done exactly as Arya had ordered. They swarmed out of the jungle to surround the mounted Rangers, engaging them in battle and forcing them to stop and defend themselves.

It saved all their lives.

The mounted soldiers were spread into the trees on either side of the trail, sweeping down. There was no room to divert off the path and flee into the jungle. And no doubt the mounted soldiers racing up behind them were doing the same thing.

They'd have to fight their way out.

But Kulan's warriors were already close to overwhelmed. They didn't have the numbers. Arya didn't slow, drawing her sword with a sharp ring. A glance back to Kulan.

"We fight to break through, then we run."

She had time to see his nod, then the fight was on them.

She swung her sword and took the first Ranger cleanly, slicing deep into his side as he lifted his sword to bring it down on her. He screamed and toppled from the saddle. She blocked the downward thrust of another rider and lunged, shoving his sword sideways and out of his hand. Recovering quickly, Arya slashed again, slicing deep into his arm.

Rorin appeared on her right, driving through two Khadini riders and only just managing to avoid being killed by either. He engaged the one on his left and with a powerful lunge, drove his sword between his adversary's ribs, overextending and leaving his side vulnerable in the process. Arya hurled her dagger at the other, embedding it in his neck a second before he could drive his blade into Rorin's side.

"Don't leave yourself open," she snapped at her brother.

He stared at her for a moment, blood spattered over his face. He'd never killed before.

"Process later," she shouted, keeping her voice hard. "Sword up, Rorin!"

He blinked, shook away his fear, then waded back into the fight, slipping between another two horses and slicing his sword across the back of the soldier on the right as he did so. Arya plunged into the gap he'd made, driving her sword into the one on the left. She lifted her blade in time to deflect a bone-jarring blow, then fell sideways to avoid the follow-up strike. She hit the ground and rolled, hearing the Ranger shout as he turned his horse after her. Cursing under her breath, she kept rolling, unable to see from which direction the horse was coming.

She stopped rolling and felt her sword snatched from her grasp. She looked up to see Darmanin leaping up behind the Khadini rider and running her sword into his back. Blood spurted from his chest and the horse stopped centimetres from her. Darmanin yanked the sword out, threw it back to her as she gaped, then shoved the dead Ranger out of the saddle, grabbed the horse's reins and went after Rorin. Arya's brother was battling one soldier while another tried to outflank him. Darmanin leaped from his saddle to land behind the second. Before the warrior was able to react to his presence, he reached around and snapped the man's neck. At the same moment, Rorin got through his opponent's guard and ran him through.

Darmanin grabbed Rorin's arm, dragging him over to Arya so all three could retreat towards Kulan and his warriors. As they ran, Arya studied the fight, quickly identifying how desperate it was becoming. The thunder of galloping hooves coming up the trail behind them was loud. They were already outnumbered, and it was soon going to be much worse. She took a breath, focused, thought about what Desomer would do.

He would never have agreed to rush into this damned summit, Arya thought. They had to shift this fight if they wanted to survive it. Take the advantage back somehow.

In between blows, Arya shouted to Kulan and his warriors, telling them to draw the mounted soldiers deeper into the jungle, where their manoeuvrability would be hampered. They did as she bade, as hard as that was while they were almost entirely on the defensive, and slowly the fight shifted further away from the trail.

"Keep together!" she shouted. "Don't scatter into the trees. Tanifa, Kiraya, with me!"

She led the two warriors at the largest group of Rangers harrying them, seeking to divide them into smaller groups that could be picked off amidst the trees and thick foliage. They'd improved their chances, but not enough. And even as Arya scanned the area, more mounted soldiers arrived—the ones who'd been coming up the trail behind them.

She took a breath, holding still for a moment to try and figure out the best strategy. If she had mounted Raiders at her back, she could take this force. But while Kulan's warriors were fierce and brave, they clearly hadn't trained on combating mounted cavalry. Their fighting was desperate and reactive, and it was going to get them killed.

Before she could settle on a plan, a violent snarl cut through the chaotic sounds of battle. The mere sound of it set the hairs on the back of her neck rising and the Rangers' horses panicking. A second snarl turned the battle into chaos. Horses reared in fear or tried to flee, and their riders were suddenly desperately focused on trying to keep them under control and stay in the saddle.

As the echoes of that second snarl faded, a terrifyingly large black shadowhound joined the fray. It launched itself at a Ranger, tearing his throat out mid-leap before landing gracefully and launching into another leap. Three Rangers were dead on the ground before Arya even blinked.

Terror now infused the soldiers as much as their horses.

"Get clear of the horses. The riders have lost control and they're about to stampede!" Arya shouted above the din. "Form a circle. Keep them contained. Kill the Rangers as they flee. Archers ready your bows."

Kulan and his warriors scrambled to follow her orders, creating a circle as best they could on the forested slope, the archers among them firing into the mounted soldiers. Darmanin continued to sow panic as he leaped, graceful and powerful, killing Ranger after Ranger. Arya watched the brutal efficiency of his movements, his killing, and she was in awe.

In moments it was done. Most of the Rangers were dead, only a handful escaping the cordon on panicked horses. The shadowhound stood, growling softly, amid the carnage he'd created. His inky black coat seemed to swallow the sunlight, dimming it.

Then with a quick movement, sped off into the trees.

Movement to her left had Arya turning. Kulan was watching the shadowhound too, shock written deep into his face. But the moment her gaze landed on him, the look disappeared, replaced with focus as he began making a head count of his warriors.

They weren't safe yet, so Arya started snapping orders. "Tanifa, scout the route back to where we camped last night, make sure no more ambushes are waiting. We won't be far behind you. Rafal, you keep a watch on the trail down into the valley, make sure no surprises approach from our rear." She paused, thinking, "Those who we lost in battle, bring them here. Those who are hurt should gather here too. We'll patch the injured up as best we can and move as soon as that's done."

Arya deliberately didn't let her gaze linger on Darmanin as he slipped back into the clearing in human form, as blood spattered as the rest of them. Instead, her gaze searched out Rorin. "You okay?"

"*I'm fine.*" Rorin was pale, blood speckled on his cheeks, arms, and clothes, hair tousled and sweaty. But his hand was steady where it still held his sword and his eyes held hers.

"Kulan?" She swung her gaze to him.

He'd been helping to carry his dead into the clearing but came over when she called. "There's no sign of Safal anywhere," he said. "Or any of the other rebel leaders."

"I'm sorry," Arya said.

"You were right. It was a trap."

"I'd bet a lot of money that Safal was the one that betrayed you to the Rangers the first time you were captured too. If you ask me, *he* wants leadership of the rebels. With you out of the way, he can have that."

Kulan's jaw tightened, and he gave a terse nod.

"That's the second time he's betrayed you," she said flatly. "You must take advantage of his betrayal."

Kulan's eyes flashed. "From here I plan to ride to every other rebel leader and tell them what Safal has done. And I will not leave until they agree to unify under me."

"Good."

His hard expression softened, and he stepped closer to her. "You saved my life today, and while I lost four warriors that I grieve, it would have been much worse if you were not here. You are a formidable commander and warrior."

She held his gaze. "And now it's time for you to hold up your end of the bargain."

Sadness flashed on his face, but he nodded. "Let's retreat with our wounded to Armani's farmhouse. From there Tanifa and Rafal will escort you to the cazaix mines and then back to the border."

***

In the pre-dawn before their departure, Arya and Kulan stood out front of Armani's farmhouse, staring out over the misty fields and surrounding jungle. He'd woken her quietly, asked for a moment to speak before she left.

"I am sad to be parting from you," he said.

"I will miss you, too." And she would. She'd miss his good humour and his easy friendship.

"Perhaps one day, Dunidaen and Khadini might be closer allies," he said. "It is a thing I hope for very much."

"I hope for that too." She searched his gaze, sensing he was holding something back. Suddenly his desire to speak with her alone made sense. "What's wrong?"

"I did not realise…" He let out a worried breath, lowered his voice. "Your friend Darmanin." Kulan hesitated. "Am I wrong that he was the one who shifted into a shadowhound during the battle yesterday?"

Arya let out a breath. Part of her had been waiting for this conversation. After all, it wasn't only Kulan who'd seen the shadowhound during the fight. And Kulan and his warriors knew it wasn't one of their own. "It was Darmanin."

"That is the magic of House Nightstalker, Arya." He shifted towards her, earnest, intense. "Their House motto is *Rule the Night*. You didn't know this?"

"I thought it was already clear I know very little," she said, an icy chill rippling down her spine. "Are you saying that Darmanin is somehow related to Lucius Nightstalker?"

He shrugged. "As far as I understand it, only members of House Nightstalker have that shapeshifting ability."

Her gaze shifted to the farmhouse, where a light had gone on in the room Darmanin shared with Rorin and Taze. They were up and dressing.

Did Darmanin know?

No, he didn't. She was sure of that. What did it mean for them all? Little tingles of unease tracked down her spine. Darmanin Nightstalker. It fit him, she realised, in ways that only made her more uneasy.

"Arya?"

"Sorry." She shook off the worry that had settled on her shoulders and smiled up at him. "Promise me you will keep his secret too, as well as Essa's. And mine. You know better than we do, I think, the consequences if you don't."

"We will not breathe a word to anyone. I swear it on our friendship, Arya Ravenstrike."

"Thank you, Kulan uq-Danresan," she said, speaking formally. "I wish you the best of luck. With everything."

"You too, Arya Ravenstrike." His formality faded. "We shall see each other again; I am certain of it. Perhaps even sooner than you think."

They hugged, warmly, and then Kulan let go and strode away, striding across the fields. Arya watched him go until he faded from sight, then turned for the farmhouse, intending to hurry up the others. She wanted to get going.

It was time to get their cazaix and go home.

Chapter 24

Arya scrambled up the hillside, keeping as low as she could. Rorin and the others followed closely behind, Leanir bringing up the rear. Down to their left, a wide road led around to a pair of tall iron gates that formed the main entrance into the cazaix smelter. They were closed and locked. Enough torches were lit that a bright pool of light dissipated the darkness of the night, making it impossible to approach the gates unseen.

When they'd scouted the area the night before, six Rangers had stood guard on the gates, and it was the same tonight. Beyond the gates, the road lead into a massive compound surrounded by low hills. A large stone building—the forge—stood along the eastern side, and directly across from it, bisected by the road, were multiple warehouses. Unlike the forge, the warehouses had been built from the same logs as those at the pit mine where Arya had been prisoner.

As soon as Arya and the others approached the crest of the hill, they dropped flat, waiting. The night air was warm, but an odd scent teased their senses; something metallic and sharp. The smelter. More torches lined the exterior of the compound, and Arya quickly spotted the patrolling pairs of Rangers. The hillside was in shadow, but once they were at the bottom, there wasn't much of anywhere to hide.

"They're late," Leanir said.

Arya glanced at him. "We're early."

And then, as if on cue, Arya's sharp hearing caught the hiss of arrow flight. Pinpricks of light shot into the air from the opposite hillside, arcing gracefully down towards the warehouses. All of them landed, thudding into wood, and breaking the silence hanging over the compound. Flame roared into life, spreading across the roofs.

Tanifa and Rafal's warriors were good shots.

Rorin shot Arya a grin. Even Darmanin looked grimly satisfied. Only Essa seemed unhappy, looking away when Arya tried to meet her gaze.

It took a few minutes for the patrolling Rangers to realise what was happening, but as smoke billowed and flames began licking down the walls of the buildings housing their precious cazaix, shouts rang out across the compound.

All but two of the gate guards ran for the burning buildings, as did most of those patrolling the grounds.

"That's our cue." Arya was up and moving in a blink. Keeping low, she scrambled down the hillside, sacrificing stealth for speed. As soon as her boots hit the ground, she sprinted for the stone wall along the back of the forge.

The crackle of fire was audible, interspersed with the crisp cries of the Rangers as they organised themselves to respond to the fire with what sounded like impressive calm and efficiency. Leanir reached them last, and instantly they headed along the wall—bypassing the locked and barred steel door at the back entrance—until they found the large, grated opening set just above Arya's head; exactly where Rafal had promised her it would be.

"The crucibles are not worked at night," he'd told her. "When they are running, poisonous air flows through the vents, but you will be safe as long as you are out well before dawn."

She hoped that Rafal had been right. Dying from poisonous gases in an air vent in Khadini was not the way she wanted to go. Taze passed her a section of rope, and she tied it securely around the grate. Then, they all took hold of the rope and gave it a hard tug. It stuck. They tried again. It screeched alarmingly but came out.

Arya pulled herself into the opening while Rorin gave Essa a leg up behind her. The moment Arya was fully inside the vent, scrambling on hands and knees, terror pressed down on her shoulders as heavily as a physical weight.

It constricted her chest, made breathing hard. She wasn't sure she'd be able to move at all if there hadn't been people behind her that she didn't want to betray her weakness to.

"Can you see anything?" Darmanin whispered.

"Only a whole lot of black," she managed, barely swallowing the panic that wanted to send her screaming back out into the fresh air.

Hand over hand, she forced herself to keep going, crawling along on all fours for what seemed like an endless amount of time. Sweat poured off her, her breathing tight and fast in her chest. Anxiety clenched so fiercely in her shoulders that they ached. She wanted out so badly she barely stopped herself from a frantic and heedless scramble back the way she'd come.

Then her hand hit only open space. She halted and felt Rorin run into her from behind. "I think we've reached the end," she said. "I'll go first. Wait for my signal before you follow."

Arya manoeuvred in the tunnel so that her legs were sticking out of the opening, and then she jumped. Luckily, it wasn't too far of a drop. No more than a second passed before she hit ground and rolled away to make room.

"Clear," she called up to the others.

Arya scanned her surroundings, her senses returning as the terror of the small crawlspace lifted and she could breathe again. A faint red glow illuminated the area enough for her to confirm they'd dropped into one of the smelting rooms. A great fire pit filled the centre of the space, its dying embers the source of the light. It was deserted. She fought the urge to hunch over her knees in relief at being out of the tunnel.

Rorin appeared beside her. "*Where to now?*"

"We need to find the storage area," Arya said.

"It would have been nice if Ranier had provided directions," Taze remarked. "We can't spend long in here."

"Don't look at me," Leanir snapped when they turned to him. "He didn't give me any secret information."

Arya's gaze lingered on him. Why *had* Leanir come on this journey with them? The question continued to nag at her. She felt like understanding that was important somehow.

"I give it barely a half hour before the fire loses its hold on their attention and they're patrolling the compound again," Essa said. "And that's if a smart Ranger doesn't consider the fact that the attack might be a diversion."

"The storage area won't be far. This way." Darmanin pointed to an exit and strode off. The exit let into a narrow, unlit corridor. Given the sound their boots made on the stone floor, Arya hoped the guards didn't patrol *inside* at night.

Darmanin's tall form disappeared through a doorway at the opposite end of the corridor, and Arya emerged behind him into another room. Once inside, Darmanin stopped so abruptly, doubling over with a grunt, that she ran right into him.

Only to suck in a shuddering breath as that *weight* from her panic in the vent crashed down over her again.

"Arya!" The voice was Taze's, but it sounded distant. Faint.

Arya forced herself to straighten, look around, but her vision was blurry at the edges, hazy. This room was massive and was well-lit by flickering wall sconces. Her gaze scanned the metres-high stacks of gleaming metal weapons, all in different sizes and shapes. To Arya's left, Essa was frozen, taking quick, gasping breaths, and Leanir was hunkered over his knees, clearly trying to draw in steady breaths and failing.

It was the cazaix doing this to them. The room was full of it.

Rorin appeared in her field of vision, immediately confirming her theory. He was completely unaffected. "*Arya, what's wrong with you all?*"

"The cazaix," she gasped.

"It affects Sky Lord magic," Taze said in realisation. The look on his face—on Rorin's too—as they realised what was happening was almost comical.

They'd never disbelieved Arya. But now suddenly it was real.

To Darmanin, too, it seemed. He'd gone white, horror in his eyes. He didn't want this.

"Just breathe." She got the words out. "The cazaix is obviously suffocating whatever magic we have because there's so much of it in here, but unless the metal pierces our skin it can't hurt us."

"You *think*," Essa gasped out.

"There are thousands of weapons in here, and this is only one storage room." Taze spoke in wonder. "These can't all be for the emperor's army."

"*He could be selling them,*" Rorin suggested.

"To who?" Darmanin asked, wincing as he straightened. "Khadini has always refused to sell more than a tiny amount of their cazaix. It gives them too much of an advantage."

Leanir stepped further into the cavern. The effort it cost him was visible. "Irrelevant. We need to get what we came for and leave. This room is too well-lit. It suggests people come in here at night."

"He's right." Arya stifled a groan as she took another step into the room. Every part of her—bone, muscle, and instinct—wanted out of here with an urgency that was impossible to ignore. It was a sensation unlike anything she'd ever felt before. "Pick something and let's go."

She approached the closest rack of weapons—a row of beautifully hand-crafted swords. The cazaix blades gleamed with a soft blue hue, and when she touched one it burned her skin. Swearing, she snatched her hand away.

Essa, who'd been about to do the same thing, wisely pulled her hand back.

"Why did your father send you to get this, or me?" Arya asked her. "He knows what we are, which means he knows what effect this stuff has on us."

"Protection," she said simply. "No Sky Lord would willingly walk around with a cazaix blade. I'm guessing it also hides our magic signature from the nazal."

Arya let out a breath. Of course. Ranier was a clever man.

She returned her attention to the rack of swords. Not only had the Khadini smiths forged the blades, but they'd also created hilts and handles with exquisite workmanship. Arya hadn't seen anything like it before.

Her hand paused at the last sword in the row. Its hilt was crafted from ivory, so it was safe for her to hold. The cross guard was fashioned in a pair of spread wings and the pommel had a single blue topaz inserted into the ivory. Polished leather wrapped the grip.

Hesitantly, she lifted it off the rack. The weight and balance felt perfect in her hand, and the cazaix rang clearly as she swung it through the air. She'd never felt so comfortable with a sword before.

As long as she didn't touch the blade, or let it cut her.

Swathes of black velvet cloth sat in a pile at the end of the rack, and Arya wrapped her new sword in the cloth and tucked it under her arm. Both Rorin and Darmanin did the same with swords they had chosen.

Near the sword rack was a long table with knives and daggers spread out along its surface. Arya hesitated, then picked up one of the daggers and wrapped it up with her sword. Then, unable to help herself, she backed up to the doorway, unable to bear the stifling pressure tugging on every muscle in her body. Essa joined her, four throwing knives wrapped in cloth. Leanir was next, a lethal-looking cazaix dagger in his hand. Taze was last, with a sword like the rest.

He and Leanir had almost reached them, Arya turning with dread to lift herself up into the vent, when the door on the other side of the room opened and five men walked in.

For a long, frozen, moment they all stared at each other.

Arya clocked three Rangers and two well dressed … merchants? The gold chains around their necks and thick robes despite the warmth of the night suggested wealth, at least.

By then Leanir had crossed half the distance between them.

The Rangers reacted almost as quickly.

The three warriors shoved the two merchants behind them and lunged forward to face Leanir's charge.

"Take them quick and quiet," Arya spoke the order as she and Darmanin launched themselves after Leanir. "Taze, get Rorin and Essa moving through the vent."

Leanir was already moving as the closest Ranger swung at him. He ducked, flipped his new dagger, and countered the blow. The screech of metal-on-metal set Arya's blood firing.

She lifted her new sword and stepped into the space between Leanir and the second Ranger who lunged at him. She caught the blow and turned it, her peripheral vision seeing Darmanin engage the third Ranger.

And then she knew nothing but the fight. The drumming of her heart, the quick rasps of her breath, the focus on her opponent, on reading his moves before he made them, looking for his weaknesses. Staying alive. The burn in her arms as she swung her new sword, its balance a delight, making her almost stumble on occasion as she adjusted to it.

All too soon she was inside the Ranger's guard, a powerful counter sending his swing out wide so that she could reverse her own swing and bring her sword slicing across his throat. Blood sprayed and she stepped back to avoid it.

Leanir had already dispatched his opponent, and Darmanin's grunt filled the room as he blocked a downward thrust, pushed it away, then darted in, quick as a striking snake, and drove the dagger in his off hand through the Ranger's heart.

"That's new," Arya commented on his move.

He gave her his little smile.

"We have to go." Leanir pointed to the swinging door, through which the two merchants had presumably fled during the fighting.

Shit. They'd quickly raise the alarm. Taze had followed her orders, and he, Rorin and Essa were already in the vent. Arya hesitated, but when Darmanin offered her his knee as a step, she forced herself to push off it and leap up to grab the edges. Panic closed over her as she hauled herself into the tunnel and kept going without pause, knowing if she let herself stop, she might never start moving again.

Night air cooled the sweat on her skin as she dropped out of the vent and padded over to where the others waited. "We're all fine," she said, reassuring them.

"We should hurry though." Darmanin joined them. "Those merchants will be raising the alarm as we speak."

Even as he said the words, a shout went up somewhere on the other side of the compound. More shouts clamoured in response. Then the sound of running feet.

They'd been discovered.

Arya saw Leanir appear from the vent. "Let's run," she said.

They were halfway up the hill when they were spotted. Cries of triumph rang out. A second later the ominous hiss of arrows sounded in the night air.

"Stay low and don't move in a straight line!" Arya bellowed.

An arrow landed in the ground an inch away from her right boot. Another tore a hole in her left pant leg. Leanir swore as another arrow clipped his arm.

They still had too far to go. One of them was going to get hit. Arya thought about stopping, letting the others go on while she drew the arrows to her. But before she could make that decision, more arrows began flying through the night.

From the top of the hill.

Rafal and his warriors laying down covering fire.

The barrage of enemy arrows slowed almost to a complete halt, and Arya and her companions managed to reach the top of the hill without serious injury. Up there stood Tanifa and Rafal, directing their archers where to shoot.

"Thank you!" she told them breathlessly.

"A debt was owed." Rafal bowed. "If we go now, we can lose them in the jungle. Quickly."

Leanir was already running down into the trees, Essa and Darmanin with him, Kulan's archers peeling off to join them. Arya glanced at Rorin, who was grinning at her despite the circumstances, and she grinned back. "Thank goodness we got good at this running thing."

"*Indeed. You first, sister dearest.*"

She snorted. "Not a chance. Taze first, then you, and I'll bring up the rear."

A sense of almost anti-climax wrapped her as they reached the cover of the jungle and the small clearing where they'd left their packs of supplies. Quickly, they strapped their cloth-wrapped cazaix to the outside of their packs, then hefted them on their shoulders. As soon as they were done, and with Tanifa in the lead, they set off at a ground-eating lope. After all the difficulties they'd had—and how long it had taken—getting to the cazaix forge, it was strange to suddenly have everything that they'd come for.

Arya promptly told herself off for thinking too far ahead—they weren't clear of the cazaix forge yet—and focused on the runners ahead of her as Tanifa turned them north.

For the Dreadwater Gate.

And home.

Chapter 25

They ran north for ten days, and when the hazy outline of the tall cliffs of the Dreadwater Gate appeared on the horizon, Arya could scarcely believe it. They reached the eastern banks of the Dreadwater river that afternoon and made camp near the water.

Tanifa told Arya as they stopped, "I think we are too far south of the border to be in danger of running into any Ranger patrols yet, but Rafal and I will scout farther up the banks, just to make sure. Our warriors will keep you safe in the meantime."

"We'll make sure there's food waiting when you return," Arya promised.

Soon after, Arya found Essa fetching water. Darmanin and Taze were organising a fire—rain threatened, apparently, so Kulan's warriors were also building a shelter—while Leanir had left to do his own patrol.

"Everything okay?" Essa asked as Arya kneeled beside her.

"For now, at least." Arya smiled. "But I've been thinking a lot while we've been running all these long days, and I wanted to talk to you about Rorin."

"Oh." Essa blinked, taken aback, and returned to filling another water flagon. "Okay. Go on."

Arya paused, and Essa waited patiently for her to find the words. "I have this feeling where Rorin is concerned," she hesitated. "Could it be possible for your magic to heal his voice?"

Essa's head came up sharply. "He wasn't born mute, was he? I remember him telling me that he was sick as a child."

"Right, he had a terrible fever and agonisingly sore throat—apparently it swelled up so much the healer worried it would constrict his airway. He was so sick he almost died, I get the sense, though he never said that directly. When he did recover, his voice was gone."

Essa frowned in thought. "It would take a lot of power to reverse such old damage, and I'd need to understand what the speech muscles are supposed to look like so that I could draw them healed."

"Then we would need Tiya's help?"

"At least. Maybe your help too—like back at the dam." She searched Arya's face. "Using our magic will draw the nazal straight to us."

Arya squashed the instinctive shudder that thought roused. She'd let herself forget the nazal in their triumph of stealing the cazaix. But the creatures were presumably in Khadini somewhere, and they knew her magic enough to recognise it. Essa's too, possibly, if they'd been close enough the night they'd broken out of the pit mine. A spurt of temper surged in response to the fear that shivered through her. She refused to be cowed by these monsters. "For Rorin, I'm willing to risk it. He has the cazaix now, Essa, but what if he walked into that State Council with his voice too? There'd be no doubt of him being named heir."

Essa nodded slowly. "We should see what he thinks about it. It's his choice."

"You should make sure you're comfortable with the idea too." Arya held her gaze. "I won't consider it unless you are."

Essa smiled. "For Rorin, it's worth it." She sobered. "But Arya, we're almost home. We can't keep living our lives hiding from the Nightstalker and his hunters. It's time to—"

"—do something about it. I know, Essa." Arya tried not to be sharp with her. "I promise you I'm not going to keep hoping he forgets about us. We'll talk, all of us, once we're home safe, and figure out a real plan."

"Thank you," Essa said quietly. "And you know that plan doesn't have to be starting a war with the Nightstalker or leaving the lives we have."

Arya looked at her with dawning hope. "You could help us come up with something that gave us another option?"

"I'll do my best."

Arya stood, stretched, feeling far more hopeful than she had. "Some kind of delicious smell is coming from camp. We'd best go investigate."

Rorin, Taze, and Darmanin looked up when Arya and Essa returned with the filled water flagons. They'd gotten a fire going and a shelter erected. One of Kulan's warriors had caught a couple of rabbits and they crackled on the spit over the flames. The rain hadn't arrived yet, so they were sprawled on the ground, resting from a long day's running.

"*What is it?*" Rorin asked immediately, presumably seeing something in their expressions.

Arya dropped to the ground with a grateful sigh, stomach growling at the scent of cooking meat. "Nothing urgent. I was just talking through an idea with Essa." She didn't want to raise the Nightstalker, not yet when they still had to get back through the Dreadwater Gate. They needed all their focus for that. They were so close to home now; she didn't want anything to distract them.

"What idea?" Taze asked.

"It's not like we're going anywhere soon," Darmanin pointed out.

Arya glanced over at Essa, wanting to make sure she was certain about their offer. Essa smiled and nodded.

"Well, you remember what Essa and Tiya did together, that night in Heathrock city?" Arya switched to Dunidae, the words feeling strange on her tongue after so long speaking Khadini. As much as she respected Kulan's warriors, the less they knew about the group of Dunidae they were protecting, the safer all of them would be.

"*Saved a little girl's life.*" Rorin directed a smile in Essa's direction.

"Right, well, something occurred to me," Arya said, then explained her idea.

Rorin stared blankly at them for a long moment once she'd trailed to a halt. Darmanin and Taze had stilled, looking towards Rorin in stunned surprise. Darmanin was the first to move. He sat up, leaning forward eagerly. "I can help give you strength, Essa. I mean ... I don't know how. But I'll try."

"*You think you could really do it?*" Rorin's hands trembled slightly as he signed.

"To be honest, we don't know. Our magic is instinctive at best. Of all of us, though, Essa has the most control. The rest of us would just be feeding her magical strength," Arya said. "And when I visited Heathrock before we left, Tiya was gone from the Arms. We'd have to find her first."

"It would risk you, though, wouldn't it?" Taze pointed out. "The nazal would be able to get a better sense of your location."

"Yes. That's probable."

Rorin turned pensive. "*Let me think on it.*"

Leanir walked into the camp a moment later, two dead and defeathered birds hanging from his right hand.

"What?" he demanded into the silence.

Arya smiled at him. "Nothing. Are those for us?"

He scowled, opening his mouth, no doubt to demand an answer, but Rafal and Tanifa fortunately chose that moment to return.

"Ah, quail!" Tanifa's eyes lit up in delight. "My favourite."

Leanir's jaw tightened, but he didn't protest further. Instead, he added the birds to the spit over the fire, and finally sat down.

"We're safe enough here, but once the food is cooked, we should douse the fire," Rafal said, sitting cross-legged by the fire. "The Ranger patrol region starts barely a mile from here. If you move fast, and leave early, you could be at the Dreadwater Gate by noon tomorrow."

"Barring any obstacles." Tanifa added with a grin.

Darmanin lifted an eyebrow. "Such as the Rangers and their dogs?"

Tanifa waved a dismissive hand. "We'll draw them away for you. When you head out in the morning, we'll strike west and split into three groups. Each of us will aim to attack a patrolling group—strike and then melt away in the jungle. Any dogs and Rangers in the area will converge on us, drawing them away from the Gate."

Concern filled Arya. "What if they catch you?"

"They will not catch us in the jungle." Rafal snorted. "Do not fear for us, Arya."

"You have done so much for us," she said. "We are in your debt."

"There is no debt." Rafal shook his head. "You saved our dostari's life, twice, and ours. We are honoured to help you."

Tanifa made a face. "But perhaps you could tell your people to stop getting themselves killed or captured stealing our cazaix?"

They all chuckled.

"*We will do our best,*" Rorin promised.

"And we'll miss all of you," Arya said.

"We will see each other again, I am sure." Tanifa shrugged. "Now, get some sleep. We will rouse you early."

***

So it was that weary, travel-stained, and slightly battered, the six of them reached the waterfall at the Dreadwater Gate just before midday the following day, soaked in sweat, but amazed to have reached it unchallenged.

All morning they'd heard shouts echo through the jungle as Kulan's warriors had taken the Rangers and their dogs on a merry dance. Not once had the barking or shouts come close to the western bank where Arya and the others ran.

She just hoped all of Rafal and Tanifa's warriors escaped unscathed into the jungle.

None of them wanted to linger, not now that they were so close to home, so after a long drink at the pool, they removed all the non-essential weight from their packs, carrying only their new weapons, rope, and water. Climbing was going to be risky on muscles weary from hours of running, but the longer they rested the stiffer they'd get. Besides, they needed to be up before nightfall.

So, they began the climb.

Darmanin led the way, with Rorin following the path he set. Taze came behind Rorin, then Arya, and Essa and Leanir last.

While their packs were much lighter than on their journey down months earlier, weariness was a factor even Arya couldn't ignore. They moved in silence, every ounce of energy needed to lift their arms, find a grip, push themselves up, then do it all over again. Spray from the waterfall cooled their overheated skin.

She made the mistake of looking down once, shuddered, and resolutely fixed her eyes on the rock before her. They were halfway up when a frantic scrabbling sounded below Arya. She steadied her grip and glanced down just as a section of cliff Essa was holding onto dislodged from the cliff wall. She gave a cry as she fell.

It happened as quick as a blink.

"Essa!" Arya screamed, reaching out helplessly.

Leanir, just below Essa, reacted with that fearsome speed she remembered from their past encounters. He leaped gracefully out into the air, swinging his body around so that he could wrap one arm around Essa's waist as she fell and reach out with his other arm to curl his fingers around a solid rocky outcropping.

As he moved, Arya recklessly slid down the cliff towards them. Leanir and Essa swung back hard against the cliff, and Leanir grunted as his right arm took both their weight. Arya was there a second later, reaching across to prop Essa up so that Leanir could get a more stable handhold.

A few moments later they were all safely balanced on the cliff, breathing hard but alive. Arya's heart beat so hard in her chest she struggled for breath, the surging panic she'd felt making her dizzy.

"Are you all okay?" Darmanin shouted down; all three men above were pale with alarm.

"We're fine, keep going!" Arya called, voice shaking despite her best efforts, then lowered her voice. "Essa, you okay?"

The woman nodded, sheet-white, and looked at Leanir. "Thank you." She shook her head.

"Now we're even," he said, and abruptly began climbing again.

Arya stared after him, then turned to look at Essa. "I've never seen anything like that before. He would have died along with you if there hadn't been a good handhold to grab and he had no time to see whether there was before he jumped. Why would he do that?"

"I have no idea," Essa murmured.

"Go," Arya said. "I'll come behind you."

The two climbed together from there on out, Arya reluctant to leave Essa's side. She needed to keep her close after how close she'd come to… Arya blinked away that thought. Essa was fine. Nothing bad had happened. She hadn't lost her.

They reached the top in the late afternoon, having made the last part of the climb as Khadini's hot sun made the space between waterfall and cliff face thick with damp humidity. Arya's arms trembled with fatigue, sweat slicked her skin, and soaked her clothes, and weariness swamped every bone and muscle in her body, but she'd never felt so triumphant as that moment she hauled herself back onto Dunidaen soil.

"Essa!" Taze scrambled straight over. "You okay?"

Rorin didn't bother with signing, he simply gathered her into a fierce hug. She let him hold on tight, which told Arya how shaken she was.

"She's okay." Arya reassured Taze, gaze shooting briefly to Leanir before returning to her friends. "We're okay."

"And we're home." Darmanin's light grey eyes glimmered.

Rorin let Essa go so he could sign, "*Just smell that sweet Dunidae air.*"

"I smell smoke from a cookfire," Leanir announced, hand sliding to the hilt of his dagger. He was already on his feet, stance tense.

Arya stood too, spinning around but seeing nothing in the dim light behind the waterfall. The echoing rush of the water hid any other sounds beyond where they stood. She sniffed the air and couldn't smell anything but damp. "Everyone up," she said quietly. On this, she'd trust the assassin's senses.

Leanir turned to Arya, gaze faintly challenging as always. "We are through the Dreadwater Gate, and that means we part ways here. As of tomorrow's dawn, the truce between us ends. My word on it. Are you agreed?"

She hesitated, but only briefly. If Leanir was one of her Sky Lords, so be it, but he couldn't know that. It was already bad enough that he'd learned she had magic, she didn't want him holding any more information he could use as a weapon against them. But more than that … he would be safer not knowing who he was and far away from her. Safer until she dealt with the

Nightstalker somehow. And if she did that, well, there'd be no more need for them to be involved in each other's lives. Arya nodded. "My word on it."

He gave her that mocking smirk. "Then goodbye, Raider, until we meet again."

They all watched as he slipped away, following the narrow trail towards the eastern side of the waterfall, rather than taking the western trail they'd initially come down.

"He's the fifth, isn't he?" Essa asked. "That's why my father sent him with us."

Arya turned back to the others. There was no surprise in Darmanin's face at Essa's words, or even in Rorin or Taze's. "He's the fifth," she confirmed.

"Does he know?" Taze asked, his protective gaze making sure Leanir did actually leave.

"No."

"Like Chiarn, we're better off well away from him, and vice versa," Darmanin said.

"*I don't know about that*," Rorin said. "*He saved Essa's life today, and literally risked his own to do it.*"

"That doesn't make him a hero," Darmanin said shortly.

"I agree," Arya said, forestalling further argument. "Now, let's move cautiously up to the western tower. I want to make sure we're not walking into a camp of Lances."

Taze glanced at Darmanin. "Let's avoid that if we can."

Darmanin gave one of his rare smiles. "We don't have to. I am eighteen now. My father can't order me to do anything anymore."

Arya fixed him with a look. "We still can't attack a shield of Lances on Crowtalon land, Dar. We will be *avoiding* any Lances we see. Clear?"

They all nodded, and Arya set off along the narrow trail, but Rorin's touch on her arm stopped her. She looked at him expectantly. He took a breath, turned so that he was facing them all, and began signing. "*Before we go back to Dunidaen and everything that entails ... I've been thinking on your offer to try and heal me—I honestly haven't been able to think of anything else since you mentioned it last night."* Rorin hesitated, then firmed his shoulders. *"I have decided not to accept it. I do not wish to be healed."*

Arya looked at him in astonishment. "Why not?"

"Being a mute does not disable me in any way from being a good warlord, and I'm going to prove that to everyone. I want to make sure the next heir born mute, or deaf, or missing a limb, knows that they can still succeed in whatever they put their minds to. That they can lead if they choose. I'm going to be the first to show them all," he signed determinedly.

"Rorin, that's foolish. You—" Darmanin started, but Essa cut him off.

"It's not. It's laudable, in fact. There is absolutely nothing wrong with Rorin, there never has been," she said fiercely. "And if he can show the stuffy, intolerant warlords that—not to mention anyone else who somehow thinks being different means being less than— then that is a good thing. Better than good."

Arya stared at Essa once she'd finished her impassioned words, mouth slightly open. Rorin beamed at Essa, gave them all a sweeping bow, then set off along the trail, Taze hurrying to get ahead of him. Darmanin trailed close behind, scowling at Rorin's back.

Arya turned to Essa, heart full, and said, "I am glad of you, Essa Varsoth. We won't always agree, in the days and years coming, but never allow me to forget how your perspective grounds me."

Essa smiled, nodded, then started along the trail behind the others. Arya followed, Essa's words still ringing in her mind. The sentiment in them was what Arya had always believed, deep down, but now she realised it wasn't how she'd always behaved. She should never have suggested that Rorin change himself, because Essa was right, he didn't need to. He was more than good enough as he was. Her eagerness for Rorin to succeed had blinded her to that.

And it wasn't just Rorin. Magic-wielders were different. But that didn't make them bad. They had the same choices in front of them as everyone else did. It was their choices that defined them.

Shadeweavers too.

Chapter 26

"Arya?" Taze's quiet word came from ahead.

Arya shook herself from her thoughts and moved up to take the lead. The late afternoon sunlight lightened their path as they made their way along the narrow trail curling up from under the waterfall towards the western tower. The scent of woodsmoke was discernible now, away from the water and mist. Arya reached back, making sure she had easy access to the cloth-wrapped sword strapped to her pack, then waved them all into line behind her, and they crept silently along the banks as Ranier had taught them.

She pressed herself against the stone wall of the tower, inching around until she had a view of the cleared ground before it. There was no sign a campsite in the open space, or visible in what she could see of the surrounding forest. She lifted a hand for the others to stay where they were and continued around the tower wall until reaching its entrance. Then, ever so slowly, she craned her head around the opening.

Unlike the last time she'd been inside, it was no longer empty.

A camp—a very lived-in-looking camp—filled the massive space. The floor was swept clean of debris and contained a cookfire, sleeping mats, and a neat pile of supplies. The men and women inside—some standing watch on the balcony, others playing a quiet game of cards— weren't wearing a uniform, but Arya recognised the camp structure of a Raider shield immediately.

And then her gaze landed on the man tending the cookfire.

She smiled and stepped away from the wall to wave the all clear to Rorin and the others, then stepped through the entryway, voice booming. "Shield

Captain Laskin Carter. What kind of half-assed lazy security do you call this? I just wandered in here without a care in the world!"

He shot to his feet then froze, weathered features shifting from shock to relief then joy. "Arya? Is that really you?"

"It's really me." She took two long strides and threw her arms around him. It took him a moment, but he hugged her back, fierce and tight, before letting go.

"You came for us?" She stared at his wonderfully familiar face, so glad to see him she felt like crying, then lifted her glance to the other men and women gathering behind their captain, delight shining in their eyes. She spotted Wattin there, Charlin too. And Etan and Allicen and Kait. Her original Icecliff shield-mates.

Laskin scowled. "Of course we did. Where is Lord Rorin, is he—"

His words died as Rorin came through the doorway, Taze and Darmanin and Essa filing in behind him. "*It's good to see you, Captain,*" Rorin signed.

Laskin's mouth fell open, and his eyes widened. His jaw worked, but he seemed unable to speak. His Raiders looked to have been struck by the same infliction. They'd seen a gangly youth leave for Khadini and a self-assured young man return. Right now, even unshaven and dirty and rumpled, Rorin Ravenstrike looked everything like a warlord's heir. Arya thought the decision he'd made about his voice only added to his aura of self-confidence.

"Something wrong, Laskin?" Arya asked, needling him.

Rorin smiled, his whole face lightening. "*It is me, Captain. Somewhat changed from when you last saw me, I grant you, but still me.*"

Laskin gathered himself and saluted, and within a second the entire shield was saluting and standing at attention. "Welcome home, Lord Rorin."

"We're all safely returned and accounted for," Arya said. "But what are you doing here? Mathas Crowtalon would have a fit if he knew Raiders were encamped in his State."

"Waiting for you," Laskin explained. "Out of uniform so we can claim to be travellers if anyone spots us, but we've been staying inside during the day—hence no watch—and avoiding fires at night, and nobody seems to come this way."

Darmanin raised an eyebrow. "We've been gone almost six months. You didn't give us up for dead?"

Laskin scratched his beard. "You took a little longer than expected."

Arya snorted, then grinned, then laughed. Rorin too. Even Essa broke into chuckles. When Taze slapped Darmanin's shoulder, grinning, even he smiled. The relief of being on home soil broke the tension that had been hovering over all of them since rafting into Khadini.

Once the laughter died, Laskin continued, "We figured you'd be wanting a good hot meal once you got up that cliff." Already a couple of his shield were placing a pot over the fire while others retrieved bread and cheese from the stack of supplies. "Is anyone hurt? Wattin has his healing supplies with him."

"No, we're all patched up." Arya said. "Food sounds wonderful though."

"*I'm absolutely ravenous*," Rorin signed enthusiastically.

Arya lingered while the others moved to sit around the fire and receive bread and cheese. She smiled to see Taze surrounded by their old shield-mates, receiving grins and shoulder punches and hearty slaps on the back. She didn't have a single qualm about the fact these Raiders had clearly been told the true purpose of Rorin's absence from Heathrock. She trusted each of them with her life, *and* Rorin's. "You brought horses?"

Laskin nodded. "Tethered in a thick area of brush near a stream and with plenty of grazing. Far enough from here that if someone stumbles across them, they won't find us too. And all the tack is in here with us so there's nothing on the horses to identify them as having come from Ravenstrike."

"Good work, Laskin." She let out a tired breath. "We're exhausted, but I think we should leave once night falls, cross Crowtalon as quickly as we can. I won't feel like we're safe until we're across the SparrowWing border."

Laskin agreed. "Sunset is less than an hour away. I'll have the shield pack up and prepare the horses. You all eat and rest until then." He hesitated. "It's good to have you safely home—it was a long wait, Arya."

She smiled. "It was a long journey."

✱✱✱

Still within the borders of Crowtalon, they made camp at dawn the following morning, and Arya and the others rolled immediately into blankets to
get the first sleep they'd had in two days.

Blinking awake as dusk fell, they gathered around a small cookfire and
received bowls of hot stew. Properly rested now, they all had questions for
Laskin.

"*Tell me about my parents, Captain,*" Rorin asked first, fingers flicking.
Laskin, who'd been his weapons' tutor as a boy, understood his sign language well enough that it didn't need translating. "*I doubt they shared your
optimism about our return.*"

Laskin hesitated only briefly. "That's right, Lord Rorin. Your parents assume you died in Khadini or were captured."

He frowned. "*What about the other warlords?*"

"Your mother has kept hidden your Dreadwater run. Her vicelords believe you are travelling Dunidaen, learning to be a future warlord." He
paused. "When I left, she and Adviser Magen and Lord Eaglesoar were
planning how to explain your death and when to announce it. I do not know
if they have made any formal announcements yet."

Rorin's face fell, and Laskin hurried to add, "Your parents are devastated,
Lord Rorin. Your mother blames herself."

"If they have made an announcement, my father will think he's struck
gold," Darmanin said.

"The State Council is less than two months away," Arya said. "Almost
straight after Winterfest. Without you or Rorin, your father can put forward
Jenka as Ravenstrike heir and Andrian as his own. Having Jenka as her heir
will make it impossible for Warlord Ravenstrike to put herself forward for
High Warlord." She looked up then, caught Darmanin's gaze with a little
smile. "Your father has another thing coming."

His eyes glimmered as he returned her smile across the fire. "Yes, he
does."

"How did you come to be waiting for us, Laskin?" Arya asked.

"I requested permission to remain at the Dreadwater Gate until your return; knowing you as I do, I thought it a decent chance that even if you were captured, you'd get free eventually. Warlord Ravenstrike allowed it, but only until Winterfest. And while the warlord had to tell General Lerin the truth of where Lord Rorin was when his absence grew so prolonged, he refused to order anyone to go with me. He said I could only take volunteers, and they couldn't be told where they were going or why until we got here. And if we were caught, he and Warlord Ravenstrike would disavow all knowledge of us."

Arya lifted her gaze, meeting the eyes of every Raider gathered around not on watch, giving them a sincere nod of acknowledgment. "Your loyalty won't be forgotten."

"It wasn't loyalty, Captain," Laskin said.

She met his gaze last. "I know."

"Can you tell us anything about what happened at the Council after we left?" Essa asked. "Are things with Andahar settled?"

"I don't know the details." Laskin looked grim. "But Arken heard from General Lerin that the Nightstalker's missive demanded Dunidaen allow his soldiers inside the border to search for Andahari rebels. The warlords voted to refuse permission at the Council, and the High Warlord sent a return missive to that effect. As far as I know, there's been nothing but silence from Andahar since."

Arya and Essa shared a glance. Was that another reason Thiara Ravenstrike had sent them to run the rapids? To remove them from the border region? Even if that were true, the Nightstalker and his nazal knew Arya's magic now, knew for certain she existed. Would that change the demands he made on Dunidaen?

"There's something else you might find interesting." Laskin hadn't missed the look between them, and his gaze was narrowed. "We left Heathrock late summer, was early autumn when we arrived. The night before reaching the Dreadwater Gate, Wattin went into a village to top up our supplies. He went to the inn—wanted to listen in a bit and make sure there were no Lances or anything else we needed to be concerned about in the area."

Arya recognised that look on Laskin's face. "What did he hear?"

Laskin glanced over at Wattin.

The bearded man cleared his throat. "Almost everyone at the inn was talking about something that had happened a few days earlier." He hesitated. "A rider in the night, galloping fast through the village, heading in the direction of the Dreadwater. Cloaked and hooded. It was notable because whoever it was rode down the village gates, pulverised them apparently. They assumed it was a magic-wielder, and there was some chatter about forming a search party to catch them, but I think they were all a bit too scared to follow through."

"When we got here, we did a bit of scouting," Laskin added. "There was evidence that someone had been preparing to run the Dreadwater after you. We must have only just missed them."

"What sort of evidence?" Darmanin asked.

"Signs of a campsite. Materials left over; materials you would use in raft building."

"You've seen nothing else since you got here?" Arya asked. "They haven't come back?"

"No. Not the same way they went, at least."

"Thanks Laskin, Wattin," Arya said. "Could you get the shield ready to mount? It's close enough to dawn we can get going."

She waited until both Raiders were out of hearing range before speaking again. "Mid-summer was when I had the nightmare. When the nazal learned where I was."

"So, it *did* come to find you," Essa said. "And if it didn't reach here till the beginning of autumn, that travel time suggests it was the nazal in Heathrock that came for you."

"*Does that mean there was only one of them in Dunidaen?*" Rorin signed.

"I hope so." Fear shivered through Arya.

Darmanin looked grim. "I hope your mother hasn't made any kind of announcement about your death while running the Dreadwater Gate yet, Rorin."

Rorin's head came up. "*Why?*"

"Because if the nazal learn that a small group of Dunidae went into Khadini shortly before they found Arya in that pit mine, they'll know that the Sky Lord they're hunting is one of us," Darmanin said.

"Not necessarily." Essa shook her head. "If I were a nazal, I would be assuming my prey was Khadini, not Dunidae."

"I don't think it's safe to assume that," Taze said.

"*How do we even know the nazal will hear of us running the rapids?*" Rorin asked. "*The elder told Arya they could pass as human, but if it's in Khadini hunting for us, how will it hear anything about our run?*"

"I think we *should* assume the Nightstalker has spies in Dunidaen who will learn of any news relevant to the warlords," Darmanin said. "He'll hear about it, and he'll put two and two together."

Arya agreed. "We need to be more careful than we've ever been. We don't talk about Andahar or magic unless strictly necessary, and then only when we're alone. Nobody uses their magic either, it doesn't matter how important it is."

"Agreed." Darmanin nodded.

"The whole point of Rorin running the Dreadwater was so that he could announce it to everyone at the State Council, firm up his bid to be made heir. Everyone will know then," Essa pointed out.

"*We have time to come up with a plan before that happens,*" Rorin said.

Conversation went on around her, but Arya felt a weight slowly settling down over her shoulders. They'd made it through the Dreadwater Gate and they'd won their cazaix.

But that also meant they were heading back home. Where she could no longer ignore the fact that her wyvern existed or that nazal were hunting them. She'd promised Essa that they would figure something out, and she couldn't keep putting it off. Once they were home, she'd have to hold to her word.

Arya just wished she had any idea of *how* to permanently deal with the Nightstalker and keep those she loved safe at the same time. And deep down, what she feared most was the creeping certainty that change was coming.

A change that none of them wanted.

Chapter 27

The moment they crossed the border into Ravenstrike Arya felt better, some of the weight of worry lifting from her shoulders.

She was almost home.

Arya let out a breath and glanced over at her brother, riding without reins as usual so he could sign.

"I want to be home for my mother's formal Winterfest eve dinner," Rorin announced.

"It's going to be a push to make it back to Heathrock in time." Arya glanced up at the sky, which was heavy with snow clouds. "Especially if this weather worsens."

"Most of the Ravenstrike vicelords will be there," he pointed out. *"What could be better than for them to see me return triumphantly from running the Dreadwater, rather than hearing about it via messages?"*

She couldn't deny it would be a powerful strategic victory for Rorin's mother—for Ravenstrike's vicelords to see their heir strong and healthy and carrying a cazaix blade. It would be next to impossible for anyone to undermine Rorin's place if his lords had seen it in person.

"What about the nazal?" Taze asked. "I don't think the vicelords are going to stay quiet about something like that. Word will get out."

"What if we alter the timing?" Essa said, sitting up eagerly in the saddle. "Nobody has to know Rorin went in there six months ago, and people would ask questions anyway about why it took so long if they knew. His mother could tell everyone that he spent nine months training for the run *before* he ran the rapids. That timing places his entry into Khadini after the nazal found Arya in the mine. That will reinforce to them that those they hunt are in Khadini, not here."

Arya wasn't so sure. She figured there had to be a reason the Nightstalker had assumed the Sky Lord potentials he hunted were near the Diamond-fang—he'd been clear on that from the beginning. But it was possible it had been a guess on his part, and the new information from the nazal could change where he was looking for them.

And when she weighed it up—having Rorin confirmed as heir was critical to everything Warlord Ravenstrike wanted to do. And a triumphant return would bring all the Ravenstrike warlords behind him immediately.

"*We have to consider that everyone will know Arya and Essa travelled with me. They've been gone the same amount of time.*" Rorin pointed out.

"Even better if Warlord Ravenstrike lies about the timing. It puts us all firmly out of suspicion." Taze said.

"Leaving us vulnerable only to Ranier claiming something different." Darmanin said. "But he gave his word to Warlord Ravenstrike. I think he'd stay silent."

"Laskin!" Arya called ahead. "Let's push the pace. I want to be back at Heathrock by Winterfest eve."

He let out a resigned sigh. "As you wish, Captain."

Heavy snowfall made the northern roads slow going, but they pushed the horses, galloping as often and as long as possible. The little spark of joy Arya had felt crossing the Ravenstrike border burst into flame at her first sight of the Diamondfang on the distant horizon.

At the sight of those dazzling snow-covered peaks, she let out a long whoop and threw her hands out, hair blowing back in the wind, the rhythm of the horse steady under her, eyes closed in bliss.

In that moment, the troubles that plagued her melted away. She could deal with it all. She'd be home. Even the deepening cold didn't bother her. It was familiar, comforting, a return to everything she knew.

When she opened her eyes, both Rorin and Darmanin were watching her. Rorin's eyes were bright blue, alight with the shared joy of homecoming, his grin as wide as hers. But Darmanin's gaze was alight with something else, something unfamiliar. Whatever it was, it blazed with intensity.

Arya laughed and urged her horse into a faster gallop.

Her Raiders whooped and whistled as they came after her.

***

On the day before Winterfest eve, they rode deep into the night, not making camp until the early hours before dawn when they were forced to rest their exhausted horses.

The Raiders not on watch curled up in their blankets to get a couple of hours rest, but Arya and the others didn't sleep, instead sitting around a fire, sipping at hot tea to keep warm. Snow drifted, but judging from the clearing skies to the west, the weather looked to clear up by morning. They chatted idly, laughing when Rorin accidentally inhaled a mouthful of tea and started coughing and spluttering. It felt like old times.

After a moment though, he sobered. *"Mother's Winterfest eve dinner doesn't start until nightfall, which gives us the whole day. If we're going to show up and announce my triumphant return, we have to look the part. We can't stumble in unshaven, filthy and smelling like we do."*

Arya looked at him, startled. He was right, but Rorin had never cared about things like that before. His gaze settled on her, sober, and he gave her a little nod. For the first time she understood how things truly were different now. Rorin didn't just *look* older and more mature. He *was* those things. Confidence flared in her. This young man was her *brother*. She would be his general one day, and she couldn't wait.

"I agree." Essa gave Rorin a contemplative glance, like her thoughts might be echoing Arya's. "Your return needs to be managed for full effect. Especially since we don't know how the last impromptu Council went. We *do* know Crowtalon will be doing everything he can to undermine Raven-strike."

"Did I just hear you right?" Tazed asked, amused. "Essa Varsoth advocating for political theatre?"

"Oh, I don't hesitate to use politics when it's to our advantage," Essa said. "Having Rorin as a future warlord means only good things for Dunidaen."

And for magic-wielders. The words went unsaid, but they all heard them.

"*That's my future chief adviser,*" Rorin signed proudly.

Darmanin sat up straighter. "We'll go into Heathrock city first. We can buy fresh clothing and clean up properly. We should arrive after the event has started, too, so that we make an entrance."

Essa sighed in bliss. "Fresh clothes. I was starting to wonder if I'd ever have that small pleasure again."

Arya shared her smile across the fire, shoulders loose, chest easy. For the first time in too long, she felt safe. She didn't need to be on constant lookout for Rangers, and she knew that they weren't out there in the darkness hunting for her.

She knew it wouldn't last. Knew the nazal would find them eventually.

But she would always have this moment with her family.

***

As sunrise broke over the road the next morning, they cantered along the road approaching the intersection splitting the road between Heathrock city and Heathrock castle. To keep their visit to the city discreet, Laskin left his shield at the intersection, and he alone stayed with them, having changed out of his uniform.

The Diamondfang loomed above the brooding city, as dark and grim as Arya remembered it. The entry gates stood wide open, the main thoroughfare already busy. She reveled in the hustle and bustle of Heathrock's streets, following Rorin as he led them to the tailor who'd served the Ravenstrike family for decades.

As they walked, Arya studied those they passed, searching for any signs of unease. But everything looked and felt normal. There were no signs of extra Raiders patrolling either. If a nazal still stalked the city, it wasn't public knowledge. Her instincts were quiet, relaxed, and she felt nothing of the quiet shivery sensation she'd felt that night.

When they reached the tailor, Laskin split off with instructions to obtain new uniforms for Taze and Arya. He also carried their new cazaix weapons; he would source sheaths and weapons' belts so they could wear them openly.

The poor tailor looked horrified at Rorin's request to come up with formal dress for Rorin, Essa, and Darmanin in the space of a few hours. Rorin's charm and smile failed to calm his frantic dithering, until Essa suggested that perhaps it would be easier to simply alter existing clothes already in his store.

After getting themselves measured, they ate a companionable lunch together at one of the quieter inns—Arya quelling her temptation to go to the Arms and see if Tiya had returned—and then headed to one of the city bathhouses. She sighed in pure bliss as she lowered her body into a pool of steaming water. Essa echoed her enjoyment nearby, and they spent a good hour luxuriating in the warmth after scrubbing months of dirt and grime from their skin and hair.

Essa broke the companionable quiet only once. "Are you afraid? Of what might have changed while we were gone."

Arya didn't hesitate. "We're home. We're safe. Whatever happens, we'll figure it out. Together."

"I wish I had your confidence in that." She sighed. "I fear losing all of it."

A bathhouse attendant appeared a couple of times with packages; the first from Laskin for Arya, the second from the tailor for Essa. When Arya finally emerged from her bath, the water had turned a filthy grey colour.

Once out, they moved with purpose, towel drying and combing out the tangles in their now-clean hair. Essa's shoulder-length brown curls had grown out during their months away, and Arya had to blink at the unusual sight of her with hair drawn back in a braid rather than framing her face.

Laskin had done well, accurately estimating Arya's size at the Raider outfitters in Heathrock and acquiring the full uniform, cloak and cowl included. She breathed in the fresh wool smell of the quilted jerkin and felt that warm rush of being home again. The black breeches fitted perfectly, as did the jerkin and cloak. Finally, she buttoned the cowl around her neck.

The cazaix sword at her waist looked perfect in the sheath that he'd found for her; tooled from black leather with hints of blood-red stitched into its edges.

"What do you think?" Essa's voice drew Arya's attention away from admiring her new sword—vaguely uncomfortable sensation of the cazaix or not, she loved it.

Rorin's tailor had altered a gown for Essa. The periwinkle fabric was dotted with little golden sunflowers, and it fitted her small frame perfectly. A fur-lined cloak in a deeper blue sat over her shoulders, and matching velvet gloves fitted to her elbows. Arya had to suppress a smile—Essa hadn't been backward in telling the tailor how easily she got cold.

"You look perfect," Arya said. "Shall we?"

The three young men waited out the front. Taze matched Arya in his new Raider uniform, now shaven and with his raven hair cut Raider short. He looked tall, sober, and grown up. A true warrior.

Rorin and Darmanin had shaved too but wore their longer hair in the short braid that was traditional for young noblemen. Rorin sported a midnight blue jacket that fell to his knees, over a navy tunic and white undershirt. He was probably cold but looked handsome and impressive. Darmanin wore a similar jacket in black over a deep violet tunic and undershirt. Both looked every inch the image of what warlords wanted in their heirs.

Laskin scratched his beard, grumbled. "I thought this was supposed to be a discreet visit to the city."

Rorin gave a sheepish look at the glances they were already getting from those passing by. Seeing Arya's Raider uniform with the young heir dressed as he was meant people were quickly recognising them.

Despite Laskin's words, Arya was glad they'd delayed their return to do this. No vicelord that saw them tonight could doubt that Rorin was a worthy heir to their State, especially once he drew that cazaix blade at his hip.

The sun was already lowering behind the mountain peaks, casting the city in a dim orange glow. A light snow drifted from the sky, but the clouds were mostly clearing.

Winterfest eve dinner would be starting right about now.

She grinned. "Let's go home."

***

Laskin's shield fell in behind them as they passed the intersection and headed out on the empty road to the castle. Arya thought she'd never been as happy to see a place in her life as she was when they rounded a corner in the road and saw Heathrock nestled in the moonlight at the northern end of the frozen lake, framed by the snow-covered mountains of the Diamond-fang.

The road leading up to the castle was lined with torches, and the massive front gates stood open and welcoming. Carriages were neatly lined up in the entry yard beyond. Despite the gates standing open, Arya was pleased to see Raiders instantly materialising to cover the opening when their horses were spotted by the guards up on the wall. They didn't draw weapons, but their alertness told her they were ready to respond quickly if needed.

They slowed the horses to a walk so as not to alarm the guards, and as soon as they were close enough, Arya kicked her horse forward and lifted a hand in greeting, addressing the closest Raider she recognised. "Derrin." She grinned. "Is it too much to ask that you remember me?"

He took two steps forward so he could see her better, before shock filled his expression. "Captain Ravenstrike! I didn't realise it was you. I'm sorry!"

"Don't apologise, you were doing your job," she said briskly. "It's good to see you, Captain."

An unbelieving smile spread across his face. "And you, Captain."

Arya gestured behind her. "As you can see, I'm escorting Lord Rorin home, and that's Captain Laskin's shield bringing up the rear. Is Warlord Ravenstrike's Winterfest dinner on tonight?"

He straightened. "Yes, Captain. It's all going smoothly so far. We've got a double guard on the walls, and all her guests have arrived. That's why we were being a little extra cautious when we spotted you approaching."

"As I said, you did well." She glanced around. "We'd best get inside. Let's get an ale in the mess soon, eh?"

"I'd like that." Derrin stepped back and the Raiders with him followed suit. "Welcome home, Lord Rorin."

Rorin gave him a grin and a wave as he rode past. The Raiders all gave a sharp salute. They reined in at the steps before the castle entry, and grooms appeared to take their horses. Their shock at the sight of Rorin and Arya returning had them both chuckling.

"Laskin, dismiss your shield and get them into the mess for a hot drink and a meal," she told him. "Two days rest before they're required back on duty."

He swallowed a smirk, saluted. "As you say, Captain Ravenstrike."

"Get out of here," she said. "I'll find you for an ale as soon as I have a moment and tell you the whole tale of our run."

"We look forward to that." He paused. "Welcome home, kid."

"Thanks, old man."

Once Laskin and his shield filed away, Arya turned to Rorin, who was shifting from foot to foot, gaze fixed on the doors at the top of the steps, eagerness in every inch of his bearing. "Ready for this?"

"*I've never been more ready for anything,*" he said, then smiled, "*Besides, I really want to see my parents, and Peemla, and everyone else here. I've missed them.*"

"Last time we were all together for Winterfest eve dinner, we were watching from Rorin's roof, too young to attend," Essa said.

"Not anymore." Arya said with a look of shared resolve with Rorin. "Now we're the future of Ravenstrike."

Chapter 28

They started up the steps and through the doors into the empty entry area. The great hall stood directly across from them, its doors flung open, light spilling out from inside along with the sound of music and chatter and glasses clinking.

But that wasn't the first thing Arya noticed.

Instead, her gaze went straight to the small huddle of people near the open doors, and she halted instead of continuing inside. The light from inside the hall was enough for her to recognise them.

Thiara Ravenstrike, her husband, and Lanna Crowtalon and *her* husband.

Rorin surged forward when he realised his parents were there, but Arya reached out to hold him back, lifting a finger to her lips then gesturing for him to listen—the group's conversation was carrying clearly across the cavernous space. Darmanin and Essa threw her a frown, but seemed content to wait, while Taze hovered protectively behind them.

"Sister, it is time you faced facts," Lanna was saying, her voice sickly sweet in tone, something that had always made Arya itch. "You need an heir to Ravenstrike, and my Jenka is most likely to be confirmed by the State Council. Wherever Rorin is—and I don't believe for a second your fanciful tale that he's travelling alone around Dunidaen—it won't change that fact."

"My wife is aware of that, Lanna," Matte Eaglesoar said. "She doesn't need to be reminded of it twice a day. Is this really what you wanted to talk about so urgently that you had to hold us up from entering our dinner? The vicelords will be wondering where we are."

"This event is the perfect time to announce that you will be putting forward Jenka as your heir at the State Council. Our vicelords will appreciate being informed ahead of time and can then bring their support behind yours for the nomination."

"*Our* vicelords?" Thiara's voice had a dangerous edge to it. "You're more Crowtalon than Ravenstrike these days, sister."

"We are all Dunidae, and this is what's best for *our* country," Lanna said. "You don't have a choice, Thiara. If you don't name an heir, you risk instability at a time when Dunidaen needs to be strong. Name Jenka and bring the vicelords behind you. He will be a popular choice and a strong warlord."

Arya glanced at Rorin, seeing her anger reflected in the tightening of his features.

"You must deal with this at once," Darmanin spoke quietly behind them.

Rorin and Arya turned simultaneously to give him a scathing look. Darmanin acknowledged their scorn with a nod of capitulation, then drew Essa and Taze back to give them some space. Arya looked at her brother and gestured for him to precede her; she would stand at his back, but this moment was all his.

"Sister, I will not be silenced on this."

Rorin and Arya started walking, moving out of the shadows across the entry foyer. Their boots echoing on the stone floor had all four adults turning in surprise. Arya didn't allow them a moment to gather themselves. "Warlord, I hope we're not too late," she said. "We rode long and hard to make it on time."

Rorin stopped a few paces from them, blue eyes bright, and signed, "*I'm sorry, Aunt, we've rudely interrupted you,*" Arya translated for him. "*What was that you were saying about manoeuvring your son into* my *rightful place?*"

"Yes, do continue. Rorin and I are quite riveted," Arya added.

Matte was the first to break out of his shock and surprise. He broke away from the group towards Rorin, wonderment written across his face. "Rorin, it's really you?"

"*Yes, Father, it's me.*" Rorin took three strides, and the two men threw their arms around each other.

Thiara Ravenstrike was only a heartbeat behind her husband, almost leaping across the intervening space to hug her son, all her usual gravitas utterly forgotten. Rorin stretched an arm out to include her, and the three of them held tight to each other for a long time.

Arya's gaze stayed on Lanna Ravenstrike, who had flushed a deep red, something hard shifting into her expression. Arya was confident it wasn't embarrassment. After snapping something at her husband, she pushed past the hugging family, striding away from the great hall.

Arya moved in a blink, reaching out to grip the woman's arm in a vicelike hold as she passed, using her superior height and strength to force her to stop. "Threaten Rorin or his position ever again, and I will destroy you. Are we clear, *Aunt*?"

Lanna's face tightened. She tore her arm from Arya's grip before stalking up the stairs and vanishing from sight. Daskinal lingered for a moment before withering under the weight of Arya's icy stare and following his wife. Once they were gone, Arya turned her attention back to her warlord, who was dis-entangling herself from her son. Both Matte and Thiara stared at Rorin, drinking him in.

"You look..." Thiara's words trailed off. "You are well?"

"*We had quite a time in Khadini, Mother.*" Rorin smiled his mischievous smile. "*But I am returned safely and successfully.*"

Thiara considered that for a moment, then her expression turned angry, lowering her voice even though they were alone. "Where have you been all this time? We were certain you'd been killed."

Matte chuckled at this wife. "Love, we just got our boy back. Let's not get too upset with him so soon."

"*It's a very long story, and I'm happy to tell you about it later.*" Rorin turned and stepped aside so Arya could join them. "*You'll be pleased to know that we all returned safely.*"

"Warlord." Arya saluted sharply.

"Welcome home, Arya," Thiara said, reaching out to take her hand. "I am so very glad to have you back with us."

Stunned to see a sheen of tears in the warlord's icy blue gaze, Arya squeezed her warlord's hand. "Thank you. I missed Heathrock. Very much."

Their grip tightened, almost painful, then Thiara let go. "I'm glad." She took a breath, her voice turning businesslike. "May I ask about the cazaix?"

Arya nodded, waving Darmanin and Taze and Essa over. "As Rorin said, we have a long tale to tell, but we all returned with cazaix blades."

"Warlord Ravenstrike, Lord Eaglesoar. Hello." Essa beamed, clearly pleased to see them, and Darmanin bowed politely.

"Welcome back, all of you. You've been missed," Matte said warmly, his eyes shining. Arya noticed his hand kept reaching out to touch Rorin's arm, as if to reassure himself that his son was truly there.

"I hope I am not imposing, Warlord Ravenstrike," Darmanin said with that grave formality of his. "I realise I have not been invited to Heathrock, or to this event."

"Nonsense," Thiara responded. "You are my son's foster-brother. You will always be welcome in my home, Darmanin, and that includes after you become warlord yourself one day."

"Thank you, Warlord Ravenstrike," he said. "I will not forget your generosity."

Before any of them could do or say anything further, Peemla appeared from inside the hall, looking worried. "Warlord, there you are!"

Her voice trailed off as she saw Rorin and Arya and the others, and for a moment she turned still. Then, a light crept into her eyes and her cheeks flushed with colour. "You're home."

"Peemla." Arya couldn't help grinning. "You're a sight for sore eyes."

Peemla lifted a hand to her mouth, and it was trembling. Tears spilled down her cheeks.

"Peemla, Lady Crowtalon and her husband have left the dinner early. Could you check that they've returned to their rooms and aren't up to anything more nefarious than fuming over Rorin's return?" Thiara asked, voice crisp.

Arya stifled a smile. Of course, her warlord had already mastered her surprise and relief and was moving to next steps.

The chamberlain startled at the warlord's words—she'd been staring at the new arrivals in wonder—then nodded and made for the stairs Lanna had taken. Rorin's fingers touched her arm as she passed him. *"It's good to see you, Peemla."*

She smiled at him, her flush deepening, then ducked her head, and left.

There was a moment's stillness once she'd gone, then Rorin began signing, *"We'd best get in there. You* are *hosting this thing after all, Mother."*

Thiara Ravenstrike smiled her wolfish smile. "Rorin, your cazaix sword is with you?"

He grinned and half-drew his sword from its sheath. The blade glimmered blue in the firelight from the hall.

Thiara nodded in satisfaction. "Well, Lanna *did* want me to announce my heir tonight. It looks like she's going to get her wish after all."

"Mother." Rorin stopped her with a touch. *"You need to tell them I crossed the Dreadwater Gate two months ago—that I spent all the months beforehand in Dunidaen training for it."*

Thiara's gaze narrowed, but Arya spoke before she could argue. "We don't want questions about why it took so long for Rorin to successfully steal his cazaix blade. Mathas will use any piece of leverage he can to undermine Rorin's achievement. The point is that he did it. Nobody needs to know the details."

The warlord's gaze settled on Arya. "The Raiders who met you at the border—they can be trusted to keep their mouths shut?"

"Implicitly, Warlord. And there are none who can dispute our account of the timing, bar Ranier."

"Then that's the tale we'll tell." She shifted her glance between the two of them. "And you'll tell Matte and I *everything*. But later."

***

When Thiara Ravenstrike and her husband appeared at the top of the steps leading down into the great hall, the hum of conversation slowly died. The warlord waited until it was fully quiet before beginning to speak.

"Thank you all for coming tonight. You are very welcome here at Heathrock, and I am genuinely pleased to see so many of you gathered." She paused for a moment, letting it draw out until all attention was focused on her. "I have an official announcement to make. I wish you to know my intentions ahead of the upcoming State Council so that we may all show a united front in support of House Ravenstrike."

Anyone who *hadn't* fully been paying attention to their warlord now was … fixedly. Arya couldn't help the triumphant grin spreading across her face as she watched from the shadows beyond the door.

"Come next month, I will be putting forward my son, Rorin Ravenstrike, to be confirmed as heir to this State." Thiara spoke loud and clear into the anticipatory silence, and as she did, Rorin walked out of the shadows to join his parents at the top of the steps. He offered the vicelords a low bow.

His mother continued into the stunned silence, "Rorin has just returned from running the Dreadwater Gate, where he successfully obtained a cazaix blade. That is the true reason for his absence from Heathrock for the past year. He spent nine months training before undertaking the run."

And as gasps of surprise swept through the gathering, Rorin drew his cazaix sword with a loud ring and held it low and ready, in the swordsman's stance Laskin had taught him as a boy. In that moment, with the light of the hall illuminating him, glimmering blue blade in his hand, Rorin Ravenstrike looked every inch a future warlord.

And he didn't need to open his mouth and speak to show that to his future vicelords.

A master of this, Thiara Ravenstrike let them look and whisper and mutter to each other, holding the moment long enough for it all to sink in. Then, she smiled, and clapped her hands once. "Thank you once again for coming tonight, my lords. Please drink and dance and enjoy yourselves. This dinner is in your honour."

The Ravenstrike family headed down into the hall, taking a glass of wine from a passing servant, and immediately stopping to talk with their vicelords. Taze slipped after them, taking up a position along the edges of the hall where he could keep an eye on Rorin.

"Shall we go and join the party?" Arya asked, smiling at the pleased looks on Essa and Darmanin's faces.

Essa shook her head. "Making small talk with insufferable nobles is the last thing I want to do. I'm going to go sleep for three months."

Arya chuckled, not surprised. She turned to Darmanin. "What about you? Will you come down and have a drink with me?"

He seemed to hesitate. "I'd like that, Arya, but I think I should leave tonight to Rorin. If I appear, they'll be gossiping about me and what I'm doing here and not about his triumphant return."

He was right. "Fine. I'll party on my own. Will I see you at breakfast tomorrow?"

"Don't expect to see me before midday," Essa said. "I *might* be there for dinner."

Even Darmanin smiled at that, his face lighting up. "I will share lunch with you, Arya. Until then."

Already she was looking forward to it. "Until then, Dar."

***

After Arya had shared a quick celebratory drink with Rorin—before his mother dragged him away to speak with more vicelords—and a quiet moment with Matte, who rarely tore his eyes away from his son—she went in search of General Lerin. After such a theatrical return, she knew he would expect her to report to him immediately to demonstrate her respect for his rank, and she thought there was no harm in keeping things civil between them.

After all, Thiara Ravenstrike had made Arya a promise.

Lerin wasn't going to be general of Ravenstrike much longer.

It didn't take her long to find the general, standing near a table lined with glasses of wine and plates of artfully arranged food, speaking with Arken. His glass was empty, Arken's still full. Arya's gaze narrowed at that pairing as she approached, but she plastered a respectful expression on her face and saluted as soon as the general saw her. She watched the anger ripple over his face, the gathering order to tell her to leave, that she didn't belong here, and then the realisation that he couldn't. She was a member of the Ravenstrike family now.

"Captain," he said, his face finally settling into an expression like he'd tasted something sour. "Welcome home."

"Thank you, General," she said, and gave Arken a brief nod.

"This isn't the place for your report," Lerin barked. "I'll debrief you first thing in the morning after drill, and we'll discuss your new duties," he said. "Don't be late."

"Yes, sir. I'll be there."

"Good." He nodded again, striding off without another word, effectively dismissing her from his presence.

Arya turned to Arken with a more genuine smile.

He regarded her for a moment over his glass of wine, eventually responding with an inscrutable, "Arya. It's good to have you back."

"You almost managed to sound like you meant that."

"It's certainly been different, without you here." His glance flickered to Lerin's departing back. She wondered if Arken now thought better of the man than he had. It was hard to tell.

She lowered her voice. "Have the passes been quiet?"

"When we've been able to check, the roadblocks were untouched," he said, still inscrutable.

"And everything has been well in Heathrock city?"

"Around the time you left," his emphasis on the last word let her know he wasn't happy about her not telling him where she was going, "there were some nasty killings. The culprit still hasn't been caught but there haven't been any for a few months now."

She relaxed slightly. "That's good news."

"I assume you'll be joining us at drill tomorrow morning?"

"As always." She lifted an eyebrow. "I hope your Raiders haven't gotten rusty while I was away."

"You'll see for yourself tomorrow morning." He tipped his wine glass at her and moved off, but then paused, "And I meant it, Captain, about being glad to see you back."

Surprised, she nodded. "Okay then."Arya paused a moment before following him, taking a deep breath of Heathrock-scented air.

She was home.

Chapter 29

Despite the bitter cold and dark of early morning, drill the following day was a delight. Word of Arya's return with Rorin had already spread through the ranks, and her arrival on the drill yard was greeted with a heart-warming display of whoops and whistles. They'd clearly been curious about her and Rorin being absent so long and without a real explanation, but the truth left them thrilled, and proud of their young heir and fellow captain.

Every greeting, every backslap, every warm grin and teasing jibe, it all cemented her feeling of being home. Of being exactly where she was supposed to be. And they all wanted to see her cazaix blade.

Eventually, Commander Randin appeared, and while he also gave Arya a warm greeting, he ordered them all to stop slacking and get started on drill. She dived into the training with alacrity.

After drill, she had breakfast in the castle kitchens before heading up to report to General Lerin as ordered. Essa, Darmanin, and Rorin were all still abed, so it was just her sitting amidst the bustling kitchen staff, soaking in the warmth from the cookfires and eating bite after bite of delicious food.

Peemla seemed to have an extra step of energy. She bustled from cookfire to cookfire, issuing orders to her staff, perfectly coordinating the simultaneous serving of breakfast to the warlord's family and the hungry Raiders out in the barracks.

"What?" Peemla stopped, noticing Arya watching her with a smile.

"Nothing." Arya shrugged. "I just missed you, that's all."

Instead of the smile Arya had expected, Peemla's eyes sheened with tears. "I thought you were gone, that you weren't coming back. You have no idea.

The thought of this place without all of you. It was..." Peemla shook her head, seemingly unable to get the words out.

Arya put her spoon down, trying to figure out what to say.

Fortunately, she was saved by the arrival of Magen, the warlord's chief adviser. Peemla cleared her throat and turned to one of the cookfires as Arya shifted her attention to him. "Hello, Magen."

"Arya!" he greeted her. "We didn't have a chance to speak last night, but welcome home."

"What brings you down here?"

"The promise of Peemla's fresh baked bread?" He shot a hopeful look in the chamberlain's direction. "And a summons from the warlord. She'd like to see you right away."

Arya rose immediately. "Understood, thanks Magen. Peemla?" She waited until the woman turned around. "I wouldn't want to be here without you, either."

The smile on the chamberlain's face was blinding.

***

The warlord looked up from scribbling on a piece of parchment when Arya knocked on her open door. "Come in, Arya, and close the door behind you."

Arya did as requested, then saluted, words tumbling out of her unexpectedly. "Good morning, Warlord. It feels good to be in here again, speaking with you."

Thiara looked up, surprised, but then smiled. "I'm forced to agree. Take a seat, over by the window. I'll join you in a moment, I just need to finish this message."

Arya sat, enjoying the view over the frozen lake and snow-covered trees of the forest surrounding Heathrock. The fire crackling in the hearth kept the room warm and the scent of spices and honey from a pot of her warlord's favourite tea—another Peemla special—filled the room. It wasn't long before Thiara put down her quill, left the parchment to dry, then crossed the room to join Arya.

"I informed Lerin this morning that you'll be taking over as general of Ravenstrike," Thiara said without preamble.

A silence fell. Arya had known that Thiara Ravenstrike would hold to her promise, but to have it happen. For it to be real. The joy unfolded inside her, deep and real and truer than anything she'd felt.

"I don't know what to say," she said.

An uncharacteristic smile crossed Thiara's face. "I hold to my word."

"How did he take the news?" Arya asked cautiously. If she was now general, Lerin was someone she was going to have to deal with under her command.

"I offered him his choice of battalion commander positions, but he declined." Her warlord's mouth twisted, and Arya suspected that Lerin's 'declining' hadn't been pleasant. "He has chosen to retire and return home to his brother's estate. I offered him the choice of announcing his retirement to the Heathrock Raiders himself, and again he declined."

From Arya's perspective this was an ideal outcome. She hadn't looked forward to dealing with a disgruntled and incompetent commander. But still ... it could have significant political ramifications. The general's brother, Vicelord Lerin, was among the most powerful and influential of Ravenstrike's vicelords.

Her warlord continued, "Arya, I ask that you let Lerin leave quietly in the manner that he wishes. There's no need to rub salt in the wound."

"I can do that." As much as she'd love to rub the awful man's face in her triumph over him, she didn't need to, not now. She had won. She took a deep breath, thinking through the implications. "I understand my appointment—and Lerin's retirement—will have implications for you. Is there anything I can do that will help limit those repercussions?"

"A triumphant return from running the Dreadwater with a cazaix sword in hand about does it," Thiara said. "Rorin's success will drown out any concern about Lerin in the short term. In the longer term—well, if you show yourself to be a competent and successful general, then we'll be fine. You are young, but no other State has a general carrying a cazaix blade."

"I will do my best for you, Warlord," Arya swore it.

"I know you will." Thiara smiled again. "Now, it's not ideal timing, but Commander Randin has given me his retirement notice, so I need to add finding his replacement to your task list right away. After that, we leave for the State Council in two weeks. You'll come, of course, and we'll be taking a full battalion with us. That's the maximum of what any warlord is allowed to bring into Gateport. You'll need to start preparing for that immediately."

Arya took a steadying breath. So much was riding on the upcoming State Council, and now her responsibilities were greater than they'd ever been. The thrill that leaped through her at the challenge almost had her jumping out of the chair with energy. She restrained herself with an effort. "Understood. Was there anything else you needed from me right away?"

"Magen will be here shortly, and there are some things we should discuss." Even as she said it, there was a sharp knock on the door. Thiara lifted her voice to tell her chief adviser to come in. "As soon as we're done, you'll be free to get started."

"General." Magen nodded to Arya when he entered, showing in a single look that he was entirely comfortable with her appointment.

"Thank you, Magen," she said, smiling wide with gratitude.

The three sat around Thiara's council table. Arya could scarcely believe it. Here she was at a meeting with Ravenstrike's warlord and chief adviser, and she was their *general.*

It was everything she'd ever wanted.

Magen began without preamble, crisp and succinct. "General, one of the reasons your appointment may not raise the furore it normally would—aside from the Dreadwater run of course—is that heavier matters are currently occupying the warlords' minds. The impromptu Council after you left was tense. The Nightstalker is convinced there are potential Sky Lords hiding in Dunidaen and he's close to outright accusing us of actively hiding them."

The words hit Arya like a blow, reminding her with an unwanted surge of fear that being home wasn't all happiness. She couldn't put the Nightstalker off any longer. She swallowed, then looked them both in the eye and asked baldly. "But the warlords have no knowledge of any potential Sky Lords here?"

"No, of course not." Magen huffed an incredulous breath. "If they are here, they're hiding well. I personally think it's ridiculous. I know General Desomer always thought King Lucius was simply planting grounds for a future invasion, and these days I find myself agreeing with him more and more."

Thiara didn't reply, but she wouldn't look directly at Arya. "What comes next?" Arya asked the chief adviser.

"It won't appease the Nightstalker to keep sending any Shadeweaver magic-wielders we catch to Andahar. Warlords Crowtalon and Falconcrest want to capture and send every magic-wielder in Dunidaen to the Nightstalker. They fought hard for it, but the other warlords are too concerned about the precedent that would set for our sovereignty to allow it," Magen said. "For now."

"What will change their minds?" Arya asked.

"If the Nightstalker follows through on his threat to openly send his hunters across the border into Dunidaen," Thiara said flatly. "Just wait until any of them set their eyes on a wraith or shadowhound. Our seasoned Raiders were troubled enough by them when they came four years ago—the softer southern armies will wilt."

"And we have to assume he *will* send them," Magen added. "Because we've not made any conciliatory gestures beyond sending Shadeweavers, and he no longer considers that enough. He might even do more."

Arya let out a shocked breath. "You both truly believe we're facing invasion?"

"Eventually, yes," Thiara said.

"But we are alone in that view, for now," Magen added. "I believe Crowtalon and Falconcrest will convince everyone that sending all magic-wielders to Andahar will permanently deal with the issue."

Arya frowned. "While I understand how dangerous Mathas Crowtalon is to us, part of that is because he's so clever and capable. Surely, he sees the threat too?"

"I would have thought so," Thiara said. "But I wonder if he has become so preoccupied with winning the High Warlord vote that it takes up all his time and attention."

Arya looked between them. "I assume you'll be pushing for the warlords to take the idea of invasion seriously at the State Council?"

"Yes," Thiara said. "Despite my fears, I want to believe there's a solution to manage Andahar that holds off the Nightstalker permanently without going to war *or* blithely handing over our citizens to be killed. But we'll need to work together to accomplish it."

And what if that meant handing herself over to the Nightstalker? Handing *all* of them over. Years on, and it came down to that same question. Thiara caught Arya's gaze, but her look was unreadable.

Arya ignored the sick twist in her stomach and let that thought go for the moment. "My understanding is that whenever there is a High Warlord vote, the leaders of Khadini, the Icelands, and Andahar are invited to Gateport to witness the vote and formally meet Dunidaen's new leader. Will the Nightstalker come?"

If he did, it would be problematic, and that was putting it mildly. Last time Arya had been in the same room as the king of Andahar, only Rorin's quick thinking had saved her from being revealed to him. She'd never forgotten the sheer power in the pull of his magic. How she'd drowned in it. None of that would have changed despite the passage of years.

Arya had no defence against it.

Magen let out a sigh. "He formally refused the invitation. That may not mean anything, as he didn't attend the Council in which Darien was voted in as High Warlord, and our borders remain officially closed."

Arya sensed there was more he hadn't said.

"His message in response to the invitation was one word. '*No*,'" Thiara said.

"He's refusing to have anything to do with us until we address his concerns in what he considers a meaningful way," Magen said. "He will be waiting to see how the new High Warlord treats his demands, so I am confident we have some time to play with before he makes any significant moves."

"It will be my first priority if I'm successful in the vote," Thiara added. "It is dangerous to allow a foreign king to keep thinking he can treat us this way."

"I'd like to help with that," Arya said. "And for my part, I'll increase our watch on the border, with a focus on the pass and the underground road. If Andahar sends anything across the border, we'll know about it immediately. I'll also increase training, make sure the Raiders are as sharp as they can be in case the worst happens."

"We'll need your help at the Council, too," Magen said. "The other States' generals—I suspect they see the Nightstalker situation more clearly than their warlords. You can help convince them to press their warlords to do more about it."

"I can do that." She nodded.

Thiara let out a breath. "You can go for now, Arya. The three of us will meet every day until departure for the State Council. I want to make sure we're as prepared as possible."

Arya rose and saluted, leaving them to it. As she walked down the hallway outside, she spotted a clerk leaving Magen's office and sent him off with another task. He scurried away, and she stopped outside the door to the general's office, pausing there, letting the moment sink in.

When she finally opened it and stepped into what was now her office, the faint scent of Desomer's cigar smoke settled around her. Lerin hadn't changed any of the furnishings, and he didn't seem to have touched any of the books or scrolls lining the walls either. The desk chair still creaked the same way it always had when she dropped into it.

This was hers now.

Arya Nameless led an army.

And she'd done it all on her own. None of it due to carrying the bloodline of a royal house. She'd earned this for herself.

A knock came, and Arken entered. To his credit, he read the scene in a blink and saluted her, crisp and respectful. "General Ravenstrike. Congratulations."

"Thank you." She leaned against the front of her desk. "The warlord just told me that Commander Randin has given her his retirement notice. The job is yours, Commander Rosenthal."

Surprise flashed on his face.

She continued before he could say anything. "And you're far too senior now to be apprenticing to anyone, but I intend to make clear to the warlord that you're my successor, if anything happens to me."

He saluted, sharper than he ever had. "General. Thank you."

"Magen and the warlord think invasion is a realistic possibility." She held his gaze. "Which means you and I need to make sure our army is as strong as it can be. We'll be the front line of defence for Dunidaen."

He took that in without a blink. "Then you and I will make sure Andahar breaks its teeth on us if it tries to take a bite, General."

A smile spread across her face. "All right, then."

"What's first, General?" he asked.

"Planning for the State Council. The problem with giving you command of Heathrock is that you'll miss out on travelling to Gateport," she said. "I need you here while I'm gone to make sure the border stays secure."

"Understood. And I'm good with that." She got a genuine smile from him then. "I've been to Gateport before, it's not that exciting."

"Take a seat." She pushed off the desk. "We've got a lot of work to do. For a start, the warlord wants to take a whole battalion with her. Who do we leave here, and who do we bring in to fill the gaps of those coming with us?"

***

Arya headed back to her room late that night, tired from a busy day, but ebullient. She and Arken had spent hours huddled together, re-gathering the reins of the Raider army under them. Lerin hadn't done much at all, they'd discovered, but simply let Desomer's finely oiled machine continue running.

"We stop the attacks on Shadeweaver encampments at once." It was the first order she gave Arken. "And begin re-training the alert shields to deploy in the event of a breach of the border."

"Good." He nodded. "In light of what you just told me about the Night-stalker threat, I propose we expand to five alert shields."

"Do it." She frowned. "But we'll need to talk about where we're going to draw those resources from."

"I have some ideas about that too."

Already she could tell he was going to be a good second. They might never be friends, but there was respect between them, and growing trust now, too. And, if Arya was honest with herself, she thought it good that someone was there who could check her worst instincts if it came to it.

Darmanin stood outside her room—it hit Arya that this was probably the last night she'd sleep there, before moving to the general's quarters.

"Is something wrong?" she asked. He'd never come to her rooms before. "I'm sorry I didn't make it to lunch or dinner like I promised."

"Not at all." He smiled. "Congratulations, Arya. We heard the news."

"Thanks, Dar." She cocked her head, pleased at the recognition from him. "But that's not why you came by."

"I spoke to Warlord Ravenstrike this afternoon. I'm leaving tomor-row—Rorin and Essa know, and I wanted you to hear it from me."

She leaned against her door, arms crossed. "And where will you be go-ing?"

"Gateport via Crowtalon." His light grey eyes glimmered in the dim light. "I intend to visit as many vicelords as I can as I travel through Crowtalon. My father has them firmly under his thumb, of course, but I would like the opportunity to introduce myself, show them my cazaix. That way, when I succeed at being named heir, I will not be a stranger."

It was a good idea, except... "Dar, your father won't stand for you being in Crowtalon, let alone visiting his vicelords. He'll come for you again."

"He can't come for me legally anymore, and I don't intend to announce my presence. No doubt word will reach him of my visits, but I'll stay one step ahead of him."

"He will send someone to kill you."

"He will try."

Arya couldn't help but chuckle. Honestly, she pitied anyone sent to kill Darmanin these days. "All right then."

"Thank you for trusting me with this."

"Always," she said, then hesitated, her last conversation with Kulan coming back to her. She'd promised herself she'd tell Darmanin what she'd learned, that she wouldn't hold back information from him ever again. If she didn't do it now, it would be weeks before she saw him again. "If you're leaving tomorrow, then ... there's something you should know."

"What is it?" he asked with concern.

"Kulan told me something after he saw you shape change during the battle in Khadini." Arya forced herself to meet his gaze. "He said that's the magic of House Nightstalker, being able to shapeshift into a shadowhound."

"And how does Kulan know that?" Darmanin's face was expressionless.

"He's spent a large part of his life living among the Andahari at Taskari. He knows more about Sky Lords than we do." When Darmanin didn't say anything, Arya forged ahead. "Look, Dar, even if you are related to the Nightstalker some way, that doesn't mean anything. Not to me, anyway. You're still Darmanin Crowtalon. You're still you."

"My mother must have been..." He trailed off.

"The Nightstalker's daughter," she said softly. "Or maybe not. Kulan implied the Sky Lord Houses were large, and that anyone carrying their bloodline had the potential to be born as a Sky Lord after one died."

"Yes, but the way Ranier described her to you..."

"Yes, I know. My question is, your father hates magic-wielders. Surely, he'd never have willingly married one?"

"Maybe he found out after they were married. Maybe that's why he..."

Arya shifted forward, touching his arm. "I'm so sorry, Dar."

A muscle ticked in his jaw. "You're right, it doesn't matter. None of it does."

She saw the denial in his face and voice, and wanted to let him keep it, but she couldn't anymore. "I promised Essa we'd come up with a real plan, something more than just hoping the Nightstalker goes away. You are part of that, Dar."

"You said when we returned that you and Rorin and Essa were the future of Ravenstrike." Darmanin shifted closer, intensity vibrating from him. "The four of us are the future of *Dunidaen*, Arya, not Andahar. Never forget that."

She didn't look away from his gaze. "The warlord thinks invasion is coming."

"Then we'll destroy the Nightstalker here, on *our* ground. And then we never have to worry about him again."

She shook her head. "I want a plan that avoids war."

"That isn't going to be possible," he said quietly. "You already know that, deep down. So does Essa."

"I'm going to try anyway."

"Then try." He gave her his little smile. "You and Essa plan. And when I see you in Gateport, I will support whatever you want to do."

"Thank you, Dar."

"Farewell, Arya. For now."

***

The following morning, when Arya stepped into the drill yard, all the Heathrock Raiders were waiting. They stood in shield formation, Arken just off to the side. Even those on guard at the walls who were in sight of the drill yards were faced inwards.

When she stopped in surprise, Arken gave a nod and every Raider there snapped out a salute. Laskin stood at the front of his shield, Derrin and his shield beside them. Both men were barely holding back smiles.

"Good morning, General Ravenstrike." Arken addressed her formally, voice carrying across the open space. "We wanted to put our best foot forward on your first day and welcome you as a group. Show you that we're ready for whatever you ask of us."

He'd thrown his support behind her. He'd dragged them all out of bed and onto the drill yard extra early so he could show that the Heathrock Raiders fully supported their new general.

"Commander Rosenthal." She couldn't keep the warmth from her voice, letting it carry through the yard like Arken had. "I honestly couldn't be prouder of any group of men and women, and I wouldn't exchange any one of you. Shall we get started together?"

"Aye, General." The roar ripped out, unanimous, filled with enthusiasm.

Arya Ravenstrike grinned, alight with their support, their respect for her. This was *her* army now.

Let the Nightstalker come.

Chapter 30

An hour later, Arya dodged between two restive horses and then ducked under a saddlebag being tossed across the yard. Individual shields were rotating through the Heathrock entry yard, packing supplies, and making sure their mounts were properly shod and their tack didn't need any repairs. As soon as one shield finished, another moved in.

Arken had them drilling for the State Council departure, wanting the battalion escorting their warlord to be as sharp as possible. More shields would arrive in coming days to bolster the Heathrock forces while they were gone, and room was being made for them too.

It was a noble intention but meant that things were currently chaotic.

Arya reached the front gates where Darmanin stood by his horse, securing his saddlebags. The others had already made their farewells, but Arya had been busy arguing with the blacksmith over how many new blades they needed.

When he spotted her approach, he straightened, pleasure shining from those eerie grey eyes of his. "I'm glad I didn't miss saying goodbye to you, Arya."

"It won't be long. I'll see you soon enough in Gateport." She paused, trying to fight back a flare of worry. "You be careful, Dar."

"I've told you before, Arya Ravenstrike. You don't need to worry about me," he said.

"Yes, well, even so," she said.

"I'll see you in Gateport." He swung up into the saddle and rode through the gates.

Tempted by a sudden urge, she instinctively tugged on that thread between them. It wasn't a firm pull, not like that night when she'd desperately been trying to stop him from killing his father. This was a feather-light touch, a little tremble along the line that joined their magic.

He turned, too far for her to see the expression on his face as he glanced back at her. But she felt a returning tug then, just as soft, and it made her smile. She watched until he was out of sight, then turned away and surveyed the chaos of the yard with a sigh.

Why had she thought being general of Ravenstrike was a good idea?

Arya weaved back through the courtyard and up the castle steps. Rorin and Essa were standing not far from the entrance, deep in conversation as Arya entered. Both looked up, their conversation abruptly cutting off.

"*Has Darmanin gone?*" Rorin asked.

"He just rode out."

"*I worry about him.*"

"He will be fine," Arya said, even though deep down she held the same concerns.

"He will," Essa agreed. "I'd better leave you both. Magen is expecting me."

Rorin's gaze followed Essa as she left, and Arya nudged him. "What's the secret?"

"*What?*" he asked, startled.

"You two were huddled together talking very intensely when I came over," she said.

He shrugged. "*Oh, that was nothing.*"

Arya frowned. Rorin very rarely lied to her, but when he did, she usually caught it. He wasn't a very good liar. "Rorin, you know that if there's a problem, you can trust me with it? Both of you can."

"*Of course, I know that!*" He smiled widely. "*But right now, I'm off to the kitchens to sneak some of Peemla's cookies. I'll see you later, Arya.*"

"General?" Captain Danil stood nearby, obviously with bad news. "I have word from the blacksmith."

"What is it?" she snapped, irritated by the interruption.

"If we want new blades before departure, he's not going to have time to also shoe all the horses that need it."

"Raven's balls, that man is going to be the death of me!" she muttered. "All right, Captain, I'll deal with it."

"Yes, General," he hesitated. "My shield won't be able to finish preparations until our horses are—"

"Shod, yes I know, Captain. I said I'll deal with it."

"General!" Danil saluted and then strode off.

Heaving an irritated sigh, Arya reined in her temper and went looking for the blasted blacksmith.

****

The night before their departure for Gateport, Laskin appeared in Arya's office door. She and Arken were huddled at the table by the window, as they had been all day, making sure things were ready. A part of her yearned for a quiet evening, her and General Desomer, playing his stones' strategy game.

A pang of loss went through her. She'd summoned her courage and ridden out to visit the general that morning—the warlord had gifted him a comfortable home and staff in Heathrock city. But she'd arrived there only to find him gone, apparently visiting family elsewhere in Ravenstrike. From there she'd gone to The Ruined Arms, but neither Tiya nor her stepfather had returned. The inn looked shabbier than the last time she'd been there, the ale not as good, fewer customers in the main room. It had only deepened her melancholy over finding Desomer gone.

Wherever she was, Arya hoped Tiya was safe and well.

Laskin's knock startled her from her thoughts. "Warlord wants to see you, General." He cleared his throat. "In her private quarters."

This time when Arya stepped into Thiara Ravenstrike's sitting room, Ranier was already there, standing by the fire. The urge to draw her new sword was still there, but this time she swallowed the impulse. She was a general now. Besides, she had a lot of remaining questions about Ranier and his relationship to her warlord.

"This is an unsettlingly familiar scene," she muttered. "We're not about to attempt more dangerously difficult challenges, are we, Warlord?"

Thiara smiled slightly, but her reply was forestalled by Essa's entrance.

Ranier's gaze went straight to his daughter, and though he did not make any move towards her, he said quietly, "I almost gave up on you."

Essa arched an eyebrow. "Almost?"

He shifted his gaze to Arya. "You did well, to get them all out alive."

"I can't take credit for that," Arya said. "In fact, it was Essa who got us out of a particularly difficult situation."

Ranier pushed off the mantle. "I offer thanks, Warlord, for allowing me to see my daughter arrived safely home."

"And in return?"

"I will keep to your ... amended timeline as regards to Rorin's departure for Khadini. I will also tell you that the attack on your son and general last year was not a Shadeweaver contract killing. Leanir acted unilaterally."

"And how can I be sure he will not come for my family again?" the warlord demanded.

"You can't, but you can be sure any further attacks won't be at my behest. I am sending Leanir away, to Gateport," he said, his gaze shifting to Arya as he spoke. "An associate there recently passed away, and I needed a replacement to fill her spot." After a moment, Ranier turned back to Thiara and bowed his head. "All agreements between us are now at an end. It is unlikely we shall see each other again."

"For the best, I'm sure." Thiara nodded. "Goodbye, Ranier."

"Hold up!" Arya acted on instinct, stepping between Ranier and the door. "I have questions before you wander off never to be seen again."

"Yet you have no payment for the answers." Ranier said.

"That ruthless mercenary act doesn't work on me as well as it used to." Arya crossed her arms over her chest. "Warlord, I assume you know Ranier is Andahari, from one of their Sky Lord Houses. Inkweaver, to be exact."

Ranier stood dangerously still, which made Arya almost reach for her weapon. Only her fierce desire not to show her fear stopped her. Essa turned watchful, her gaze fixedly on her father's.

Thiara's expressionless mask was impressive, but at her side the fingers of her left hand twitched. "I know that Ranier is not a Sky Lord, and therefore not one of those that the Nightstalker hunts, if that is what you're getting at, Arya. He has no magic."

And how did Thiara know that? It was Arya's hesitation to confront her warlord that gave Ranier the moment he needed. "Whatever I may have been in the past," Ranier said. "I am now no more and no less than the leader of the Shadeweavers. Something you should keep in mind when considering tangling with me, girl."

"What is going on here, really?" Arya questioned, turning to Thiara.

"Ranier and I met once, in the past." Thiara said. "Do not mistake us for friends or even allies, Arya, but we have, on occasion, had shared goals. That ends now. I swear it."

"As do I." Ranier gave a sharp nod and left, drawing his hood up over his head.

Arya hesitated, glancing at Essa, then straightening her shoulders in resolve. "Warlord, we need to talk about the Nightstalker, about what you said that time—"

"You are dismissed." Thiara Ravenstrike's voice was ice-cold, the look on her face uncompromising. "That's an order, General."

Arya didn't dare push her. So, she followed Essa out the door.

"She wasn't surprised," Essa said immediately.

"What?" Arya asked, distracted by her thoughts.

"The warlord. She wasn't surprised when you announced Ranier's identity. Shocked that we knew, yes, scrambling to figure out what to say, but not surprised."

"I know." She let out a sigh, rubbed at suddenly aching temples.

"What does she know about us, Arya?"

"You heard her back there. She won't talk about it."

Essa stopped in front of her, forcing her to stop too. "What's the plan?"

Arya took a breath. She *had* been thinking on this, in the occasional spare minute she wasn't busy with her new role. "We go to the State Council, we make Rorin and Darmanin heirs and Rorin's mother High Warlord."

"You're putting it off again," Essa cut over her.

"No, I'm not, I swear. Essa, we can't make plans while everything is in flux. Once the leadership of Dunidaen is settled, then we can start preparing for invasion. Our goals align for now. Making Thiara High Warlord is the first step in dealing with the Nightstalker."

"Invasion?" Essa stared at her. "What about *preventing* a war? What about the nazal that was hunting the streets of Heathrock before we left, that followed us into Khadini?"

"I will protect you."

"How?"

Arya's jaw clenched. "What else do you expect me to do? If we cross into Andahar now, claim our heritage and fight the Nightstalker, that *is* war. Worse, it's a war we can't win. And unless we hand ourselves over, the Nightstalker will come for us, which means war in Dunidaen. At least here we are on home ground, we have a chance of winning, of destroying him for good."

"You've been listening to Darmanin." Essa's words were short, clipped. "You're both so fiercely in denial about this whole thing you think it can be solved by just doing what you want anyway."

"What do you want me to do, Essa?" Arya threw her hands in the air. "Tell me what the solution is to avoid war and my closest friends and family being killed, and I'll do it."

Silence fell between them, filling the empty space with its weight.

"You are the one with uncanny strategic instincts, trained by a master general," Essa snapped. "What will *you* do when a nazal comes for us?"

"You want my uncanny instincts?" Arya snapped right back. "They tell me to *hide* from the nazal, Essa, to avoid a fight Salyarin and Ranier believe we can't win. *That* is what will keep us safe. Wearing our cazaix and not touching our magic."

"Hiding is not a plan."

"It's the best one I've got." Arya said.

"What about doing what Salyarin says, going to the Etherean and learning our magic so we—"

Arya shook her head. "The Nightstalker killed four fully trained Sky Lords and every potential born since. We need more than our magic to fight these creatures, to fight the Nightstalker. We need Dunidaen's army. And we don't have that unless Thiara Ravenstrike is High Warlord."

Arya only realised as she threw out the words how true they were. That had to be their plan. It didn't give her any relief though; it only filled her with dread.

Essa crumpled. "I don't want war."

"The only way to avoid it is for all five of us to march across the Diamond-fang and give ourselves up to be killed. That is the *only* thing that will hold the Nightstalker at bay."

Essa nodded, hand over her mouth.

"If it were just me, I would do it, Ess. But he won't be satisfied with just me. He wants all of us." Arya said. "And I'm too selfish to sacrifice any of you, not even if it stops war. That's the bald truth."

Essa stepped forward and Arya wrapped her arms around the woman's smaller frame. They didn't say anything, just stood there together in silent understanding. But eventually Essa let go, turning and leaving without a word.

Arya watched her go, heart heavy. Maybe with time, she could think up something better. Maybe they could do it together.

But she had a sinking feeling war was inevitable. And she didn't want it any more than Essa did. As much as Arya loved her Raiders, loved the swing of a sword in her hand, war meant death. And pain. And suffering.

And she didn't want that for her home or her family.

Chapter 31

Thiara Ravenstrike and her retinue departed Heathrock on schedule. Travelling were all members of the Ravenstrike family, Arya's battalion of two hundred Raiders, Peemla and a handful of staff. As well as Magen and Essa and his clerks.

Morale was high among the battalion, and Arya used that to her advantage. Each day she rode with a different shield, taking them away from the main column and drilling them in battlefield manoeuvres. She learned how they operated together and identified the weak points. Then she pushed them to get better, eventually drawing in more and more shields to practice larger manoeuvres.

She was acutely aware that her strength and experience lay in leading individual shields. Her strategic training with Desomer had been cut short, and while she'd absorbed all the theory he'd taught her, she'd yet to have a chance to put it into practice.

That was okay. She'd focus on improving those skills. Dunidaen might find itself at war, but Arya was determined that she and Arken would have the Raider army ready if that happened.

Spending so much time away from the main column meant she didn't see much of Rorin, Taze, and Essa, and after all they'd been through in Khadini she found herself constantly checking for their presence, wanting to make sure they were safe and well. Something inside her always relaxed when she returned to camp each night and saw them. Her thoughts were frequently with Darmanin, too, hoping he was staying safe in Crowtalon.

The weather grew warmer as they travelled south, which made things easier, and a competitive spirit infected each shield as they strained to be the best of the battalion.

"General Desomer once told me that an army often takes on the characteristics of its leader," Thiara Ravenstrike commented one evening as Arya returned from a training exercise and reported in.

"He told me the same thing, Warlord."

"His army was steady, deliberate, and well-trained," Thiara said. "Yours is already showing signs of being flashier, sharper, *and* more confident."

Arya nodded, not sure where the warlord was going.

"Don't let the confidence become cockiness, Arya. We need a skilled, capable force, not one that will cause us embarrassment." Thiara let those words sink in while Arya did her best not to bristle, understanding that this was a test. "I have made you my general, but you are still young and have little experience. We reach Gateport tomorrow, and I will keep you on a short leash."

Arya bowed her head. "I understand, Warlord. I won't let you down."

Leaving the warlord, she searched for Rorin and Essa. She found the latter at one of the campfires shared by Magen's clerks, deep in conversation. Arya offered a wave but left her to it. Rorin wasn't in his tent, but she eventually found him with the small group of household staff Peemla had brought. They were dancing near their fire, one of the cooks playing a merry tune on a flute. Arya was tempted to join them.

"General?"

She turned at Laskin's approach. She'd left Derrin and Arken's alert shields at Heathrock, bringing the least experienced shields with her, wanting her home kept safe while she was away. Bringing Laskin had been one of only two indulgences she'd allowed herself. The other was reforming his shield so that it contained the volunteers who'd gone with him to wait for her and Rorin at the Dreadwater Gate. She still thought of them as her shield, even though she never said that aloud.

"Laskin. Everything all right?"

"One of the horses is sick. I worry it might be infectious, so I've ordered it be separated from the rest. That okay with you?"

"You don't need my approval for that. What did you really come to ask me?"

He cleared his throat. "I was just wondering if you'd noticed that situation." He gestured towards the laughing and singing staff, Rorin among them, dancing with Peemla.

"Rorin enjoying himself is a situation?"

"It's going to be," Laskin said. "Best go see to that horse. See you in the morning, General."

***

Gateport, the capital city of Dunidaen, was positioned between Eaglesoar and Crowtalon States but belonged to neither. For a twenty-mile radius out from the city centre, the land was neutral and fell under the control of the High Warlord of Dunidaen and his ceremonial guard force, the Defenders.

Arya let out a long whistle when she got her first sight of it.

It was an enormous city sitting at the mouth of a long, narrow bay crowded with merchant shipping. Encircled by two concentric stone walls—one that surrounded a rise in the centre of the city, and the second an outer wall, the only un-walled area was where the southern end of the city sprawled along the harbour. To the north and west were rolling plains of emerald farmland, and to the east the sunlit woods of Eaglesoar.

They approached the city along the northern road which brought them to Gateport's entry gates. Arya cantered Zeke up and down the Raider column, checking that their formation was faultless. Then she reined in beside Laskin. "If I see even one toe out of line, I'll fire you as well as the toe. Clear?"

"Crystal, General," he said with an admirably straight face.

Arya settled a final glare on him before urging Zeke back along the column, coming to a halt beside the warlord's carriage and reining in with a flourish. Rorin and Taze, riding alongside, smiled in welcome, but Rorin's mother gave her a faintly disapproving glance through the open window.

The road grew busy as they approached the gates, and it meant a substantial delay getting through as the High Warlord's Defenders—who also functioned as city guards—conducted a cursory check of everyone passing through.

The warlord gestured for Arya's attention once they were through. "I'll take Rorin's shield with us. They can alternate shifts with my personal shield to guard the residence while we're here. Take the remainder of your battalion to the designated Raider barracks, and then come and find me at the residence please," Thiara said, then gave a quick series of directions.

"Yes, Warlord." Arya reined in as Thiara's carriage rolled on, those of her staff and advisers following, then repeated the instructions she'd been given to the residence, trying to set them in her memory. But first she had to find the Raider barracks. Thiara hadn't thought to mention where those were.

"General?" Laskin brought his horse over. "One of the Defenders just told me where to find the barracks we've been assigned."

"Thank everything for you, Laskin," she said. "Please lead on."

The streets were thronged with people. It was a bustling city, and on a much greater scale than Heathrock. Vendors shouted their wares from street corners, and inn staff stood along the pavement, promising the best ale or lamb pie in Dunidaen inside their premises. On top of this, horses neighed, people talked, laughed, and shouted to each other, birds squawked, and dogs barked.

The pungent smells of the city were almost as chaotic as the noise. The scent of baking bread mixed with brewing ale, cooked and uncooked meat, and various ripe fruits and vegetables spread on the air. Layered under that was the faint tang of sewage and stale smoke. The final undercurrent was a hint of salt and seaweed in the faint breeze.

She loved every bit of it.

The energy of the city made Arya feel like she could take on the world. Citizens stood aside respectfully for the column of two hundred Raiders, and Arya kept them to a walk, so they wouldn't risk an accident.

Eventually, when her faith in Laskin's navigational abilities was beginning to waver, they arrived outside a stone-walled compound. The flag of Ravenstrike hung from the entrance gates to welcome them. They weren't far from the harbour and the salty scent of ocean and seaweed was stronger here. While the air wasn't as humid as Khadini, it was warmer than Heathrock, even though spring was still a few weeks away.

Arya rode through first, Zeke's hooves clattering into a cobblestone yard. Stables stood directly to her right, barracks to her left, and directly ahead were what looked like a mess hall and privies, sizeable enough to hold her two hundred Raiders comfortably.

"Laskin, Rarik?" She got their attention. "You're in charge of dismount and settling in, as well as setting a watch. I've been ordered to report to the warlord, but I'll be back this evening."

At their salutes, she weaved Zeke back out of the gates, recalling her warlord's directions. As she rode through the bustling streets, Arya spotted the green and brown livery of the Hawkesdale Longbows, the black and violet of the Crowtalon Lances and the gold and blue Eaglesoar Knights. Their armour glinted in the afternoon sun.

To reach the Ravenstrike residence, she had to pass through the city's inner wall, where more Defenders stood guard. The streets beyond the wall were far cleaner than anything she'd seen yet, and the gardens along the pavement edges were bright and carefully maintained. She eventually arrived at a distinguished looking townhouse in a quiet street. Again, the Ravenstrike banner hung above the gated entry.

Two Raiders from Taze's shield opened the gates as soon as they saw Arya. Inside was a circular entry yard, a small bubbling fountain in the middle, the drive only just big enough for a single carriage at a time. The four-level townhouse took up most of the space, with a path leading around the side of the house to where Arya assumed the stables were.

She dismounted and handed Zeke's reins to a waiting groom before striding up the steps. A hush filled the inside of the house. The entry foyer was empty, although the coat racks near the door bristled with cloaks.

Directly opposite the front doors was an elegant, sweeping staircase, and closed doors led away to her left and right.

Shrugging, Arya headed up the stairs, her boots echoing on the marble flooring. On reaching the top, she paused, when Peemla appeared. "Hello, Arya. She's in her office—just down the hall and around to the right."

"A saviour as always, Peemla." Arya swept into a graceful bow, making the woman blush—exactly as she'd intended—before following her directions.

The warlord's office took up a large part of the second floor, with arched windows that looked over the street and a fireplace that was only just coming to life. On one side of the room, Magen and some of his clerks, including Essa, were busy planning something or other. Thiara sat behind her desk, writing furiously.

"Warlord." Arya stopped and saluted. "The Raiders are settled in the barracks. What do you need from me?"

"For now, nothing." Thiara looked up, distracted. "Keep the battalion drilled and sharp, and—of utmost importance—well behaved. I will not have tales of undisciplined Raiders in their off duty hours undermining my work here."

"Understood, Warlord."

"The Council officially starts in three days. Between the formal sessions there will be dinners, receptions, social events. I will require you at some of those—especially where the other generals will be present. Magen's people will keep you informed of where you need to be and when. Outside that, your time is your own." Thiara finally looked up. "It would be nice if you could make family dinners."

"I'll be wherever you need me," Arya promised. Even the thought of painful small talk at social events where everybody would be talking politics didn't deter her. She owed her warlord so much; she was determined to be the general Thiara Ravenstrike needed, no matter how tedious or uncomfortable.

Footsteps sounded outside and Peemla knocked a moment later. "Warlord, I have Lord Andrian Crowtalon and Darmanin for you?"

Arya spun in surprise, relief filling her at the sight of Darmanin entering at his brother's side, safe and well. He gave her a nod, then a wave at Essa across the room.

"Warlord." Andrian bowed respectfully, an easy smile crossing his face. "It is a pleasure to see you. When we heard you'd arrived in Gateport, my brother wanted to come immediately, and I hope you don't mind that I joined him."

"Lord Andrian, not at all. And it's good to see you, Darmanin." Thiara stood, her tone also formal but respectful. "Do I take this to mean your father is in Gateport?"

"We arrived two days ago." Andrian nodded. "For now, he is unaware that Darmanin is here."

Arya regarded Andrian thoughtfully. Darmanin obviously trusted his brother enough to tell him he'd arrived in Gateport, and that was telling. Darmanin trusted so few.

"Darmanin, where are you staying?" Thiara asked the question burning in Arya's mind.

"With one of our vicelords," Darmanin replied. "He is no great supporter of our father's, and I am safe enough there."

"We won't take up any more of your time." Andrian spoke. "But Arya, I hope you and Lord Rorin would be willing to join us in exploring the city. We're at your disposal, so just let us know a time that suits you."

"I'd like that." Arya tried not to sound too eager in front of her warlord.

"Lord Andrian, I'd be pleased if you and Darmanin dined with us while we're here," Thiara said crisply. "I'll send a servant with a formal invite."

"That would be a pleasure. Until then." Andrian bowed and left, Darmanin with him.

When Arya turned back to her warlord, the woman's smile had widened, and that steely determination flashed in her eyes. "It's time, Arya."

She knew exactly what Thiara meant.

Time to make Darmanin the Crowtalon heir and strike a powerful blow against Mathas Crowtalon. Time to make Ravenstrike's future secure in

Rorin's hands. Time for Thiara Ravenstrike to be voted High Warlord of Dunidaen.

Arya matched that wolfish smile. "I can't wait, Warlord."

Chapter 32

Two days later, on the eve of the formal opening of the State Council, after drill with her battalion, Arya rode to the Ravenstrike townhouse. She was supposed to meet Rorin and Essa there before joining Andrian and Darmanin in the city for an early lunch. But neither were waiting out front.

Arya went inside, but she'd barely reached the top of the magnificent staircase when the slamming of a door echoed through the house. Moments later, Rorin stormed around the corner, almost colliding with her. His features were tight with anger, something she'd rarely seen before. "What's going on?" she asked in astonishment.

"*Arya!*" He halted his onrush and tried a smile. "*Perfect timing, I need to get out of here. Let's go.*"

"What's got you so riled?"

He made a face. "*I just want to get out of the house and see Dar.*"

"And what about Essa?"

"*She knows we were supposed to meet, she's probably in the stables already. Come on,*" he urged, and set off down the stairs.

Swallowing her irritation at his high-handed tone—something was clearly upsetting him, but it wasn't her—Arya followed. Rorin pushed open the front doors and called one of the grooms to bring their horses.

She cleared her throat. "Where's Taze?"

"*You can protect me, surely?*" Rorin gave her a winning smile. "*After all, you are the general of my army.*"

"I'm the general of your mother's army, Rorin." Arya waved over Charlin, on guard at the front gates. "Where's Captain Nameless?"

"Doing a patrol of the grounds, I believe, General."

"Go and get him, please, and tell the grooms to bring out his horse as well."

"*Arya, come on*," Rorin urged her.

"You know you have to bring Taze with you, so why are you fighting me on this?" she said, trying not to be irritated. Taze appeared a moment later, looking surprised.

"I'm sorry, Rorin, I didn't realise you were leaving already. The shield won't be long in gathering."

"He's in a strange mood," Arya said to her Raider. "Any idea why?"

Taze shrugged. "Not a clue."

Essa's voice called out as she rounded the corner of the house with her horse. "Oh good, you're all here. The grooms are bringing your horses, and your shield is on its way, Taze."

Essa seemed to pick up on the odd tension, because she sent Rorin and Arya a puzzled glance. Rorin ignored her, and Arya gave a helpless shrug. The horses were led out moments later and the three of them mounted and rode out. In silent agreement, Taze and Essa hung back to give Arya a chance to talk to Rorin. "So why were you slamming doors and ranting about the place?" she asked him.

"*My mother's tendency to make absolute and final decisions, and then refuse to discuss them, irritates me.*"

"She's a warlord. That's what she's supposed to do."

"*You're as bad as she is.*" Rorin's signing was sharp with frustration. "*You both think your view of things is the right one and refuse to consider anything else. Look, Arya, I don't want to argue. Let's just go and have some fun.*"

"Okay." She lifted her hands in the air in mock surrender. Rorin was genuinely angry, and they'd only end up in a fight if she pushed it, so instead she let the matter drop.

For now.

Rorin in a mood like this was the last thing he needed if he wanted to be confirmed heir, so she'd have to get to the bottom of it sooner rather than later.

***

Later that evening, Arya sat comfortably in a booth, which had grown from the initial five of them to include a handful of Hawkesdale Longbows Rorin and Darmanin knew from their fostering in Hawkesdale. Andrian sat on one side of her, Rorin on the other. It was warm and cosy and her head was growing fuzzy from the delicious mugs of mead Andrian kept supplying them with.

As she finished her mug, resolving that it would be her last, Andrian turned towards her, warm smile on his handsome face, voice lowering. "Tell, how is Arya Nameless these days? You've come a long way since we first met."

"Arya Ravenstrike is doing great." She chuckled. "And Andrian Crowtalon?"

"Glad beyond belief to be out of Crowtalon and able to spend some time with my brother. It's no easy thing living in a draughty old castle with my father's attention constantly on me, constantly disapproving." He winked flirtatiously. "But that's boring talk. I have to say, Arya, that you're even more stunning these days than you were when I met you."

"Is that so?" she asked dryly.

He smiled and leaned closer. She gave him a little shake of her head. "That's a polite but firm no, Andrian." She was flattered, but uninterested in tangling with the son of Warlord Crowtalon and all those potential implications.

"Let me know if you ever change your mind." He smiled in capitulation, and shifted away. "Standing offer."

Rorin and Essa were grinning at a joke that had just been told by one of the Longbows, while Taze stood behind his charge, scanning the crowd for danger. His shield was arrayed between the exits, a discreet but watchful presence. Darmanin sat on Rorin's other side. He'd been reserved and quiet all afternoon. She hoped whatever was bothering Rorin hadn't affected him too.

The inn door opened, and a group of sky-blue cloaked Falconcrest Aggressors entered. From their stumbling gait and loud voices, they'd obviously already been drinking somewhere else. They cast their gazes around the full inn, and one of them straightened and pointed when they saw Rorin and his party. All of them sharpened then, and she wondered how drunk they actually were.

This wasn't good.

Essa's gaze landed on Arya's, warning written in it, but Darmanin moved before Arya could respond. "Let's make a move." He stood. "The Council opening is tomorrow morning, and we should get our rest."

"*The night is still young,*" Rorin protested, already onto his fifth mug.

"I don't think your mother will appreciate you attending the first meeting of the State Council with a hangover, Rorin," Darmanin said pointedly.

"*I'm not feeling particularly well disposed towards my mother at the moment Dar, so don't pull that card with me.*"

Darmanin shot Arya and Essa a questioning glance, but they both shrugged. Rorin's angry mood from earlier hadn't faded. If anything, it had gotten worse. Arya glanced back at the Aggressors. They'd gathered around a table near the door, but were frequently glancing in Rorin's direction. It hadn't escaped Arya that Falconcrest was Crowtalon's closest ally. Something told her these Aggressors weren't here by chance.

"Is there a back way out?" she asked Taze.

"Asked when we arrived." He shook his head. "Innkeeper won't let bar customers through the back."

Arya swung around to Rorin. The sooner they left, the better. "Rorin, I must be up at dawn for drill tomorrow. So does Taze and his shield." She tried a different tack. "Give us a break."

"I'd like to go too," Essa added, finishing her mug. "SparrowWing and Crowtalon are having a spat over the taxes SparrowWing is charging to store goods in transit through Seelan. Magen wants me to draft up some ways we could take advantage of the dispute by tomorrow."

"*You all go then. Andrian and I will stay here and have some real fun.*"

Arya sighed. "Rorin, let's go."

"You cannot order me around, Arya. Do as you wish, but I'm staying."

Arya's temper—which she thought had held up admirably— snapped. "I am general of Ravenstrike, Rorin. Since you aren't even confirmed as heir yet, and certainly won't be if you keep up this behaviour, I damn well can order you around. Now get off your ass. We're leaving."

At Arya's tone, Taze snapped to attention and began signalling his shield for departure. Rorin flushed a deep red, jaw clenching. He purposely took his time draining his mug, then stood, and slid insolently out of the booth. Darmanin and Essa kept their heads down and filed out after him. Their Raider escort closed around them.

To get out, they had to pass the Aggressors near the door. They were laughing and whispering, and one of them spoke loudly as they approached. "You're right, Nathy, there's no way I'd want to ride into battle with a mute leading me."

Rorin bristled. Arya swore under her breath. Taze tried to move between Rorin and the Aggressors, but Rorin pushed him out of the way, fingers flickering as he challenged the Aggressor.

The man grinned. "Sorry, I can't hear you. Maybe you should try speaking up." His gaze shifted to Arya, then he sneered, "A woman general. What happens when you break a nail amid battle? Do you drop your sword and start crying?"

"Rorin!" Both Andrian and Darmanin shouted a warning, but Rorin was already launching himself at the Aggressor, knocking him back off his chair and landing a solid punch on his jaw. Rorin raised his fist to land another punch. By then, though, the other Aggressors were responding. Two of them grabbed Rorin by the arms and dragged him off their companion.

The sight of anyone with hands on Rorin had Arya's temper imploding and with it the surge of magic wanting to escape.

She and Taze dived in.

By then Rorin had shaken one Aggressor loose and launched himself at the second, sending them crashing to the floor. Arya shouldered into another Aggressor before he could try and drag Rorin off, and with angry shouts, the remaining Aggressors joined in.

Arya ducked a flying punch, came up under the man's guard and sucker-punched him in the ribs. This left her wide open for a moment, however, and she collected a solid hit to the side. Cursing with pain, she lashed out at her attacker, catching him on the jaw. He staggered back, and behind him she saw her Raiders enthusiastically joining the fight to help their heir and general. The Longbows dived into too, whooping with glee.

Arya swore. This was bad. This was very, very, bad.

But it was also out of control, and there was no stopping it. Within moments, the inn was a mass of bodies punching and kicking and wrestling on the floor. Arya focused on keeping Rorin safe. She took another hit in the jaw, and another to her gut, but dealt out just as much punishment before someone shouted a warning that the Defenders were coming. The fighters scattered and suddenly the fight was over, the inn emptying in a blink.

Arya looked up from the fight, breathing hard but filled with an energetic glee. Her magic roiled inside her until she shoved it down and out of sight. Rorin stood nearby with a bloodied lip but otherwise unharmed, Taze and his shield close around him. With a single gesture from her, they all stumbled out onto the street.

Essa watched from the other side of the road—arms crossed over her chest, thoroughly disapproving. She looked Rorin up and down. "Are you okay?"

"*I'm fine,*" he signed, then rounded angrily on Arya. "*I don't know why you kept pulling me out. I was holding my own.*"

She rolled her eyes. Hard. "It's like you've forgotten who I am and what my job is."

Andrian appeared, breathing hard, a bruise forming under his left eye. Darmanin was at his side, unharmed. "Arya, you should go. Defenders are only a block away."

She nodded. "See you at Council tomorrow?"

He grinned, sketched a wave. "See you then."

"What are the chances Rorin's mother hears about this?" Arya muttered to Taze as the shield closed around Rorin and they headed to the public stables where they'd left their horses.

Taze winced. "Depends on what the innkeeper tells the Defenders."

"I doubt it will be the innkeeper," Arya muttered. "That was a set up." She sighed. "This isn't good. This isn't good at all."

Chapter 33

Arya woke early and joined her Raiders for drill, anxious about the opening of the State Council later in the morning and the fallout from the events of the night before. Murder seemed like the best-case scenario if Thiara Ravenstrike learned Arya had let Rorin start a brawl. And underneath all that was worry about what had caused Rorin to act like he had—it was completely unlike him.

She was going to have to tell her warlord what had happened, which she looked forward to about as much as having a rotten tooth extracted.

Darmanin appeared at the barracks just as drill was wrapping up. As soon as she saw him, she roared, "Enemy at the gate!"

Immediately, the shield closest to the gates wheeled their horses and hurtled towards Darmanin. With skill born of endless practice, they surrounded Darmanin in seconds and levelled their drawn swords at his head. At the same time, the shield on watch duty turned the winch holding the front gates, closing them with a reverberating clang. Soon after, the walls either side of the gate were lined with Raider archers, bows drawn and ready to fire.

Darmanin, in the seconds before he was surrounded, had dropped to a crouch and drawn his sword. The cazaix glittered in the morning light, and Arya could tell her Raiders were impressed by his quickness, though they didn't back off.

"Good work," she told them. "You reacted swiftly and effectively. Drill is done for today. See to your horses then breakfast in the mess."

Hooves clattered as her Raiders broke the circle, and metal screeched as the front gates were raised again.

"They look sharp," Darmanin noted as he sheathed his sword.

"They were already good. Desomer was an excellent general," she said. "I'm just adding a few personal tweaks."

"Like the ability to react to unexpected situations just as effectively as in planned battle," Darmanin said.

Arya gave him a pleased smile. It was rare that somebody was able to read her intentions so clearly. "What brings you here this morning?"

"Two reasons." He glanced around, lowering his voice. "Chiarn is in Gateport."

She stiffened. "How do you know?"

"One of the Longbows mentioned it last night. He's playing at The Rotting Log." Darmanin continued before she could reply, "I came to tell you because I knew you'd eventually hear about it anyway, but I think you should leave him alone. It's bad enough we're all in one place for the duration of the State Council."

Arya frowned in puzzlement, then remembered that Ranier had sent Leanir to Gateport weeks ago. "Thanks for telling me. You're probably right about leaving him alone. The less we have to do with each other, the safer he'll be while this nazal is hunting."

"So leave him alone," Darmanin said.

She chuckled at his serious expression. "What else did you want to talk about?"

"Rorin—what's happened to put him in that mood?"

Arya gave a helpless shrug. "He seemed fine on the journey from Heathrock, so I don't know what's gotten into him."

"I don't think those Aggressors were there by accident last night, Arya."

"And Rorin played right into their hands."

Darmanin frowned. "You should talk to him. This is the worst time for him to be throwing tantrums. All of our plans rely on Rorin being confirmed heir."

"Don't take that high-handed tone with me, Darmanin," she warned. "Besides, you're his brother in everything but blood. Have *you* tried talking to him? Maybe it's something he can't talk to me about. Maybe he's having romance trouble."

She'd been mostly joking, but Darmanin looked distinctly uncomfortable about that possibility, and Arya couldn't help but chuckle. Ever since she'd met the Crowtalon son, he'd been reserved almost to the point of coldness. It was obvious he didn't like the idea of discussing emotions, even with his best friend. "I'll try," he said eventually.

"Good. Let me know how it goes. Now, the State Council is opening in an hour, so I need to go and pull on my gaudiest uniform."

***

The State Council building was the centrepiece of the inner circle of Gateport; a high domed chamber rising several stories high and surrounded by smaller buildings where clerks and Defenders worked busily to support the High Warlord in running Dunidaen.

The compound was surrounded by wide, paved streets that gave it the air of an island amidst the closely packed density of the city outside the inner walls. To its north was the quiet, expensive quarter where warlords and those vicelords who could afford it had their city residences.

Gateport had been cleverly designed around a low hill that meant the Council building sat higher than anywhere else in the city. The rambling streets were laid out in all directions around it—the inner ring of stone wall wasn't high enough to obstruct the view—the waters of the harbour a deep blue, ships rocking at anchor.

The heart of Dunidaen, as it were. Or maybe the brain. Arya made a face at her philosophical thoughts and promptly dismissed them. That kind of thinking was for Essa.

Despite it being late winter, the morning was sunny, so Arya's first sight was of the white walls of the domed building bathed in a golden glow. The entrance doors stood open, and a steady stream of people were making their way up the steps and inside. Two Defenders stood at each side of the doorway, tall and impressive in their pristine white and gold uniforms.

Thiara Ravenstrike strode a pace ahead of Arya. Despite her diminutive size, she was a prepossessing sight, with neatly braided blonde hair, and those piercing faded blue eyes. She wore an expensive but simple gown in deep red, with a rich cloak that had been cleverly tailored to make her look taller. The heels on her boots gave her a few extra inches too.

The anger coming off her stiff shoulders was chilly enough to make Arya glad of her cloak. To say she'd been unimpressed by Arya's earlier report of the night before was an understatement.

"What were you all *thinking*?" she'd snapped viciously.

Arya had braced her shoulders. "My read is that Falconcrest sent his Aggressors out looking for us, hoping for exactly what happened. Starting a brawl undermines Rorin's competency for heir."

"You think I need to be told that?" Thiara had rounded on her. "You should have stopped him, General. It is inexcusable that you didn't."

"I know."

"Rorin now has a curfew. And not just because of this. The Defenders reported a violent robbery at one of SparrowWing's properties two nights ago—a relative of his lives there. The man stumbled across the thief and was beaten half to death. By all accounts the beating was so bad his mind was broken. Apparently, he's raving about red eyes and voices in his head."

Arya had opened her mouth. Closed it. Violent crime was far from unusual in large cities, but of course someone in a warlord's sphere expected it not to taint *their* lives. And given Rorin's current mood, she didn't think it a bad idea to restrict his ability to frequent the inns of Gateport.

"I won't take Rorin to any of the Council hearings either. Not until his confirmation hearing." Thiara paced.

"Won't that undermine his case, if the warlords don't get a good look at him, get to know him, before the confirmation hearings?" Arya asked.

"If he can't control himself, then it's even riskier to have him there where he could do or say something to undermine his case," she said, still seething. "Besides, my vicelords will be gossiping all over the city about him and his Dreadwater run. Maybe it's best to let everyone hear only the whispers and rumours and build their anticipation."

With an effort, Arya shifted her glance from her still-furious warlord to take in the domed building ahead of them. She'd made an extra effort before leaving the barracks. Her golden hair was neatly braided at the base of her neck. Her breeches and jerkin fit her like a glove, and she'd polished her black leather boots to a high shine. Atop this sat the cloak Thiara Ravenstrike had gifted her the previous day. Made from blood-red velvet, it was thick and fur-lined, with a high collar. The emblem of a black striking raven emblazoned across the back had been outlined in pure gold stitching, marking Arya's status as general.

Behind them marched Laskin's shield, Arya deciding to go with the veteran Raider's experience and steady head for the first day. He'd taken one look at her when she'd collected Zeke from the stables and let out a long whistle of appreciation. "My, don't you look the part, General Ravenstrike."

"That's the point, Laskin. I need the warlords and their people to take me seriously."

"They will," he assured her. "And if they don't, just shoot them that glare you like to use so much. That'll straighten 'em out right quick."

"You're a laugh riot," she'd muttered, before yanking the reins from his grasp and mounting up.

The Defenders stationed at the entrance gave their party a quick, assessing glance as they reached the top of the steps. Arya noted this. Given the relatively small size of the Defender force—only five battalions in total—she had assumed them to be mostly ceremonial. Yet those looks had indicated a sharpness that impressed her.

One of Arya's gloved hands rested on the hilt of her sword as they walked inside, instinct making her cautious. An assassination attempt, while unlikely, was not out of the realm of possibility. She wouldn't put anything past Mathas Crowtalon.

A wide hallway, floored with a polished, light-coloured wood, and thronged with people, circled the main Council chamber on the ground floor. Benches and chairs, along with small potted plants, lined the walls, but Arya saw no indications of danger. Pairs of Defenders stood at each entrance to the chamber.

Arya instantly stiffened when a familiar voice hailed them, as if summoned by her thoughts. "Warlord Ravenstrike!"

Mathas Crowtalon's tall, powerful figure strode towards them, followed by his own guard of Lances, Andrian, and his chief adviser, Nain. It didn't appear he'd brought his general with him. The adviser wore the same voluminous cloak he had been wearing the last time they'd met. He had all the appearance of a voracious crow.

The last time she'd seen Mathas Crowtalon, she'd been shouting at him to leave before Darmanin's shadowhound ripped his throat out. The sword of knowledge hung over both their heads now; that Mathas had fathered a magic-wielder, and that Arya had attacked his Lances and him to rescue Darmanin.

None of that was on the warlord's face. He looked as self-assured as always, perfectly groomed, his broad frame accentuated by his well-tailored clothing.

"Warlord Crowtalon," Thiara said. Her words were polite but cool.

"It's good to see you've arrived safely in Gateport," Mathas said.

"Is it?" She raised an eyebrow, tone faint with condescension. "I'm glad you think so."

Mathas' face tightened, and he turned his gaze to Arya. "I was disappointed to hear of General Lerin's retirement. He was an excellent tactician and a highly experienced commander. It is a shame that someone so young and inexperienced must take his place."

"Father," Andrian spoke, discomfort rippling over his face. "Arya is—"

"Arya is a fitting replacement for Lerin," Thiara cut over him, sounding almost bored with his provocation. "Not that my choice of general affects Crowtalon in any way."

Mathas Crowtalon smiled in private amusement, dismissing Arya with his gaze as he turned back to Thiara. Arya fumed but kept her face expressionless. A display of temper was exactly what Mathas wanted.

"Your son is not here, Thiara? The confirmation hearings begin next week. Given his, shall we say, *disadvantage*, don't you think it would be best to expose him to the warlords early, so they can get to know him. It will be hard work to convince them he can lead a State by himself. I'm already hearing worrying things about his character and suitability."

Thiara smiled. "I appreciate your sound advice, Mathas. Permit me to offer some of my own. I don't see Darmanin here. You don't think he might be a better candidate to be your heir than Andrian?"

Arya's gaze went straight to the handsome elder son, but Andrian seemed unperturbed by the comment. He was able to control his expression better than she'd expected. She wondered if Darmanin had spoken to his brother about his ambitions to be warlord. And if so, how Andrian felt about it.

Mathas' expression stilled, and his voice was quiet but vicious when he responded. "I warned you on that score, Thiara. I hope you haven't taken my warning lightly."

Those pale blue eyes flashed. "In all honesty, I don't take anything you say with any weight, *Mathas*."

"Darmanin is not fit to be a warlord's son, let alone my heir." Mathas remained outwardly calm, but Arya didn't miss the vein throbbing in his temple or the way his left hand shifted fractionally towards the sword at his hip.

"And why is that?" She cocked her head.

Arya tried not to stiffen. Thiara Ravenstrike didn't know about Darmanin's magical ability. It was in Crowtalon's best interests to keep it hidden, but if he was provoked, she wasn't sure what he'd do.

"My family is my business, Warlord, and Darmanin is no longer a member of it, despite the liberties you've taken with him," he said.

"We'll see about that." Thiara's gaze shifted to the entry to the chamber. "Shall we go in? I think the first session is about to start."

He swept out his hand in a magnanimous gesture. "After you, Warlord."

Arya watched Mathas Crowtalon for any threat to her warlord, so it was a few moments before she got a good look at the inside of the State Council chamber. It was a cavernous space, the walls curving up to the apex of the domed building, where great skylights sent morning sunlight shining down into the space. The floor was polished oak. Tapestries depicting the

State emblems hung along the walls. The table sat in the centre of the space, along with its cushioned chairs, the only pieces of furniture in the room. On the second level of the building, viewing alcoves had been built into the chamber wall so interested citizens could watch the proceedings.

Andrian stopped beside Arya. "It's impressive, isn't it?" he said in a low voice. "A bit over the top though."

"The grandeur is necessary," she said. "An entire country is ruled from within this room. The space needs to reflect that."

Andrian mock-shuddered. "A horrible job, if you ask me. Who could want all that responsibility, and all the administration that comes with it?"

Mathas called his son over with a sharp word before Arya could reply, but as she walked over to stand behind her warlord's chair and the proceedings started, she thought on Andrian's words.

All the responsibility of running a country; being able to make the decisions, to have the power to do things the way she thought was right? It was far more power than a general held.

Now there was a tempting thought indeed. And one that could one day be fulfilled if she did what Salyarin and Ranier wanted.

No. Her home was here. Her family here. And she had power enough.

She ignored the little voice in her head that added *'for now'*

Chapter 34

The night after the opening of the Council, Arya dreamed of her wyvern again. The enjoyable dream she'd been having about sitting on a roof eating Peemla's iced cakes with Rorin ended right before she was able to bite into the cake, and she found herself staring down onto a field.

The image lost the faintly unreal quality of a normal dream and became as clear as if she were awake. The grass, between patches of pristine white snow, was a bright emerald colour. The call of a wyvern shivered through her mind, and then he flew into sight.

He'd grown bigger since he'd come to her defence against the nazal, so many months ago now, the size of an adult draft horse. His scales shone a stunning burnished gold, and the wings extending from his sides were a paler golden colour. At this moment, he was a bundle of frustrated anger. Something had driven him away from his hunt, higher into the mountains where he now was.

Was he in the Diamondfang?

The wyvern propped suddenly. He'd felt her. With a graceful sweep of wings and tail he circled down and landed on the snowy grass.

"*Mine,*" he stated confidently. He wasn't speaking, exactly—at least, it wasn't words and a voice like she heard in her mind when the Etherean elder spoke to her in her dreams. It was more like a strong sense of intent.

"*Mine,*" she agreed, because she simply wasn't able to say otherwise.

"*Where? Where? Where?*" he demanded.

"*They hunt us. We must hide. Be careful.*" She wasn't sure how much of her words he understood. She also was suddenly aware of how quickly the nazal might be able to find them and terror shivered through her. *"We can't talk like this. Danger."*

She felt assent, then his long head lifted, mouth opening to reveal rows of deadly-sharp teeth. With two steps, he spread his wings and lifted into the sky. *"Coming!"*

To her? Shit! Arya tried to tell him to stop, but before she could do anything, she felt herself being pulled from the dream.

The familiar darkness associated with the nazal swept over her. It was closer than ever before, she could *feel* its stench and power crawling along her skin. But it hadn't quite gotten a proper hold of her mind yet—its magic was still grasping for her. Arya hauled herself away with the strength of sheer panic and woke up with a gasp, covered in sweat.

As her breathing rasped, and her heart thudded in her chest, she came to a realisation. The nazal was close. She'd *felt* it. Every dream in the past where they'd found her, she'd sensed distance. But this time it was nearby. At least, the one who could trap her mind was nearby. So close she'd been surprised to wake up and not find it beside her bed.

Was it in Gateport?

***

Several days passed in a flurry of Council meetings and social gatherings. Arya did her best to be a sober, thoughtful ambassador of Ravenstrike, but it was a struggle. She was distracted by constantly looking over her shoulder, scanning her surroundings, wondering if a nazal was stalking her. Worse, none of the other States' generals apart from the Fireman general took her seriously, and she was hard pressed to hold her temper at the condescending looks and regular barrage of pointed comments about her youth, gender, and inexperience.

It took her only a handful of days to realise that talking to these men wasn't going to convince them of anything. Not until she proved herself to them. And that wasn't going to happen in conversation. Even so, she persisted. Thiara needed her to convince the generals that the Nightstalker was a genuine military threat, and that Thiara Ravenstrike as High Warlord was capable of repelling that threat.

Magen didn't seem pleased with their overall progress either. While having an informal dinner together one evening, Essa confided to Arya that the chief adviser didn't think they were anywhere close to Thiara being taken seriously as a candidate for High Warlord.

"She's convinced most of the warlords and vicelords that she's capable, with her quick and decisive management of the border and action against the Shadeweavers, but none of them are making the leap from that to consider her as High Warlord." Essa snorted. "They don't want to, that's my view. Mathas Crowtalon is everything they see as right in a warlord, so they're not even interested in looking at anyone else, especially a woman. Not to mention he's been the assumed successor for Darien for years now."

That was the sense Arya had gotten too. "How do we change that?"

Essa shrugged. "Change the warlords."

"That's never going to happen," Arya said. "Did you end up helping Magen take advantage of the SparrowWing-Crowtalon dispute?"

Essa sat up eagerly. "I figured out a way to make up the costs of SparrowWing's taxes when storing our trade goods in Seelan—which meant Rorin's mother could argue in SparrowWing's favour when Crowtalon brought it up in the Council hearing yesterday. Warlord SparrowWing won the argument, and he owes it to Ravenstrike."

"Well done, Ess!" Arya beamed at her.

"A good thing, too. He needs those taxes," Essa said. "SparrowWing recently lost a significant amount of money. A thief got a hold of one of his companies' banking codes and siphoned off a large amount of coin from his stores before it was discovered."

"A thief? The same one that broke into one of his properties and almost beat the resident to death?"

Essa shrugged. "I'm not sure."

They finished off their meal and sipped tea. One of Peemla's servants came in to clear their dishes, and as soon as he'd gone, Arya shifted her chair closer to Essa and lowered her voice. "I dreamed of my wyvern again last night. The nazal came for us, and I only just avoided it. I'm pretty sure you're right, Essa, that only one of the creatures can trap and attack our minds. What I don't know is if that's the same creature that went into Khadini after us. If it is, it's back, and I think it's here in Gateport. That's how close it felt."

"And even if it's not, we have to question why a nazal is here." Essa didn't have to speak her fear aloud. What if somehow, they knew Arya was in Gateport?

"Do you think telling Rorin's mother everything after the Council is over is the right move?" Arya asked.

Essa cocked her head. "Yes. I know you think some kind of fighting is inevitable, and we need Dunidaen's army behind us, but if Rorin's mother knew the full truth, as High Warlord she could help us develop a strategy to avoid that."

Arya huffed a laugh. "If she doesn't kick us all out of her household for hiding the truth all these years."

Essa gave her an appraising look. "Somehow I don't think it will come to that."

But what if the warlord stripped Arya of her general-ship?

That couldn't matter, not anymore. She'd promised Essa she'd make a firm plan regarding the Nightstalker after the Council was done, and she'd meant it. They would need help. It would be a gamble, seeking help from Thiara Ravenstrike, but something inside Arya told her it just might be the right gamble.

Arya said, "And if she loses the vote?"

"Then Mathas Crowtalon rules Dunidaen. He'll be no ally of ours, but he's not going to be a weak High Warlord, not like Darien Eaglesoar. He won't let the Nightstalker traipse all over Dunidaen."

"No," Arya said. "But he'll happily send all magic-wielders to Andahar to be killed."

"Will you let that happen in Ravenstrike?"

"No, Ess, I won't." Arya didn't look away from Essa's gaze. The question was fair. As apprentice to General Desomer, Arya hadn't made any effort to prevent Shadeweaver magic-wielders being rounded up in Ravenstrike to be sent to Andahar. A niggle of shame twisted her stomach at the thought. She would never stand aside like that again.

"Good." Then she gave Arya a curious look. "If Rorin's mother does become High Warlord, what will you do?"

"We haven't discussed it yet," Arya admitted. "It will depend on how she takes the conversation we need to have with her. Hopefully I will be involved in the planning for dealing with the Nightstalker."

"That doesn't bother you? Not having a say in where you go and what you do."

"I love being a Raider, and I love being general even more. That outweighs the less attractive parts of the job," Arya said. "I haven't seen Rorin properly in days and I was hoping to catch him for dinner while his mother is out dining with Hawkesdale. Do you know where he is?"

At their family dinner the previous night, Rorin had still been in a foul mood, his mother furious with him, and Arya firmly stuck in the middle. Peemla was unusually subdued as she'd directed the servants serving their food. Her constant glances in Rorin's direction indicated she wondered what was wrong with him too.

"He's been out every night, abiding by his mother's curfew but only just. Usually with Andrian, sometimes with sons and daughters of the Ravenstrike vicelords. SparrowWing's likely heir, Amius, was over here the other night, playing cards. At least he seemed a sensible influence."

Arya didn't miss the note of disapproval in Essa's voice. "What has gotten into him? He's never behaved like this before."

"What does that tell you?"

Arya huffed a breath. "If you've got something to say, spit it out, Essa, otherwise I need to get back to the barracks."

"His confirmation hearing is only two days away. SparrowWing the day after. Crowtalon after that."

Arya stilled. She knew. It was why she'd initially come over, hoping to talk to Rorin. "I'll come by early tomorrow, talk to him, and if he's not here, I'll wait till he comes back. Night, Ess."

***

"Night, Arya."

Arya emerged from the townhouse and took a deep breath of the cool evening air before sitting on the steps. As blithely as she'd played it off, her conversation with Essa troubled her. She should have been paying more attention to Rorin, but she'd been so busy keeping to Magen's schedule and managing the battalion, there hadn't been enough time.

And it wasn't just Rorin's confirmation that felt under threat. The sense of impending danger hadn't left her since she'd dreamed of her wyvern, no matter how hard she tried to shake it. How close *was* the nazal? Would the cazaix hide them well enough if the Nightstalker's hunters were in Gateport?

Arya took a steadying breath.

She just had to hold things together, support Ravenstrike as best she could, until the Council was over and the leadership of Dunidaen was settled. Then they'd go to Thiara Ravenstrike, make a firm plan. The thought of confiding in her warlord gave Arya an unreasonable sense of comfort. Maybe she should have asked for help years ago.

At that thought, she was tempted to wait for her warlord's return from dinner and do it tonight. But that would be horribly unfair to Thiara and for no real gain. Let her concentrate on winning High Warlord. Then Arya would go to her and tell her everything.

"Copper piece for your thoughts?"

Arya startled as Darmanin's familiar figure strolled through the gates, acknowledging the Raider guards with a nod.

"Dar. What are you doing here?"

He shrugged, leaning against the pillar at the bottom of the steps. "I came by to try talking to Rorin."

"I had a similar intention, but he's out, apparently, and Essa's giving me her disapproving look, which means she thinks I'm missing something obvious, or not doing something I'm supposed to be doing," she said.

He cracked a smile. "Let me walk you back to the barracks."

"I *can* take care of myself," she said, getting up.

"I know," he said simply. "But the company would be nice."

It wasn't too much longer until Rorin's curfew—within an hour of nightfall—meant he'd be arriving home, but waiting around wasn't really Arya's style. She'd talk to him first thing. "I can agree to that." She rose to her feet and joined Darmanin.

They fell into step, strolling through the inner residential quarter. It was a quiet evening, and the temperature was cool but not cold.

"Why the glum demeanour just now?" Darmanin asked. "You're not just worried about Rorin, I gather?"

"I'm worried about everything," she said. "Rorin's confirmation hearing in two days, the nazal, your father. I don't know how to protect those I care about from all these dangers at once."

He lifted an eyebrow. "Has anyone ever mentioned to you that you're not the hub of the world? That perhaps everything that happens is not directly under your control."

"You think I'm arrogant?"

"It's not a bad thing, Arya, especially in a general. But you do have to learn to recognise the difference between the things you *can* control, and those you can't."

"I'll take that under advisement," she snapped, bristling at the condescension in his voice. It was insufferable sometimes.

"You're not the only person in the world with faults," he said. "I have plenty. Rorin has plenty, even your beloved warlord has them."

"That's true enough." She grinned, turning to him. "Can I start listing out yours now? We could start with 'irritatingly stubborn'."

"Maybe leave that for another night," he grumbled good naturedly.

They turned onto one of the busier streets. Around them people spilled in and out of inns or stood in small groups talking and eating food purchased from street vendors.

"General!" Taze's voice called out, making them both turn in surprise.

Rorin was emerging from one of the inns, Taze at his back. Arya's adopted brother looked as if he'd been drinking; his face was flushed, and his blue eyes glittered.

"*Arya! Darmanin! What are you two doing out?*" he asked.

"I'm going back to the barracks," she said. "Your curfew is about up."

"*I'm having a good time.*" He grinned. "*I probably need a walk in the fresh air before going home, though. Taze and I will join you.*"

"What is going on with you?" Arya asked.

"*I told you, I'm having a good time, and I'd really prefer you not ruin it with your high-handed bossiness right now.*"

Arya gaped at him, more stunned than upset by his uncharacteristic insult.

"Your confirmation hearing is in two days, Rorin," Darmanin said.

"*Are you under the impression I don't know that?*"

"Quit being a petulant child. It doesn't suit you," Darmanin said, his tone shocking them all into silence.

Rorin bristled. "*You have no right to talk to me like that!*"

"You know how much is riding on you being confirmed heir," he said. "Yet you're treating it like it's a holiday picnic."

"Enough," Arya said to them both.

"If you want Crowtalon as an ally when you become warlord, you'd better straighten yourself out, Rorin Ravenstrike," Darmanin said. "Because I *will* be confirmed as heir to my State, and I won't tolerate childishness in my allies."

Darmanin stalked ahead, leaving the rest of them staring after him in astonishment. Arya recovered first. She gave Rorin a pointed look, then jogged to catch up with Darmanin.

"I suppose I did ask you to talk to him," she said. "I'm not sure that's quite what I had in mind."

"He needs a good thrashing to shake him out of this," Darmanin said, the remnants of anger still in his voice.

"*I don't want to fight with you, Dar, so let's just leave it,*" Rorin caught up, cheeks flushed.

"Maybe a fight would do you some good," Darmanin said.

"*I wish you'd all stop thinking you know what is best for me,*" Rorin signed in tight, abrupt gesture. "*Can you please just leave it alone?*"

"Fine." Arya conceded, flicking a quelling look at Darmanin. "Let's walk. Some silence might do us all some good."

They made their way through the area where the warlord residences were, heading for the gate in the inner wall that would take Arya to the Raider barracks. They emerged into a square only a block away from the wall; across the other side of the square was a well-lit and busy street of inns and theatre houses.

Arya swore when the scar on her right forearm flared white-hot. She rolled up her sleeve, but by the time she did, the pain had vanished as if it had never been there. The scar was reddened, though. Just as quickly, she rolled her sleeve back down, instinct warning her to do so.

"Something wrong?" Darmanin asked.

Before she could reply, a gaggle of raised voices erupted off to their right. The source was a group gathering outside Warlord SparrowWing's townhouse where it faced onto the square. Two Firemen were carrying something away from the front of the house, shooting fearful glances over their shoulder, their movements hurried.

Arya and Darmanin headed straight toward the huddle, Taze and Rorin quick to follow. As she came closer, Arya saw that most of those gathered were Firemen, dressed in the SparrowWing brown and gold. And they were gathered around three bodies.

Her heartbeat quickened and she increased her pace, snapping an order at Taze to hold Rorin back. "What's going on?" she called out.

The Firemen turned, and Arya was surprised to see Warlord SparrowWing among them. Belatedly, she straightened. "I'm sorry, Warlord. I didn't see you there."

"General Ravenstrike." His spare features were taught with worry. "I've just returned from a late dinner to find a madman has gotten into my home. He's barricaded himself upstairs with a bow and is shooting at anyone who gets in range. He's already killed three of my Firemen."

Shocked, Arya shot a glance at the house, then looked back at the warlord. A madman shooting arrows at people? What in raven's balls was going on. "What does he want?"

"I don't know, but Amius was home when I left earlier, and he hasn't come out," SparrowWing replied, jaw tensing.

Concern shivered through her. Amius was Helden's only son, and about to be confirmed as SparrowWing heir in three days.

Arya glanced at Rorin over her shoulder, eyebrows raised, and he gave her a quick nod. She turned back to SparrowWing. "Warlord, I'd like to offer our help, if you'll accept it?"

"My Firemen are primarily trained for fighting fires, General. They can fight if it comes to it, but your experience would be welcome. I was about to send for the Defenders." He took a breath. "What do you suggest?"

Before she could reply, something clattered onto the cobblestones near the warlord's feet.

"Move back!" Arya bellowed, giving Rorin a hard shove. "We're in the archer's range. Move back!"

Firemen instantly circled the warlord and pushed him farther away from the house. Everyone else backed up several paces. "Taze, run to the barracks," Arya said. "Get me Laskin, Zamarin, and Rarik's Shields. I want sixty Raiders in this square five minutes ago."

"General!" Taze saluted and dashed off at a sprint.

She spun. "Dar, Rorin, I need somebody we can trust among the Hawkesdale Longbows. What about the men we drank with the other night?"

"Yale and Keepa," Darmanin said to Rorin's firm nod.

"*They were our guards during our fostering,*" Rorin explained. "*They're good men, and they'll be happy to help.*"

"Take Taze's shield and go get them." Another arrow clattered to the ground where they'd just been standing. Arya clapped her hands and bellowed, "GO!"

Rorin and Darmanin took to their heels, Taze's shield pouring after them. Arya scanned the darkened windows of the SparrowWing townhouse. It looked to have a similar layout to the Ravenstrike residence, which was helpful. "Which floor is the archer on?" she asked the warlord.

"Fourth floor, east corner," he replied. "Amius' room."

She gave him a quick glance. "You think he's in there?"

"He spends most of his time there. He likes his books and parchment," Helden said. "We made a deal that he'd attend every dinner I asked this week, and he has, so I said he could have this evening to himself."

"Do you have any idea who the archer is, or who might have hired them?" she asked, thinking of Shadeweaver mercenaries.

Helden's narrow face was taut and pale, a vein ticking in his neck. He was maintaining his composure well, but this man was terrified for his son. "No, nothing. I'm not planning to put my hand up for High Warlord and Amius is an uncontroversial nomination for my heir."

"What about the robbery you had recently?"

"A thief looking for my banking codes to steal money from me." Helden looked blank. "What could that have to do with this?"

"It seems coincidental to have two attacks on your property within such a short period of time." Arya stared at the house, thinking out loud. "The archer went up there for a reason, and it's not a coincidence that he's in Lord Amius' room."

"I'd like to act before Amius is hurt, General," Helden said.

Arya felt a flicker of sympathy for him but ruthlessly quashed it. Emotion wasn't going to get Amius SparrowWing out. "Warlord, I'd like to take command of your Firemen and set up a cordon. If the archer was going to kill your son, he'd have done it already, so if Lord Amius is still alive up there, the archer wants something." She ignored Helden's flinch and forged ahead. "To give us room to work, we need to keep people out of this square and out of range of those arrows. I don't want bystanders or citizens out for an evening walk wandering close enough to get themselves killed."

"Do it," he said tersely, then waved over one of the Firemen lingering protectively nearby. "Captain Taska? You'll do as General Ravenstrike says."

"Warlord." The woman saluted and turned expectantly to Arya.

"A cordon is the first priority. Do you have enough Firemen to do it?"

"Yes, General." Taska glanced around. "I'd recommend we empty the square and extend the cordon a full block beyond the back of the residence."

"Agreed. Go to it. Nobody gets inside the cordon unless they're a Defender captain or one of my Raiders."

Taska hesitated, glanced at her warlord, and got a firm nod. "Yes, General."

While the Fireman went to work, and Helden SparrowWing paced incessantly, gaze not straying from his home, Arya set up a command post in the middle of the square, well out of range of the archer.

The Firemen had just finished completing the cordon when cries of surprise came from the opposite side of the square. A crowd—formed from those who'd been visiting the inns and theatre houses when all the ruckus started—had started gathering along the edges of the cordon. Their cries signalled the arrival of Taze, now mounted and leading three shields of Raiders at a canter.

Pride flared through Arya at how quickly they'd mustered. The four captains rode forward and dismounted to join her, the warlord, and his Fireman bodyguard.

"We've got a man up in the townhouse loosing arrows at anyone who gets too close," Arya told them. "He is probably holding the warlord's son hostage. He's on the fourth floor, in the eastern corner."

Laskin absorbed that while his gaze studied the building. The presence of him and his experienced shield settled her. "What do you need from us, General?"

"My first priority is containing the scene, but the Firemen are spread thin on the cordon, and if we end up with panicked citizens, it might not hold. Zamarin, take your shield and help them bolster it. Laskin, Rarik, keep your Raiders inside the square, weapons drawn and looking intimidating. That archer needs to look out and see that there's no escape for him."

"Aye, General!" They saluted and returned to their shields.

Her captains' voices were crisp on the night air as they rapped out their orders. The Raiders moved quickly into their positions, disciplined and efficient. Arya relaxed, felt some of her worry replaced by burgeoning confidence. Her Raiders were here now.

They had this.

Arya's gaze shifted to Taze. "We're going to have Defenders descending upon us as soon as they hear about this. I need you to find whoever is in command when they arrive and send them through to me."

"What now, General?" the warlord asked, impatience edging his tone. "I understand you want to make citizens in the area safe, but my son is in that house."

"If that truly is a madman up there, rushing in might only serve to get Lord Amius killed," Arya cautioned. "I want to make sure we understand the situation fully before moving."

"What more information do you need?" he asked.

Movement at the western edge of the cordon resolved to the arrival of Darmanin and Rorin and his shield, accompanied by two men wearing Hawkesdale green and brown. They weren't much older than Arya, with brown skin and messy dark hair. They each carried a bow taller than they were and looked and moved alike enough that they had to be brothers. She pointed. "Advice from the experts, sir."

Rorin reached them first, already signing. *"Arya, this is Keepa and Yale. Dar and I have told them what's going on. They're off duty and happy to help."*

"General Ravenstrike." Keepa saluted. "What can we do?"

"Warlord?" Arya was conscious he was right beside her and thought it best to defer to his rank.

"We have what appears to be one archer up on the fourth level of the townhouse. My Firemen place him at the fourth window from the centre, in the eastern wing." Helden SparrowWing paused, looked to Arya.

"The first thing I'd like to know is the archer's range. How close can we get before being at risk?" she asked the Longbows.

The brothers studied the townhouse, and one of them tested the breeze with his finger. Then they took a close look at one of the arrows on the ground before conferring briefly in low tones.

Yale broke the silence. "It's a regular recurve bow he's using, we reckon. We're just outside the range of one of those now, Warlord. We could probably move a few paces closer, but no more than that."

"Could either of you take him out from here?" Arya asked.

"Certainly, our longbows have far greater range. And the archer has helpfully left the window open, which is a bit of luck. But we'd need to get eyes on him, General," Yale said. "Has anyone spotted this man near the windows yet?"

"No," SparrowWing said, jaw tightening. He was growing more impatient. Anxious. She hoped he held onto his patience long enough for her to do this right and not be forced into rash action. The echo of Desomer's barking laugh drifted through her mind.

"Do either of you know what Amius SparrowWing looks like?" Arya asked the Longbows.

"Yes, General. We were drinking with the young man's Fireman guard some nights ago," Keepa replied. "They speak well of him. He's a good lad."

Helden SparrowWing's face softened, and he turned to Arya. "What do you suggest, General?"

While they'd been waiting for Yale and Keepa, she'd already worked through several different tactical approaches, and now she had advice from the Longbows it was easy to settle on the best one.

"I recommend sending two soldiers into the residence. Their goal will be to herd the archer towards the open window. As soon as Yale or Keeper have a shot, they take it. They know what your son looks like, so they won't mistake him for the archer."

"How are you going to get anyone inside without the archer firing on them as they approach?" Darmanin asked, pre-empting whatever the warlord had been about to say. "He's got line of sight on the front door, and we can't be certain he doesn't have accomplices watching the back or any other entrances."

"See that ridge of brick sticking out of the wall down the centre of the townhouse? Covering the drainage pipe from the roof gutters, I'd guess."

She pointed. "It's thick enough that if someone climbed along the inside of it, they'd be invisible to the archer because of how close it is to the window."

"She's right, sir." Yale and Keepa spoke after another brief conference. "The angle means he won't have a clean shot from the window even if he could see around the ridge."

"*You still have to make it to the wall without getting shot,*" Rorin signed.

"A risk, but a necessary one." Arya nodded. "We can't do anything without getting inside the house first."

"General, you couldn't just go through the front door?" Taze asked.

She shook her head. "Dar already made a good point that the archer might have accomplices. If he does, they'll be guarding the obvious entries to the house. We need to get to the cover of the wall and up it before anyone in that house realises what we're doing and responds."

"We?" Darmanin asked.

She hesitated, then, "You and I, Dar. It's a tricky climb. There's nobody here as good at that as the four of us after our Khadini training, and I'd prefer Taze down here watching Rorin."

A little smile flashed over his face and his eyes gleamed. "Agreed."

SparrowWing looked unconvinced. "General, the room is four levels up and that's not an easy climb. If you fall, you risk serious injury or death. Are you sure that's the right approach?"

"I have a knack when it comes to heights, Warlord," she assured him.

SparrowWing stared at her for a beat longer, then his jaw firmed and he nodded. "All right. But please remember that's my son in there."

"I won't forget it," she assured him.

Arya and Darmanin began shedding their cloaks and slinging their swords over their backs so the weapons wouldn't hinder them as they climbed.

"*Arya, wait!*" Rorin gripped her arm. "*I want to come with you. I can make that climb too.*"

"I'm sorry, Rorin, but the way you've been behaving lately, I can't trust you enough for this. Besides, your mother would skin me alive if I risked your life. I need you to stay here with Warlord SparrowWing," she told him firmly.

He didn't look happy, but he released her arm and stepped back. "*Good luck, Arya. You too, Dar.*"

"Be safe, General." Taze saluted. "And be confident your Raiders will keep the area safe and secure until you're out."

"I don't doubt it." She reached out to grip his shoulder. "See you soon."

"Ready?" Darmanin asked.

Arya smiled, seeing the challenge in his grey eyes. "Ten copper pieces I beat you to the wall."

"I'll take that bet, General."

And they ran.

Chapter 35

They moved at the same moment, breaking into a sprint towards the townhouse. Almost immediately, the hiss of arrows sliced through the air. It sent a shiver through Arya. Not only did this mysterious attacker know how to use a bow, but he could fire at a rate comparable to the famous Hawkesdale archers.

How many arrows did he have up there?

Arya hurled her body to the side to avoid the first arrow, and then ran in a zig-zag pattern. Darmanin followed suit, and the single archer was hard pressed to aim at both targets.

Even so, an arrow ripped through Arya's jerkin, grazing her side, just before she reached the wall, and she hurled herself the rest of the distance, rolling into the hard brick with a grunt.

"You okay?" Darmanin demanded as he rolled to stop beside her. He glanced at a rent in his breeches, then dismissed the trickle of blood. "Just a graze for me."

"Nothing more than a scratch," she said, wincing as she pressed her ribs, ascertaining the wound was shallow. "Let's get a move on."

Arya leaped up, just managing to grip the brick windowsill of a first-floor window. She hung there for a moment, then pulled herself up, scrambling for purchase until she was balanced on the sill. From there she stood carefully, then reached upwards to curl her fingers around the top of the window frame and pull herself up again.

She moved quickly, using tiny protrusions in the rough brick to push off, not giving herself time to lose balance or slip. She kept her momentum, not at all afraid of the yawning drop below.

Darmanin followed right behind her, perfectly in sync. She could feel the thread between them enlivening, giving her an extra sense of where he was in relation to her, when he was about to move, the calm focus in his mind.

When Arya reached the fourth floor window, she drew her dagger, then used the hilt to tap the corner of the glass as hard as she could. It broke with a tinkle, and she reached inside to unlatch the window. Her boots made no sound on the plush carpet inside as she swung through. Darmanin came in behind her, and they paused to gain their bearings.

The room was empty and dim, and though she'd kept hold of her dagger, nothing leaped out to attack them. She let out a breath and came to her feet. Darmanin tapped Arya's shoulder, then pointed to the floor between the doorframe of the room's entrance. She followed his gaze and saw four pieces of taut wire running about an inch above the carpet.

"Tripwire?" she asked.

He nodded.

Arya began reordering her assumptions about the archer. SparrowWing had said he was a madman, and that had made sense given there didn't seem to be any obvious motive for this attack, but laying down tripwires suggested an ordered and planned strike. Tripwires to set off what, though?

"This isn't a civilian," Darmanin said, echoing her thoughts.

They stepped carefully over the wire and into the hall beyond, placing each step carefully in case there were more tripwires. All the doors in the corridor stood open, including the one at the far end where the archer was.

The faint sound of muttering drifted out of that room. It had an oddly frantic note to it. As they crept closer, she could just make out the words.

"I know you're in here. I know you're here. I know you're here."

Arya froze, turned to Darmanin, but as she did so, her gaze caught on where the tripwires ran along the skirting boards. There was trembling, and then ... a hard tug on one of them.

The sharp twang of a bow echoed into the silence, flint sparked, and then a whoosh of bursting flame tore through the corridor, coming from the opposite end of the hallway. And then she smelled it. A scent indelibly burned into her senses after their trip to SparrowWing the year before.

Smoke and fire. Well, that explained what the tripwires were set to do.

Arya turned to Darmanin. "He knows we're here."

A quick nod. "And nobody else has come to intercept us, so—"

"No accomplices."

"If there is Khadini oil in those traps…"

"This whole place is going to go up fast."

Arya moved purposefully for the room at the end of the hall. She flattened herself against the wall and inched closer, risking a quick look into the room. The interior was dim, the only light that of the streetlamps outside.

And a figure was tied to a chair near the window.

She drew back, and Darmanin leaned down so she could murmur in his ear. "He's got Amius SparrowWing tied to a chair in there. Over by the window."

Darmanin's gaze narrowed. The scent of smoke was strengthening, and she could see wisps of it curling along the floor at the far end of the hall. Arya stifled a cough as it tickled her throat. Flames wouldn't be far behind.

Arya murmured. "I say we burst in there and take him by surprise. I'll go for the archer, either take him out or push him close enough to the window for the Longbows to take him down, while you get Amius free."

He gave a minute shake of his head. "It's too risky. If the archer reacts quickly enough, he could take us both out before we get anywhere near him or Amius."

"Not if we take him by surprise," she said.

"And what if he decides to shoot at Amius first?" Darmanin shook his head. "Arya, it's too reckless. I say one of us goes in there with hands up. We try talking to him, calm him down, herd him towards the window."

"Have you noticed the fire rapidly getting closer?" she asked. "We don't have time to talk him down. If he's a contract assassin, he'll shoot first and ask questions later, and he certainly won't be stupid enough to walk in front of the window."

"If he's a contract assassin, why is he holding Amius hostage rather than killing him? He hasn't made any demands."

An exploding window somewhere down the hall cut off Darmanin's words. An incoherent shout came from inside the room and another trip-wire pulled taut. Even over the crackle of flames Arya heard the bow twang and a subsequent whoosh of flame. The orange glow of fire spilled out from another room further along the hall, closer to them.

Arya shook her head. "We have to move or we're all going to burn in here. I'll go in first. He'll shoot as soon as he spots me, so I'll avoid the first shot, then attack in the moment before he can reload. Once I've engaged him, you go for Amius. Ready?"

"He's got a pretty quick reload, Arya," Darmanin said, then shook his head and lifted his hands in capitulation. "All right. I'll go for Amius. Please take out the archer before I get shot."

"I won't let anyone hurt you Dar, you know that."

He smiled that little smile of his, and their gazes caught and held.

Then Arya drew her sword, the crackling of oncoming fire hiding the ringing sound it made. She risked one more look around the door, her sweeping gaze taking in Amius still in the chair and an indistinct figure pacing along the side wall, bow knocked and ready.

She waited for the right moment when his gaze flicked away from the door. Then, cazaix blade balanced in her hand, Arya turned the corner and exploded into the room. A bow twanged, but she'd been expecting that, already ducking low two steps inside the door, before surging to her feet and diving at the archer before he could knock another arrow.

But he moved too, even faster on his feet, re-positioning to fire another arrow from the quiver at his waist. Swearing, Arya dropped and rolled to the side. The second arrow thudded into the carpet where she'd been standing. She kept rolling until she was behind the bed. Once there, she peered over it. Another arrow slammed into the bedding inches from her head. "Raven's balls!" she swore.

Well, that hadn't gone as planned.

At least Darmanin had stayed outside the door on seeing her plan go awry. She breathed a sigh of relief. If she could distract the archer, he could capitalise on that.

"I'll kill you!" the archer screamed, sounding both frantic and angry.

She looked up again, using the voice to orient where he was. Closer now, she could see him better—he was an older man, brown hair threaded with grey, bulky frame tense as he paced up and down. His gaze was in constant motion.

"Hey!" she called out, trying to draw his attention to her. If he turned to look at her, his back would be to the door where Darmanin waited.

Her words were greeted with two more arrows slamming into the mattress above her head. The *thing* inside Arya surged powerfully as the threat she faced increased, and for a long moment she curled over, fighting her magic down.

"Raven's balls," she muttered, breathing hard and fast as she let out a grunt of effort. "I don't have time for this."

A groan escaped her, but she finally got her surging magic under control. By then, the archer was pacing again, rubbing at his eyes. He almost looked sick. And he seemed content with holding her at bay behind the bed rather than leaving Amius to seek her out.

"I don't want to. No. I won't." He let out a groan.

None of what he was doing made sense. His manner was erratic, incoherent, his actions not logical, all signs of madness or severe illness. But his reaction times, his planning, his skill with the bow—it all suggested the opposite.

"I just want to talk," she called out, trying Darmanin's idea. "I won't hurt you if you put down the bow."

Silence greeted her words. Taking a deep breath, she sheathed her sword, then put her hands in the air and stood up slowly. Each step of the way she expected an arrow to the chest, but surprisingly it didn't come.

The archer glanced at her, back to the window, then the door, then back to her. His eyes were glazed. "They're making me do this. They're making me do this. I can't—"

Arya risked a quick glance at Amius. He was conscious, and he met her gaze with a little nod. His mouth was gagged but he seemed unhurt. She looked back at the archer. "Who's making you?" she asked.

"They're making me do this." He shuddered, shook his head. "They're making me."

Arya shifted, intending to try and edge her way close enough to take him down in a single jump, but as soon as she moved, he raised the bow. She froze instantly, hands high. "What's your name?" she asked, as if they were just meeting at a bar for the first time. "I'm Arya."

"Bralin." He swallowed. "They're making me."

She slowly lowered her hands. "Bralin, the man you have tied up, his name is Amius. Has he hurt you at all? Did he do something to you?"

"They're making me." The voice was a whisper.

"If you don't want to do this, then I can help you. Why don't we start with you letting Amius go, and then you and I can keep talking?"

"I can't! THEY'RE MAKING ME!!" he screamed.

The air in the room was growing hazy, and Arya could taste smoke on her tongue and feel it drying out her eyes. Urgency beat at her, but she tried to show only calm.

"Okay, I hear you." She kept part of her attention on the bow in his hand. He kept jerking it up and down as he paced. She began making small movements with her fingers, using Rorin's sign language to tell Darmanin that Amius was unhurt. "Who's making you? Maybe I can stop them."

"I don't know," he shouted, eyes wild. "I can't stop them; I can't make them go away!"

Arya watched as Bralin smacked himself in the head several times. His eyes were bloodshot, skin pale, breathing quick and shallow. All signs of being incredibly overwrought. Had he accidentally eaten something hallucinatory? But if that was the case, why had he come after Amius, and what did he want?

She could see the smoke in the room now, eddies of it swirling in the faint breeze coming from the open window. Flames crackled nearby. The temperature in the room felt like a sauna and sweat slicked her skin.

"Bralin, do you know what they want?"

His voice lifted into a roar. "THEY WANT ME TO KILL HIM!"

Arya winced. Whatever reason or sanity Bralin had left, it was rapidly fading away. "Why Amius?"

"THEY'RE MAKING ME!"

Arya caught a flicker of movement in the doorway. Darmanin was gesturing urgently down the hall. Bralin turned, suspicious, and he ducked back out of sight. Still, she'd caught enough of Darmanin's sign language.

"I signed to Rorin through another window—told him to send the Firemen in. Keep the archer distracted so he doesn't fire on them. I'll go for Amius as soon as there's an opening."

Arya glanced between the door and Bralin. Amius was between them, still tied to the chair. The young SparrowWing heir looked scared, but alert. The temperature had risen uncomfortably.

Pulse racing, Arya waited until Bralin turned in his pacing and moved back towards her. He was still muttering to himself. Arya balanced on her toes, watching him come, calculating the distance between them in her head. He was holding the bow firmly in his right hand, an arrow already knocked and ready to fire.

She waited until he stopped at the end of his pacing line, and turned to head back in the other direction, towards the window and away from the door. He'd become well enough accustomed to her presence now that he wasn't watching her as carefully.

At the instant he turned, she leaped for him.

He caught the movement out of the corner of his eye but couldn't bring his bow to bear in time to get off the shot. She crashed into his side, and they fell to the ground right in front of Amius.

Bralin shouted in agitation and fought to get her off him, but she managed to pin his wrists to the floor and straddle his chest. Darmanin flashed into sight a second later, his dagger out to cut the ropes binding Amius.

"He's okay, sir!" Darmanin called out as the warlord came into the room, two Firemen at his side.

"Warlord." Arya looked up in shock. "Sir, you shouldn't be here. Please—"

Bralin let out an unholy roar and *surged* upwards. His forehead crashed into her chin, and she reeled back, stunned. He shoved her off him with an inhuman strength and she went flying, hitting the wall hard. Blackness loomed in her vision, and she fought to stay conscious.

By the time Arya struggled back to her feet, blinking through blurred vision and garbled thoughts, Darmanin had freed Amius. Bralin lunged towards them both and Darmanin reacted fast, shoving Amius towards the window and stepping into Bralin's path.

Bralin crashed into Darmanin with that same unexpected force, sending him staggering backwards into the bed, then turned after Amius with a fixed, glazed, look on his face. That look sent horror tingling down Arya's spine.

Whatever Bralin had been fighting. Whatever resolve or sanity he had left.

It was gone.

Only Arya could see that look, and therefore the danger to Amius. She dived for Bralin.

She wasn't fast enough.

Helden SparrowWing roared in anguish as Bralin collided with his son and dragged him to the open window.

Time seemed to slow. Arya caught the warlord's expression of utter despair as his son fought uselessly—it was clear Bralin had some source of extra strength. Was he a magic-wielder of some kind?

"They're making me. They're making me." Bralin kept repeating those words as he muscled Amius' struggling form up against the windowsill. They were too entangled for the Longbows outside to take out Bralin.

Everyone in the room was diving towards Amius and Bralin, but Arya was the only one close enough to reach them before Bralin could shove Amius all the way through the opening. But she knew even as she reached him, wrapped an arm around his neck and tried to yank him backwards, that it wasn't going to work. He was too strong.

He simply squared his shoulders against her hold and kept pushing the struggling Amius out the window. She drew her dagger, drove it into his side, angling towards his heart.

But aside from a bellow of pain, he didn't stop. Arya swore. Who was this man? She needed more to stop him. Her strength was no match for his. Not unless…

"Dar, be ready to grab Amius," she shouted.

Then she closed her eyes, pressed her free hand against the small of Bralin's back, and she let go of the surging magic she'd been fighting back since first stepping foot in this room and coming under threat.

"Arya, NO!" Darmanin roared at her.

Her magic exploded out of her, crackling blue sparks lighting up her spread fingers as she pressed them into Bralin. His body arched, every single muscle going rigid, and his hold on Amius froze. In a blink Darmanin was there, helping the young man fight entirely free of Bralin's hold and stagger away from the window.

Warlord SparrowWing swept his son into his arms, tears of relief sliding down his cheeks. Firemen gathered protectively around them.

"Get out, get clear!" Darmanin called to the warlord after a quick glance in Arya's direction. "We'll deal with the archer."

As if on cue, another Fireman ran into the room, soot-stained and sweaty. "Warlord. The entire floor is in flame, but we've contained a narrow path to get you out!"

SparrowWing nodded, pushed Amius ahead of him, and the Firemen took him safely from the room.

Arya let go then, gasping, staggering away from Bralin as energy drained out of her in a flood. She barely managed to suck in a breath before Bralin recovered and spun towards her. His brown eyes were now red and gleaming. He snarled, teeth bared. "You!" his voice was a hiss. Surprise and delight rang through that sound.

Dread sank through Arya, deep and insidious. Bralin wasn't crazy.

There *was* something in his head.

A nazal. She felt it deep in her bones. But why would a nazal attack Amius SparrowWing?

She backed up, shaky and disoriented. Bralin's red eyes gleamed in triumph. Agonising pain flared along her lightning scar, and she screamed, dropping to her knees clutching her right arm.

"BEGONE!" Darmanin roared. He leaped at Bralin, cazaix sword glinting in the orange of the flames, grey eyes luminous.

Bralin ducked away, let out a matching snarl, then knocked Darmanin's sword aside and crashed into him. He slammed Darmanin against the wall, winding him, then turned on Arya. She staggered to her feet, swordless, and faced him.

"You can't kill us," she told it defiantly.

It laughed.

When it lunged at her, instinct took over. Arya drew tight on all four of the threads inside her, the ones she'd been aware of for a long time now, and she pulled.

Strength flooded her. Clarity of purpose.

But there was another thread there too, one she hadn't noticed before. It was—

The nazal screamed in triumph, eyes flaring bright red, and then she *felt* it, grabbing those threads, following them, the snuffling sound it made as it tracked an unbearable noise in her head. Frantically, she let go, realising her mistake, but it was too late, the thing had already—

Bralin crashed into her, and they hit the floor. She fought bitterly, kicking and clawing, just managing to get him off her. Darmanin had recovered by then, and he straddled the man, dagger raised. Bralin knocked it aside and Darmanin went for his throat instead, closing both hands around it. His snarl tore through the room, low and deadly.

By then Arya had reached her sword. And as she sent a warning along the thread between her and Darmanin, they acted in perfect concert. He loosened his hold on Bralin's throat, throwing himself backwards.

At the same moment, Arya brought her cazaix blade down on Bralin's neck, severing his head from his body. A shriek of pain resonated through her head, sending her swaying, and then it was gone, cut off as quick as a link.

A momentary silence fell over the room. Arya blinked, breathing hard, regaining her senses. "Darmanin." She was at a loss for words.

"We have to go." Darmanin dragged her into the hallway. All she could see was smoke and orange flame, the heat blistering her skin. They stumbled through it together, coughing and spluttering, somehow getting down the hall and the stairs until eventually they stumbled out the front door and into the square.

Arya gulped in the fresh night air, sooty, sweat-soaked, and exhausted. She forced herself to stand straight and take stock of the situation. A shield of Firemen surrounded the warlord and his son nearby. A quick sweep showed the cordon holding, though a large crowd had massed around the edges of the square.

Rorin appeared then, Taze hovering at his shoulder, her three shield captains trailing them. "*Are you both all right?*"

"We're fine," Darmanin replied, jaw tense.

"General," Taze asked. "Your orders?"

She glanced over her shoulder, saw Firemen crawling all over the still-burning townhouse, making sure it didn't spread to neighbouring properties. The situation seemed well in hand.

"Laskin, make sure the cordon remains in place until the Fireman are confident there is no more danger to residents. Zamarin, take your shield and escort Warlord SparrowWing and his son safely wherever they're going tonight. If the warlord allows it, stay with them, and ensure they get to the Council meeting tomorrow safely."

"*I'll speak with the warlord now, offer him the Ravenstrike townhouse to stay,*" Rorin said. "*Captain Zamarin, please come with me.*"

He strode off without another word, making his way to the huddle where SparrowWing was consulting with his captains about the fire, Zamarin trailing him after Taze translated Rorin's order.

Arya turned to her remaining captain. "Rarik, take your shield back to the barracks. Make sure there's a double guard on the walls tonight, then get some rest."

They dispersed, leaving Arya standing with Darmanin and Taze.

"What is it?" Taze asked warily, glancing between them.

Arya swallowed, meeting Darmanin's gaze. "It was a nazal."

"We don't know that," Darmanin said immediately. "Bralin might just as likely have been a magic-wielder, driven mad by his magic, or an illness, or a drug of some kind."

"He might have been," she said. "Except for the fact that as soon as I used my magic the thing inside him recognised me. Don't tell me you didn't feel its surprise when it recognised me."

"You…" Taze trailed off, then his shoulders straightened, and a soldier's focus settled over his face. "A nazal is in Gateport. Are you sure, General?"

She nodded, stomach sinking. "I'm sure."

Darmanin crossed his arms and glared at her. "What were you *thinking*?"

A shudder went through Arya at the memory of Bralin's glowing red eyes. "Amius would have died, Dar."

"Amius SparrowWing is not our responsibility."

"If you think I'm ever going to stand by while someone's life is threatened and do nothing, you don't know me very well," she snapped.

"You are a general. You don't get to make decisions like that anymore. You *have* to stand by if it's for the good of your army or your State."

"I don't have to do anything," she told him, temper flaring. "Including taking condescending as shit orders from you."

"You're the one that keeps saying you want power enough to influence things," he said. "But the price for power like that is that you don't get to always do things your own way."

She didn't look away from his gaze. "We'll see about that."

Chapter 36

Arya went for a long run in the pre-dawn hours, feet pounding against the Gateport streets as she allowed her thoughts free rein. She hadn't even tried sleeping after the night's events.

If a nazal was in Gateport...

Darmanin's words from the morning before kept echoing through her mind.

"It's bad enough we're all in one place for the duration of the State Council."

All the Sky Lords were here. Gateport was a massive city, but the nazal knew Arya's identity now. Her cazaix blade would keep her hidden from them no longer.

And now, thanks to her pulling on the threads linking her to the other Sky Lords when the nazal attacked her, well, the nazal won't know who they were, but it was possible they could now recognise their magic. Guilt swamped Arya. Why had she pulled on those threads? It had been instinctive, a plea for strength and something else. But it had been exactly what the nazal wanted.

And there had been that fifth thread, hidden—it was how the nazal had been able to latch onto her, she was sure of it. It had used that thread to find the others *through* her. A shudder went through her at the memory of it, even hours later. She wanted it gone, but didn't dare try and reach for any of those bonds in case it allowed the monster to attack.

She had to fix it, somehow. And that started with a warning to all of them. *And* the full truth of what she knew. If they then chose to go their own way, at least they'd go armed with as much information as possible to keep themselves safe.

Even Leanir.

The sun was rising above the horizon as Arya returned from her run, feeling marginally better. She went straight to where Laskin was drilling with his shield. He saluted in greeting. "General. Pulled up all right after last night?"

"I'm fine." She drew him aside, lowered her voice. "Do you have any way of contacting the Shadeweaver network in Gateport?"

He stared at her for a long moment, then walked a few paces even further away. "Dare I ask why the general of Ravenstrike is even considering talking to a Shadeweaver?"

"I need to get a message to Leanir. I can't tell you why, but it's important."

"Arya, the implications if *anyone* found out you were talking to—"

"I know, Laskin, but I still need you to do it."

He sighed. "What's the message?"

She passed him a folded piece of paper.

Still jittery, Arya joined drill, hoping more physical exercise would help calm her. But just over an hour later, as she followed her warlord into the domed Council chamber, her chest was still tight with anxiety. Her gaze constantly scanned their surroundings, looking for a monster ready to leap out at them. But everything seemed so normal. She supposed it couldn't risk attacking in broad daylight in front of so many soldiers.

She didn't even know what they *looked* like. Could they pass as human enough to escape notice? One of them could clearly take over a human's mind and force them to do its bidding, but could it control *any* human, or were there limitations? Why hadn't she asked for more details from Salyarin when he'd warned her about the nazal. She'd been too damn stubborn.

"Arya?" Thiara's voice was sharp, as if she'd been trying and failing to get her attention.

"I'm sorry, Warlord. What did you say?" She forced herself to focus.

"You look tired." Thiara's gaze roved her face. "Did you get any sleep after last night?"

Both Arya and Rorin had briefed his mother late the night before on the events of the evening. "Not really. I'm fine, though."

"You won't be if you don't get enough rest. I need you sharp for the confirmation hearing tomorrow. Go back to barracks, I don't need you today."

"I'm fine to—"

"Go," Thiara ordered. "Rest."

Reluctantly, Arya let her go on ahead, then waved over the captain of the warlord's personal shield. "Keep a close eye today, Robem. Until the Defenders get to the bottom of last night's events, I want to be extra careful."

"General." He saluted. "We'll keep her safe, don't worry."

Instead of going back to the barracks, Arya rode to the Ravenstrike townhouse, where she found Rorin and Essa sitting in the little gazebo in the garden at the back of the townhouse, finishing off the remains of a midday meal.

"*Hello, Arya. What brings you by?*" Rorin asked. There were shadows under his eyes and his usual energy seemed dimmed, but that had been the case almost since their arrival in Gateport.

"Are you alright?" Essa asked, concern written in her eyes. "Rorin told me what happened last night."

"I am," Arya said. "Did you feel it last night, when I—"

Essa nodded. "It was this sharp tug in my chest, like a summons I couldn't ignore. I was sitting at the time and almost leaped from my chair. But just as quickly as I felt it, it vanished, like you shut it down."

Had she done it fast enough, before the nazal got a good read on the four of them? Arya sighed, sank into one of the chairs.

"*What's wrong?*" Rorin asked.

"I need to ask a favour."

"*What is it?*"

"We need to talk, as soon as possible. Somewhere discreet so nobody knows we're meeting. Any ideas?"

"Who's *we*?" Essa asked.

"The three of us, Dar, and a couple of others." Arya looked around, lowered her voice. "Better for me not to say aloud."

Essa looked at Rorin. "What happened last night?"

He frowned. *"I told you everything I know."*

Arya leaned over the table, lowering her voice to a murmur. "Essa, I'll explain everything tonight, I promise."

Rorin considered, *"Wouldn't it look normal for Dar to come here rather than all of us sneaking out to meet somewhere? He's already visited plenty of times. Arya, could your guests come here? You and Taze could get them in through the back so that none of the Raiders see."*

"The shed in the back corner there could work. Peemla uses it to store unused furniture," Essa said thoughtfully.

"That works," Arya said. "Will you speak to Taze about it? Emphasise to him that nobody can see these guests coming in or out. I'll see you there tonight, an hour before midnight?"

"We'll be there," Rorin nodded.

***

After giving Laskin the location of the meeting to pass to Leanir, Arya snatched a couple hours of sleep at the barracks, then, unable to lie still any longer, she rode over to The Rotting Log inn. Not even the cheerful atmosphere of a popular inn served to calm her as she bought herself a mug of ale at the bar before taking a seat in the corner of the room.

More patrons filed in as the afternoon deepened. Chiarn appeared on the stage filling the top end of the room and introduced himself to the crowd, receiving a round of enthusiastic applause. With a smile he began to play.

Arya listened to the musician's full set, in no rush, genuinely enjoying his music as she sipped her ale. He played for a good hour before taking a break and a seat at the bar. The bartender gave him a glass of ale and plate of food, then left him to it.

She waited until Chiarn started on his food before slowly wending her way through the crowd and dropping into the empty seat beside him. "Hello Chiarn. Long time, no see."

The copper-haired musician started violently when he saw her, and promptly choked on his mouthful. She gave him a sympathetic pat on the back and waited until he coughed himself hoarse, drained several swallows of ale, then turned watery eyes on her. "What do you want?"

She spread her hands in an innocent gesture. "I just want to talk."

"Yes, well, I don't want to talk to you. And even if I did, I don't have time for a chat."

She smiled, rested her elbow on the bar and propped her head on her hand. "You're not really going to brush me off, are you? Considering what I know about you."

Panic flashed in his blue eyes. "You know nothing."

"You have nothing to fear from me. But we do need to talk."

"I'm not interested in whatever you have to say," he said flatly.

"Sure, you are," she said. "Because you've been running your whole life, right? First because you didn't want anyone to know about your ... secret. And now..." She leaned closer. "Now you're running because you're being hunted."

His face tightened. "I have no idea what you're talking about."

"You've had the nightmares." Arya didn't know this for a fact, but she and Essa had both had them. Darmanin too, probably, though he hadn't admitted to it. There was a good chance Chiarn had too.

"Everyone has nightmares."

Her mouth thinned. "Do I really have to sit here and tell you every detail of my nightmares to prove to you that they're the same?"

His shoulders sagged and he ran a hand through his copper curls. "What do you want from me?"

"To start, I want to share with you the information that I have."

"I have a few minutes before I go back on." He pushed his plate of food away, drained the remnants of his ale, and swivelled on his chair to face her. "You have until then."

As succinctly as she could, Arya told him everything the elder of the Etherean had told her. She told him about the dreams she'd had, and about the nazal. By the time she'd finished, Chiarn was grinning in amusement. "That's a great story. I could make a famous ballad out of that."

"That's what I thought when I first heard it."

His grin widened, but fear lurked in his eyes. "And now you believe it?"

"I believe that I am the heir to the Andahari throne, whether I want to be or not," she said. "I believe the Nightstalker considers me, and you, a threat, and wants us dead more than anything. I even believe he has sent these nazal to do the job, and after last night, I'm sure at least one of them is in Gateport."

His grin faded. "You said it yourself; I've been running my whole life. I'm a musician, not a hero. I want no part of this fairy tale about dethroning an evil king in a country I've barely even heard of, let alone stepped foot in."

"That's exactly how I feel," she admitted. "I'm general of Ravenstrike, and this is my life. But that doesn't mean I can ignore the consequences of who I am."

"It will go away," he said. "If we do nothing."

"I tried that. It didn't work." She leaned closer. "I'm here to offer you my protection, Chiarn. This thing is in the city hunting us."

"It's not hunting me," he said determinedly. "And unless you keep coming here, things should stay that way."

"I want you to come to one meeting," she said, voice intense. "We need to talk, all five of us together, and then, if you want to go your own way afterward, I won't stop you. Please."

He let out a sigh. "I'm no general or master strategist, but if this nazal knows who you are, doesn't gathering together put us all at risk?"

"It's at the Ravenstrike townhouse, so if they *are* watching me—which, yes, you're right, they likely are—they're watching for me to leave and go somewhere, see who I meet with. One of my soldiers, one I trust with my life, will sneak you in the back. We can make sure the street is clear—the warlord's personal shield does that as a security measure anyway."

"And what if they're watching you now?"

Chiarn was no idiot, despite his cowardice and lackadaisical demeanour. Arya smiled, leaned in to murmur in his ear. "Put your hand on my leg, and smile. We're flirting, Chiarn."

A smile flickered over his face despite himself. His hand slid onto her knee, fingers caressing. "When?"

"An hour before midnight." Arya kept a flirtatious smile on her face as she stood. "Come to the back gate. Make sure nobody follows you there."

"I'll think about it." The words were sour, but he gave her a wink and a smile for the benefit of anyone watching.

He'd come. Arya saw the fear in his eyes. She didn't like leveraging that, but it was for his own protection. Before leaving, she leaned in once more, left hand running up the outside of his leg while her right hand placed a cloth-wrapped bundle in his lap. She'd carried that bundle all the way from Khadini. "Keep this with you, always."

He whistled when he discreetly slid the cloth away. "A cazaix dagger. What's this for?"

"It will hide you from the nazal. But I recommend you avoid cutting yourself with it—cazaix can apparently make Sky Lords very sick."

Arya's stomach turned as she left the inn, any temporary relaxation she'd felt from Chiarn's music fading entirely. All her Sky Lords together for the first time. So dangerous. But necessary.

The need to keep them safe wasn't a choice for her, she'd realised. It was an instinct she couldn't ignore, like the threads inside her that connected them all. Like a noose around her neck.

She wished more than anything she could be free of it.

Chapter 37

At the appointed time, Arya waited with Rorin, Darmanin, and Essa in the cluttered but tidy shed at the back of the garden. Darmanin was silent, brooding, and Essa merely looked unhappy and tired. Rorin sat quietly, shoulders hunched, gaze on the floor. It wasn't the most bolstering of atmospheres.

When Taze knocked, Arya went to the door, hesitating only a moment before opening it and allowing Leanir to slide through. "No one saw you?"

He gave her a disgusted look.

"What the hell is he doing here?" Darmanin stepped forward, hand going to the hilt of his sword.

"What do you think he's doing here?" Arya snapped, in no more mood for Darmanin's petulance than she was Rorin's.

Rorin glanced between them, clearly putting two and two together. "*The attack on Amius last night had something to do with the nazal, didn't it?*"

"One more person will be here soon, and then I'll explain," Arya said. "Leanir, you agree to the terms of my message?" She'd given her word that she wouldn't seek to arrest or harm him in any way if he agreed not to threaten anyone in attendance.

"I'm here, aren't I?" The Shadeweaver's gaze was wary as he looked around the room, one hand on the hilt of his cazaix dagger. "This better not be a trap."

"It's not." She paused, forced the words out. "My word on it."

He looked unconvinced, backing away to the farthest corner of the shed. Even so, he said, "Safe passage agreement goes both ways."

Arya took a breath, hesitated, then forged ahead. "There's something you need to know, Leanir. You—"

"Arya, stop." Darmanin stepped forward. "You can't tell him."

"I have to," she said. "I don't have a choice."

"What does that mean?" He searched her gaze.

"He's one of us. And after what I did last night, I owe him the information he needs to protect himself."

"*And what if he uses the information to betray you to the warlords? If they find out who you are, they'll have you arrested and shipped off to Andahar in a blink. Besides, I thought you* wanted *him dead?*" Rorin asked, as confused as Darmanin.

"Yes." She expelled a breath and glanced at Essa, who merely gave her a small smile and a nod. "I did. I do ... I think. But this is different."

"That doesn't make any—" Darmanin started.

"I *am* standing right here," Leanir snarled. "What in raven's balls is going on?"

Arya faced him, crossed her arms. "Ranier sent you with us to run the Dreadwater because you are a Sky Lord of Andahar, just as I am, and Dar, and Essa. The Nightstalker knows we exist, and he's been hunting us for years. The cazaix blade you stole hides your magic from the Nightstalker's hunters—monsters called nazal. By all accounts they are incredibly dangerous to us."

A long silence fell. Leanir held her gaze, expressionless. A killer's look. Eventually he spoke, deadly quiet. "If all this is true, why choose to tell me now?"

"You don't look entirely surprised, Leanir." Her gaze narrowed. "As if you know what a Sky Lord is and what it means already."

"What I know is none of your business, Raider."

A second tap came at the door, forestalling Arya's response. She opened it to wave Taze and Chiarn inside. A quick glance at Chiarn's hip showed he wore the dagger she'd given him.

"The shield is arranged in such a way that there are no eyes on this shed," Taze confirmed. "And nobody is stationed within hearing distance."

A gap in Rorin's guard she didn't like, but at least she and Taze were with him. And having this meeting at all was already too big a risk for all of them. They couldn't afford anyone else knowing about it.

Chiarn sighed as he looked around the room. "Secret meeting, is it? Is that a Shadeweaver standing over in the corner—he looks like he's about to start slitting our throats any second now. Should I take it these are my supposed fellow Sky Lords?"

A snarl ripped from Leanir's throat. "You *told* him?"

Arya stepped between the two men, facing down Leanir. "I just told you, didn't I?"

"That is ridiculous." Leanir looked at Chiarn in disgust. "You think I'm destined to be on a team with *that?* The Nightstalker must be shaking in his boots at the thought of being sung to death."

"I'm inclined to agree, but I'll tell you the same thing I told Chiarn," Arya said. "If you want to walk after this meeting and never look back, that's fine by me. I'd prefer you did. But I owe you all a warning and the information you need to make an informed decision."

"What did you do, Raider?" That dangerously flat expression settled over Leanir's dark features again.

There was no point in prevaricating, so she told them everything about the events of the night before. "At least one of the nazal hunting us is here in Gateport. It knows who I am, and there's a chance it can recognise the rest of your magic. I think it's connected to me somehow."

"What does that mean?" Chiarn looked white as a sheet.

Arya hesitated. "They already knew my magic—from trapping me in my nightmares—but last night one of them saw my face, which means they will soon know my name, if they don't already. And through their connection to me, they can ... see or track my bonds to the rest of you. I cut them off quickly last night, but I don't know how much the monster saw."

"Then it's safe to assume they can recognise *our* magic now too, even if they don't know our faces or identities," Leanir said, cold and cutting in his disgust. "It was beyond stupid of you to use your magic."

"Watch the insults, Leanir," Arya warned. "You weren't the one standing in a burning-down house wrestling with a madman trying to kill a warlord's son."

"He has a point," Darmanin said. "What if Bralin took Amius to draw you out?"

"How could the nazal know that one of the Sky Lords they're hunting would come to Amius' rescue?" Essa gave him a scathing look. "If *I* took hostage a warlord's son, I would expect that warlord's soldiers to come for me, not a Sky Lord."

"She's right, but Dar has a point. What did the nazal want with Amius SparrowWing?" Taze said as Darmanin opened his mouth, looking like he was about to disagree.

"I don't give a single raven's ball about that. Your recklessness has put all of us at risk," Leanir rounded on Arya. "What were you thinking?"

Arya stiffened, took a step closer to him. "I wasn't going to let Amius die."

Leanir didn't back down. "A rich warlord's son is worth more than any of us, is that it?"

His dark gaze challenged hers, and his hand shifted, moving towards his knife. She snapped, pushing forward, and getting in his face. "He's certainly worth more than you, Shadeweaver."

Leanir watched her with that tell-tale smirk. A heavy silence fell over the shed, and Essa broke it by asking bluntly, "Who else is dreaming of a wyvern?"

Arya lifted a hand. So did Essa. Darmanin and Leanir didn't. Chiarn twitched, eyes dropping to the floor, but didn't move his arm. So that was a yes.

"When were you going to mention that?" Darmanin snapped.

"Don't take that tone, Dar," Essa said. "The nazal can find us when we dream of the wyverns, but we can't control those dreams. None of this is Arya's fault."

"Her choices are," Chiarn said. "If these creatures are after Arya—"

"They're after *all of us*, Chiarn," Arya said. "The cazaix blades we wear *might* hide us from the nazal, but unless none of you plan on never using your magic ever again, even accidentally, they'll find you eventually. The Nightstalker isn't going to give up, not as long as we live."

"And even if we wear our cazaix everywhere and never touch our magic again, we can't stop the dreams of our wyverns when they come," Essa pointed out. "The nazal will have us then. They haven't been able to hurt us in our nightmares so far, but I'd prefer not to test that. Even if they can't, the more times they trap out minds, the more chances they have to learn our identities."

"You said at least one," Leanir said. "How many nazal are there?"

"Four or five." Arya shrugged. "But that's a guess. Only one seems to have the ability to trap our minds, but I've always been able to sense more of them in the nightmares. Hard to get an exact count while I'm panicked and trying to escape, though." Chiarn paled. Leanir raised his eyebrows but said nothing. Darmanin merely crossed his arms and brooded.

"*Can we fight these nazal?*" Rorin asked.

"Not according to Salyarin," Arya huffed a breath in annoyance. "He went to great pains to impress upon me how powerful they are and how we'd have no hope of defending ourselves against one until we took up our heritage and learned our magic."

"But you killed one last night?" Taze pointed out.

Arya shared a glance with Darmanin. "No, we killed the human body it was riding, and it took two of us to do it. I think we should assume in its natural form it will be much more dangerous."

"Can't you reach out to the Etherean?" Darmanin asked. "Ask for more information. At the very least, maybe he can teach us how to stop having the wyvern dreams?"

"We're too far from the Diamondfang for Salyarin to reach my dreams, even if I had some way of contacting him," Arya said. "But there are some sensible precautions we can take immediately. We never speak of this aloud, ever. Chiarn, Leanir, it's crucial neither of you are seen associated with me after tonight. Leanir, you should leave Gateport and return to the Diamondfang. You'll be safer with Ranier and the Shadeweavers."

"I don't take orders from you," he said. "Magical destiny or no."

Her gaze narrowed, but Darmanin spoke before she could respond. "Leanir and Chiarn can do as they like. The rest of us just need to keep our heads down and focus on the State Council. If they only know us by sense, then we can stay hidden as long as we wear our cazaix and don't use our magic."

Arya fumed at Darmanin's high-handed orders but kept quiet. He wasn't wrong.

"The nazal might not go after you immediately, Arya," Essa said, thoughtful. "I mean, if that was their intention, they'd be here right now, right? So either it *can't* come after you openly for some reason, or ..." Her eyes brightened and she looked up. "What if the nazal thinks it can use you to track the rest of us?"

Rorin smiled at her. "*Of course. They would be smarter to wait and find out who all of you are before striking. That way none of you are left alive.*"

"Now we're assuming these monsters are capable of thinking intelligently, are we?" Leanir snapped.

"They've remained hidden from us so far," Darmanin said. "That indicates both patience and the ability to plan. I don't think it's a good idea to underestimate them."

"*So what then? We let Arya stay in the city so the nazal can use her to find the rest of you too?*" Rorin asked.

"I'm not leaving, Rorin," Arya said. "I refuse to be chased off by some monster just because it wants to kill me. Let it come. I'll destroy it, no matter what the elder said."

He raised his arms in surrender and backed off.

A tense silence permeated the room as everyone either glared at the floor or at someone else. Arya could feel the weight of Darmanin's impassive stare, but refused to look at him, not in the mood for the censure she would see in his eyes.

"I've done just fine all these years on my own, and I intend to keep doing so," Chiarn said into the ensuing silence.

"And if the nazal finds you?" Leanir sauntered over, fingering his knife. "You want to deal with that all alone too?"

"I'm willing to take those odds," Chiarn said.

Leanir shrugged and turned to Arya. "Your thoughts on a deal, Raider?"

Her gaze narrowed. "That depends on what you want."

"If this monster comes for me, I'll expect your help. The same in reverse. You will have mine."

Arya didn't hesitate. She still didn't trust Leanir, owed him his death one day for the things he'd done, but she'd believed Salyarin when he'd told her how dangerous the nazal were. If she wanted to protect those she loved, it would be foolish to discount the help of an assassin of Leanir's skills. She nodded. "My word on it."

"And my word on it." Leanir gave her a cold smile. "If you need me, light two candles on the windowsill of your quarters here or at your barracks. Send another clumsy Raider looking for me and I'll kill them."

He left without another word, opening the door and vanishing into the shadows beyond.

Chiarn gave them an elegant bow. "I wish I could say it has been a pleasure. Please do me a favour and stay away."

"Taze will make sure you get out without being spotted." It was on the tip of Arya's tongue to recommend that he leave the city too, but if he did that he'd be even more isolated.

"I don't need luck," he said before sweeping out the door.

Taze followed behind.

It closed with a click and heavy silence permeated the dim space. Arya leaned against the wall, weary to the bone.

"Now they're gone, we need to talk about Warlord SparrowWing." Essa spoke, breaking the silence.

Rorin started. "*Why?*"

"He saw Arya use her magic to save Amius," Darmanin said.

"He *might* have seen," Arya corrected. "My hand was pressed against Bralin's back when I did it. It could very well just have looked like me using an unarmed combat manoeuvre to get him off Amius."

"An unarmed combat manoeuvre with a crackling blue light?" Darmanin snorted. "You should *never* have—"

"Darmanin, will you stop harping on that, it's not constructive!" Essa rounded on him. "Arya did what she thought best at the time. No matter what your opinion is, the deed is done. Leave it."

Darmanin's jaw tightened, and he withdrew into himself. "I won't apologise for being right, Essa."

"Which would be fine if you were actually angry at Arya, but you're not." Essa didn't back down. "You're angry at the situation. Don't take it out on us."

More silence fell.

Essa continued, "That's not what I meant, even though it's a very good point. Why did a nazal take Amius hostage? And Arya, how you described Bralin ... it sounds very similar to the description of the intruder who broke into one of SparrowWing's properties a couple of weeks ago to steal his banking codes, don't you think?"

Startled, Arya's head came up. "You're right. So Bralin was the thief—and we have to assume he was controlled by the nazal that night too."

The door clicked open and Taze returned. "Nobody saw Chiarn leave. He was heading for The Rotting Log when I left him."

Essa frowned. "So a nazal stole a bunch of money from Warlord SparrowWing and then took his son hostage, but there was no ransom. Why?"

Arya's brain felt like it was melting. "I can't even begin to imagine why, Essa. What does SparrowWing have to do with nazal hunting Sky Lords? It's not like he has any connection to us, or knowledge of us."

"*Maybe they think he does, for some reason?*" Rorin ventured.

"Even if so, how does stealing money or kidnapping his son help them find us?" Darmanin looked as confounded as the rest of them.

"I think maybe the nazal did plan on killing Amius," Arya said slowly, thinking back. "Bralin seemed reluctant. I think he was fighting the nazal's control. If we hadn't been there, he would have lost that fight and Amius would be dead."

"Either way, we have to assume the nazal have another purpose in messing with SparrowWing," Essa said, thinking. "The nazal are the Nightstalker's Sky Lord hunters, but what if they're not *just* that? What if they serve him in other ways too?"

"What we need to worry about most is the nazal coming after us," Arya said.

"*And if SparrowWing saw you use magic.*" Rorin pointed out. "*SparrowWing can be very tough on his people, but fair at the same time. My mother respects him. But I also know that he hates magic-wielders.*"

"Many of the outcasts Ranier receives into the Shadeweavers are from SparrowWing State," Darmanin added.

Arya rubbed a hand at suddenly aching temples.

"You saved his son's life," Essa said. "Surely that will count for something?"

"*There's no more we can do tonight except talk in circles,*" Rorin said. "*The confirmation hearings are only a few hours away. We need rest. Today will unfold how it will.*"

"See you in the Council chamber in a few hours," Darmanin said.

Rorin reached out and took hold of his arm to stop him. "*Dar, wait.*"

"What is it?"

"*Before you go … I need to apologise to you all. My behaviour since we arrived in Gateport has been childish and selfish. The events of tonight have made me realise that I'm only adding to your worries. My problems are my own to manage, and how I've been behaving isn't the right way to do that. Will you accept my apology?*"

"You are my brother," Darmanin said.

Rorin smiled. "*Thank you.*"

"I accept your apology also," Arya said. "You know I will always have your back, Rorin. And you know we're here to help with whatever problem you're having."

"*This isn't something you can help with,*" he signed, sadness in his eyes. "*But I thank you anyway.*"

Arya thought about pushing further, but he left the shed before she decided, and in the end she was glad. Exhaustion tugged at her and instead of following the others, she leaned against the shed door, breathing in the night air. Worrying.

She wondered if distance would be enough. Or if they were all kidding themselves that the nazal wouldn't eventually find Chiarn and Leanir too. After all, the Nightstalker had apparently found and killed all Sky Lords born since his coup.

Maybe it would be easier to go on the offensive.

Slay the creature before it could trap and kill them.

Chapter 38

Once again, Arya walked a step behind her warlord as they ascended the marble steps to the domed Council chamber. For the first time since the Council had opened, Rorin walked with them.

He'd surprised them all that morning, appearing downstairs resplendent in a long velvet jacket over blood-red vest and white shirt. He was clean-shaven, and his blonde curls were tied back neatly in a short braid. His cazaix sword hung at his waist. While his natural ebullience remained dimmed, he'd been civil to everyone, including his mother.

Arya's stomach tightened with anxiety. She'd barely slept again the previous night, and weariness tugged at her. *Had* SparrowWing seen her use magic? Or guessed at it? She swallowed and glanced at Thiara. What would her warlord do if SparrowWing started making claims that Arya was a magic-wielder? He had no evidence, after all. But just the claims would be enough to damage Thiara's High Warlord bid. Especially since SparrowWing was one of the warlords they needed to vote in her favour.

Today was about Rorin, though. He hadn't been there that night, but if SparrowWing sought to make problems for Ravenstrike's warlord because of Arya, then this would be the time to do it. Her palms sweated, and she tried to calm her breathing.

Should she have said something to warn her warlord? No. Even if the worst happened, it was best she knew nothing at all, that her shock and dismay were genuine. That way she could cut Arya loose and salvage the situation the best she could. Arya's stomach curled with nausea at the thought.

Darmanin's tall figure approached as they entered the wide hall circling the Council chamber, as if he'd been waiting for them. He, too, had been absent from the Council hearings so far, and his appearance was causing a visible buzz of muttered whispers.

He wore black breeches, shirt, and violet waistcoat. His cuffs were trimmed in matching violet, and his cazaix sword was prominent at his waist. He wore his raven hair similar to Rorin's in a single short braid. Arya found it hard to credit this imposing young man with the skinny wildling boy who'd come to Heathrock to live all those years ago.

"It was the biggest gamble I've ever made," Thiara murmured to Arya as Darmanin approached. "But look at what we made of him."

Look at what he made of himself, Arya thought instead.

"Warlord Ravenstrike." He greeted them with a graceful bow. "I am glad to see you here."

"Darmanin. I'm surprised to see you—your hearing isn't until tomorrow."

"I wanted to be here to support Rorin, and perhaps create some distraction to keep those here from focusing too much on his muteness," Darmanin said. "Andrian is here too and wanted me to make it known to you that whatever our father says, Andrian's support lies with Rorin."

"Ravenstrike is appreciative," Thiara Ravenstrike said formally. "We should go in."

Their footsteps echoed in the cavernous space as Arya followed Thiara Ravenstrike to her chair at the central table. Magen was already there, seated in the chair beside his warlord's. Directly behind them, hanging down the circular wall, was the Ravenstrike tapestry; an impressive red striking raven displayed on black.

"Warlord Ravenstrike." Gelfrey Hawkesdale's voice boomed. He wore a green waistcoat, the gold-edged buttons straining over his girth. His cufflinks were set with glittering emeralds, but otherwise his attire was simple.

"Warlord Hawkesdale." Thiara smiled with genuine warmth before nodding coolly at the younger man seated beside him, as well as the two respective chief advisers. "Warlord Falconcrest. I hope you're both well this morning?"

Arya watched as the three exchanged pleasantries. Nashdar Falconcrest, a slim man with dark skin and tight curls of raven hair, was the youngest of the six warlords, only in his early thirties. He had a reputation for being aggressive and impulsive, a reputation mirrored by his Aggressors. Arya was certain he'd been behind sending his Aggressors out to bait Rorin that night. His general—also his husband—stood stiff behind Nashdar's chair, staring into the distance, and ignoring Arya's attempts to meet his gaze and offer a greeting.

Mathas Crowtalon and Helden SparrowWing arrived then. Darmanin's father looked suave, strong, and confident. His brown hair and beard were neatly trimmed, and he looked every inch a future High Warlord. Beside him, Andrian was a handsome young man, but didn't hold the commanding presence his father did. Nain was with them, supercilious expression firmly in place.

Striding at Mathas Crowtalon's side was Jenka Crowtalon. He'd grown into a tall man, with his mother's heavyset build and the Crowtalon broad shoulders. Thiara's expression narrowed at the sight of him, but none of the Ravenstrike contingent were surprised to see her nephew there.

With Helden SparrowWing came Amius, and the general of his Fireman army. The general gave Arya a nod as he took up the position behind his warlord's chair. She smiled back at him. None of the other generals had acknowledged her presence. Amius stopped by Darmanin and Rorin to greet them. He was a thin, serious looking young man, just like his father, but he also offered Arya a nod of acknowledgment. "Thank you, General Ravenstrike. I'm sorry I haven't had a chance to say that to you yet."

"You're welcome, Lord SparrowWing." She bowed her head respectfully.

SparrowWing's features were unreadable as he took his seat at the table and exchanged greetings with the others. Amius' gratitude had seemed sincere but reserved. Had *he* seen what Arya had done? Had his father told him? Arya's anxiety tightened to a fierce knot in her chest that made it hard to breathe.

Andrian greeted his brother cheerfully, but Mathas' face tightened at the sight of Darmanin. He would not readily display a lack of control in front of the warlords, but Arya could sense his anger seething beneath the surface. She saw the internal struggle play out on his face—demand that Darmanin leave the room or forgo a distraction that might paint him in a poor light. Before he could decide, Nain leaned over and murmured something in his ear. Mathas' shoulders relaxed, and he stayed quiet. Darmanin took up a position beside his brother behind the Crowtalon chair.

Finally, the doors at the opposite end of the room opened and the Eaglesoar contingent entered in a large group. Darien Eaglesoar, the elderly High Warlord, led the way, helped by his youngest son, Matte Eaglesoar. Striding behind them was the tall, rangy Roan Eaglesoar, warlord of Eaglesoar State.

With them came two Defenders, the Eaglesoar general and the two chief advisers, along with a gaggle of clerks whose job it was to record the events of the session. The Defenders took up position behind the High Warlord's chair, while the clerks arrayed themselves at the base of the table, ink and parchment ready.

Servants appeared to cover the table with jugs and cups, as well as plates of food. Once they were done, and had filed out of the chamber, the High Warlord spoke. "Greetings all."

"High Warlord," came the respectful response.

"Today marks the start of our heir confirmation hearings," he spoke.

Quills scratched on parchment as the clerks went to work.

"The first on our agenda is that of Ravenstrike."

From what Arya had observed in the Council sessions so far, Darien Eaglesoar might be elderly and physically frail, but his mind was still sharp. His eyes were bright, and they crackled with intelligence as he shifted his gaze to Ravenstrike's warlord. "Are you ready to begin, Warlord Ravenstrike?"

"Yes, my Lord," Thiara spoke.

"If I may, High Warlord?" Helden SparrowWing spoke before Darien could reply. "I'd like to propose that we confirm both Ravenstrike and Crowtalon heirs this morning. I have information on the candidates for both States that is relevant to their claims, and I feel it is important to deal with both issues at once."

Arya let out a shaken breath. Nausea roiled in her stomach and sweat prickled under her heavy layers. It was all she could do to keep an expressionless mask on her face. She didn't dare look at Rorin or Darmanin. But a quick look at the Crowtalon warlord showed his surprise in the faint narrowing of his eyes.

He hadn't been expecting this. Thiara Ravenstrike appeared curious, but not unduly worried. Arya squirmed, horrified that her warlord had no idea of what was coming. Thiara Ravenstrike wouldn't forgive Arya this, and nor should she. If SparrowWing outed Arya, then all her warlord's careful planning and strategising was about to go up in flames. Arya could only hope that her ignorance of it all would save her.

What had she been thinking? Darmanin was right. So was Leanir. She should never have used her magic.

Darien broke Arya from her spiralling thoughts. "It's an unusual request, Warlord SparrowWing, but I don't have a problem with it. We shall proceed with the confirmations for both Ravenstrike and Crowtalon today."

Mathas cleared his throat. "High Warlord, I don't think—"

"Oh hush, Mathas. It's not going to take all day to confirm Ravenstrike. We might as well get your State done in the one sitting," the High Warlord said irritably. "Then we get a free morning tomorrow."

"My Lord." Mathas subsided.

Thiara Ravenstrike stood. "High Warlord, my fellow warlords. You all know my son, Rorin Ravenstrike. He is of age, and my only child. I propose to confirm him as heir to Ravenstrike. I have no doubt that he will make a fine warlord after me."

She sat, and Darien waved to Hawkesdale, sitting on his right.

Gelfrey shrugged. "The boy is legitimate, and a direct heir. I had the opportunity to foster him in my home, and it is clear to me that his lack of voice is no reflection of his sense, intelligence, or judgement. I support his confirmation."

Darian nodded and turned to Mathas. "Warlord Crowtalon?"

"I am wary, High Warlord. Warlord Hawkesdale too easily dismisses the boy's disability. How would he lead an army without a voice? How would we communicate with him in Council?" Mathas spoke with a tone of considered sympathy. "Think also of his conduct since arriving at Gateport. He seems to have caroused his way through every inn in the city, not to mention starting a brawl which damaged property. My young nephew, Jenka Crowtalon, is a sensible, clever lad. He has the same education and is also a direct heir of the Ravenstrike line."

Darien frowned. "Are you formally putting forward your nephew for contention?"

"I am, High Warlord. In my view, Rorin is not a suitable candidate. My vote is for Jenka Crowtalon as the Ravenstrike heir."

"Jenka will never have my support." Thiara's voice was cold as a winter's day.

"I agree with Crowtalon." Falconcrest sat with his arms folded across his chest. "Your boy can't lead if he can't speak, and he's a wastrel. Jenka has my vote too."

Into the silence that followed, Rorin took a step forward, standing directly behind his mother's chair. When he began signing, Arya translated, keeping her voice crisp and clear. "*Warlord Crowtalon, Warlord Falconcrest, I appreciate that you have not had the opportunity to know me as Warlord Hawkesdale has. But I respectfully disagree with your view of me. I am as strong as a warlord needs to be, and I can prove that to you. Last month, I successfully ran the Dreadwater Gate.*" Rorin drew his cazaix blade. The metal gleamed blue in the morning sun shining from above.

The warlords stared.

"Nobody has run the Dreadwater and survived since Crowtalon," Hawkesdale said.

Mathas frowned but kept his polite air. "Ravenstrike's vicelords have been spreading rumours of this since arriving in Gateport. A carefully crafted story to bolster the boy's claims, no doubt. It takes more steel than he has to survive the Dreadwater."

Rorin offered Crowtalon the hilt of his sword. *"This blade is cazaix, my Lord. Are you claiming that I am lying about how I obtained it?"*

"If you are, I can verify his word," Arya spoke once she had translated. "As can many others."

"Including me." Darmanin stepped forward, in one smooth movement drawing his cazaix blade. The blue metal sang clearly, and the warlords were visibly astonished. "I ran the Dreadwater with Rorin."

Mathas' eyes widened slightly when he got a closer look at the blade, but he didn't say anything, merely pushing it away with a huff.

"Dreadwater or not, the boy's character is in question," Falconcrest said.

"It hasn't escaped any of our notice that the brawl he supposedly started was with your Aggressors." Hawkesdale grumbled. "Or that there haven't been any other reports of bad behaviour—including in the three years he lived with me. And if you try and tell me that you never did anything stupid when you were drunk at his age, I'll eat my hat."

Arya risked a glance at her warlord. Sending Rorin to foster with Hawkesdale had been a masterstroke. He was no biased warlord. He was experienced and respected and his words carried a lot of weight.

"Young Rorin is my nephew." Roan Eaglesoar gave Falconcrest a mildly disapproving glance. "He's a good lad as far as I can tell, and his lack of voice cannot be too much of a liability if he survived the Dreadwater run. I'll support him as heir to Ravenstrike."

"I find myself siding with Crowtalon," the High Warlord said surprisingly. "My vote is to suspend the confirmation until the next Council, to give Rorin time to prove himself and verify his claims of running the Dreadwater. We will decide between Rorin and Jenka then."

Thiara Ravenstrike's face went cold with anger, matching the surge of frustration leaping in Arya's chest. Ravenstrike was one vote away from having Rorin's confirmation denied. It all now rode on Helden SparrowWing, the last to cast his vote.

Arya sent a glance in Darmanin's direction. His normally grave expression had deepened to frustrated anger. This was just as bad for him. His claim for Crowtalon was already tenuous, and SparrowWing's nay vote for Rorin would destroy his chances.

Helden SparrowWing sat straight in his chair, his expression still unreadable. Arya desperately wanted to sink into the floor and disappear.

"Well, Helden?" Darien asked impatiently. "You said you had information relevant to Rorin's nomination to tell us? Now might be the time since it's your vote."

"Warlords," Helden said. "I first met Rorin Ravenstrike over a year ago when he and his Raiders assisted my Firemen during a particularly bad fire season—in fact it was his Raider battalion that was critical to the saving of Seelan. I have come to know him a little better since his arrival in Gateport, and as such, I feel I am more qualified to speak to his character than any of you here apart from his mother and Hawkesdale. I firmly support Rorin Ravenstrike being confirmed as heir to his State."

Arya stared at SparrowWing in astonishment as Darien Eaglesoar, High Warlord of Dunidaen, nodded acceptance. The dour SparrowWing warlord was demonstrating a flair for the theatrical that she hadn't known was in him.

"It is official," Darien spoke over the outbreak of chatter, silencing the table. "Lord Rorin Ravenstrike is confirmed as the heir to Ravenstrike State."

"If I may continue?" Helden SparrowWing asked politely.

"Yes, yes, go on." Darien waved a hand.

"We face a threat from the northwest that we have not faced in decades. It is imperative that Dunidaen is as strong as it can be, and that includes having strong warlords with reliable successors in place. I therefore nominate Darmanin Crowtalon to be confirmed as heir to the State of Crowtalon."

It was like someone had dropped an angry cat on the table. Falconcrest half rose from his chair, a furious scowl on his face. Hawkesdale snorted in amusement, loudly. Eaglesoar rolled his eyes before slumping back in his chair. Mathas Crowtalon turned rigid with fury. Everyone else in the room began muttering to each other.

All the warlords except for Thiara had fully expected to be confirming Andrian as the heir to Crowtalon.

"Let him speak!" Roan Eaglesoar roared at a gesture from his father. "Quiet! You'll all get your turn."

Slowly the chatter faded, and everyone stared expectantly at Helden SparrowWing.

"Last night, Darmanin Crowtalon—along with General Ravenstrike—risked his life for my son, even when it could have cost him everything to do so." Helden paused. "The Ravenstrike family has, more than once, shown itself to be one of nobility and honour. If we want to assure ourselves of Dunidaen's future, then we need men like Darmanin and Rorin ruling their States in the future."

Having said his piece, Helden nodded, folded his arms, and settled back in his chair. Mathas almost exploded out of his in fury. All his veneer of politeness was gone.

"What right has Warlord SparrowWing to suggest an heir for my State? Andrian is my eldest son, and he is my choice. I do not submit Darmanin for consideration."

"You were just allowed to submit an alternate heir for Ravenstrike, Mathas, were you not?" Hawkesdale asked mildly, face twitching in what might have been smothered amusement.

Thiara Ravenstrike spoke. "My Lords, I too support Darmanin Crowtalon to be confirmed as heir to Crowtalon. I echo everything SparrowWing has said as regards his character, and I remind you I am in a position to do so given he fostered in my home for many years. I will also raise Mathas' objections to Rorin. Andrian spends even more time at the Gateport inns than my son."

Darien shifted uncomfortably. "Darmanin is hereby nominated along with his brother Andrian."

"Your argument is compelling, Warlord Ravenstrike, and I like the lad," Hawkesdale said. "Mathas, are you sure you don't want Darmanin as your heir? He is clearly someone to be reckoned with."

"Andrian is my choice for heir," Mathas said. "Darmanin is a weakling. Clearly, he relied on his friends to survive running the rapids. I wouldn't be surprised if he'd spent his time in Khadini hiding on the border while the others went to get the cazaix."

"*That's not true!*" Rorin said, echoing the indignant anger that swept through Arya.

"I am uncomfortable going against Mathas' wishes for his own State," Gelfrey said. "I will vote for Andrian."

"I too vote for Andrian," Falconcrest said.

"If I may, High Warlord." Andrian stepped forward. He gave his father a wary look, but his voice was firm. "I do not wish to be heir to Crowtalon. My brother is the better candidate, and I would be honoured to serve under him as my future warlord."

Stunned silence permeated the chamber so thoroughly that the slightest rustle of parchment could be heard. Arya was hard pressed to stop a smirk. She wondered if an heir had ever refused being confirmed before. She risked a glance at Andrian—he was visibly quailing, sweat beading on his forehead, but he didn't take his words back.

"I formally withdraw from consideration." Andrian finished, gave Darmanin a firm nod, then stepped back into place. Mathas turned a deep red, a vein pulsing in his neck.

Again, looking like he was struggling to contain amusement, Hawkesdale cleared his throat and broke the silence. "In that case, Darmanin has my vote."

"And mine," Roan Eaglesoar added, shooting a wary glance at Mathas.

"The Council confirms Lord Darmanin Crowtalon as heir to Crowtalon State," Darien said with evident surprise.

"Thank you, my lords." Darmanin bowed. Everything about him was calm and composed ... expect for the tiny twitch of his mouth. He was elated.

"Are there any other revelations for today?" Darien asked the table with a raised eyebrow. "No? Very well, the session is over. We'll resume tomorrow afternoon for SparrowWing's confirmation."

Chairs screeched as they were pushed back, and the warlords and their advisers rose to their feet. Darmanin and Rorin moved to shake hands warmly, grinning at each other. The warlords grouped around to offer their congratulations to the two young men. Mathas Crowtalon even offered his stiff regards. His eyes burned with anger though, and Arya knew that he would not let this lie.

"Arya!"

She turned at the sound of Darmanin's voice. "Congratulations, Lord Crowtalon," she said, grinning in pleasure for him.

"Thank you, General." He gave her a low bow, and when he straightened, his grey eyes were alight with pleased satisfaction.

She reached out to briefly squeeze his arm. "You're going to make an impressive warlord one day."

"I will never be able to repay you properly for getting me here, Arya Ravenstrike," he said fiercely, surprising her. "I thank you with everything I have."

She shook her head. "Dar, it was all you."

"No, it wasn't, and we both know it. Because of you, and Warlord Ravenstrike, my future is assured. I can start building my life now."

She smiled at him. "I'm glad. You know I just want you to be happy."

"*Dar, Arya!*" Rorin joined them, a wide grin on his face. "*We did it!*" he said, slinging an arm around Arya's shoulder and clapping Darmanin on the back.

"We certainly did." She laughed up at him.

"*Come on, I want to go and tell Essa and Taze and Peemla the good news.*"

"You go ahead. I'll catch up, I need to speak with your mother."

Arya waited as Thiara finished speaking with the other warlords and gave Magen some quick instructions. Then Arya approached, unable to help smiling, and saluted sharply. "Congratulations, Warlord."

"Today went better than I could have expected." Thiara eyed her. "I believe it was your actions, in addition to those of Rorin and Darmanin, that sealed our victory today."

She felt a squirm of guilt at those words. It could so easily have gone the other way. "It has always been your plan, Warlord," she said. "I am only glad I could help bring it to fruition."

"Even so," Thiara said. "We have one more goal to reach, you and I."

Arya smiled. "We'll get there."

"I have things to get done before this afternoon's session," Thiara said. "But I look forward to seeing you at dinner later, Arya."

Arya watched her warlord walk away, accompanied by Matte and Magen. She walked purposefully, as always, and Arya found herself anxiously anticipating the day when Thiara Ravenstrike would be High Warlord of Dunidaen.

Then what power she would wield.

She let out a breath full of pent-up anxiety. It was going to be all right. Dunidaen would come together under Thiara Ravenstrike and they'd force the Nightstalker and his nazal back into Andahar.

Arya would make sure of it.

Chapter 39

Arya offered the Raider guards at the residence gate a wave as she took the front steps of the townhouse two at a time. The confirmation hearings had marked the halfway point of the State Council. Its successful outcome meant they could now concentrate entirely on getting the majority vote for Thiara Ravenstrike to be made High Warlord.

Although there were still worries aplenty—a nazal was hunting her and looking for the others, and Mathas Crowtalon was still in the lead for the vote—a warm sun shone today, presaging the arrival of spring, and it buoyed Arya's mood. As she stepped inside, Peemla called a greeting from where she arranged flowers by the stairs.

"Morning, Peemla." Arya smiled. "I'm looking for the errant lordling. He was supposed to be at drill with Taze's shield this morning, but he never showed."

"I believe he was invited to breakfast with Warlord Hawkesdale." Peemla returned her attention to the flowers, gaze downcast. "He's not yet come back. The house is rather empty this morning. Only the warlord is home."

"I'll go up and say hello," she said. "Thanks, Peemla."

"I'll have some tea sent up. Warlord Ravenstrike is in her office."

Arya paused. Something about the chamberlain's manner was off and had been ever since they arrived in Gateport. She performed her duties with her usual ruthless efficiency, but it was like some of her energy had dimmed. She'd originally thought it a response to Rorin's bad mood—which had affected them all—but Rorin had been making a clear effort to return to his usual cheerful self recently. "Everything okay, Peemla?"

"It is, Arya, thank you," she said, and left before Arya could probe further.

Shrugging, Arya jogged up the staircase and walked along the hall to the warlord's office.

"Enter," called Thiara when Arya knocked.

And so Arya did, saluting as she entered. "Warlord, good morning."

Thiara smiled. "It's good to see you."

Arya removed her cloak and took a seat in a chair by the desk. The fire was unlit this morning, plenty of warmth coming through in the morning sun through the window. Thiara finished signing some papers just as a servant sent by Peemla appeared with a tray of hot tea.

"So, Arya, what brings you by this morning?" Thiara sipped at her cup.

"I was looking for Rorin, but when Peemla said you were here, I thought I'd come up and say hello. Is there anything I could be doing to help with the vote? I know I've been busy, and we haven't had a chance to talk much."

"Yes, very busy indeed," Thiara said. "Running around risking your lives and winning me Lord SparrowWing's vote on the Council."

Arya smiled. "Something like that, yes."

"This has been the most interesting State Council I've ever attended." Thiara shook her head as she sat comfortably back in her chair. She seemed to fully relax in Arya's presence these days, perhaps finally able to rely on her the way she'd always needed to. It made Arya feel warm inside. And determined to keep being worthy of it. "Surprise allies, marriage proposals, I wonder what will come next."

"Marriage proposals?" Arya asked, startled.

Thiara let out a sigh. "I'm sure you noticed the tension between me and my son since our arrival in Gateport."

"I've certainly noticed his mood. We all have." Arya winced. "What's that got to do with marriage proposals?"

"He wants to marry Peemla."

For a long moment Arya stared at Thiara, at first unsure she'd heard properly, and then wondering if her ruthless warlord was attempting a joke. "He *what*?"

"You didn't know?"

"I had no idea," Arya said in genuine astonishment. Peemla and Rorin? When and how had that happened? And how hadn't she noticed it?

"Yes, well, apparently, he's formed some sort of attachment to her. I refused him, of course. There are several young noblewomen I'm considering for him, all of whom will bring us a significant amount of influence in the election."

Arya reeled. This was why Rorin had been behaving so out of character, why he'd been so angry at his mother. "I see."

"You really knew nothing about this?" Thiara sounded surprised. "I've honestly expected you to come charging in here at some point arguing fiercely on Rorin's behalf."

Arya shook her head slowly. "We all wondered what was bothering him, but he wouldn't tell us."

"Well, there you have it." Thiara smiled and waited a moment, before leaning forward and continuing. "Then two days ago I get a marriage offer for you. From the Crowtalon boy."

Andrian wanted to marry her?

Thiara raised an eyebrow at the expression on her face. "I take it you knew nothing about that, either?"

"Well, he has shown interest," she admitted. "I didn't think it was a serious one. What did you say?"

"No, of course. As an adopted member of the Ravenstrike house, you have some value in a marriage alliance, but I need you as my general."

"Thank you ... I think." Thiara Ravenstrike held ultimate power where Arya's life was concerned. If she'd wanted to, she could have married her off to a man she barely knew for a stronger power base.

Abruptly, her vision swam. *"Near!"*

"What?" Arya blinked, straightened in her chair, and stared around, searching for the source of the voice.

"What? I didn't say anything." Thiara was looking at Arya in confusion. *"Near! Come now!"*

Arya almost swore aloud in horror. It was her wyvern, his voice she was hearing.

In her waking mind in the middle of Thiara Ravenstrike's office.

Oblivious to Arya's panic, Thiara continued, "Please don't tell me you're going to be mad at me too. I won't tolerate it."

"Oh no, it's not that," she said. "I have no desire to marry anyone. It's just that I should get moving, Warlord. I have three shields waiting for training."

"I'd like it if you came to dinner tonight. We have a rare night off from socialising. Perhaps now that Rorin's mood has improved we could have a nice evening together." Thiara said. "One can hope, anyway."

She stood, still trying to regain her equilibrium. "I'll see you then, Warlord."

***

Arya's thoughts swam as she made her way downstairs, her warlord's revelations mixing with the shock of her wyvern pushing himself into her consciousness.

He couldn't really be nearby, could he?

Almost as if reading her thoughts, he crashed back into her mind again. *"Come? Come? Come?"*

She halted, slapping a palm against the wall for balance as dizziness overwhelmed her. *"Wait."* She sent the word and feeling behind it as firmly as she knew how.

"Wait." Came the very unhappy response.

Arya sighed, opened her eyes. She had a feeling his patience wasn't going to hold long. She was going to have to figure out what to do about him quickly. A loud groan almost escaped her as she envisioned the look on the warlords' faces if a wyvern suddenly appeared flying over Gateport.

On her way back through the house, she spotted Essa sitting outside in the gazebo, reading a book. Arya hesitated, but then headed outside. Talking to Essa always helped when she felt overwhelmed.

"Arya!" Essa looked up with a smile. "I didn't know you were dropping by this morning."

"I just had a word with the warlord. How goes the bid for High Warlord?" Arya asked, seeking a distraction from panicking about her wyvern. There was nothing she could do about it right now.

Essa put the book down. "Better since the confirmation hearings. Darmanin's confirmation undermined Crowtalon. Now, even if he wins High Warlord, he faces an enemy warlord ruling his State. But it's going to take a lot. I'm not sure we can get there."

Arya nodded. "I see."

"And I'm going to paint my hair yellow for dinner this evening."

"Wait, what?" Arya's head came up.

Essa chuckled. "What's on your mind?"

Arya shifted in her chair. "The warlord had some interesting news."

"Really? What was it?"

"Apparently Andrian made a request to marry me."

"*Andrian* did?" Essa looked as surprised as Arya had been. "What did you say?"

"Not much. The warlord had already said no on my behalf."

Essa cocked her head. "Does that bother you?"

Arya smiled. "Not in the slightest. I like Andrian well enough, but I don't want to marry him."

"Fair enough, but that's not what I meant. I wanted to know if it bothered you that the warlord had made such a decision without even consulting you?"

"She is my warlord. Everything I am today I owe to her. I trust her to do what is best for our family."

Essa rolled her eyes. "I see you've never been in love."

Arya paused, lifted a pointed eyebrow. "And you have?"

"No, I haven't, and like you, I have no desire to be." She trailed off, looking uncomfortable. Their gazes held, then slid away from each other.

Arya let it go. "What about this thing with Rorin and Peemla? The warlord told me about that, too. Did you know?"

Essa hesitated. "I wish she hadn't told you."

"Why, did you imagine it would be a secret forever?" Irritation flashed through Arya. "How could you both keep me in the dark over this?"

"I didn't want Rorin to be hurt any more than he already was, so I encouraged him to keep it to himself."

Bewildered, and not failing to notice the edge in her friend's tone, Arya asked, "Why?"

"If he'd told you, would you have gone to his mother to plead his case?"

Arya slumped back in her chair, let out a breath. "No, I wouldn't have."

"Why?"

Arya sighed. "Because the warlord is right. Rorin needs to marry someone of his own station. Our State has a chance of holding the position of High Warlord. Rorin's marriage will never be simple, he should have known that."

"And if Peemla loves him back, and they both want to marry?" Essa seemed incredulous. "That would truly be the stance you'd take?"

Arya was unsure how to respond to that.

Essa shook her head and stood. "I'll see you later, Arya."

"Essa..." Arya called, but the woman had already gone. "Dammit!"

She kicked the table hard, stubbing her toe in the process and sending the lemonade jar crashing to the ground.

"General?" A startled Peemla appeared in the kitchen doorway. "Is everything all right?"

Arya couldn't face her. Not knowing what she knew. Not knowing if it were up to her, she'd be ruining Peemla's happiness too. "I'm sorry, Peemla, I have to go." Arya brushed past her and escaped out the front door.

***

Darmanin strode through the gates of the barracks late that evening. Arya was busy securing saddlebags on Zeke's back, while throughout the yard, her shields were preparing for departure.

The afternoon's developments had been a tipping point. It was all too much—knowing the nazal was in Gateport and trying to find her friends, the Rorin and Peemla mess, Essa's anger at her, her *wyvern* announcing himself as nearby. The weight of it all on her shoulders had become unbearably heavy and she needed to do *something* or she felt she'd go spare.

A strained family dinner had been the last straw. Arya hadn't been able to meet Rorin's eyes the entire meal and had mostly played with the food before her. As soon as dinner had finished, Arya had requested her warlord's approval to take the battalion out of the city for a week to undertake training exercises. Thiara had considered it, a speculative gleam coming into her eyes, before granting approval. "No more than a week, Arya. I want you back here before the foreign leaders arrive."

"Darmanin." She scowled now at his appearance. "Are you here to tell me what a terrible friend I am too? Perhaps you'd like to take your turn having a go at me because I think it's a bad idea for you to marry a tavern wench."

"How did you find out about my tavern wench?" he asked in mock surprise.

She glared at him.

He seemed unfazed. "May I ask where you're all going?"

"The High Warlord vote is a fortnight away, and my Raiders are getting restive. I'm taking them out on training manoeuvres."

"And where exactly did you get the impression that it was a good idea to leave the city when a nazal is here hunting you?"

"Don't start, Dar," she warned him. "It already knows who I am, so if it wanted to attack me it would. And if it's using me to track others, then even better that I'm away from you all for a while."

What she didn't say was that this trip served two purposes. It gave her cover to find her wyvern and figure out what to do about him—and she had no intention of telling anyone about him until she managed that situation.

But the trip also took her out of the city and gave the nazal an opportunity to strike.

It would be safer for all of those she loved if she dealt with the nazal alone. *Then* she could throw herself into the High Warlord vote with her full focus and worry about a long-term solution to the Nightstalker once it was done, as she'd originally planned.

He paused, studying her for a long moment. She got the uncomfortable sense that he knew exactly what she was thinking. "What's got you in such a mood?"

"What makes you think I'm in a mood?" she countered.

"You usually only do absurdly stupid or reckless things when you're in a temper. And this is stupid and reckless." He huffed a breath. "It's night, Arya. Why the rush in leaving? You could ride out with your battalion in the morning."

"This is just wonderful," she said, tightening the girth strap. "Essa thinks I'm an awful person, and you think I'm stupid and reckless. I wonder what everyone else thinks."

He eyed her. "Self-pity doesn't suit you. Tell me what's really going on."

She sighed. "Did you know Andrian made an offer to marry me?"

"He did?" Darmanin looked anything but surprised. "Who told you that?"

"Warlord Ravenstrike."

"That's interesting."

She laughed, momentarily breaking out of her funk of irritation and worry. "That's all you have to say? I could have been your sister by marriage."

"Trust me when I say that's the absolute last thing I want, Arya." His eyes glimmered in the dark. "I take it your warlord said no?"

"She did." Arya was unaccountably stung by his response but shook it off. "She also said no to Rorin marrying Peemla."

Darmanin let out a long whistle. "So that's why Rorin was acting so badly? I didn't see that coming. Rorin clearly adores her, but I always thought it was in the same way he adores you or I or Essa. Does she...?"

"I think so. Which must make things even harder." With one movement, Arya hauled herself into the saddle. Zeke danced around, and she tightened her grip on the reins. "Be kind to him if you see him, Dar. None of us really understands how he's feeling."

"Maybe we do," he murmured, mostly to himself, then blinked and looked at her. "So what you're actually doing is escaping Rorin and Peemla because you can't bear to face them?"

"Tensions are getting high, I'm sure you've noticed. If I don't run some of this energy out of my Raiders, the little digs and provocations from the Lances and Aggressors will result in a brawl or some other incident while they're off duty."

His look told her he was thoroughly unconvinced by this line of reasoning. "You'll miss the arrival of the Khadini emperor and Icelands rulers. All that pomp and ceremony leading up to the High Warlord vote; the stuff you love."

"They don't arrive for a week. I'll be back for that. See you, Dar."

"Arya, wait!"

Arya pulled Zeke into a halt and turned back to look at him.

"Were you disappointed? About Andrian?"

She smiled. "Not even a little bit."

***

As she led her battalion out of the city, and breathed the crisp night air of the plains beyond the walls, Arya felt some of the weight lifting from her shoulders, exactly as she'd hoped. The nazal might be hunting her, but it wouldn't find the others while she was away from the city, and she hoped it *would* come for her. It would feel good to actually deal with a problem rather than hide from it.

And not just the nazal problem.

Almost as terrifying as the Nightstalker's hunters going after her family was the reality of her wyvern coming into Dunidaen. She had to deal with that before any Gateport citizens noticed a golden wyvern flying about.

If that happened, utter chaos would follow.

"*Danger?*" The questioning thought from her wyvern slid into her mind. He *was* close. She could feel it in his presence in her mind.

This time Arya didn't startle. "*Maybe,*" she sent back. "*I'll deal with it.*"

"*We.*" Determination.

Then.

"*Coming?*" Hopeful.

"*Soon,*" she promised. "*Very soon.*"

A little thrill of anticipation whispered through Arya then. She'd been so preoccupied about figuring out what to do if her wyvern really *had* come to her, she hadn't let the idea settle in her mind that she was going to see him.

Her wyvern. A smile tugged at her mouth.

What would he be like?

Chapter 40

The following day, Arya walked alone through the forest east of Gateport. In comparison to the Wraith Forest back home, this one was sunlit and airy. It was early afternoon, and spring sunlight poured through the canopy above, dancing off the emerald foliage and warm enough that Arya had discarded her cloak hours earlier.

Not far off, near the forest's western edge, her Raiders were performing exercises. One half of the battalion had been tasked with setting an ambush, while the other half was supposed to try and spring it without getting caught.

Arya had left her captains to it while she answered a summons.

She'd barely rolled out of her blankets that morning when her wyvern had pushed himself into her mind. *"Coming?"*

She'd tried holding him off during breakfast with her captains, but he'd persisted, until she was rubbing at throbbing temples and her captains were throwing her odd looks.

She'd sighed, and capitulated. *"Coming."*

When she let herself, she could *feel* that he was near.

Now as she moved through the forest, she arrowed in on the clear sense of him tugging at her. The distant roar of the ocean drifted on the breeze. Soon, Arya emerged from the trees onto open cliff top. She stopped and admired the view. A salty sea breeze whipped back her unbound blonde hair and cooled her sweaty skin.

A long line of cliffs spread out to her right and left, and she could see the sprawling city of Gateport to the west. Deep blue ocean ran all the way south to the horizon. It was a peaceful spot, and she basked in the sunshine, allowing all her worries and anxiousness of the previous weeks fade away.

"*Here*," she announced, feeling him close by.

A rustling sounded behind her, and she spun away from the view, body tensing. Everything inside her knew what was coming through the trees. Anticipation flared like a lit match, and she took an unconscious step forward, hands clenching and unclenching at her sides.

A long, serpentine head appeared, then a taloned foot, and then a golden wyvern emerged onto the clifftop.

Arya stared.

He'd grown again since the last time she'd seen him in their dreams. He was larger than a cart horse now, with burnished gold scales that rippled in the sunlight, and paler gold wings that were currently curled against his long, sinuous body.

She moved forward without thought, reaching out to run her fingers over the scales above his nose. He snorted and shied away, mouth opening to reveal long, razor-sharp, fangs. "I won't hurt you," she soothed.

He stilled at the sound of her voice.

Then he lowered his head towards her reaching hand, allowing Arya to press her palm against his jaw, right below those fearsome teeth. As soon as her skin touched his scales, a rush of *something* heady swept through them both.

"*Mine*," he whispered.

"*Mine*," she agreed, a blinding smile stretching across her face.

She took a deep breath, stepping closer, her palm pressing more firmly against his jaw, her gaze shifting to meet his fierce eyes, dark gold and luminous. Her shoulders relaxed entirely and the magic inside her she'd been fighting for months simply unfolded. There was no other way to describe it. It was like a rose opening to the spring sun. A lock unsealing.

Then everything went black.

Arya was tumbling, free falling through an endless void.

Wind rushed past her ears, and the ground was far, far below. Treetops flashed past at a dizzying speed. Clouds surrounded her, and she felt like the ruler of the world. She saw a sword being raised, flashing with blue lightning.

Then she saw a city on fire, thick smoke hovering over the orange flames. A scream of anger rippled through the air. The ringing sound of clashing blades cut through that, and then she saw a man in a silken blue cloak fall through the sky, blood spreading from a gaping wound in his chest.

The scream of a wyvern ripped through the vision.

Arya's eyes snapped open.

She found herself on a wide balcony, the ice-capped peaks of the Diamondfang spread out at her feet. The Etherean elder stood nearby, staring at her in astonishment.

"Salyarin? What's happening?" Arya asked, staring around her. Part of her reveled in the joy of the cold and the mountains around her. Home. She'd been away in Gateport too long.

"I could ask you the same thing!" His voice was crystal clear, but they *were* dream-walking. It was clear from the blurring at the edges of her vision.

"How are you able to reach me so far away? I didn't think you were strong enough for that."

"I'm not! You got yourself here, Arya." His voice was still infused with shock and surprise.

Arya was completely lost. *"I have no idea how that happened."*

The surprise on Salyarin's face melted to awe as he shifted his gaze over her shoulder. She turned to look at whatever had caught his attention and saw the shadowy form of her wyvern balanced on the railing, wings spread outward, dwarfing both of them.

"Now I see," Salyarin said. *"You bonded with your wyvern."*

Arya rolled her eyes. *"Oh, that explains everything."*

"I don't have time to explain it fully." Exasperation flashed over his face. *"Which is why you need to come to us. Why do you persist in refusing to do what you need to do?"*

"Salyarin, I'm in Gateport and my wyvern has found me. Can you at least tell me what I need to know to keep us both safe until the Council is over and we return to Heathrock? I promise I will come and see you then."

Salyarin shook his head, then he spoke, bluntly. *"You are descended from the royal house of Andahar—House Stormrider. Now that your wyvern has found you, your magic will stir, if it hasn't already. That makes you dangerous, to others, as well as yourself. There is no way to be safe until you learn."*

"What does that mean?"

"Carrying Stormrider blood is as much a curse as it is a blessing," the elder said. *"Your family is named for its volatile power—a line of quick tempers and recklessness. Stormriders have the capacity for great compassion and kindness, but just as much a capacity for ruthlessness and arrogance. As the rightful monarch, you will be the strongest of all your Sky Lords. If you don't learn how to use it, your magic will be a danger to yourself and others. It can't be repressed forever, and if you lose control over it, it will do what it wants."*

Arya processed that. *"Tell me about my wyvern. Can he help me control it?"*

"Your Valheran is a conduit for your magic. Linked with him, you are far more powerful than when you are alone, which only compounds the danger if neither of you learn to wield control. That is why you must—"

"Learn my magic. I get it, Elder." She hesitated. The dream rippled, as it usually did when Salyarin was losing his grip on it.

"The initial burst of magic from your bonding is fading," Salyarin glanced around. *"And once it does, I won't be able to hold the dream. We haven't got long."*

Arya nodded. *"I need advice on one more thing. There's a nazal in Gateport. It knows me and I think it's using me to find the others. Can you tell me how we can protect ourselves, or at least stop dreaming of our wyverns so they can't track us through our dreams?"*

Horror rippled over his face. *"Arya, there is no protection other than growing into your magic."* His voice took on an urgent, frantic tone. *"The dreams will persist until your Sky Lords have bonded with their wyverns—they cannot be stopped. You must get out of Gateport. Now. If your wyvern is there too then you are both more vulnerable than you have ever been. You have no choice anymore."*

"I always have a choice," Arya said, trying and partially succeeding in wrangling her temper. Salyarin was right, and her situation wasn't his fault. He was only trying to help her. *"I will come to you, after the High Warlord vote. Until then, my duty is with my warlord."*

"*That is not your home*," Salyarin insisted.

"*I will heed your warning as best I can. And I will come to you and learn to use my magic, as soon as I return to Heathrock,*" she said to him. "*My word on—*"

A wrenching shift of perception, a flash of blackness, and Salyarin and the mountains were gone.

Arya blinked her eyes open and found herself back on the clifftop, palm still pressed against the wyvern's scales. Her head throbbed. He snorted, then shook himself, spreading his wings to catch the breeze coming off the ocean. "*Nice.*"

"You can't be here," she told him. "The people here fear magic, they would fear us if they knew what we were. If they see you, they will kill you. And if the nazal finds you, it will kill you too." She huffed an uncertain breath. "Do you understand what I'm saying?"

He gave her a look heavy with condescension. "*Yours. Stay.*"

"Yes, I know." Her shoulders sagged. She didn't want him to go anywhere. Something had changed in that moment of their magic connecting. It was more than just knowing he was hers and she was his. Having him there felt right in a way nothing in her life ever had before. It made her feel safe. It was an anchor in the unsteadiness of all the worries crowding her mind.

But along with all of that was a growing fear of the danger he was in. "This is not the right place for you," she whispered, pressing her forehead against his nose. "You won't be safe here. You can't live here."

"*Yours.*" He snorted, then suggested what she assumed was a compromise. "*Hide?*"

Arya let out a breath. "Hide here in the forest until I can go back home? Is there enough game in this forest for you?"

His head swung upwards, and it almost looked like he rolled his eyes at her.

"All right," she chuckled. "If you must fly, only at night, understand me? Nobody can see you. And remember what Salyarin said about how dangerous the nazal is."

In fact, after the look on the elder's face, Arya was already thinking about taking her battalion straight back to the city. Facing the nazal alone no longer seemed like a good idea.

His head lowered and he bumped his nose against her shoulder. "*Danger. Hide.*"

"Exactly." She stepped away, looking him over. He was beautiful. The pride that filled her at the realisation that this was *her* wyvern was undeniable. "Your name ... when we bonded, I think I felt it?"

He snorted, looked at her questioningly, as if leaving to her to choose his name.

"Elendryl," she said quietly. "Your name is Elendryl."

His head snaked upwards, and he opened his wings wide. "*Elendryl.*"

Chapter 41

A messenger galloped into camp the following morning as Arya observed her shields practicing formation manoeuvres on the open plains before the forest's edge. In the back of her mind sat Elendryl's presence, lazily contented with a full belly. As new a sensation as it was to have him there, so close, it also didn't feel strange or uncomfortable.

In fact, it felt like a piece that had been missing her entire life had been filled.

She was still trying to think of a good reason to pack up her battalion and return to the city early—her hope of the nazal coming after her had now turned to dread after her conversation with Salyarin.

The message from Thiara Ravenstrike solved her problem instantly.

After reading it, she looked up and gestured to Laskin, observing his shield nearby. He came over and saluted. "General?"

"It seems the warlords have taken it into their heads to organise some exhibition war games between the States to pass the time before the foreign leaders arrive and the High Warlord vote takes place," she told him. "We'll have to ride back to Gateport today."

"If they're bored, why don't they just hold the damn vote so everyone can go home?" he asked.

"That would break with tradition, Laskin. We can't do that."

He gave her one of his looks. "Any information on what the warlord expects from us?"

"Absolutely none. Once this exercise is done, let's get them all packing up. I want to be back by nightfall."

Elendryl sensed her relief and excitement. *"Coming?"*

"Not yet. It's too dangerous for us to meet."

Protest followed her words. An image of the nazal pushed into her mind.

"I can look after myself. If I need you, I'll call for you, I promise."

Stronger discontent.

She smiled. *"We'll go home soon,"* she promised. *"And then we'll be able to see each other more often."*

At least, she hoped so. There would be more opportunity in the wilds of the Diamondfang and Wraith Forest for the two of them to see each other without being observed. At the least, the isolated mountains would be much safer for Elendryl.

And once she'd worked with her warlord and Essa and the others to come up with a plan for the Nightstalker, it would be time to go to Salyarin.

And learn her magic.

***

Arya arrived at the townhouse late that evening, having left the Raiders settling into the barracks. As she approached the front gates, she did a now habitual sweep of the street around the residence. There was no sign of anyone watching the place, watching for her. In fact, since the attack on Amius SparrowWing, Arya hadn't sensed any danger nearby. It made her itch. What were the nazal planning?

She dismounted and nodded a greeting to the guards on duty at the door as she passed through.

"Arya!" Rorin was coming down the stairs as she crossed the foyer. His welcome smile was bright. *"You're back already."*

"I was summoned." She smiled, hugging him tightly when he threw his arms around her. "How have you been?"

"I'm good," he said. *"I've been busy courting the warlords and vicelords on Mother's instructions. It seems to be going well. How was your time away?"*

"Good for the Raiders, even though it was cut short," she said. "Is your mother here?"

"She is, but she's in the middle of something. She asked me to tell you to wait in the library if you came in tonight."

Arya hesitated. It was time she stopped avoiding her brother and talked to him about Peemla, as uncomfortable as the prospect made her. "Care to keep me company while I wait?"

"I'd love to, but I'm supposed to be having a late supper at the Eaglesoar residence," Rorin sighed. *"I'll see you in the morning."*

Arya grinned. "Better you than me. Night, Rorin."

A fire crackled in the hearth when Arya stepped into the library. She shrugged off her Raider cloak and tossed it over a nearby chair before tugging off her leather riding gloves and dropping them on the cloak.

"Hello, Arya." Essa's voice sounded.

Arya turned in surprise; she hadn't noticed the figure curled in the chair by the fire, reading. "Essa, hello. I'm sorry, I didn't mean to disturb you."

Essa nodded and closed her book before standing up. "Was the extra training beneficial?"

"It was."

"I'm glad."

Arya wanted to growl in frustration at this stilted politeness, but knew she probably deserved it. "Essa, about what happened before I left—"

"We don't need to talk about it." Essa was already turning away, even more uncomfortable than Arya with awkward conversations.

"I'd like to." Arya pushed on determinedly. "I know you feel like I'm letting Rorin down by agreeing with his mother's position on his marriage, and I understand why you think that."

Essa stopped, as if conceding to having the discussion. "But you haven't changed your mind?"

"Is it so terrible that I have a different opinion than you?"

"Of course not," Essa said. "But this is different. Your opinion is against the happiness of your own brother."

"Essa, I want what's best for Rorin. If he wants to be warlord, then he needs to accept that—"

"You mean if Thiara Ravenstrike wants to be High Warlord?" Essa cut her off. "This isn't about Rorin; he's already been confirmed as heir to the State. Marrying who he wants wouldn't change that."

"All right," Arya conceded. "Essa, the warlord gave me everything I have today. I owe all of it to her. I would do anything to support her bid for High Warlord."

"Even over Rorin's happiness?"

"That's not how I see it."

"Of course, you wouldn't understand," Essa said, her ire seemingly now sufficient to dispel her discomfort with confrontation. "You have no idea what it's like to love someone fully; you'd never allow yourself to, it would interfere with your desperate need to control everything in your life."

Stung, Arya reeled.

"I'm not trying to be cruel, Arya, and I know you aren't either. But you are making decisions for Rorin without considering what he wants. Worse, you think you're entitled to do that."

"I haven't made any decisions. They are the warlord's to make," she said.

"Yet if the decision *was* yours, you would make the same one."

Arya huffed a breath. "Essa, that doesn't change how I feel about you or Rorin, or Dar. I would protect all of you with my life. I don't want to lose your friendship."

"Rorin loves you too much to ever let anything come between you. He understands you like nobody else and so he already knows and accepts your position on this. It's why he hasn't confronted you about it," Essa said. "And I am still your friend, Arya. It's just not the friendship that I thought we had."

"Essa, that's not fair."

"You told me you valued my honest thoughts, always."

"I do, always."

"Good night, Arya. Sleep well."

The woman left with a sad smile. Arya watched her go, then turned around and kicked the nearest chair, cursing under her breath as pain stabbed through her toes.

"*Danger?*" Elendryl demanded. "*Upset?*"

"*No danger. I'm safe,*" she assured him. "*I'm just annoyed with myself.*"

He withdrew with a little mental tap of affection, which took the edge off some of her frustration.

"It's not always easy, is it?"

"Warlord." Arya straightened as Thiara Ravenstrike walked in. "Good evening."

"It's good to see you, Arya," Thiara said. "Have a seat, please."

They took chairs before the crackling fire, and a comfortable silence fell for a brief time before the warlord broke it. "It's difficult to be a strong, decisive leader," Thiara said in contemplation. "It's even harder when you're dealing with people you love. Sometimes the decisions you make hurt them, and sometimes you must put your job and your duty above what makes them happy."

"Which is what you're doing with Rorin." Arya said. "I understand."

"I know you do." Thiara met her eyes. "It's why I chose you to become Desomer's apprentice, and why I know you'll one day be the finest general Ravenstrike has ever had."

"Thank you, Warlord." As always, Arya was warmed from head to toe by her warlord's praise.

She waved a hand. "Enough of that. We need to discuss plans for the war games. They start tomorrow."

Arya leaned forward eagerly, a little zip of energy running through her, all melancholy gone. "Ravenstrike will be involved?"

"We have to be," Thiara said. "I'm sure you've learned from Essa and Magen that Mathas remains the front runner for the High Warlord vote. Even though Darmanin's confirmation was a blow, it wasn't enough of one."

"They've said as much, yes."

"At every Council session, I've been pushing the need to do something more decisive about the Nightstalker, and yesterday Warlord Falconcrest suggested war games as a way to test the sharpness of our armies. It was a clever suggestion that ostensibly deals with my concerns so that I stop nagging them on the subject." Frustration rippled across Thiara's features. "An idea Mathas quickly jumped on."

Neither of them had to verbalise the underlying source of Thiara's frustration. If none of the warlords were taking her warnings about the Nightstalker's invasion plans seriously, then they certainly didn't respect her enough to vote for her to be their High Warlord.

Still ... her warlord was a formidable leader even if none of the other warlords recognised it. Arya gave a little smile. "I'm guessing you've figured out a way to turn these exhibition games to our advantage?"

"Not entirely, not yet." Thiara smiled, then stood up. "Get some rest. I want you sharp and ready to go as soon as I have figured out how to use these war games to win the High Warlord vote."

***

Despite her warlord's instructions, Arya took a long walk through the streets of Gateport rather than going directly back to the barracks. She felt too uneasy to sleep. She hated being at odds with Essa, and she still didn't feel settled about Rorin and Peemla. Essa wasn't wrong, but Arya also didn't disagree with her warlord.

"Danger?"

Arya couldn't help but smile. It was going to take Elendryl some time to figure out that not every emotion she felt meant danger. *"No danger. Rest."*

His response reverberated with grumpiness. *"Hiding."*

People thronged the streets, out enjoying the warm evening. She relaxed into their energy, allowing it to soothe her. Arya turned down a side street, taking a short cut she'd found that would set her in the direction of the barracks. The street was empty, and her boots tapped loudly on the cobblestones. A scuffing sound behind made her turn, but there was nothing there. A voice called out drunkenly a couple of streets over. A group of people laughed nearby.

The scuffing came again as she was halfway down the street, and this time she stopped and scanned the shadows behind her. Her hand fell to the hilt of her sword, and she sucked in a breath as the scar on her right arm flared briefly with a sharp pain. Nothing moved in the shadows, so she turned and continued walking, faster now.

Another sound echoed through the empty street, this time coming from the roof above. She stopped, half drawing her sword as she scanned the skyline above. The cazaix glimmered blue in the dim light. By now she'd grown so accustomed to the faint dissonance it caused her senses that she didn't even notice it.

The shadows lining the edges of the street had grown noticeably darker, and when Arya concentrated, the sounds of the lively Gateport streets receded.

Fear crept down her spine. Was the nazal finally coming for her?

"*Danger?*" Elendryl sounded sleepy.

"*Maybe,*" she said this time, then hurriedly, "*Don't come. Wait.*"

She could *feel* the presence of something nearby, and whatever it was, it wasn't friendly. Her heart picked up speed, and she couldn't forget the look of panic on Salyarin's face at the idea of her facing a nazal.

She *hated* being afraid of this thing.

"Come on, then," she said loudly, circling. "Come and get me."

"*Arya Ravenstrike.*" The words hissed through the street, a sibilant hiss.

Arya turned still. It was impossible to tell where the voice had come from. Fear and dread pounded at her bones, but she fought it back. "Are you here to eat me or whisper at me? Whichever it is, hurry it up because I have somewhere to be."

The darkness closed in, but it was all formless. Wherever the nazal was, it wasn't physically in the street with her. Tendrils of magic whispered over her, sank into her thoughts, holding her in place. Pain burned in her head. "*Arya Ravenstrike. We come for you. We come for all of you.*"

She snarled, tried to fight free, felt her magic surging. And then Elendryl was there, a pulsing warmth of reassurance in her chest. It gave her just enough presence of mind to press her bare palm against her cazaix blade, ignoring the sickly feeling it gave her.

Just as panic began setting in, the hold on her mind disappeared. The shadows in the street cleared and the sounds of revelry from surrounding blocks became audible once again.

"*Calm,*" she told Elendryl, when it was clear the nazal had gone. "*Danger gone. Hide.*"

"*Nazal?*" A questioning thought.

"*Yes.*"

Sober reflection. "*Danger.*"

There was a whisper of movement at the top of the street. She spun and drew her sword. Everything was still, and then a hooded figure emerged from the shadows. "Hello, Raider."

"Leanir?" She lowered her blade. "Raven's balls."

Leanir glanced around, then gestured for her to join him in the shadows along the wall. Once there, he pushed back his hood. After only a moment's hesitation, Arya sheathed her blade and joined him. He was almost a welcome sight after her encounter with the nazal. Her hands still trembled and sweat sat sticky on her skin.

He looked her up and down. "What are you doing standing in the street with your sword drawn?"

"A nazal." She glanced up at the roofs, gaze narrowed. Had touching the cazaix scared it off? "I think it was here to bloody *taunt* me."

Leanir's entire bearing turned watchful, his gaze narrowed, and then he copied her and scanned the roofs around them. "You're still in one piece, so I assume it didn't attack?"

"Is that disappointment I hear?" She smirked.

Instead of scowling, or snapping back, Leanir merely looked wary. "As I approached, there was *something* here." He shook his head.

"It's good you didn't come a few minutes earlier," she said. "It might have sensed you, even with your cazaix."

His dark eyes glimmered. "Are you protecting me now, Raider?"

"I'm honestly not sure," she shot back. "You saved Essa's life, but that doesn't erase the fact you murdered my Raider comrades or attacked my brother." But it was *something*. "And now we're linked by all this infuriating *magic*."

"I'll stop you right there." He lifted a gloved hand. "We're not friends, we're not even allies, and I have no interest in changing that."

He was right. She expelled a weary breath. "Then why are you here?"

"I came to find you because we made a deal," he said. He paused, jaw tightening. "I've been having dreams. Nightmares. Like the ones you described at our last meeting, but different."

"Go on," she said.

He crossed his arms, almost a protective gesture. "I hear voices talking. Planning. But they're not human, not really, though they almost sound like it. I think it's the nazal I'm hearing. In fact, after what I sensed just now approaching this street, I'm sure of it. It was the same darkness."

"Do you *see* the nazal in these dreams of yours?"

A terse nod. "I sometimes get flashes of their faces."

"White skin, papery complexion, narrow features?" Arya asked. "Dark red eyes, voices that scratch at you like sandpaper?"

Leanir's eyes met hers. "Yes, exactly like that."

"Then you're in danger. If they sense you, they can trap you in the dream, Leanir." Arya said.

"They don't know I'm there." His fists clenched at his side. "I can hide from them."

"You can *hide*? How?" Realisation filled her. "Your magic. You can shift perception, so your magic has to do with the mind. You're reading theirs, dream-walking them somehow?"

"Something like that, yes."

A thought niggled at the back of her mind then, but she couldn't quite capture it. She stepped closer. "You said you overheard them planning."

"To kill us," he said flatly. "I've heard your name mentioned specifically, but they speak as if they don't know, or aren't sure, who the rest of us are—there's a lot of frustration sometimes," he replied, then shuddered. "It *burns*. I get the feeling they've made some guesses though and aren't too indiscriminate about who they take out."

She held his gaze. "How are they going to kill us? When?"

"I don't hear all the details, just snippets, and because I must hide, it makes them even more indistinct." Leanir took a breath. "But here's what I've cobbled together. High Warlord Eaglesoar is going to make a speech, and they're planning an ambush of some kind. They think it's the best time because those they want will all be there, but also because…" He faltered.

"Because what?"

"The Nightstalker is coming. He wants to arrive after you're dead. I don't know why—I haven't been able to hear enough to figure it out."

"It was High Warlord Eaglesoar they spoke of? Not whoever the new High Warlord is going to be?"

"They specifically mentioned Eaglesoar giving a speech."

Arya considered that for a few moments, then realised, "The last night of the State Council, there's always a formal celebration, a ball. This year it will be a bigger event than ever, because the new High Warlord would have just been voted in, and all the foreign leaders will still be here. Eaglesoar will make a formal speech to step down and welcome the new High Warlord. It's already been scheduled."

"And you'll be there," Leanir said.

"But *you* won't." She narrowed her gaze. "If there's no threat to you, then why are you here?"

He bared his teeth in a snarl. "Like I said, I'm not hearing all their planning. I can't know for certain that they don't know about me, that they don't plan to come for me too. We made a deal, Raider."

"Fair enough." Arya nodded slowly. For all she felt about Leanir, he had proven during the Dreadwater run that he held to his word. "Thank you for the warning. If you hear more details, tell me."

"There is one more thing. It sounded like they were talking about you having a cazaix blade. I heard that specific word. I think it scared them. Or worried them." He frowned. "I wish I could get a clearer sense of them talking."

Arya's gaze narrowed. "The nazal that was riding Bralin when I killed him might have felt the cazaix blade I used when I cut his head off. That's interesting. *Very* interesting."

Leanir nodded. "They wouldn't be worried unless—"

"Cazaix could hurt them." Arya huffed a breath.

He pulled his hood back up over his face. "Hopefully this is the last time we see each other."

As he walked away, disappearing quickly into the night, Arya wasn't as sure if she felt the same way.

Everything was becoming so complicated. She still didn't fully understand what the nazal wanted. To kill her and the other Sky Lord potentials, yes. But how did SparrowWing fit into any of that? She didn't like forming a strategy without knowing all the pieces of the puzzle. It meant things could go wrong. At least, thanks to Leanir, they knew when the nazal planned to attack now.

And she'd make sure they were prepared.

Chapter 42

Arya's orders were to keep her battalion in the barracks for the first morning of the war games, so she skipped drill and went to the residence for breakfast. Fortunately, Rorin was already up, eating with Taze. One look at Arya's face, and Taze slipped off to wake Essa.

Rorin and Arya filled some plates with the food laid out on the table, then headed out to the back garden. It was still cool, but a morning sun promised a warm day ahead.

"*I'll wait for Essa, but … you're okay?*" Rorin's gaze searched hers as they sat inside the small gazebo near the shed.

"I am." She smiled and forced herself to pick up one of the sweet pastries. She hadn't slept well again but needed to eat.

Essa was still rumpled and bleary eyed when she appeared with Taze, and Arya immediately poured her a cup from the steaming teapot. The dark shadows under her eyes spoke of more than being woken early. "Nightmare?"

"I saw my wyvern properly. He's beautiful." A smile whispered across her pale face. "But then the nazal came. We got out before it could trap us, but it felt so close, Arya." She shuddered. "We could feel how badly it wants us. I'm scared to go back to sleep."

"That fits with what happened last night," Arya said, "But before I tell you about that, you should know that my wyvern is here. He's currently hiding in the woods to the west of the city."

Rorin's eyes widened to saucers. "*That's why you took your battalion out?*"

Taze's mouth had fallen open. "There's a wyvern flying around?"

"Yes," she answered, chuckling a little at their reactions. "I've managed to convince him to stay hidden until I can leave Gateport. When I first saw him, there was a flare of magic. It allowed Salyarin to reach me. I'm sorry, Essa, but in the brief time we had to talk he told me there's no way to stop the dreams of our wyverns. Not until we bond with them."

Taze was still staring at her. "You're a Sky Lord. Like, really, truly a Sky Lord."

"I am," she said.

Rorin reached over the table, squeezed her hand. "*I can't wait to meet him.*"

Essa seemed troubled, but changed the subject, "What happened last night?"

Arya cleared her throat, took a sip of tea, then filled them in on her encounter with the nazal and Leanir's information. Once she'd finished, silence reigned.

Taze was the one to break it. "I suppose the first thing is, we don't go to the ball."

"It's not that simple," Arya said. "Doing that will avoid the trap they're setting, but it won't stop them coming for us. They've obviously given up on using me to track the others. And what concerns me most is Leanir seemed to think they weren't being particularly discriminate in who they killed. That puts everyone in my orbit in danger."

"But we've got a plan, right," Essa said. "We get through the High Warlord vote then focus on the Nightstalker, with Rorin's mother's help. We can still do that, just with some more urgency."

"*So we stay for the vote, then leave immediately after it, make sure we're not in the city by the time the ball happens.*" Rorin signed.

"I don't like this at all," Arya admitted. "I don't like running."

"*Neither do I,*" Rorin said. "*But until we learn how to combat these things, it's the safest choice.*"

"It's going to be all right," Taze said, trying to clear the worried expressions on everyone's face. "We will find a way to kill these creatures and deal with the Nightstalker for good. We can do this together."

Arya looked at him, wanting to believe his words, but unable to quell the flicker of doubt in her mind; she wasn't sure it was going to be so easy.

"Should we tell the warlords that the Nightstalker is coming?" Essa asked.

"And how would we explain that we know that?" Arya let out a frustrated sigh. "I do think we should tell your mother, Rorin. If she wins the High Warlord vote, we'll go to her with everything. Then she can help us leave the city quietly before the ball."

"*I agree. I'd really like to stop keeping secrets from my parents.*" Rorin glanced between Arya and Essa. "*The way you looked at each other just now. Does my mother already know something about you?*"

"We think so, yes," Arya said, sharing a glance with Essa. "But we don't know what, exactly. She refuses to discuss it."

Taze glanced at the house, where a Raider had appeared heading towards them. "Rorin, you and I are supposed to be leaving for the games."

Arya stood with them. "Rorin, can you speak to Darmanin today? Let him know all of this. And let's figure out a time to meet soon, plan out how we're going to leave the city after the vote."

"*I will.*" Rorin stood and looked between Essa and Arya. "*You know that Ravenstrike stands behind you? Anything you need, resources, aid, you have it. I am heir now, and you have my word.*"

Arya stepped up to her brother. "And the same goes for you."

***

The second afternoon of the war games was bright and sunny, spring having fully arrived in the south of Dunidaen. A large square space was roped off north of the city walls to form a field for the exhibition battles, with an area along its eastern side sectioned off for the warlords and their participating shields. The open plains surrounding the field were filled with spectators; the city's residents mingling with the visiting States' warriors and entourages.

A festival-like atmosphere reigned. Music from busking minstrels filled the afternoon air, mixing with the delicious scents emanating from the myriad of stalls set up by enterprising citizens selling food and drink. It wasn't often a new High Warlord of Dunidaen was chosen during a State Council, and the citizens of Gateport were making the most of the influx of people to the city.

Arya rode Zeke through the crowds, looking for the distinctive red tent of Ravenstrike House. They hadn't yet participated in any of the events, and for the entire first day Arya had chafed relentlessly as she watched the other State's armies show themselves off. But her warlord had told her to be patient.

Still, they were fast approaching the end of the two-day festival, and her restlessness was growing. When she reached the Ravenstrike pavilion, Thiara Ravenstrike was speaking with a Defender captain and a Crowtalon Lance captain, while Rorin, Matte, and Magen stood a short distance off, sipping from cups and laughing over something. Taze and his shield were dispersed in a loose protective cordon around the space. The two captains turned to leave just as Arya rode up and dismounted. She gave the Lance captain a suspicious look. He ignored her.

At Arya's arrival, Rorin, Matte, and Magen drifted over, looking curious—presumably about the conversation Thiara had just had.

"Warlord." Arya saluted. "I've five shields mounted and ready to deploy. I assume you're going to need us soon?"

Thiara smiled at Arya's impatience. "It's almost time for the final exhibition battle, and that's the one we've been invited to participate in. I just formally agreed on behalf of Ravenstrike."

Her heart leaped. "What can you tell me about it?" she asked eagerly.

"It will be a pitched battle. Our Raiders against the Crowtalon Lances," the warlord said crisply.

Rorin looked shocked. "*Mother, you can't agree to put the Raiders into a contained battle against heavy cavalry.*"

She settled a cool gaze on her son. "Why not?"

"*Because their greatest vulnerability is facing heavily armoured cavalry in a contained area. Without manoeuvrability and distance, we have no advantage. You see that field. There won't be enough space for them to operate,*" he replied.

Arya smothered a smile—Rorin clearly *had* been paying attention to Desomer and Laskin all these years. Magen was frowning too, presumably finding Rorin's argument compelling.

Thiara spoke before her chief adviser could weigh in, "The idea was Mathas Crowtalon's. He and I are the two candidates for the High Warlord's position, and everybody knows it. If he wins this contest, it will solidify the vote for him. If I back down from the contest, I look like a coward, and the outcome is even more certain to go in his favour," Thiara said. "I had no choice but to accept."

"You look utterly unsurprised that this is how it turned out," Matte observed, giving his wife a knowing look. "You wanted him to challenge you. That's why you haven't agreed to participate in any of the events yet."

Thiara smiled. "I will field the Raiders, and Arya will ensure they win against the odds. Then I get the votes moving in *my* favour."

Matte frowned. "Thiara, you might be the warlord of the two of us, but I had the same strategy lessons growing up as our son. Crowtalon will be using his best shields. Wooden swords and arrowheads will have no effect on the Lances' armour, so all they have to do is wait the Raiders out until they're exhausted and then ride them down."

"You telling me things I already know doesn't change the fact that I cannot back down from Mathas' challenge," Thiara snapped at her husband, including Magen and Rorin in her glare.

Mindful of Magen and other listening ears nearby, Arya hesitated. "Warlord, Rorin and Lord Eaglesoar have valid points. Out in the open, I'd have an excellent chance of defeating the Lances, but the confined field heavily favours them. I'm not sure—"

"This is a clever but rather obvious strategic move by Crowtalon. It's one that appears to have only good outcomes for him." Thiara met her gaze. "Are you telling me you cannot counter his move?"

Arya ignored the increasing rapidity of her heartbeat. "I'll figure something out, Warlord."

"You need to do better than that." Thiara held her gaze, those pale blue eyes seeing right through her. "Win this war game for me, or I lose the vote. It is as simple as that."

Thiara Ravenstrike was an appallingly terrifying tactician. She'd known she was losing the vote. She'd known she had to do something decisive enough to get herself in the running.

And so, she'd gambled on Arya pulling off the impossible, and manoeuvred Crowtalon into making the challenge.

"I understand, Warlord." Arya saluted. Her gaze caught Magen's worried look as she turned to head down the pavilion steps to where Zeke waited.

Rorin touched her arm as she passed him, then signed, "*I spoke to Dar. He knows what he needs to. So you forget worrying about us for a time, and go get them, Arya.*"

"I'll see you once this is done."

Arya had just swung into the saddle when Thiara called out her name. She'd crossed to the top of the steps.

"Was there something else?" Arya asked.

Her warlord came down the steps and walked up to Arya's stirrup, so there was no chance anyone could see or hear what she was saying. "I want you to win today, Arya, don't underestimate that. But if you fail, don't think I'll turn you out."

"Warlord?" Arya asked in confusion.

"I know that I can be harsh and unforgiving. It's how I survive as the first female warlord in this world, and one with ambition." Thiara paused. "But I love you like my own daughter, Arya Ravenstrike. Losing today won't change that."

For a long moment Arya was silent, struck completely dumb. She wished for a moment that so many eyes weren't on her, so that she could freely say what she wanted to. Instead, she murmured the words she wanted to scream in defiance. "I'm going to do everything I can for you, Warlord."

"I never doubted it."

***

Zeke carried Arya the short distance to where her five shields waited. A quick roving glance told her they were calm and focused, despite having been sitting there for hours in the warm sun.

"General!" Arya's five captains saluted smartly as she approached.

"Listen up!" she called out. "We'll be taking part in the final exhibition match—a challenge from Warlord Crowtalon to a pitched battle."

Laskin raised an eyebrow. "Against his Lances?"

"Correct, Laskin! Who said you didn't have to be clever to be a shield captain?"

The five captains shared a glance, then they turned back to her, and Zamarin said, "What are your orders, General?"

"Warlord Crowtalon will no doubt be fielding his sharpest and most heavily armoured shields," Arya explained. "They will expect to be impervious to our attack, and so their best plan will be to charge us in their defensive formation and tire us out before going on the offensive."

"Seems like a reasonable strategy to me," Laskin commented.

"Eminently sensible," Rarik agreed.

"What any half-decent war leader would do," Zamarin added.

"It is, isn't it?" Arya lifted her voice so all hundred Raiders could hear her. "Shall we?"

"Aye, General!"

***

A short time later, a trumpet sounded to call both forces to the field. Crowtalon appeared first, a hundred mounted Lances, their black armour glinting in the sunlight. Each carried a long wooden lance in the hand not resting on the reins of their big war horses. They moved into place at the north end of the field, stopping in perfect formation.

Ten rows of ten riders waiting.

The Raiders cantered onto the field in equally well-ordered fashion and lined up opposite the Lances. The crowd was already in an enthusiastic mood—no doubt enhanced by the many stalls selling mead, ale, and wine—and began cheering loudly in anticipation of the fight.

The mood was raucous and highly strung.

It wasn't only Dunidaen's warlords and vicelords and their advisers who understood the stakes. The citizens of Gateport understood the High Warlord vote would come down to Ravenstrike and Crowtalon, and they were clearly incredibly eager to watch a showdown between the two armies.

Arya reined in at the head of her shields and saluted her warlord, who'd left her pavilion and stood at the rope marking the eastern edge of the field. Rorin stood at her side, waving madly. Mathas Crowtalon and Nain, along with Nashar Falconcrest and his husband, stood close together at the opposite end of the rope line, with the other warlords and their entourages filling up the space in between. Arya caught a snatch of Hawkesdale's booming voice on the afternoon breeze. Darmanin and his brother were with Amius and the SparrowWing contingent.

The spectators lining the other three sides of the roped field now spread out for a distance, those further away craning their heads or standing on boxes to get a clearer view.

"Remember." Arya turned to address her shields. "Let them get up a good pace. It's vital that we limit their manoeuvrability as much as possible."

"We hear you," Zamarin said.

Laskin scratched his beard. "I believe this might actually be fun, General,"

"You bet your ass it will." She grinned at him, then turned Zeke back to face the Lances. Finally, she was going to be able to let her Raiders loose. Her first battle as general. She couldn't wait.

The Defender captain refereeing the match stepped up onto a dais, a white flag flapping in his right hand. Arya watched him carefully, squinting against the bright afternoon sun. Abruptly, he dropped his hand and let the flag go.

The Lance general—he stood at the edge of the field, not participating—shouted an order, and the shields lurched into movement. Arya lifted a hand, signalling her Raiders to sit tight. The Lances moved into a trot, and then a canter. A susurrus of murmurs swept through the spectators, most wondering why the Raiders weren't moving.

Ignoring the crowd, entirely focused on the battle now, Arya kept her hand raised, waited until the Lances were well into a canter before she dropped a hand and shouted a crisp order. "Raiders on me!"

An echoing shout from her soldiers roared over the field and the Raider shields moved seamlessly into a swift trot towards their adversary, Arya at their head. The heavily laden cavalry horses were picking up more momentum, moving from canter into a gallop. As soon as this happened, Arya called another order and the Raiders sped up into a canter.

The two groups bore down on each other.

The whispers of the crowd faded to an anticipatory hush.

The Lances were a fearsome sight as they rode down their opponents, an unbreachable wall of armour and weapons. Undaunted, Arya lifted her wooden sword high, and behind her, the Raiders did the same.

The hush of the crowd deepened, spreading over the plains, every gaze riveted on the two hundred soldiers barrelling towards each other with increasing speed, the gap between the forces growing smaller and smaller. The Lances reached their top speed, and as they did so, they lowered their lances into strike readiness.

The hush broke and a loud roar swept through the crowd as they anticipated the two forces crashing together.

The gap closed. Arya, in the lead, waited for the very last second.

Then she roared. "Break off!" She brought her sword down sharply. "Now!"

Almost instantly, a hundred Raiders split smoothly into two groups, and, at full gallop, wheeled sharply to the left and right. Instead of crashing into the oncoming Lances, they raced down the sides of the Lance formation.

The crowds were momentarily stunned into silence by the sheer precision of the Raider manoeuvre. It was something that shouldn't be possible without hours of practice and drill.

It wasn't.

Because Arya had known. She'd known for years now that if trouble came inside the borders of Dunidaen, it would come from Crowtalon. And it had been Desomer that had taught her that winning or losing in a civil war would come down to each general's ability to weaponise their oppositions' strengths and weaknesses.

So, Arya had trained her shields to fight Lances under every circumstance she could imagine. And these five shields had just spent days out on the plains beyond the city honing the sharpness of those manoeuvres.

Now, Arya's Raiders pushed their horses into a flying gallop down the flanks of the Lance formation, reaching the end and wheeling back around with the same seamless precision. Arya thought her chest might burst with the pride she felt in watching them do as she'd taught them. Mixed with the rush of racing down the field on Zeke's back, the feeling was indescribable.

"Ropes!" she shouted.

As one the Raiders sheathed their swords and reached down to grab the coiled lassos hooked underneath their saddles, hidden from casual sight. The Lances, having worked up a bulldozing speed, were still moving south down the field. Though their general had shouted the order for them to halt and turn, the horses were too heavily laden to slow with any speed, and it was this that the Raiders now took advantage of.

"Take 'em down!" Arya called her final order a loud whoop. She wheeled Zeke around and led her Raiders racing up behind the slowing cavalry. They still had a good few seconds before the Lances would be able to get themselves turned around in formation and be ready to counter-attack.

Again, the hundred riders split evenly and galloped alongside the outer line of Lances. Picking her man, riding in the first line of Lances, Arya bought Zeke up beside him, and tossed her lasso around his midsection before he even knew what was happening.

"HA!" she urged Zeke faster, and they raced forward.

The lasso caught firmly on the man's armour, and as Arya galloped ahead, it pulled him cleanly off his horse. As soon as he hit the ground, she reined in her stallion and leaped out of the saddle. Two strides bought her to his fallen body, and now she drew her wooden sword and levelled it at his throat. "Do you concede?"

His eyes were bitterly disappointed inside his helmet, but he nodded. "I concede."

All over the field, one by one, the Lances were dragged off their mounts and onto the ground, the Raiders moving with such perfect coordination that their opponents didn't have time to see what was happening and respond.

Soon, a Raider stood above each fallen Lance with a sword levelled at the man's throat.

It had taken no more than a few minutes for Arya's army to win.

"Laskin!" Arya called out. "I think we won."

"You might be right, General," he called back, failing to hold back his smile.

Only then did Arya become aware of the roaring crowd. The cheering rose in volume, shock and jubilation both. It swept over the field and into her racing blood, her beating heart, stirring the triumph flooding through her into a conflagration.

She stepped away from the fallen Lance and lifted her sword the air in jubilation. Around her, every Raider followed suit, and the crowd screamed for them.

Arya let the moment hold, then she lowered the sword and returned to Zeke. Once she was back in the saddle, she called out the order for her shields to re-form. Disciplined despite their victory and the screaming crowds, they were in formation and riding to the northern edge of the field within moments.

Arya rode Zeke up to where Mathas Crowtalon stood with Nain. "I'd like to thank you, Warlord Crowtalon," she said. "I understand this war game was your idea. My Raiders and I enjoyed it immensely."

"Get out of my sight, girl," he snarled, face twisting with some unsettling combination of menace and contempt. "You have made yourself an enemy here today."

"I think we're already enemies. It's nice to see you're not pretending anymore, though," she said, then glanced at Nain. The Crowtalon adviser was smiling slightly, but it wasn't a warm smile. Something about it was familiar, and a chill ran down her spine. "Good day, Warlord."

Not giving him a chance to say anything further, she turned Zeke and cantered along the rope towards the Ravenstrike contingent, soaking in the cheers of the crowd as she rode. She reined Zeke in before Thiara Ravenstrike and dismounted before saluting sharply. "The battle is yours, Warlord Ravenstrike."

"Well done, Arya." Thiara's smile was fierce. "Very well done indeed."

"*Agreed*." Rorin grinned, ducking under the rope so he could unceremoniously throw his arms around her. "*You just delivered my mother the High Warlord vote.*"

"Let's not get too far ahead of ourselves," Thiara warned. "We've managed to undermine Crowtalon further, but that doesn't necessarily mean they'll turn to me."

Magen nodded, but he looked pensive, and hopeful. "We certainly have a lot of work to do between now and the vote."

"Then let's get started," Thiara said. "Congratulations again, Arya. Please pass my gratitude to your shields and ensure they get the night off."

Arya saluted, then watched as the Ravenstrike contingent left, Rorin waving at her with a grin. Success and triumph flooded her.

They were going to succeed. Arya had just delivered her warlord her best chance of winning the High Warlord vote. Soon, they'd be done in Gateport, and if Rorin sat ruling Ravenstrike and his mother ruled as High Warlord...

Then Arya would have Dunidaen's support to deal with the Nightstalker.

For once and for all.

Chapter 43

Almost as soon as the war games were over, fresh excitement swept through the city. For the first time since the election of Darien Eaglesoar as High Warlord almost two decades earlier, Gateport played host to foreign leaders, come to witness the election of a new ruler of Dunidaen.

On the afternoon following Arya's Raiders defeating Crowtalon, Emperor Atan uq-Danresan sailed into the harbour with a fifty-strong escort of his elite Rangers. Causing even more of a stir the following morning was the arrival of the delegation from the Icelands. Prince At'eir Is'heim came overland, representing his mother, queen of the Icefolk, with a small group of warriors. Their snow-white hair, styled in intricate braids, and the silver furs they wore despite the warmth made them stand out in a crowd, but it was the blades they had strapped all over their bodies that turned heads wherever they went.

Only King Lucius Nightstalker of Andahar and Elder Salyarin of the Etherean were missing. Even if he had been invited, Arya doubted the Etherean leader would risk the Dunidae hatred of magic.

But the excitement in the air was edged with unmistakable tension, and it increased with each day that passed, winding tighter and tighter, an explosive mix. The presence of foreign visitors provided a diversion for the city's residents as they explored the streets of Gateport and drew stares and excitement, but the nobility was not so easily distracted.

A vote for a new leader of Dunidaen rarely happened more than once a generation. A High Warlord remained in their position until they either died, voluntarily stepped down, or were voted out by a unanimous State

Council vote. Both Mathas and Thiara were relatively young, and so the upcoming vote would have long-term repercussions for Dunidaen.

A formal reception was held two nights before the vote to welcome the foreign leaders to Dunidaen. Arya, dressed in her formal best, accompanied a resplendently dressed Thiara Ravenstrike, Rorin, and Matte Eaglesoar.

The Council chamber had been entirely transformed, chairs and tables swept aside to create an open space filled with dancing couples and groups of richly dressed guests drinking, eating, and talking.

Entering a pace behind her warlord, Arya was immediately too hot in her thick, gold-edged cloak with its high neck, but she knew it made her look tall and impressive, offsetting her youth, so she ignored the discomfort.

Her gaze roved those gathered, recognising many of the various States' nobility now that she'd been to so many dinners and receptions. She couldn't see anyone from Crowtalon, but both the foreign entourages were there.

"Rorin, Matte, please go and speak with the Falconcrest vicelords, as we discussed," Thiara said. "Arya, with me."

Thiara Ravenstrike made straight for where the High Warlord stood speaking with the Khadini entourage, and as they approached, Arya immediately picked out the man who must be the emperor. The two men who stood with him were overtly deferential in their manner despite the fact the swords at their waists and the rippling muscle of their bared arms indicated they were elite Rangers. Arya quickly checked that the sleeve of her Raider jerkin covered the labour camp scar on the inside of her right arm.

The sight of the emperor sent a little sizzle of anger through her. This was the man who kept thousands of his people in slave-like conditions in his pit mines, who'd imprisoned *Arya*. Who'd murdered his siblings to assure his place on the throne.

With a breath, Arya caught the anger at its root and crushed it. This night was far too important to her warlord to risk ruffling feathers.

No matter how much she'd like to strangle Emperor uq-Danresan with the gaudy belt tied at his waist.

"Warlord Ravenstrike," Darien Eaglesoar said politely. "Allow me to introduce you to Emperor uq-Danresan."

"Emperor." Thiara bowed her head, but not too much; she already appeared diminutive standing so close to the big Khadini man. "It's a pleasure to host you in Gateport."

"Warlord." Atan uq-Danresan gave a brusque nod, his Dunidae heavily accented. There was resemblance to Kulan in his green eyes and olive skin, but his face was harder, broader than his younger brother. And there was no light of humour in his expression. "You will be standing as a candidate for High Warlord, I understand?"

"That's right, Your Grace."

Arya stiffened at the flicker of contempt that crossed the emperor's face, but she kept the tight stranglehold on her temper. It mattered little what the Khadini emperor thought of the candidates for High Warlord.

"A pleasure." The emperor nodded again, then strode off, his two companions following him.

Even Darien Eaglesoar blinked in surprise at the emperor's abrupt departure, but before either he or Thiara could say anything, one of the Icefolk swept up. Arya looked over the empty sheaths strapped to his body and the warrior's calluses on his hands, placing him a good ten years or so older than her. He, too, was intimidatingly tall, with tumbling white braids and bright blue eyes, but he wore a ready smile and she marked his willingness to come to the event without weapons. "High Warlord, a fine party you have here."

"Prince At'eir Is'heim." Darien smiled and bowed his head. "Let me introduce you to Warlord Ravenstrike."

At'eir bowed, smooth and graceful and spoke Dunidae far better than the Khadini emperor. "I admit I came over here in the hopes of just such an introduction. Warlord Ravenstrike, it is an honour to meet you. It was many years ago, I realise, but I would like to take this opportunity to thank you for your efforts repelling the Andahari threat. If the Nightstalker rouses, it will threaten my country also."

"Thank you, Er'fin," Thiara replied, using the correct honorific for an Icefolk prince. "I fear that it may be 'when', not 'if', but I hope that I am wrong. I was fortunate to have the help of excellent commanders. This is General Arya Ravenstrike, who was instrumental in dealing so decisively with that threat."

"Well met, General Ravenstrike. You are young for such a lofty position." At'eir's ice-blue eyes locked on Arya's. "You must be an impressive woman."

Arya smiled a little. "Thank you, Er'fin. I like to think so."

A crooked smile curled his mouth. "I am pleased to meet you both. Warlord Ravenstrike, perhaps I could steal you for a dance, later? It would be timely to discuss the northern border situation." At'eir bowed and then moved to greet Warlord Falconcrest nearby. He glanced back at Arya as he moved away, and she wondered at the source of the curiosity she saw in his eyes.

"High Warlord. Thiara!" Hawkesdale's booming voice cut over the nearby chatter, causing them to turn. Eaglesoar gave Hawkesdale a nod.

Thiara smiled. "Gelfrey. A pleasant evening to you."

"I'm glad I found you both," Hawkesdale said. "There's something I wanted to discuss."

The three began discussing some kind of trade deal in Hawkesdale cotton—Arya's warlord never *not* angling for the High Warlord vote—and her attention wandered.

"Arya!"

She turned at Andrian's voice. He was weaving through the room towards her, handsome in a violet tunic and high collared shirt. "Hello, Andrian."

He gave her a warm smile. "You look stunning tonight." He raised her hand and kissed it.

She chuckled. "I thought you would have given up on me by now."

He looked at her strangely. "What do you mean?"

"Andrian." A sharp voice cut him off, and a little shiver went through Arya at Nain's appearance. "Your father wants you."

"I just left him, Nain. What can he want so soon?"

Nain said nothing, merely levelled a look on the young man. Andrian's mouth tightened, and he gave a short nod. "I'm sorry, Arya. Will you have a drink with me after the vote? I promise to buy the round if your warlord wins."

"We'll see." Arya didn't plan to be around after the vote, of course, but couldn't tell him that.

"I'll find you," he said, winking rakishly before stepping away and disappearing into the crowd.

Nain merely gave her a cold look before striding off.

Supressing another shiver, Arya turned back to her warlord—she and Hawkesdale had moved on from cotton to something about border taxes, and Eaglesoar had wandered off—only to see Darmanin crossing the floor towards her. He bowed slightly. "Dance with me?"

Arya opened her mouth to refuse—but realised in the next breath he was offering her an escape from the tedious conversation happening between Thiara and Hawkesdale. So, she took his hand and let him lead her onto the dance floor.

"Rorin told me what happened the other night." Darmanin's voice was so low she barely heard him. "I agree that the best plan is to make sure we're all out of Gateport by the night of the ball. But Arya, you must make sure your wyvern stays hidden."

"I do know what the reaction would be if someone saw a wyvern flying over Gateport, Dar." She gave him a look. "And it certainly wouldn't be voting for Rorin's mother if they found out it was my wyvern."

"Right." He expelled a breath. "Listen, I've been doing some quiet digging on Bralin. He was a Hawkesdale Longbow."

Her eyebrows shot up. "That explains how good he was with that bow. Though I can't see Warlord Hawkesdale sending one of his Longbows after SparrowWing."

"He retired several years ago. In disgrace, I get the impression." Darmanin said. "And Hawkesdale has no current tension with SparrowWing anyway. The only one who does right now is my—"

Someone bumped into them. Arya swallowed a sharp retort when she recognised Warlord Falconcrest and his husband; the warlord's flushed cheeks and awkward stepping suggested he'd been drinking.

"My apologies, Warlord," she said as politely as she could.

He scowled at her. "Watch where you're going."

Arya and Darmanin smirked at each other as the two men moved off.

"How do you think the nazal got to Bralin?" Arya asked. "And why Bralin? If it wanted Amius dead, why didn't it just attack *his* mind, force him to jump out of his own window?"

"I've been thinking on that too. The only answer I can come up with is that the nazal couldn't get into Amius's mind. Which might mean not all human minds are susceptible to its magic."

"Makes sense." She thought about it. "Something about Bralin made him vulnerable to the nazal's magic?"

"You're still sure only one of the nazal has that ability?"

"Reasonably sure." She shrugged. "But I can't be certain."

Darmanin frowned. "Let's assume it can't access *all* minds. And we can perhaps also assume each of the nazal has a different magic?"

"*And* that they're vulnerable to cazaix," she added.

Something niggled at her then, a tendril of a thought that kept wanting to surface. Something about the nazal, and the things they were learning—

"About talking to Rorin's mother." Darmanin said.

"I'm not hiding from this anymore, I've told you that." She held his gaze. "The nazal will go after those we both love. It's time to deal with the Nightstalker, and we can't do it alone. I know you know this, so stop making me repeat it. Thiara Ravenstrike can bring Dunidaen behind us if she wins. And even if she doesn't, we need her help."

"I'm sorry," he said unexpectedly. "For being so angry about it all. I know you're right, and I know it's not your fault. It's past time we do something. I'll support what you think is best."

She stared at him. "Really?"

"I just want it done, Arya, so we can go back to our lives."

She squeezed his hand and changed the subject to lighter topics. "Have you met either of the foreign leaders yet?"

"Both." He stepped confidently, which she was glad of, because she'd never had any formal dance training. "I liked Prince At'eir. From how he talks about her, I suspect his mother is an impressive woman. It's a shame she couldn't make it."

"Whereas I'm pretty certain Emperor uq-Danresan is personally offended at the idea of a woman becoming High Warlord of Dunidaen," she said dryly.

Darmanin's eyebrows lifted. "Is that so? It doesn't surprise me. A few minutes with the man and I understand Kulan and his rebels far better now."

"We could be in a similar situation." She lowered her voice. "If your father—"

"He won't."

"You don't know that," she pointed out gently. "From talking with Magen and Essa, it sounds like Rorin's mother might have the edge in the vote after the exhibition match, but it's still too close to call."

"That match was astonishing." Darmanin's face lit up. "*You* were astonishing, Arya Ravenstrike."

"Yes," she said, arching her eyebrow. "I know."

His stern features dissolved into a grin at that, and Arya's breath caught. "That smile," she murmured. "So rare, but so wonderful."

His hand tightened on hers and he pulled her closer. "Arya."

But whatever he was going to stay trailed off when her gaze—always roving the room to ensure Rorin and her warlord would be safe—landed on a familiar face standing near one of the entrances amidst a huddle of Khadini Rangers and servants. She did a double-take, then glanced away. Astonishment and shock filled her.

What was Kulan doing here?

"What is it?" Darmanin frowned.

Arya forced herself to look at him and smile. "Tell you later."

As soon as the dance was finished, she excused herself and made her way casually through the room towards the group near the doors where Kulan stood. He saw her approaching, and after glancing around, moved discreetly towards her.

She picked up a glass of wine from a passing servant, then came to a stop near Kulan, her gaze on the dancers, and took a sip of the wine. "What are you doing here?" she hissed.

"It's good to see you, Arya." She could hear the smile in his voice. "I'm here with the emperor's small army of personal attendants. We are ready to leap at his slightest whim."

"Aren't you risking him recognising you?"

"He hasn't seen me since I was fourteen, and we rarely saw each other before that. Besides, my brother barely even looks at his servants, let alone takes note of what they look like."

They fell silent for moment, both making the appearance of being lost in their thoughts, gazes in different directions.

"Why pretend to be a servant and come here?" Arya asked. "It *is* a risk, Kulan, no matter how much you downplay it."

"I came to take the measure of the new High Warlord in the hopes he or she may be willing to ally with us."

Arya's eyebrows shot up. "Ally with your rebels against the emperor?"

"I know it is a gamble." His gaze briefly flicked to hers. "But we've come a long way since you left. Many of the rebel groups have agreed to unite. I must be bold if I am going to succeed, but I will not succeed without allies."

"I understand," she said quietly.

"Will you meet with me, somewhere privately, so we can talk? We shouldn't linger here any longer, someone will notice."

"I don't know." She hesitated. "There's a lot going on right now, Kulan, and meeting in person could be dangerous for both of us."

"Please. I need your help. I will make sure nobody sees us meeting." He glanced at her. "There is an inn not far from the Khadini quarters called the Icy Fish. I will be off duty at midnight and sneak out to meet you there."

Arya hesitated again. Her gaze fell on Thiara Ravenstrike, now talking to Falconcrest, her mouth in a tight line as he gesticulated wildly. If she won the vote, then understanding the political situation in Khadini would be beneficial. Especially if the Nightstalker invaded and they needed cazaix. "All right," she agreed. "I'll see you there."

Arya moved off without another word, in search of Rorin this time. For the moment she put Kulan's sudden appearance to the back of her mind.

She still had a lot of work to do on her warlord's behalf before this evening was over.

Chapter 44

"Congratulations, Arya. I know how badly you wanted to become general." Kulan's face lit up as Arya finished telling the story of what had happened since her return to Dunidaen. He looked different than she remembered. He'd filled out with flesh and muscle since escaping the pit mine, and he was clean-shaven, his light brown hair in a neat bun on top of his head—the required appearance for the emperor's servants, she'd learned. Her fingers itched to undo the bun and mess it all up.

On arriving at the Icy Fish, Arya had paid for a private room, and Kulan had discreetly followed her up to it. She was weary after a long night speaking with vicelords and generals, matching Rorin as best she could in his charm offensive. After her victory, the generals were at least willing to engage her in conversation now, even if some still seemed to think the win had come by chance or luck. It felt good to take off her heavy cloak and boots and sit with a friend to unwind over a mug of mead.

She refilled both their mugs. "Thank you. It's been wonderful so far. I just wish I could focus on it completely."

He nodded. His hands cradled his mug. "I had such grand plans in coming here, but the emperor wants to leave immediately after the vote. He is already growing impatient and bored in Gateport."

"I only met him briefly, but I didn't sense a lot of respect for Dunidaen," she said.

"He cares little for anything outside his own circle. Our people suffer for it, but not just in the high taxes they pay and the food shortages," Kulan said, a fierce light in his eyes. "This is a time when we must strengthen our alliances, both with Dunidaen and the Icelands. The Etherean too."

Arya let out a breath. "You can't tell anyone this, and I can't tell you how I know, but despite refusing an invitation to come, the Nightstalker is planning to show up after the High Warlord vote—at the formal ball to welcome the new High Warlord."

Concern rippled over Kulan's face. "You can't be there, if he comes."

"I can do as I like," she said with an edge. "But you're not wrong. I'll be leaving the city immediately after the vote."

He nodded, and a comfortable silence fell for a moment, before Kulan lifted his gaze to hers. "It has been interesting, wandering these streets and seeing more of your country and people. Not that we are given much time off, but still. Gateport seems bustling, thriving, even. But on several occasions, I have seen your citizens begging on the street corners."

She lifted an eyebrow. "You don't have beggars in Aq Dale'a?"

"Of course, many hundreds more than here thanks to my brother." He made a disgusted gesture. "But I noted yours because almost all wore a nasty looking brand on their faces."

Arya's hand absently traced the scar on her own forearm. "Magic-wielders. Dunidaen is terrified of them, so when they're discovered, they're branded so everyone knows what they are."

Kulan looked horrified. "Why? What is to be feared so badly?"

"The Nightstalker."

"He is one man. Not every magic-wielder is evil."

"Try telling that to the Dunidae warlords." Arya stretched, weariness turning into relaxation. "I think what they truly fear is that magic is a threat to their power."

"But Arya..." The horror had not cleared from his face. "That means if they discovered what you were, they would..."

"I know." She said softly. "Essa and Dar too."

"I don't understand. You told me in Taskari that you didn't want to be the Stormrider heir because you loved Dunidaen and wanted to serve it as general. But now you're telling me Dunidaen would brand you and throw you out on the streets if they found out what you are. And not just you, but your family too."

Arya shifted uncomfortably. "Kulan, they're not all like that. There are good people here."

He stared at her, clearly not comprehending. Her relaxation was beginning to turn to discomfort at this blunt appraisal of the conflict that had been roiling inside her for months, so she cleared her throat. "You said you wanted my help? That's why we had to meet."

"If your warlord wins the vote," he said, "will she consider speaking with me and the rebels about an alliance against my brother?"

"It's unlikely," Arya said honestly. "She'll need to spend the next few years consolidating her power, especially since Crowtalon and his allies will be trying to undermine her at every turn. But once she's done that, I think she'd at least agree to a meeting with you."

"And what if Warlord Crowtalon wins?" Kulan asked.

"He will be no ally to you," Arya said. "He doesn't think Dunidaen needs help from anyone, and I don't see him being willing to risk our army in a Khadini civil war, even if there *was* a strategic gain in it for Dunidaen."

Kulan let out a breath. "That is not the news I was hoping to hear. But I needed to know it either way. For what it's worth, my people are in your warlord's corner, Arya."

"My first loyalty is to my warlord, but I will do what I can for you. For both our country's sakes." Arya hesitated. "But Kulan..."

"Go on."

"With the Nightstalker threat looming, all our countries need to be strong. Do you think this is a good time to start a civil war in Khadini?"

His mouth tightened. "We are far from being able to do that yet. And we cannot keep allowing our people to suffer because an Andahari despot has thoughts of invasion."

"If the Nightstalker invades Dunidaen, will your brother come to our aid?"

"No," Kulan said. "I say that not to try and convince you to ally with me, but because it is the truth. He cares nothing for anything outside Khadini."

"He'll have to care if Andahar runs through Dunidaen and comes for Khadini next."

"I fear that," Kulan said. "Even with our cazaix, we would not be able to hold the Nightstalker off alone. We have no magic of our own."

She nodded, understanding his distress. There wasn't anything that could be done about either of their situations tonight, so she leaned forward and slid her hand over his, tangling their fingers. Standing, she tugged him towards the bed. "The best I can offer you now is an excellent distraction from both our troubles."

A grin spread over his face as he allowed himself to be led. "Offer accepted, General Ravenstrike."

Elendryl roused in her head, curious.

"*Private*," she told him, then chuckled when he didn't seem to understand what that meant. "*I'm fine. Just stay away for a little while. Until morning.*"

"Something wrong?" Kulan murmured, sliding his hands around her waist.

"Nothing." She leaned up to kiss him. "Just my wyvern wondering what I'm up to."

He jerked away, eyes widening. "You're not actually joking, are you?"

Arya laughed aloud. "I'm not. This first, then I'll tell you all about it."

****

Arya arrived at the townhouse for breakfast with Rorin and the others the following morning slightly late. Though she'd had little sleep, the pleasurable distraction of a few hours in Kulan's bed had eased some of the edge of anxiety that hung constantly from her shoulders these days.

"*You're late*," Rorin chided as Arya reached the table and slipped off her cloak before taking a seat. "*Wasn't that what you wore last night?*"

"I got caught up visiting a friend." She accepted the mug of tea he passed her, then asked before he could press any further. "What's your schedule like for today?"

"*It's as boring as the last several days*," Rorin replied. "*At least Dar is coming with me today to help charm the vicelords, so it won't be all bad.*"

"Dar being charming?" Arya raised an eyebrow. "I'll believe that when I see it."

Essa and Rorin laughed, while Darmanin promptly scowled.

"*What about your day, Arya?*"

"Magen's schedule tells me I'm lunching with Hawkesdale's general. It will be interminable—he's so stuck in his ways it's hard to get him to take me seriously let alone talk about anything interesting," she said. "I'll be glad when all of this is over."

"Speaking of." Essa lowered her voice and glanced around. "Dar, what are your plans?"

"If my father wins the vote, I'll leave immediately and go to Anduil with Andrian to take up my place as Warlord Crowtalon. As soon as I've consolidated my position there, I'll leave Andrian in charge and come to Heathrock to be part of your planning against the Nightstalker. Perhaps with my vote added to Rorin's mother's, we can force the warlords into action," Darmanin said.

"*And if my mother wins?*"

"That will be easier." Darmanin gave his little smile. "If you're willing, I'll join you while you speak to her as High Warlord and tell her everything."

"After which we will all immediately decamp from Gateport and head north to Heathrock," Arya said. "I think I should travel separately, though. Dar too, just to be cautious."

"*Essa, if my mother wins and I become Warlord Ravenstrike, you'll be my chief adviser, so it will make sense for you to travel with me,*" Rorin mused.

Essa stared at him. Arya and Darmanin both stifled smiles.

"*What?*" Rorin blinked at her. "*Ess, I told you you'd be my chief adviser when I became warlord.*"

"Yes, but that was a long time ago and—"

"*Nothing has changed.*"

It seemed to take her a moment for that to settle, then her face lit up and she sat forward. "Rorin! There's so much we'll be able to start doing."

His smile was wide. "*I know.*"

"First though." Arya let out a resigned breath. "You and I need to go into the Diamondfang and see Salyarin, Essa. We must start learning enough about our magic to protect ourselves and those we love."

"I will go with you too," Darmanin said after a moment's hesitation.

She tossed him a grateful smile across the table. He inclined his head, eyes glimmering.

Rorin let out a sigh and rubbed his forehead as if he had a headache. Arya saw how worry was weighing on him, not to mention how heartsick he must be about Peemla, but he'd been handling it admirably so far.

"Everything will be fine," Darmanin said, as if noticing the same thing. "We've only got today and tomorrow to get through before the vote, and thanks to Leanir we know the nazal won't act before the ball. We'll be okay."

"*You always say that,*" Rorin said. "*You and Arya are as bad as each other; so confident that you think if you say something will be so, it will.*"

"Hey, I'm insulted by that," Arya said in protest. "I'm nothing like Dar."

Rorin grinned, then broke into silent laughter, his amusement deepening so much he had to brace himself against the table as his shoulders shook. Essa too, grinned from ear to ear.

Darmanin rose with a grumble. "Come on Rorin, we'd best start our schmoozing for the day. Taze and his shield will be waiting."

"Have fun." Arya waved them off.

"Two days," Essa mused once they'd gone. "And then everything changes."

"Not forever," Arya said. "You can still have your cottage, *after* you change the world with Rorin of course."

"*If* we all make it through facing the Nightstalker alive." Essa's green gaze was troubled. "You talk about facing him, about bringing Dunidaen behind us, as if that's going to solve everything."

"I know it won't." Arya leaned towards her. "But I bet on us, Essa. I bet on us every single time. We'll figure this out together."

Chapter 45

The day of the High Warlord vote arrived without any fanfare. Arya spent most of it at the Raider barracks drilling the anxiety and anticipatory energy out of herself and her troops. She didn't want any trouble started, especially if tensions from the vote spilled out to the respective warlord's warriors. She certainly didn't think Nain or Mathas Crowtalon were above having their Lances provoke the Raiders into some kind of confrontation if they thought it would give them an advantage. Falconcrest had already proved they were up for it.

The Ravenstrike townhouse was a hive of activity when Arya made a quick visit in the late afternoon. She ran into Peemla on her way upstairs. The chamberlain carried herself with her usual bustling air, but as always had a bright smile of welcome for Arya.

"You look busy," Arya noted.

Peemla glanced upstairs. "Don't tell them, but I'm planning a surprise celebration supper for after the vote. I've even ordered in the warlord's favourite wine."

At the woman's shy smile, Arya's heart clenched. This woman could have been her sister-in-law.

And she would be wonderful for Rorin. Why had Arya refused to acknowledge that?

"Something wrong?" Peemla looked worried.

"Things are still looking positive, though it will go down to the wire." Arya said. "It's good of you. The way you look after us. Even when..."

"Are you sure you're okay?"

"I am." Arya cleared her throat. "I can't wait to see what you've organised for later. It will be the highlight of my day."

Peemla's cheeks pinked. "Oh, get away with you. I'd best get on with things."

Arya watched her go for a moment, then headed upstairs, heart heavy. Essa was right—Arya had been a poor friend to Peemla and Rorin.

Her brother was closeted with Taze and a bevy of servants whose job it was to make the Ravenstrike heir look as polished and warlord-like as possible.

"*Arya, save me please?*" He directed a pleading look her way when he spotted her hovering in the doorway.

"I wish I could." She lifted her hands in surrender when the horde of servants turned frowns on her, then slowly backed away. "I'll see you at the Council chamber later."

Thiara Ravenstrike was equally occupied, although those gathered in her office included her husband, Essa, and Magen, along with some of Magen's clerks. Only Magen would be attending the actual vote. Arya had been disappointed on Essa's behalf, until the woman had pointed out she'd hear soon enough about the outcome and was entirely happy spending the evening reading in front of the fire rather than sitting for hours in the Council chamber.

"Arya." Thiara looked up briefly at her entrance. "Do you need something?"

"No, Warlord. The Raiders are settled, and I've made it clear they're to be on their best behaviour tonight. I just came by to see if you needed me for anything before I get ready myself?"

"I've got plenty on my plate, but nothing you can help with." Thiara's eyes were already returning to her notes. "Please don't be late, Arya."

"I won't," she promised. Nothing would stop her from being at this vote tonight. The combined cocktail of nerves and anticipation already had her shifting from foot to foot.

"I'm just about to drag her away to dress so we won't be late," Matte told Arya with a smile. "We'll meet you there."

Arya returned his smile. "See you then."

Back at the barracks, Arya washed and changed. For what would be the final time in Gateport, she pulled on her formal cloak and adjusted it over her shoulders, making a face instantly at how warm and heavy it was. She couldn't wait to get back to the cold snows of home.

As she headed to the door, her gaze fell on the saddlebags packed and ready on her bed. No matter how things went tonight, they would be speaking with Thiara first thing in the morning and leaving the city before nightfall. They'd be gone from the city a full day and a half before the formal ball to close the State Council and the Nightstalker's arrival.

She took a breath. If only they won tonight, then she truly believed they could work together to find a solution to the Nightstalker. But even if they didn't, she'd make sure those she loved were safe before the nazal struck.

Shoulders squared, Arya opened her door, only to find Laskin loitering in the hall outside. He saluted. "General."

"Something wrong?"

"I just wanted to check in." He shifted his stance. "It's a big night for you."

"For all of us," she said.

"We're all wishing our warlord the best," Laskin said. "The Raiders are proud of her. And you."

"We've come a long way, you and I, haven't we?"

He gave a rueful shake of his head. "Farther than I thought we'd come, if I'm honest. But you deserve every bit of this, Arya Ravenstrike. I'm proud to serve under you."

His support and reassurance soothed her in the way it always had. Arya hesitated. "Will you bring your shield with me tonight? I know it's late notice, but I'd like to have you there. Watching my back as always."

He bowed his head. "They're already mounted and waiting at the gates, General."

***

Dusk had fallen, and the roads surrounding the domed Council building were thronged with people, horses, and ornate carriages when they arrived. Arya and Laskin dismounted, tethered their horses to the hitching post, and headed up the stone steps.

Arya paused on the threshold. A glance back showed Laskin's shield sitting their horses straight-backed and calm, alert and ready for anything despite the chaos surrounding them. Charlin's axe was strapped to his back, Wattin's beard was beyond regulation length as always, and Kait was talking to Etan while both kept a close eye on their surroundings. Allicen leaned forward and tapped them both on the shoulder, a chiding look on her face.

Arya smiled and went through the doors.

Inside, she weaved her way through the small groups of people gathered in the wide corridor circling the chamber. The main chamber had been transformed again following the ball. Hundreds of cushioned chairs lined up in rows before a dais where the High Warlord would sit. Many of them were already filled with warlords, vicelords, advisers, and generals.

Emperor uq-Danresan stood speaking with Prince At'eir in a section reserved for the foreign leaders in front of the dais. Their entourages otherwise sat separately. A quick glance showed no sign of Kulan, though the distance was too great to tell properly. Arya ignored a niggle of guilt that she wasn't going to have the time or opportunity to farewell her rebel friend before disappearing from Gateport the next day.

"There's Lord Rorin." Laskin pointed.

"Thanks, Laskin. Will you stay close?"

He scratched at his beard. "You worried about something?"

"I just like knowing you're near." She paused. "That's always made me feel safe. I don't think I've ever properly thanked you for it."

"It goes both ways, General. I'll be just outside the doors. Good luck tonight." He saluted and left her to it.

Arya made her way down an aisle to where Rorin sat with Taze, close to the front. Across the aisle to their right, and two rows ahead, sat the Crowtalon contingent. Mathas and Nain were just arriving and taking their seats, Darmanin sitting in the row behind. Arya noted Andrian making his way to sit beside Darmanin instead of his father.

Father and youngest son clearly and deliberately ignored each other. The look Nain sent Darmanin's way chilled Arya to the bone, however. Then the chief adviser turned and looked at Arya, as if sensing her gaze on him.

The look in the man's expression. It was…

"General?" Taze's voice in her ear. "Something wrong?"

Arya tore her gaze away from Nain, shaken. "He knows something."

"Nain?" Now Taze looked worried.

Arya gave herself a little shake. Nain had always been creepy and supercilious, that was nothing new. Besides, she'd be rid of him soon. "Ignore me. I'm just jumpy."

Rorin gave her a little wave as she sat next to him, Taze resuming his seat as well.

"Where are your parents?" Arya asked.

"*They're running late,*" Rorin explained. "*They were almost ready to go when I left the townhouse. I stopped at Vicelord Sayler's on the way here. He was wavering a week ago, but I think he's made the decision to cast his vote our way.*"

"Good news." Arya sat back in her chair, telling herself to relax. She watched as people entered through the doors and made their way to seats. Thiara Ravenstrike and her husband were not among them. "Did your parents mention stopping somewhere on their way here?" she asked.

Rorin shook his head. "*I thought Mother had spoken to everyone she needed to.*"

The Eaglesoar House arrived together, and Arya scanned the group for Matte. He wasn't with them. The time of the vote was rapidly approaching. The last of those attending drifted through the doors. As soon as the corridor outside cleared, the Defenders closed with doors with an audible a clang, and then stood to attention either side.

"Maybe they're behind the dais," Taze suggested.

"They didn't say anything about that." Arya's feeling of unease deepened. She felt as if there was something she'd missed but couldn't put her finger on what. "Your mother should be here, Rorin."

Ahead of them, Darmanin turned to catch their gazes. His hands flickered. *"Is everything all right? Where is Warlord Ravenstrike?"*

"We don't know," Arya responded.

He frowned, but realising he was attracting looks, turned to resume looking at the front. Beside him, Andrian murmured something. Darmanin shrugged and shook his head.

"Danger."

Arya started as Elendryl pushed into her mind. She waved off Rorin and Taze's concerned look and tried to paste on an expressionless mask. *"Danger where?"*

"Near," he insisted. *"It hunts."*

"If it comes near you, you flee," Arya drove that thought home with as much force as she could. *"Flee, Elendryl."*

Reluctant agreement, then, *"Careful!"* The wyvern dropped that single feeling with a firmness that made her head ache, then withdrew in a huff as the Defender general appeared on the dais, looking resplendent in white and gold.

Suddenly Arya wished she wasn't stuck in this room for what would likely be a lengthy vote. If the nazal was hunting Elendryl, she needed to get to him, protect him. She just hoped he would listen to her and flee. Her knee jiggled up and down.

"General, do you want me to go and look for the warlord?" Taze asked in an undertone.

"You can't. The Defenders have closed the room down for the vote. We'll just have to hope they're here somewhere."

Arya just hoped this was part of some plan of her warlord's. That she was inside somewhere.

"It's not going to look good if the leading candidate is not even here for the vote," Rorin commented. *"Do you think I should put myself forward instead?"*

She glanced at him, but there was no humour in his face, despite his joking words. He leaned into her, and they silently shared support. As she leaned away, General Radaen, head of the Defender force, appeared on the dais.

"Warlords and Vicelords, Emperor uq-Danresan, and Prince At'eir, welcome," Radaen said, voice booming through the chamber. "Thank you all for being here. Tonight, we will vote for a new High Warlord of Dunidaen. I entreat you to choose wisely." He paused to allow a solemn silence to spread over the gathering. "Before we begin the proceedings, our High Warlord would like to address you one final time while you're all gathered. Please, welcome High Warlord Darien Eaglesoar."

Arya froze as respectful clapping broke out across the room to welcome Darian Eaglesoar to the dais.

"I know I was scheduled to give this speech two nights hence." Eaglesoar spoke once the clapping faded. "But that night belongs to our new High Warlord, whoever that may be, and so I will address you tonight instead. Perhaps there is something in what I have to say that will help you vote wisely."

Arya's breath escaped in a shocked rush.

The High Warlord was speaking tonight.

Chapter 46

Beside Arya, Rorin and Taze had gone rigid. Taze's grip on the arm of his chair was white knuckled, and she could see him surreptitiously scanning the room for danger.

"*Arya?*" Rorin signed, still looking forward, jaw tense.

"Calm, Rorin."

"*It's tonight, isn't it?*" he signed. "*The ambush?*"

"He changed the night of his speech." she said.

"How could the nazal have known he was going to speak tonight if nobody else did?" Taze said. "Maybe we're fine."

"Maybe." Arya's heart was sinking, dread beginning to creep through her with shivery tendrils. "But where are Rorin's parents?"

There was nothing that could keep Thiara Ravenstrike from this vote, and it was now clear she was nowhere in the building. Dread clutched at her chest in a way it hadn't since she'd heard a wyvern's cry for the first time all those years ago when Xaphistryl had arrived with the Nightstalker at Windfall Fort.

Taze gave her a quick look, that soldier's focus setting in. "Okay. Then we have to get you and Rorin out of here."

"If we stand up and try to leave now, we'll be open targets and give the nazal exactly what it wants," she said, fighting desperately for calm. At least the nazal didn't have all of them in this room; Essa, Leanir, and Chiarn were well away. That was something, and she held into it fiercely. All she and Taze needed to do was get Rorin and Darmanin safely out. "Can you see any obvious attack points?"

Rorin said, "*This whole place is lit up like a beacon. It won't be hard for any semi-skilled archer in the viewing balconies above to take you out.*"

"You cannot be here when the Nightstalker arrives, Arya," Taze said.

Arya swore under her breath. If the nazal *was* here, then they were well and truly trapped. She had no idea how to get out of the chamber unseen. But Taze was right—if she was still here when the Nightstalker arrived … she'd never forgotten how he'd used his magic on her all those years ago in SheerRock Fort. Imminent danger sank over her like a cloud. She felt the threat of the nazal, felt their subtle power, their anticipation of triumph.

Heart thudding, she looked over at Darmanin and Andrian. Andrian sat relaxed, unaware of the danger surrounding them. Beside him, Darmanin's posture was as rigid as Rorin. His fingers twitched in his lap. He turned, risking a quick glance back at them.

Arya's breath stilled. He had such an expression of love and reassurance on his face that it cut right through the miasma of fear that was clouding her spirit.

He was not afraid.

"*Follow my lead,*" he signed as he rose to his feet. Arya watched, heart in her throat, as Darmanin inched his way along the row and then walked with quick strides down the aisle to the nearest exit. Murmuring broke out and everyone turned to look at him, wondering why the Crowtalon heir was leaving in the middle of an important speech. The whole way, she was sure he would be taken down by an archer with an arrow and she could barely breathe.

"*What's he doing?*" Rorin signed.

"Trying to get us out of this," Arya said tautly.

"He's an open target," Taze muttered.

Nothing happened, though, and Darmanin made it safely to one of the side exits. The guards let him through. Just before leaving, he turned back to Arya and signed briefly. "*Be ready.*"

She nodded, and leaned forward slightly, surreptitiously loosening her muscles. "Be ready."

"*For what?*" Rorin asked.

She merely shook her head. Darien continued his speech, unbothered by the distraction of Darmanin's exit, but she didn't hear a word he was saying. Her throat was dry, hands curled into fists in her lap.

Then, with a suddenness that had Arya reacting as strongly as everyone else in the room, the main entrance doors exploded inwards.

They'd barely turned in their seats to see who was entering when a shadowhound leaped into the chamber, pausing at the top of the main aisle, and letting out a bone-rattling snarl, jaw open and fangs flashing.

Darmanin's snarl set even her teeth on edge.

A man screamed, then another, and then the whole chamber exploded into chaos. People leaped out of their seats in terror and fled for the doorways. The Rangers dived on their emperor, while Prince At'eir waved back his warriors at the same time as he drew his sword. Defenders swarmed, dragging Darien Eaglesoar off the dais.

The shadowhound dodged among the fleeing crowd, creating as much panic and chaos as possible.

"Move!" Arya jumped up and grabbed Rorin's hand.

Taze drew his sword and together they pushed and shoved their way to the nearest exit. In the corridor outside, people milled about in fear while Defenders shouted for everyone to calm down, that they would take care of the threat, but their calls were falling on deaf ears.

"We have to find your parents, Rorin," Arya shouted over the noise.

"*What about Darmanin?*" Rorin signed. "*If the nazal is in there it might know who Darmanin is now he's used magic.*"

"He knows how to look after himself." Arya held his gaze. It was a wrench to leave Darmanin, but... "We need to find your parents, Rorin."

He paled as he saw something in her eyes. "*Okay then.*"

✳✳✳

They pushed through the panicked crowd and emerged into the warm evening, taking the steps two at a time. Carriages and tethered horses lined the streets surrounding the Council chamber, but they headed directly for Laskin and Taze's shields.

The Raiders had clearly heard the ruckus, because they had weapons out and were ready for a fight yet disciplined enough to hold formation.

Arya started bellowing orders as soon as she was in hearing distance. "Laskin, get to the barracks as fast as you can. I want yours and another shield of Raiders at the townhouse as fast as you can get them there. The rest of the battalion is to be awake, mounted, weaponed, and ready to move on my order."

Laskin didn't hesitate. Didn't pause to ask questions. He snapped an order to his shield, and as one, they wheeled and set off at a gallop for the barracks.

"On me!" Taze called to his shield as he, Rorin, and Arya mounted. "Close watch on Lord Rorin all the way to the residence. We're going in fast."

Too frantic to wait for anyone to keep up, Arya urged Zeke into a full gallop, hurtling along the cobble-stoned streets, heedless of the risk. Rorin and the Raiders weren't far behind. It wasn't a great distance back to the townhouse, but she couldn't fight the urgency that had her in its cold grasp, the feeling that she wasn't moving fast enough.

Zeke thundered around the corner into the right street, the iron gates of the townhouse visible in the distance.

They were wide open.

Panic flooded Arya. Zeke hurtled right up to the gates and into the court-yard beyond. Arya was out of the saddle mid-stride, hitting the ground in a jarring leap. She took the front steps two at a time, almost tripping over the two dead Raiders by the door.

"Shit, shit, shit." Arya kneeled beside the nearest body. Blood soaked his chest, and she could feel no pulse under the clammy skin of his neck. It was Robem—captain of the warlord's personal shield. The creeping panic engulfed her completely now.

Taze came racing up the steps behind her, propping at the sight of Robem dead on the ground. Rorin pushed past them and through the front door before either could stop him. Swearing again, Arya leaped to her feet and followed as Taze sprinted after him. They ran across the dark foyer and up the marble staircase. The hall leading down to Thiara's bedchamber was well lit.

"Essa!" Taze's anguished shout reverberated in Arya's ears as she rounded a corner a few steps behind him to see Essa slumped against the wall. Her expression was glazed, filled with horror and grief. Fresh blood spattered across her dress. A parchment lay discarded at her side, a piece of charcoal falling from nerveless fingers.

Rorin reached her first, dropping to his knees and drawing her into his arms, uncaring of the blood that smeared his fine clothes.

"Ess, are you okay?" Taze got there next. "Are you hurt?"

She managed a shake of her head, then turned wide, horror filled eyes on Arya. "Not my blood. I didn't... I couldn't."

Her entire body shuddered, tears spilling down her cheeks, and Rorin cradled her to his chest, running his hand soothingly down her back. He looked at Arya and Taze, imploring, and signed. "*Peemla?*"

Arya tore her gaze from Essa, swallowed, but it failed to calm her rising panic and terror. Her breathing came too quick, her heart racing too fast. "Taze, you go for Peemla. I'll look for Rorin's parents."

She continued down the hall at a sprint, breath burning in her chest. She burst into the warlord's bedchamber and skidded to a halt, letting out an involuntary cry. Her stomach heaved, and she came close to emptying her stomach all over the carpet.

Blood liberally coated the walls, floor, and bedding. Two dead Raiders lay on the floor near the door, their throats ripped out. Matte Eaglesoar sprawled prone across the bed, blood soaking the bedding around him, eyes staring sightlessly up at the roof. "No," she whispered, eyes turning with inevitable finality to the other body in the room.

Thiara Ravenstrike, warlord of Ravenstrike, lay fallen by the side of the bed.

A knife hung loosely from her hand. The front of her dress had been torn apart and was dark with blood. Gaping wounds ripped open her torso.

Arya screamed.

She lurched across the room, dropping to her knees beside the warlord. She reached out to cradle the woman's neck with her hand and checked for a pulse. Thiara's eyelids flickered at the touch, and Arya sobbed in relief as the faded blue eyes opened.

"Matte?" The warlord's voice was a whisper.

Rorin appeared in Arya's vision, face bone white as he kneeled on his mother's other side, staring in horror at her wounds. He went to sign something, realised his mother couldn't see it, and grabbed hold of her hand instead, cradling it in both of his.

"Get a healer! Wattin will be here soon," Arya screamed at the Raider from Taze's shield, who had halted in the doorway, stricken. "GO!"

Tears streaked Rorin's face as he gripped his mother's hand, eyes pleading with her to stay, to be okay. Arya tore off her cloak, bundled it up, used it to staunch the open wounds, to try and stop the blood loss. But part of her knew it was a losing effort.

She wasn't sure even Tiya could fix this.

Thiara's eyes closed over. Arya tapped her cheek, trying to get her to stay conscious. "Stay awake, Warlord. Please, stay with us. Rorin and I are here, and a healer is coming. Just stay here with us. Please."

Thiara swallowed, clearly seeking to summon the energy to speak, even as her lifeblood drained out of her. "It's a nazal, Arya. You have to … flee." She trailed off, breath slowing almost to a stop.

"Warlord," Arya whispered. "Please."

Her eyes snapped open, and that ruthless strength Arya had always admired shone bright like a lantern. "Arya, it was Nain. He is … the nazal. You must … run."

But that was all she could manage.

Rorin leaned down, pressed his forehead to his mother's cheek, his tears soaking her skin.

A faint smile flittered over Thiara Ravenstrike's face then. "Love you both. So much. I am … proud."

Rorin keened soundlessly as his mother died in his arms. Arya couldn't bear the look on his face, or the giant void of grief that opened inside her.

This was her fault.

She should have told Thiara everything sooner. Then she would have known. She could have protected herself. Arya dragged in a sobbing, tortured breath. She'd done this. Guilt burned so badly she couldn't bear it, couldn't think of it. So instead, she focused on the knowledge the warlord had just given her.

Nain was the nazal.

A dark, ice-cold fury swept through her. It swept away Arya's grief and shock, giving her a cold clarity and purpose. She welcomed it. Welcomed how it dispelled the pain. Blue light sparked along her palms as her fury rose, and her magic surged with it. A picture frame hanging on the wall flew off and crashed to the floor. A wind sprung up, gusting throughout the room, and slamming open the balcony doors.

"*Danger?*" Elendryl was there, demanding.

"*Time to hunt,*" she told him with a snarl.

"*Hunt!*" he echoed fiercely.

"Arya!"

She turned as Darmanin burst into the room, watched as he propped, wide-eyed, at whatever look was on her face.

"They will pay for what they've done," she said, voice terrible with power and grief. "I will kill him for it."

"Arya, no!" Darmanin reached out to stop her, but she shoved past him and ran out the door.

Nain was going to die tonight.

Chapter 47

Laskin was arriving with the two shields when Arya came flying out of the front door of the townhouse. He took in her expression and the blood on her hands in one glance and his entire posture sagged. "What's happened?"

"They've killed the warlord," she snapped, swinging onto Zeke's back, and urging him into a canter out of the gates. Dimly, she heard Laskin order his shield to follow and the second to stay with Lord Rorin.

Arya raced back through the streets as quickly as she had come, focused on only one thing: killing the nazal. Fury raged through her, threatening to erupt at any second. Her hands sparked from repressed magic, nearly melting right through the reins where they touched her skin.

Zeke came to a skidding halt at the base of the steps leading up to the Council chamber, snorting and lathered with sweat. People still milled about, and Defenders were loudly proclaiming that they had secured the area and asking that everybody go back inside for the vote.

The Defenders at the entrance took one look at Arya's wild and bloodied appearance and moved to stop her. But she slipped past them, weaving between their outreached hands, quick and agile.

"Arya!" Laskin's voice sounded against the rage swirling through her, but she swatted it away like an irritating insect. Magic sparked from her hands, her emotions too great for her to focus enough to repress it, even if she'd wanted to.

The chamber was half full of people returning for the vote. Mathas Crowtalon stood with Nain and his entourage on the dais. Arya sprinted down the aisle, straight for them, drawing her cazaix sword with a clear ring. Voices cried out in alarm, alerting her quarry.

But it was too late.

Arya leaped onto the dais in one stride. Her sword drove deep into Nain's chest, her magic-fuelled blow powerful enough to punch the blade right through his body and out the other side. At the first touch of cazaix Nain screamed; a shrill, piercing sound that was a combination of human voice and nazal shriek.

They crashed in a heap to the ground. As they fell, a burning sensation erupted from Arya's scar seared through her entire body. Beneath her, Nain still screamed, head arched backwards, eyes rolling back in his head. She snarled, bloodied hand still curled around the hilt of her blade, twisting it through flesh and bone, ignoring the pain in her arm as she soaked in the sound of his agony.

But then the screams cut off and Nain's body slumped, lifeless, a pool of blood forming in the floor under him.

"Guards!" Crowtalon bellowed, staring in genuine shock at his chief adviser on the ground with a sword through his middle. "Arrest her!"

Hands closed around Arya's arms, too many for her to fight off, and she found herself hauled off Nain's body and dragged away. She kicked out at the nearest Defender, sent him stumbling away, winded. Another kick broke a second Defender's knee. Part of her realised that Nain wasn't the nazal, that the nazal had been riding his body, that the monster was still alive. The rest of her was still maddened with fury and she fought bitterly, screaming at Mathas Crowtalon. "He killed her. He killed them both!"

"She's mad." Mathas snapped, staring at her blood spattered form in astonishment and rapidly spreading triumph. "Get her out of here and lock her up. The new High Warlord can decide what to do with her."

A Defender chained her wrists behind her back despite her struggles. As the lock clicked, Arya sagged in their hold, gasping for air, the fight draining out of her. Nausea roiled in her stomach and her body felt as if she'd been run over by a herd of horses.

The Defenders dragged Arya from the chamber, a door swinging closed behind them, and along an empty corridor. The wooden flooring beneath her blurred as Arya's vision blanked in and out.

A hissing voice cut through her dizziness. "Release her and leave us."

The Defenders halted, some reaching for weapons, and Arya looked up blearily to see a hooded figure standing several paces ahead of them. The hallway was otherwise empty.

"Leave us. You've done your job." The inhuman voice was firmer this time, wrapped in dark magic.

As if under some compulsion, the guards silently undid her chains and let go of her before marching back the way they'd come.

Arya staggered and almost fell but managed to right herself. Her pride would never let her kneel before this creature, even if everything about this situation suggested she was beaten.

"Well, we finally have you." The nazal's voice gloated from inside the concealment of the hood, the sound of it scraping along all her nerves. "What a tragedy that you were killed trying to escape from custody. I doubt many will mourn you though, not once they learn you murdered the Crow-talon chief adviser in cold blood."

She took a deep breath, summoned enough fire to spit, "You won't get away with this. There are more Defenders in this building than you can control with your magic."

"On the contrary, you've implicated yourself quite nicely, and now you'll die in custody before telling your side of the story." His eyes glittered. "Exactly how I planned it, of course. You are so *very* predictable, General Ravenstrike. You thought to kill me, but all you did was drive me out of my human host. Annoying, granted, but in my true form I'm even stronger."

"*I come.*"

Elendryl's presence thundered through Arya's mind, and she gained some measure of reassurance from it. She said nothing, staring at the nazal only a few paces in front of her and wishing she had her cazaix sword. It had driven him from Nain's body, but could it kill his natural form like it harmed

Sky Lords? She suspected, from the scream of pain he'd let out when she stabbed Nain, that it might.

"And if I had my cazaix sword with me right now?" she taunted. "I don't think you'd be so brave then. It can hurt you, can't it, the cazaix?"

Nothing but silence from the creature. She smirked. "I'm right, aren't I? So cazaix can hurt Sky Lords *and* ...." She trailed off, realisation hitting her like a sledgehammer to the head.

The nazal wheezed out a rasping laugh. "It took you this long to figure it out. What a pitiful Sky Lord you would have made."

"You're a Sky Lord," she whispered. "Or you *were*. You can't be anymore or none of us would have been born." Salyarin had insisted there were only ever five Sky Lords. "He hasn't been killing all the potentials, has he?" Horror filled her. "He's turned you into monsters."

The nazal hissed in contempt. "We're more powerful than we ever would have been as mere Sky Lords. More powerful. More dangerous. More alive." The sibilant hiss tore at her ears.

Her thoughts raced. If the nazal had started off as Sky Lord potentials, then did they only have one magical ability, or had the Nightstalker given them more? This creature could clearly invade and control minds, which meant ... Arya fiercely buried any and all thoughts of Leanir, terrified the creature might be able to read it in her mind.

No wonder Salyarin had been so afraid of them.

In the next breath, the monster was inside her mind. She fought, bitterly, but could not dislodge him as he locked her body into rigid stillness. She had neither the skill nor strength to fight off the nazal's sublime, dark magic. Agony burst through her body, and she screamed soundlessly.

"As soon as I learn who the others are, you can die. That's all he wants."

His whisper was like claws raking across her brain, and she didn't know how to hide from him, how to protect those precious threads linking her to the others. Already she could feel him using that *other* thread, the hidden one inside her, following it inexorably toward the others. And then, an echoing cry rattled the walls around them, penetrating through stone and floor and roof, deep and bone-rattling. It sounded like it came from everywhere all at once.

The cry of a full grown wyvern.

The nazal let go of her mind. Her eyes blinked open, watery from pain, struggling to fix on the monster in front of her. The wyvern cried again, defiant, challenging. The urge to run, to hide, to flee pounded through her. Arya had heard that sound only once before. From Xaphistryl, the Nightstalker's Valheran.

And then the nazal pushed back the hood of his cloak.

There was nothing human beneath that hood. His form grew larger, taller, skin papery white, red eyes with veins spidering outwards from his eye sockets. When he hissed again, she saw pointed teeth. "My master is here."

The delight in its voice was terrifying. Growing desperate, Arya turned, trying to flee, but the nazal wrapped her mind in its magic, halting her feet and freezing her to the spot despite how hard she fought.

"Leave, monster!"

The commanding voice filled the corridor around them. Footsteps thundered, and as the nazal left her mind, she turned, gasping, to see Darmanin there, cazaix sword drawn, Laskin and his shield behind him.

The creature hissed, eyes going straight to the cazaix.

Her Raiders swarmed the corridor, putting themselves between the nazal and Arya. Laskin stepped up at her side, while Darmanin took her arm. "I can get you out, but we have to go now."

Stunned and in shock, Arya simply stared at him.

"We can't hold it for long," Laskin shouted as his Raiders began fighting. The nazal was fast and seemed to be able to attack in multiple places at once. Even as Arya watched, one of her Raiders went down, claws having opened his chest, blood spraying a macabre pattern on the white walls. Etan stepped in to hold off a killing blow but barely avoided being decapitated.

Xaphistryl screamed again. The sound shuddered through her body.

"Hurry, Arya," Darmanin urged.

"Laskin." Arya managed, trying to collect her scattered wits. She was exhausted, stunned, from the nazal's attacks on her, and grief and shock. She didn't know what to do.

"I've got your back, kid," he reassured her, smiling. "Now go."

Darmanin tugged her after him as he fled down the corridor at a run. The movement, being free of the nazal, it started to focus Arya's thoughts. "Where are we going?" she asked.

"The Defenders are swarming. Mathas is demanding to know where you were taken, but the Nightstalker's arrival will throw everything into chaos. Our only priority is getting you out of this building. We're heading for the smaller side entrance in the outer corridor—you know the one on the eastern side of the building?"

"I know it. It's within sight of the main entry, though. There will be Defenders there."

"It's the best option we have."

Needing to feel some control over her situation, she lengthened her stride, taking the lead. Darmanin ceded it to her without a word. Arya's quick reckoning had them emerging from this hallway into the wide corridor that encircled the main chamber. Her memory estimated ten strides to reach the eastern exit door once they left this hallway. And for those ten strides they'd be in full view of anyone in the hallway, or stationed at the main entrance.

The door at the end of the corridor stood open. Arya slowed long enough to glance both ways into the dim space beyond—someone had blown out many of the wall sconces—and ascertain it was empty, before continuing through.

She took her first step out into the wide hallway, muscles bunching as she prepared to push herself back into a run—the eastern exit door was within sight, as close as she'd estimated. But at the same moment, her soldier's scanning gaze shifted ahead to the main entry.

It remained well-lit, and so she had a perfect view as King Lucius Nightstalker stepped through those doors.

Her first thought was to protect Darmanin. The Nightstalker couldn't see him.

So instead of pushing forward into the sprint, to dash for the exit, she took the millisecond of time in which the Nightstalker turned towards her to use Rorin's sign language.

"*STAY BACK! FLEE! PLEASE GO!*"

When she'd finished, Arya stood, eyes fixed on the king of Andahar, pushing Darmanin out of her mind, desperately running through her options.

Then his gaze met hers and the whole world turned still. Something like avarice, or delight, or contempt, she couldn't tell—maybe it was all of them—flashed over the Nightstalker's ascetic pale features. There was at least fifty metres between them, maybe more, but he knew who she was.

"How nice of you to finally appear," he said, voice light, conversational.

And then Arya was right back in that room in SheerRock Fort. She felt that sharp tug in her chest, a closing grip that demanded submission. Cold sweat broke out over her skin at the sensation of that touch. It was different to the nazal's dark magic. This was a compulsion, a need, to do whatever the Nightstalker wanted.

The hidden thread, the one the nazal had used … it connected her to the Nightstalker. He controlled her with it. Horror shuddered through her at that realisation.

She took a jolting step forward.

"Arya!"

The voice was distant, as was the sensation of a hand closing around her wrist hard enough to bruise.

Anger flickered over the Nightstalker's face and the compulsion grew so fierce it stole all the breath from her chest.

"ARYA!" The words were bellowed in her ear this time, accompanied by a furious tug on her wrist.

She blinked, tore her gaze away from the Nightstalker and saw Kulan, fear and determination mixed on his face. She stared, unable to process what he was doing there, the Nightstalker yanking at her, merciless and determined.

"Arya, we have to run!" Kulan's mouth moved, the words pattering against her consciousness like stones on a window.

She couldn't fight the Nightstalker, but she didn't have to fight Kulan. And the Nightstalker held no sway over the Khadini prince. She met his eyes, nodded, and he seemed to understand what he needed to do.

His free arm wrapping around her waist, muscles bunching, Kulan hauled her after him.

Stumbling, almost falling, she let Kulan drag her, and as she passed the hallway she'd emerged from, she saw Darmanin still standing there, white faced. She didn't have enough control over herself to sign for him to run but tried to communicate it with her eyes.

A roar of anger swept down the hall and a magical force exploded into the ground at their feet. Wood chips flew and Arya's ears rang. The compulsion strengthened.

But then Kulan had dragged her around a corner, further backwards, speeding up as the Nightstalker began striding towards them. "Servants' entrance," he explained as he shouldered through another door, bringing her with him.

He kept a hand on her arm, helping hold her up, as they stumbled together down a warren of dark corridors, then burst through swinging doors into a dark kitchen. The further they got from the Nightstalker, the more she was free of his compulsion.

Their panting breath echoed as Kulan took them up a side staircase, one that brought them out at a servant's exit, a quiet area on the opposite side of the building from the main entrance.

Here, Taze and Rorin waited with two horses. Arya stumbled, barely able to put one foot in front of the other. Kulan wrapped an arm around her waist to help her keep moving.

"He almost had her," Kulan said. "I dragged her away through the servants' corridors, but he'll be looking for us."

"Thank you, Kulan," Taze said, voice full of relief. "Arya, we need to get you out."

"Everyone, hold up a minute." Arya blinked, trying to organise her scattered thoughts, then turned to Rorin. "Essa? Peemla?"

There were dark shadows under his eyes and lines of grief around his mouth that had never been there before. But he signed crisply. *"They're okay, I'll make sure of it. The nazal doesn't know who Essa is, Arya, that's why it didn't kill her earlier."*

Ok, that was good. But there was still … she tried to take a steadying breath. "Taze, go to The Rotting Log. That's where Chiarn is playing. Tell him what happened, and that the Nightstalker is in the city. Tell him he must flee, tonight." She paused. "Tell him he should go to the Etherean, to learn how to protect himself."

Leanir would have to look after himself. She had no way of reaching him without putting whoever she sent in danger—he had threatened to kill the next person who tried to deliver a message, after all.

"And if he doesn't listen?" Tazed asked.

"That's his choice, Taze. Please, hurry."

"It's okay, Taze. Your shield is waiting just inside. I'll be going straight back in. After all, I'm Warlord Ravenstrike now. I'll keep them close to me until you get back, I promise," Rorin responded before the Raider could speak the protest forming on his face.

He hesitated once more, then nodded and took off.

"Arya, come on, the Nightstalker could be here any second." Rorin turned to the horses. *"And Kulan, you should go too before you're seen with us."*

Footsteps ascended the stairs. They all reached for weapons, but it was Darmanin, relief flooding his face when he saw them.

"You shouldn't have waited for me," he snapped. "Is everything ready?"

Rorin nodded, then turned to Arya. *"Arya, go with Dar. He can't be near the Nightstalker either. You need to get out of the city before they shut it down in the search for you. I'll be fine. I have your Raiders with me. And I'll come up with a good cover story for Dar leaving."*

She shook her head. She couldn't just leave him.

Rorin smiled his beatific smile. *"Go and be safe. Both of you. Trust me to do this."*

"I'm sorry," she mumbled, still struggling to think clearly. "Rorin, I'm sorry."

Grief flashed in his blue eyes, but he managed another smile for her. *"I love you, Arya. You'll always be my sister. Now you must go."*

"Wait!" Kulan stepped forward then. "Come to Taskari, Arya, Darmanin. Bring this Chiarn too. We can protect you there."

"There's no time for this," Darmanin snapped. "We can protect ourselves just fine here, Kulan."

Kulan ignored him, stepping closer to Arya. "We are friends and allies, you and I. Always. Come to Taskari if you need a safe place. The invitation remains open."

"Thank you." She threw her arms around him in a fierce hug. "If I can get there, I will come, but I need to get clear of Gateport first. Go back to your emperor's entourage, Kulan, before you put yourself at risk."

"Farewell, Arya Ravenstrike." He smiled, kissed her forehead, then whirled, and ducked back inside the servant's entrance.

Darmanin was already mounted, tight-mouthed, gaze scanning their surroundings. Rorin helped her onto one of the horses, giving her his cloak to cover her bloody clothes. His hand reached out to squeeze hers. *"Good luck, Arya."*

She leaned down, framed his jaw with her bloodied hand, and whispered fiercely in his ear. "Marry Peemla, Rorin. If she's your person, then marry her. I'm sorry I ever made you feel like you shouldn't."

He stared at her, eyes wide.

She held that gaze, tried to communicate all the love she felt for them. Then, she dropped her hand, righted herself, and urged her horse into a gallop out of the yard.

Darmanin led them through the city, keeping to the main streets and not moving fast enough to call any attention to themselves. Eventually, they made it to the western city gate, and Darmanin gave the Defender guards a friendly nod as they rode through.

They were still in sight of the gates when Xaphistryl's scream tore through the night.

The sound froze Arya and Darmanin at the same time as it sent a thundering compulsion to hide flooding through her body. Their horses whinnied in fright, Arya's rearing so suddenly she almost fell from the saddle.

A shadow swept over the city as another scream tore through the air, challenging, both deep and high pitched all at once.

"Xaphistryl is searching for us," Arya said, fighting for control of her horse.

The compulsion to flee and hide was close to unbearable.

"Then we have to get clear of the city before she starts searching outside it," Darmanin shouted. "Come on, Arya."

Again, he took the lead, moving along the main road until they were out of sight of Gateport, before diverging off onto a dirt track that led into the empty plains. Another cry sounded nearby, and Arya reined in, her gaze scanning the skies. That wasn't Xaphistryl.

"Arya?" Darmanin asked. "We should keep moving."

A dark shape swept over them, coming to a graceful landing a short distance away, his wings remaining poised and ready for flight. Arya immediately dismounted and ran to Elendryl, strengthened by his presence.

"*Fly*." He pushed into her mind.

"You must be careful!" She couldn't hold back the fear in her words. "Another wyvern hunts us."

"*Careful. Hide.*" He promised, nose nuzzling her shoulder, and from the shiver in his mental message, she knew he'd felt Xaphistryl's presence too. They were so close to disaster. She couldn't stop scanning the skies, looking for her enormous dark shape to come swooping down at them.

Abruptly, Elendryl uncurled, a snarl ripping from his throat, his serpentine neck swinging towards Darmanin as he approached, teeth bared. Darmanin halted with almost amusing speed, hands in the air.

"Friend," Arya assured the wyvern.

She stepped away from Elendryl and crossed to Darmanin. She felt better with Elendryl's presence, more centred, the shock and exhaustion fading enough to give her a clearer head. "Thanks for getting me out of there. You saved my life. I'm so sorry."

"It's okay," he said gently. "Here, I managed to grab this." Darmanin unslung her cazaix sword from his shoulder and passed it to her. "We should keep moving. If we push the pace, we'll make Anduil in four or five days."

Arya shook her head. "I can't go to Anduil," she said, buckling the sword on. Her hands still trembled, making it difficult. "I murdered a chief adviser in full view of vicelords and warlords. I have to disappear, or I'll make things worse for Rorin, and you too, Dar. And the nazal is still there, and the Nightstalker."

"Arya." Something in his voice stopped her rambling. The night breeze teased tendrils of raven hair from his braid, whipping it about his face. "It wasn't Andrian who asked Rorin's mother for your hand in marriage," he said. "It was me. Stay with me. I will protect you." He reached out to trail his fingers down her cheek, the barest of touches. "We can protect each other."

"It was you?" She stilled, looking at him in confusion. "But why? I don't understand."

"You know why," he said with devastating simplicity.

Did she? That light in his eyes when he looked at her sometimes. His protectiveness. His frustration with anything that put her at risk. The way he touched her cheek right now.

She couldn't. It was too much.

"Now's not the time." She shook her head. "Rorin's parents are dead." Her breath hitched as that realisation hit her again. Grief stole her breath and clenched her stomach so fiercely she almost hunched over. What was she going to do? "I can't go to Anduil. I have to stay away from you, from all of you. This was my fault."

Darmanin's touch on her cheek shifted, his palm cradling her jaw. He stepped closer. "I love you, Arya Ravenstrike, and I dare the nazal to come for us. You don't have to run."

For a moment she was held in his gaze, in the feeling it held for her, but then she stepped away from him, utterly confused. "Darmanin, no," she said. "The Nightstalker is in Gateport. With Rorin's mother dead…" Her breath hitched, and she bit her lip so hard she broke skin. "Dunidaen has never been more vulnerable. Rorin needs you now. The both of you have to do what you can to keep Dunidaen stable. You can't do that if you're associated with me in any way, not after what just happened."

His hand dropped to his side. He didn't look surprised, merely resigned. "Where will you go? To Taskari?"

"Away. Far away." She backed away until she reached her horse. There, she turned abruptly, hauling herself onto his back, every muscle protesting the movement. Elendryl spread his wings and gave himself a shake, ready to launch into flight.

Darmanin called after her. "Be safe, Arya, wherever you go. And don't stay away too long. Come home to us, where you belong."

"I'll see you, Dar." Her gaze settled on him for one last look. He stood, legs apart and arms crossed over his chest. His face was as grave as it ever was, though now for the first time she saw the love in his eyes. For her.

Elendryl lunged forward, spreading his wings, and soaring into the night. He stayed low to the ground though, harder to spot if Xaphistryl did come near.

Tears blurred in Arya's eyes as she twitched the reins, urging her horse after her wyvern. Turning back one last time, she raised a hand in farewell.

Darmanin didn't move for a long moment, then he too, lifted his hand.

"Farewell," she whispered.

THE END

***

The story continues in *The Wyvern's Cry* - Available now.

The Dock City Chronicle

Become an Inkweaver?

This is your invitation.

I'd love to welcome you into my **Inkweaver Community**—a private space for readers who love epic fantasy, found family, and all the feels.

.

Whether you've read *The Inkweaver Archive*, *A Tale of Stars and Shadow*, *The Mage Chronicles*, or *Heir to the Darkmage*, you'll find fellow readers who are just as invested as you are.

Inside my Inkweaver community, you can:

Discuss characters, moments, and theories

Chat with me directly

Access behind-the-scenes insights, sneak peeks, and the occasional spoiler

.

It's also a place to talk fantasy more broadly — to share recommendations, discover new favourites, and connect with readers who speak your language.

The adventure doesn't end on the last page.

Join me in the Inkweaver Community:

(https://inkweavers.mn.co)

About me

I'm a self-published fantasy author by day and book nerd in every other spare moment I have. I'm also self-confessed coffee snob (don't try coming near her with any of that instant coffee rubbish) but I am willing to accept all other hot drink aficionados, even tea drinkers. I live in Australia's capital city, Canberra, and like all Australians, I'm in pretty much constant danger from highly poisonous spiders, crocodiles, sharks, and drop bears, to name a few. As you can see, I am also pro-Oxford comma.

A 2019 SPFBO finalist, and finalist for the 2020 ACT Writers Fiction award, I'm the author of young adult fantasy series *The Mage Chronicles* and *Heir to the Darkmage*, and epic fantasy series *A Tale of Stars and Shadow* and *The Inkweaver Archive*. I'm currently working on a sequel to *A Tale of Stars and Shadow*.

As part of my writing journey, I've partnered up with One Girl, a charity working to build a world where all girls have access to quality education. A world where all girls — no matter where they are born or how much money they have — enjoy the same rights and opportunities as boys. A percentage of all my royalties go to One Girl.

You can follow me on Facebook and Instagram. I also have a fantasy reading community – The Inkweavers - where you can jump in and talk about anything and everything relating to books and reading.

I also have an author street team. I call them the *Wolves*, after Prince Cuinn's fierce personal guard in *A Tale of Stars and Shadow*. If you'd be interested in becoming a Wolf, you can email me at wolves@tatehousebooks.com. Everyone is welcome, and I'd be more than happy to answer any questions you have.

If you want to learn more about me and my books, head on over to my website at lisacassidyauthor.com

BORROWED FROM
The Inkweaver Archive